The Barnabas Chronicles

Volume 3

Breck: Encouraged to Love
Book 13

Barnabas: Encouraged to Live
Book 14

By

Ronna M. Bacon

Breck: Encouraged to Love Book 13

When Breck Curran is run down by an ATV, he little expects that the lady he tries to protect will become a large part of his life. The beautiful red-haired Neasa Deakin finds that she needs protection from an unknown stalker and turns to Breck instead of her family.

Driven to find out who is stalking the lady he is quickly learning to love, despite kidnappings and attempts on their lives, Breck turns to his friends at the Barnabas Foundation and their ladies to once more solve the mystery.

Twists and turns and unexpected news try Neasa's faith in God and her love for Breck. The complications of step parents and natural grandparents complicate it even more. When she is mentally incompetent in order for a family member to regain control of her, Breck and his friends step in.

Who will survive? And will their love stand the test of the trials? Learning to love one another and learning to love God in a new way is just part of their journey, a journey neither one expected to find themselves on.

Barnabas: Encouraged to Live Book 14

When Barnabas Carey heads on a mission to find the lady that he had loved in university, kept in touch with and then lost track of, little does he suspect that he will find that the beautiful Aubrey Dorsett would have been kept captive by a so-called guardian for ten years. Rescuing her and then marrying her, they set off on an adventure that will test their love for one another and their love for God.

Twists and turns send the two fleeing across Ontario before heading for the Barnabas Foundation. Even there, neither are safe. Injured in an attempted abduction, Aubrey struggles to heal. Beaten and left in the elements, Barnabas battles hypothermia.

The answer as to who is really after them stuns them and their friends, drawing in Barnabas' father and mother. Will they solve the mystery and survive?

Their love for one another grows stronger. With Barnabas' help, Aubrey learns to live in freedom once more. And they both realize that they have come to trust God in a whole new way.

Table of Contents

Breck: Encouraged to Love

The Barnabas Chronicles
Book 13

By

Ronna M. Bacon

ISBN 978-1-989699-54-6

Psalm 32:8

I will instruct you and teach you in the way you should go; I will guide you with My eye.

NKJV

Table of Contents

Standing at his office window, a mug of fresh coffee in his hand, Breck Curran stared out at the falling leaves. He had just returned from a two-week vacation that he had desperately needed, heading up to a northern park in Ontario, to a favourite camping spot. He felt refreshed, he thought, but he still had concerns about the men of the Barnabas Foundation, the twelve of whom had undergone what they termed as adventures but in fact, had been life and death situations. He sighed as he rubbed at his dark auburn hair.

Breck turned finally, heading for his desk and then searching his schedule. This afternoon, he realized, he was due to meet with the landscaping contractor about the new playground and gardens that the Barnabas Foundation was planning at the local shelter. He was looking forward to that. Until then, Breck had paperwork to look over and complete. Being second in command under his friend, Barnabas Carey, at the Foundation was work he usually enjoyed. At the moment, though, he was restless. Even the vacation had not calmed that feeling.

Parking his truck near the shelter, he waved at the older couple who ran it for the Foundation. Cadee, one of the men's wives, had seen her parents leave the mission field that they loved and then take over the shelter at Barnabas' request. They were loved by all the inhabitants.

Breck moved around the building, heading for the activity that he could see. He stopped, waiting for the equipment to move past him, and then headed towards the contractor.

"Ben Deakin, it's good to be working with you." Breck's hand was out to shake the older man's.

"Breck! It is good. I hear tell that you had a vacation. Hope you enjoyed it."

"I did. Way up north, camping in a park. Peaceful. I think every doctor should prescribe that for patients."

Ben laughed. "I agree. We don't get to camp much now, not when we are so busy, but we used to." He nodded towards the grounds. "We're just getting started as you can see. These are the plans that the board approved."

The two men studied the blueprints and then walked the boundary, Breck asking all the right questions, Ben thought. He knows his stuff, this young man. If he didn't have work with the Foundation, I'd hire him.

Nevin approached his father, pulling off his hard hat and wiping at his face. Even though it was late into the fall, the sun was warm that day.

"Dad? We're about ready to start the dig. Any further instructions?"

Ben turned, watching the small skid steer as it moved into place. "No, I think we're ready. Go for it. You two always enjoy playing in the dirt."

Nevin grinned. "That we do." He turned and ran for the equipment, hopping up to speak with the operator, before he was off and to the side, watching as it was driven forward, and the first scoop of dirt moved.

Breck watched closely before he frowned. He turned, finding Ben back at his truck, just pocketing his phone.

"Ben?"

Ben looked up at Breck's call and then moved his way. "What's up, Breck?"

"I don't like something there. Can we stop for a moment?"

"We can." Ben waved off the equipment operator and then walked forward with Breck. Breck bent over and then straightened up.

"It's what I thought. Bones."

"Bones?" Ben took a look and paled. "We have never found bones before on any dig." He sighed, waving Nevin over. "Nevin, call off the dig. We just found human bones."

Nevin stopped short, not sure of what his father was saying. "Bones?"

"Bones. Get Neasa and get back to the truck. The equipment stays where it is."

Breck walked back towards Ben after speaking with the responding officers. He sighed. This was not how he had planned his first day back. He had spoken with Barnabas, who was on his way to the site. Now, how did he explain it to Ben?

"Breck? How long?" Ben was waiting for him.

"They don't know. They have to wait for a medical examiner to come in. The techs are working around that. This will put you behind."

"Not a problem. We'll work to get it started at least this fall." Ben turned. "It's those two I'm worried about."

"Who?" Breck squinted, the motion narrowing his dark brown eyes.

"Nevin and Neasa. Neasa is the one who was on the equipment."

"Neasa? I don't know that I've met Neasa."

"No, I don't think that you have. She's been away all summer, working on her grandfather's farm, helping him out. She's back now." Ben moved towards his children. "I'll introduce you, although she does say that she has seen you around church."

"More than likely. I seem to get more and more involved. I need to pull back some."

"And you will. Neasa? This is Breck Curran. He's from the Foundation."

Neasa Deakin looked up, way up, she thought, as she smiled at Breck. He's tall and good looking. Likely taken too. She sighed to herself.

"Hi. It's good to meet you. Sorry about this."

"Sorry? It's not your fault. You didn't bury a body there, did you?" Breck grinned as she frowned at him, studying the long golden blond hair in a braid and the cornflower blue eyes.

"Certainly not. Dad, we can still lay out what we need to do, can't we? That way, we'll be ready to get back to work once the site is released."

"That we can. How be you and Breck take a walk around the perimeter? I think that should be okay." Ben frowned for a moment and then shrugged. "See what we need to do."

Breck waited for Neasa to refuse but she headed off, making him almost run to catch up with her. He walked beside her, his attention on the activity around the dig.

"This has never happened before." Neasa finally stopped, watching her father. "I don't know what Dad will do."

"He'll wait for clearance and then start again. He seemed to think that you could get a lot done this fall yet."

"We can if the weather holds." She turned suddenly, her hand shading her eyes. "Do you hear that?"

"Hear what?" Breck spun. "An ATV. There shouldn't be one around here." He grabbed for her hand, pulling her with him, heading for a small shed near the shelter.

Only, they never made it in time. The large ATV was in their path without warning and then heading directly for them. Breck could hear shouts around him as he dove out of the way, Neasa wrapped in his arms. Struck a glancing blow, he rolled, his head hitting hard on the packed dirt, and then lay still, Neasa not moving either. The ATV slowed and then sped off, even as patrol officers raced for their vehicles and followed. Ben gave a shout and ran for his daughter, Nevin racing from where he had stood watching the activity.

Ben's hand shook as he knelt beside the pair, reaching out for Neasa. Nevin was beside him, a hand on his shoulder.

"Dad?"

"She's alive, son." He reached for Breck. "So is Breck, but they're hurt." He stood back as patrol officers moved in and then the paramedics. "We'll follow them."

Ben turned as he felt a hand on his shoulder again, to find Barnabas Carey standing there.

"Ben? What happened?"

"They were walking around the plot, trying to determine what they could do, when an ATV appeared. It ran them down." Ben turned back as he watched the activity around the pair. "Who?"

"Likely related to the find." Barnabas was torn. He felt that he needed to stay with his life-long friend, Breck, but he also needed to talk to the investigators. He sighed. "You're heading in? I'll follow as soon as I can."

—

13

Late that night, or rather early the next morning, Breck shifted uncomfortably in his hospital bed, pulling at the plastic bracelet around his wrist. He wanted out of there, not having to lay there and listen to the squeak of rubber-soled shoes as the nurses moved around. He wanted to find the person responsible for running him down. But, more importantly, he wanted to find Neasa Deakin and make sure for himself that she was not harmed. Barnabas had been around, checking up on him. He had reassured Breck that she was okay and in a room just down the hall from him. That didn't suit Breck at all. He needed to see for himself that she was fine.

He looked up as he heard a whisper of sound and squinted through the low lighting, his headache pounding. He watched as the form at the door looked behind itself and then moved towards him.

"Breck?" Neasa stood beside his bed, a large bandage on her cheek. "How are you? I escaped from the nurse. She'll be looking for me shortly."

Breck stared at her. "You escaped your nurse? And you're dressed. Planning to escape the hospital as well? Take me with you?"

"Breck!" Neasa shook a finger at him. "That's not what I asked."

"I have a headache if I must answer, as well as assorted bumps and bruises. How are you?" Breck watched her eyes, seeing a slight flicker of pain in them. "And don't tell me that you are fine. I know you're hurting."

"I am, Breck, but not as much as I could. You took the brunt of it." Neasa sounded frustrated.

"Of course I would. That's what we do for ladies." Breck sat up in bed. "Are you leaving the hospital?"

"I was hoping to. Nevin left transportation for me." She turned away and then back. "Why? You planning on leaving as well?"

"If I can catch a ride with you."

Neasa grinned. "You can. I'll tell Sue that we're leaving. She said that she had our discharge papers for the morning. As far as I'm concerned, it's morning."

"It is. Give me five minutes and I'll be with you." Breck waited until she had left the room and then rushed to dress, staring at the dirt stains on his clothing. Just how close was it, Lord? Just how close?

He watched from the hallway as Neasa headed his way, waving his paperwork, trying to walk as quietly as she could. But he could see her limping. Lord, who was that person after? Me or Neasa? And did I just start an adventure like my friends?

Neasa pointed to the stairs and then shoved open the door.

"This will take us down to the Emergency Department and then we can make our great escape." She grinned at him.

"You think this is an adventure, do you?" Breck followed her down the stairs, stifling his groans at the pain.

"I do. I've heard of these kinds of adventures. Always wanted one." She walked through the opening door to the outside, waving at the security guard as she did so.

"Twelve of my friends have had them. You don't want one." Breck paused, looking around for her vehicle. "Where did your brother leave your car?"

"Car?" Neasa began to laugh. "This way." She paused beside a nice shiny brown and chrome motorcycle. "This is our transportation. But I can call for a cab if you would prefer that."

Breck stared at her and then the bike, walking around it, a soft whistle coming from him.

"Nice. I haven't ridden in years, even though I keep my license up to date." He grinned suddenly. "You driving?"

Neasa stared at him before her eyes narrowed. The lighting in the parking lot was just bright enough for her to see the mischief on his face.

"Of course." She looked around, suddenly shivering. "Can we leave? I don't feel safe."

"We can." Breck waited until she had seated herself before he climbed on behind her, taking the helmet he was handed and putting it on. He looked down at his hands before he set them gently on her waist. It was not him, Breck thought, to do this to a lady, but he didn't have much choice. "Before we leave, can I pray?"

Neasa twisted to stare at him and then nodded. When he had finished, she looked at him. "Where do you want to go?"

"On a nice long ride with a beautiful lady?" He grinned again, knowing that he was flirting with her, not something he did either. "The Foundation building or wherever."

"I was heading for Dad's. I've been staying there since I came back. I hadn't settled into an apartment yet."

"Then, head there. I won't have you on the road on your own at this time of night."

"I've done it before." Neasa sounded disgruntled.

"You may have, but not from dropping me off. I refuse to let you."

Barnabas stood the next morning, frowning at Breck's apartment door. He had talked to Breck the night before and Breck had been told to call him if he needed a ride home. That had not happened. He sighed. Breck, where are you? Barnabas rubbed at his head, suddenly exhausted. We don't need Breck to disappear, he thought.

Finally standing in his own office, Barnabas stared at his phone, scrolling through all his messages and then checking his email. Not a word from Breck. That was not him, he thought. He soon was immersed in his paperwork, looking up in surprise at the tap at his office door. Branigan and Brody, two of the men from the building, stood there.

"Barnabas, have you seen Breck? We were to meet with him today and he's not around." Brody sat in one of the chairs in front of the desk.

Barnabas leaned back in his own chair. "No, I haven't. Not since I saw him last night just as visiting hours ended. He was hoping to be home today."

"That's what we thought you'd say." Branigan leaned against the door frame. "So, where is he?"

Barnabas held up a finger as he dialed a number.

"Dan? It's Barnabas. How are you today?"

"I'm fine. Just heading in to pick up Neasa."

Barnabas could hear the house doors closing and the sound of Dan walking across the pavement.

"Barnabas, her bike's not here. I wonder if Nevin took it in for her."

"And if he did, she'd be home. Right?"

"Right. Hang on, let me call him. I'll call you right back."

Dan frantically dialed Nevin's number, only reaching his voice mail. "Nevin? It's Dad. Did you take Neasa her bike? We can't find her or Breck."

Barnabas was on his feet, not waiting for Dan to call him back, Branigan and Brody right behind him.

"Your truck?" Brody's question halted Barnabas for a moment before he nodded.

"My truck. Let's move, fellows. I don't like this."

"We don't either."

The three carefully watched the sides of the roads as they drove back in to the hospital, running for the doors and then the stairs inside the building.

Barnabas stared at the charge nurse before he ran his hand through his hair, frustration in his moves.

"He left? During the night?"

"That's what Sue said. Their discharge papers were all ready. She watched Neasa and Breck head down for the stairs. Is there a problem?"

"There is. Neither of them is answering their phones." Barnabas moved away to take a call. "Dan?"

"No sign of her bike. I can't raise Nevin, but if he's running equipment, he can't hear me. I'm heading towards that job site."

"I'm at the hospital. Neasa and Breck left real early this morning."

"They did? That's not like her." Dan sighed. "But then, she's become a lot more independent and withdrawn with us. She's not always opening up to us with where she's going."

"No? Did something happen to trigger that?"

"We're not sure. Even Nevin has commented on that." Dan reached to start his truck. "I'll be in touch as soon as I talk to Nevin. In the meanwhile, I guess we call the police?"

"I'll call it in." Barnabas turned to face the two other men. "No sign of Neasa at home. Dan says her motorbike is gone."

———

18

"Motorbike?" Brody shook his head. "Does Breck know she has one?"

"I would suspect so, by now." Barnabas had walked away and then returned shortly. "Dan called. Nevin dropped off her bike here late last night. He had talked to her briefly. She was planning on heading to Dan's."

"And if Breck knew, then he would have asked her for a ride. And he would not have let her bring him to the building." Branigan's hand slapped at the brick wall he was standing beside, frustrated. "So, where are they?"

"I spoke with Will, eventually. He's going to have a couple of patrol cars search for them." Barnabas stood for a moment before he headed back down the stairs. "We'll search as well. Where are the others?"

"At work. Other than for Burnie and he had a conference call with his publisher today." Branigan fastened his seat belt. "Let's pray, fellows. Breck needs that."

Three days had gone by and still no sign of Breck or Neasa. Dan had been out, worried about his daughter, but he could provide little help. Nevin had been around as much as he could, seeking information but also company as he tried to find his sister. The men of the building had searched the roads surrounding the Foundation lands, had been through the town, talked to the people on the street, talked to Cadee's parents, and still had found no sign of Breck or Neasa.

Barnabas looked up that day and rose, walking towards his father, Bruce.

"Dad? I wasn't expecting you here this week. Mom with you?"

"She is. Anna and she headed into town, to see what they could do. Anna talked to Dan this morning. He's not even able to work, and he needs to. I talked to him last night. The authorities have released the land by the shelter and they want to get started on it. But they don't have the heart to do that. I'm talking with the board. Given the circumstances, we may delay that work until the spring."

"Likely a good idea. I am sure that the police will want to go back there at some point. I talked to Dallas last night. Will asked him to get involved."

"Good. He's got a head on his shoulders." Bruce poured them both a mug of coffee before he leant back against the counter in the kitchenette, one hand resting on it. "What are your feelings, son?"

"I don't know, Dad. This is not Breck. He stays in touch unless he's away on vacation." Barnabas paced. "Where are they?"

"God knows, son. The prayer chains are working. Breck is too well-liked by everyone not to have that happen."

"I know, Dad. We have had our differences over the years, but nothing really major. We've always been able to talk things through. Or at least pray over them." The younger man stood staring out the window across the lands. "They haven't found Neasa's bike yet, either."

"So, someone has hidden it. It would not be either one of them. I don't think that Breck has any enemies, not that we know of. Have you talked to his parents?"

"I wish I could. They're off somewhere in another province, with no phone service. He had told me that they expected to be gone for a couple of months. If I need to, I'll have Dallas track them down."

Barnabas reached for the phone on his belt, pulling it out and staring at it.

"That's Breck's ring." He tapped the phone, bringing up the text messages. "Oh, man! Where are you, Breck? And what did you do?"

Bruce was at his son's side, studying the picture that had arrived. "He's in rough shape, son. Any way to determine where he is?"

"I'm not sure, Dad. Look. Behind him. What do you see?"

"A shadow of a cross? Where is that?"

"I don't know." Barnabas sent the photo on to Dallas. "Maybe Dallas or his team can work wonders." Barnabas began to pace, his eyes studying the picture. "I know, Dad. It's near the shelter. That old rundown church that we were looking at buying to turn into apartments. Do you think?" His voice died away, even as his father reached for his arm and pulled him with him.

"Who's around today?"

"Brady was. Brandon. Blair. Which one?"

"All of them. Brady needs to bring his supplies. We may need his medical experience. It won't be the first time we've used his paramedic skills."

The three men stared at Barnabas for a moment before Brady ran for the well-stocked infirmary in the building and then for Blair's truck, following Barnabas as he shot out of the driveway.

Bruce watched closely as they neared the church, finally pointing to a parking lot.

"In there, I think, son. We can walk in from here. It's only a couple of minutes, I would think."

"I think so, Dad." Barnabas checked his phone. "No word from Dallas. We're on our own, I guess." He slipped from the truck, meeting the other three. "Dad, pray for us. We'll need that."

"Absolutely, son."

The five walked quickly towards the building, their eyes searching but not seeing anyone, which they found strange. There were always people in the area.

"This is strange." Blair kept his voice low. "Where is everyone?"

"It's like they were scared away. What did Breck get involved in?" Brandon stopped, his eyes on the church. "Do we go in or do we wait?"

"I'm going in." Barnabas stood for a moment, his heart raised in prayer. "Brandon, stay here. Send a message if anyone shows up."

The four men ran quickly for the building, ducking inside and then stopping to listen. They exchanged puzzled glances before they moved forward, around the debris and broken pews, towards the front of the church. Brady's hand went up, as he tilted his head.

"Do you hear that?"

"Hear what?" Bruce didn't hear anything. Not at first. "A female voice."

They moved forward cautiously, stopping outside a closed door, their eyes on one another before Barnabas reached for the doorknob and turned it slowly, the door opening inch by inch under his touch. He stepped through, the other three behind him, as he searched the room, finding startled blue eyes on him before his own eyes dropped to the floor.

"Breck!"

Brady was past Barnabas, dropping to his knees beside Breck before he looked up at the lady.

"Are you okay?" His voice was low.

"I am. But Breck isn't. Please? Will you help him?"

"We can. We need to get you up and out of here." Barnabas reached for her, finding her drawing back.

"I can't." She lifted an arm, showing them the shackle that held her imprisoned, near to Breck but not near enough to touch him. "They did this to me. To make me stay. I couldn't stop them." Her eyes filled with tears as she looked over at Breck. "He tried to stop them, to make them leave me alone. They did that to him."

Blair had followed the chain to the floor as Neasa had spoken, a muttered word or two coming from him. Bruce was at his side, a pocketknife out as he dug at the eye-bolt that held the chain, Blair tugging at it to free it.

"Neasa? Come with me." Bruce had her on her feet, the chain gathered in his hand. "They'll bring Breck."

Neasa refused to move, watching as Brady and Barnabas spoke quietly and then lifted Breck to his feet and over Brady's shoulders. She finally moved at the tug on her arm, trying to watch where she was going at the same time as she watched Breck. Bruce finally just shook his head and swept her up into his arms, almost running for the door, the men following closely.

Brandon took one look and then ran for the trucks, the key fobs in his hands clicking to unlock the door.

"Who goes where?" He paused as he studied first Breck and then Neasa.

"Breck and Neasa in the back. Brady, you're with them. Dad?"

"I'm in front. Blair? Brandon?"

"We'll follow. Doc's on duty today."

"The Lord was working things out there." Barnabas pulled out his phone, tossing it to his father as he sped off. "Answer that please, Dad."

"Bruce? You have Barnabas' phone?" Dallas' voice held puzzlement.

"I do. We have Breck and Neasa. We're heading to the hospital with them. They were in that old abandoned church near the shelter."

"The old church? We searched it, two days ago. They were there?" Dallas' attention went to the traffic ahead of him. "Just a moment, Bruce. I am heading back your way, once I can get out of traffic." His hands-free device disconnected, leaving him muttering at it.

Bruce dropped the phone into the cup holder on the centre console before he glanced to the back seat. "Brady?"

Brady shook his head. "Sorry, Bruce. I'm not sure. He's hurting, I know that, but from where all? I can't do a proper assessment."

Bruce's eyes turned to Neasa, finding her watching Breck intently. "Neasa? May I call you that?" He gave a half-smile as she nodded without looking at him. "Did they hurt you?"

"No, just the shackle. We tried to escape. That's when they did that. They hid my motorbike somewhere. I don't know where though." She looked up, anger sparking briefly. "Why?"

"That's what we'll work on. We'll get you two seen to first." Bruce turned his head to watch the hospital appear. "Emergency doors, son?"

"You've got it, Dad." Barnabas had regressed to his teens with his language and phrases, his concern on Breck. He parked and then was out, helping Brady as he moved Breck to a stretcher and then reaching for Neasa, only to find that she wasn't there. "Where'd she go?"

Bruce grinned at his son. "You didn't see her moves? She was around you and ahead of the stretcher before I could stop her. Blair and Brandon were right behind her."

Barnabas stared at his father and then the closed doors. "I never saw her. Let me park, Dad, and then we'll head in."

"No, son. Let me. You'll be needed, I think." Bruce watched as his son nodded and then moved quickly to enter the department, before he shook his head, his eyes raised to the sky. Dear Lord, I don't know what's going on, but You do. Heal our boy, dear Lord.

Doc finally came to find Barnabas, stopping as he saw all the men from the building there. He had been told that they were and that the ladies had gathered in the chapel. He shook his head. Lord, this boy is going to go through something, something bad. Protect him and his lady. He turned for a moment to stare behind him, a slight smile on his face. Neasa had refused to move from Breck's side, insisting that she needed to be there. That he had been hurt because of her.

Barnabas was on his feet, moving towards Doc, a frown on his face, hearing the steps behind him as the men gathered there.

"Doc?"

"He's a fortunate man, Barnabas. Lots of bruisings. Defensive wounds on his hands and arms. No broken bones. He's been for imaging and so far, we don't see any internal bleeding. He's rousing, now that we've been able to start an IV and rehydrate him."

"Thank God. You'll be keeping in overnight?"

"I would like to, but I don't see that happening. I'll take him back to our place. I'm off tomorrow so that should work."

"And Neasa?" Bruce spoke up, worry for the young lady on his face.

"Neasa? The lady who won't leave Breck? What's the story there?" Doc searched the faces, seeing understanding on some but curiosity on others.

"Neasa? She was with him when they were run down four days ago it is now." Barnabas didn't catch the speculative glance Doc sent his way. "She's okay?"

"She is. She just won't leave him. And he's clinging tight to her hand. We can't get him to release it."

Breck raised his head from the pillow during the night, squinting as he glanced around in the low light. At least not the hospital this time, he thought, but I'm not sure where I am. His head was pounding, harder than it had been, and he sought relief by rolling on his side to face the wall, his head back on the pillow before he raised it again.

I do hear something. But what? He looked around. Lord, I know I'm free but just where am I? He jumped slightly as he felt a hand touch his face and then heard a voice muttering to him, that was the only way that he could describe it.

"Breck? Are you awake? Breck?" Neasa knelt by the bed, her hand on Breck's face, the other hand on his hair. "Breck? Please?"

"Where am I?" He had to clear his throat before he could speak.

"He said he was Doc. I had to come with you, Breck. It's my fault that you were hurt."

"It was?" Breck groaned as he rolled to his back and then pushed himself up on the pillows Neasa stacked behind him.

"It was. You tried to keep them from hurting me and they beat you up." Neasa felt the anger growing in her. "I don't know who they were or why they did this."

"We'll figure it out." Breck reached out a tentative hand to finger a lock of her hair. "You have beautiful hair."

Neasa frowned at him for a moment. "Breck?"

Breck sighed and then looked at her. "Are you sure that you're okay?"

"I am." Neasa settled on the floor beside the bed, one arm on it to prop up her head. "I couldn't leave you when they brought you in."

"You couldn't? Who?"

"Brought you in? Some friends of yours, Doc said. And one of their fathers."

"Barnabas and his father, Bruce. Was there a Brady?"

Neasa wrinkled her brow, in a very adorable manner Breck privately thought, before she nodded. "There was. He's a paramedic?"

"That he is. Listen, what time is it?"

"The time? Around four or five. Why?"

"Because I need up and I need my coffee."

Neasa just stared at him. "You need your coffee?"

"I do, Neasa. Now, if you'll excuse me, I need that bathrobe there at the end of the bed." He took it as Neasa handed it to him and then watched as he shifted to sit on the side of the bed. "It's okay, Neasa. I'll be okay. How be you go find the coffee? Do you drink that?"

"No, I don't. I like my hot chocolate but I doubt that I can find any."

Breck laughed softly. "Go and check out the tall cupboard by the fridge. I think you'll find some there. Even some mint-flavoured chocolate if I know Anna."

He was right, Neasa thought to herself, standing staring at the cupboard before she pulled out mint-flavoured hot chocolate. I need this. She had already started the coffee, Anna telling her the night before just to make herself at home.

Breck paused in the hallway, watching Neasa as she worked away in the dim light that she had put on. Lord, there is something about this lady that draws me to her. She is in difficulty and I don't know why. And I don't think it's all related to that find at the shelter. There is more going on. He walked quietly into the kitchen, startling Neasa as she turned.

"You're quiet."

"I know. I guess it's living on my own that has done that. Although Mom has always told me that I walked like a cat."

—

Neasa began to giggle, bringing a grin to his face. "A cat? What mother tells her son that?"

"Mine. She's just pointing out that cats walk quietly too."

"They can. Or they can be very loud." Neasa sat at the table, her mug in front of her, watching at Breck poured his coffee and then sat. "Nothing in it?"

"Sometimes I like it this way. This morning, I need a shot of just plain caffeine."

"I don't think that will work." Neasa grew quiet, lost in her thoughts, not seeing Breck rise again, and make toast for them. She just reached for a piece of what he set in front of her and began to eat it. "Breck? Do you know why it happened?"

Breck shook his head. "No, and that puzzles me. They seemed to be waiting for someone that first day."

"I think they were and that person never showed. I don't understand why they moved us."

"To keep us hidden." Breck reached for her hand, his thumb rubbing along it. "Did they hurt you?"

"No, just put that shackle on me. Didn't we talk about that?"

"I'm sorry, I can't remember. I do remember trying to protect you at the first house."

"You did. They beat you for that, Breck. I thought that they would kill you."

Breck nodded, his hand tightening on hers, a sense of foreboding coming over him. "May I pray with you? I think we are going to need it."

Neasa shrugged. "I guess. Breck?"

He shook his head at the unspoken question in her voice. "We'll pray, Neasa. Then we'll talk."

Doc hesitated in the doorway as he listened to Breck pray. He has a powerful way of talking to You, Lord, now doesn't he? He turned and walked away, his own prayers spoken in his heart.

———

Chapter 7

Neasa wandered Doc's living room, studying the artwork on the walls, the Scripture verses on the photos, and then the knickknacks. She was restless, she knew, and not just from the last few days. Something had happened over the past few months, something that she had not spoken to anyone about. Threats had been made against her, threats that she didn't understand. Neasa finally reached for the blanket on the back of the couch and plopped down into a corner of the couch, the blanket covering her. She was suddenly chilled, and that from fright.

Breck had watched her from where he stood in the doorway speaking with Dallas, a police officer friend who had shown up. He moved towards Neasa, sitting beside her, finding her shifting to lean against him, his hand reaching for hers.

"Dallas? You wanted to speak with us? We have given our statements." Breck frowned. "At least, I think we did." He turned to stare at Neasa as she giggled. "What?"

"We did, Breck, but I know you don't remember doing that. Not that you had much of a one to give."

"Is that right?" His hand tightened on hers. "And how would you know that?"

"Because you gave it in the Emergency Department and you wouldn't let go of me." She grinned at him. "Not that I was leaving anyway."

"You weren't?" Breck watched her intently, reading something on her face that gave him hope that just maybe he had found a lady who would be willing to date him.

Dallas simply shook his head. "Come back to the present, you two. I need to ask you some questions."

"Ask away. We may or may not answer." Breck's gaze never left Neasa.

—

Staring at his friend, Dallas was not sure of what was going on. This was not Breck, he thought. Lord? Can You help, just a little? I need to talk to him and it doesn't look as if it's going to happen. "Breck? Please?"

"What is it you want to know?" Breck finally looked at Dallas.

"I need you to walk back through what happened. You have told the officers, but I would like to hear it again, from you two. Sometimes there is something that you don't remember when you give your statements. You know that from the other twelve."

"Twelve?" Neasa's free hand was waving in the air. "What are you two talking about?"

"The twelve men who live here. You've met them?" Breck watched her closely as he spoke

"I think so. And their wives." She stared between the two for them. "Wait a minute. You told me that some of your friends had had adventures and that I shouldn't be wanting one. That night when we escaped the hospital, you said that."

"That's right." Breck grinned at her again. "I did say that. All twelve of the men who live here, other than for Barnabas and myself, have had adventures, life-threatening in many cases, but through that, they found their lady loves."

"They did? I thought that only happened in books or movies or on television." Neasa stared at him, not sure if it was really what had happened.

"No, it happens in real life, Neasa." Breck looked past Dallas, not focusing on anything in particular. "It happens, Neasa." He finally turned to Dallas. "Where do you want us to start?"

"I think he wants us to start at the beginning." Neasa smirked at Breck as he looked at her. "Isn't that what they usually say?"

Dallas grinned, even as he shook his head. "You're right, Neasa. Now, which one of you goes first?"

"He can. He has less to say than I do." Neasa settled down tighter to Breck, finding comfort from just being near him, her eyes on their joined hands.

"I guess then, Dallas, I go first." Breck shut his eyes, trying to envision what had actually happened.

"I remember us leaving on your bike, Neasa, from the hospital. We didn't get very far before we realized that we were being followed. Neasa tried to evade them, but it didn't seem to work. At one point, we were able to switch places. She actually let me operate her motorbike." Breck looked down at her. "We headed for the downtown area, and I was able to back into an alleyway, with the lights off, watching as the two vehicles passed by. I thought that we had fooled them. I took off again, heading for Dan's when I was boxed in. I didn't have any choice but to stop. We were forced into a vehicle that took off at high speed. One of the men stayed with Neasa's bike.

"We were taken to a house just outside town. The old Millar place, Dallas. We were kept there for a day or so, I think. They tried to forced Neasa to sign some kind of paperwork and she refused. I stepped in when it looked as if they would start with an assault against her. I don't remember much after that.

"It did seem as if they were waiting for someone else to arrive. Only that person never did. They keep referring to the boss."

"The boss? Male or female?" Dallas looked up from his notes.

"I'm not sure. They didn't say much other than calling whoever it was that they were waiting for the boss." Breck sighed. "I can't even give a proper description of them, Dallas. They had on bulky jackets and hoodies with the hoods up and bandanas or masks of some kind across their lower faces."

Dallas turned to Neasa, to find her watching him intently. Breck, you have yourself a very serious lady here, underneath all her fun. Something is going on with her, and I somehow think that you have just gotten involved over your head. Lord, protect my friend.

"Neasa? What is your story?"

"My story? I have no idea. All I did was unbury those bones." She sighed, leaning harder against Breck without realizing that she was and she felt his hand tighten on hers. "Okay. So, after they had beaten Breck and knocked him out. Or did they?" She looked up at Breck. "I think you fell, Breck, and hit your head on the edge of the table. You didn't move after that." She looked over at Dallas. "They moved us the next day to the old church. That's when they put the shackle on my wrist. They made sure that I couldn't reach Breck, even though I begged them to let me. They just laughed. There were three of them that day, four the day before. It's strange that they didn't take our phones. Mine had no charge left, but Breck roused enough to pull his out. He muttered something about sending a text message, but I'm not sure that he did."

"He sent a photo of some kind, Neasa. That allowed Barnabas and his father to recognize the building and find you two. Were they back at all after they left you there?"

"No. They left us there one day and then never came back. Breck's friends showed up the next day. I don't get it. Why us?" Neasa looked up at Breck, finding him watching her intently. "Breck?"

Breck shook his head. "I'm not sure, Neasa. I'm not sure that it is all related to those bones. It just doesn't make sense that it would be." He shared a look with Dallas. "Is there anything in your past that would have someone after you?"

"Me?" Neasa shrugged before she sighed. "Did Dad tell you that I was away for the last six months or so, working on his father's farm?" When Breck nodded, she sighed again. "I was getting threats by letter, on my phone. I don't know who was doing that. It doesn't make sense. I haven't seen anything I should have. I behave myself. I don't associate with criminals or wannabe criminals or the shady side of life in town." She became quiet. "Nor does Nevin. This started about a month after I got there."

"Did you keep everything?" Dallas hoped that she had.

"I did. I have it all in a safety deposit box. They were text messages, so I was able to save them that way." She reached into her pocket. "You'll want my phone. I have another one that I can use. With a different number."

"That's good. Who all has that number?" Dallas looked up as she remained quiet. "Neasa? Who all has your new phone number?"

"No one at present. I just got the phone the day before we found the bones. I was planning on letting my family know and just a couple of friends."

"Good. Let me have the number. Breck will want it. I would suggest that the fellows here have it as well."

"Really?" Neasa looked mutinous for a moment.

"It's for your own safety, Neasa." Breck spoke up. "If for some reason you need me and I can't make it, you can call any one of the fellows or their ladies for that matter, and they will come and help you."

Neasa finally nodded before she whispered. "Okay. But it's at home. If someone is after me, how do I go there? I would only bring trouble to Dad and Nevin and then Mom when she comes home."

Breck blew out a breath, his eyes on Dallas. "I will take you, Neasa. And there is an apartment here in the building that you can use. Right beside me."

"There is?" Neasa looked up at him. "That would be okay? I mean, I don't want to bring any trouble here." She frowned as the two men began to laugh. "What did I say that was so funny?"

Breck wrapped his arm around her, their hands still joined, and hugged her. "It's okay, Neasa. It's just that there has been trouble brought to the building before. Twelve times in fact."

"Your twelve friends, right? What else should I know before I move in here? And I'm not saying that I am." Neasa stared up at

Breck as he tried hard to smother his grin. "And wipe that smirk off your face, buster."

Dallas began to laugh even harder. "Breck, your lady is a spitfire. You have your hands full."

Neasa glared at Dallas. "Whose lady? And when was I to be informed of that fact?"

Neasa looked around her childhood bedroom, wiping a tear from her face. She was moving out and moving on, she thought. She had had an apartment away from here, she thought, before she had moved home the previous year, but this was different. She just hadn't settled into one since then and being away at her grandparents' meant that she hadn't needed one. Neasa drew the zipper closed on her bag and then looked around once more, just ensuring that she had what she really needed. She knew that she could come back and forth but this was the move that she needed to make.

Breck stood in the hallway watching her, before he walked towards her, just reaching to draw her into a hug, feeling her hug him back. His voice whispered a prayer in her ear. Neasa was sure that she felt him kiss the top of her head when he finished but decided that she was imagining things.

"Ready?" Breck's voice was quiet before he reached for the duffel bags on her bed.

"I think so. I hate doing this when Dad's at work. But I'm not sure if I should be around him."

"We can stop by the job site. Does he expect you to be working?" Breck was concerned about her doing just that.

"He hasn't said. I should though, but it's almost the end of the season for us. The job at the shelter was the last one." Neasa searched Breck's face, seeing nothing but caring and compassion on it. "Breck? I'm not sure what to do now. He usually doesn't do much over the winter, just plans for the next year."

"Are you going to be working for him next year?" Breck shut the back door of his truck, and then stood, leaning against it, watching her.

Neasa shrugged. "I doubt it. I wanted to get back to what I had trained as, but I'm not sure now that I even want to do that." She sighed, a woebegone look on her face.

"And what had you trained in?"

"I had trained as a chef and had been working in a really nice restaurant, but it just got to be too much. I didn't like the big city living."

"Then, take the time you need to decide. Volunteer if you want to. I know Cadee's parents would be glad if you did. They prepare meals for the shelter residents." Breck held up a hand. "I'm not saying that's what you should do. Just think about what you want to do." He helped her into the truck and then stood, staring around. Someone is out there, I can feel them watching us. Lord, protect my lady. He was not aware of how he had just prayed, he was that concerned about Neasa.

Neasa watched as Breck pulled back onto the Barnabas Foundation grounds and into his designated spot before he turned off his truck and just sat.

"Breck?" Neasa finally spoke, not sure what was going on with him.

"Neasa? This worried me, what you said about someone sending you those messages. You never said anything to anyone?" He looked over at her.

"No, I really didn't believe it at first, and then it was so busy on the farm that I just sort of ignored them. I guess I shouldn't have, but it really didn't register with me that it was dangerous." She stared out the side window, biting at her lip. "What do I do, Breck? How do I stay safe?"

"That we can work on. Dallas will be around again, I'm sure of that. He'll need to talk with you about the messages and what they have found out. But that could take a while."

"I know. It's not a high priority. It's not life and death for me, at least not yet."

"No, it's not, but you are a lady being threatened. That doesn't happen."

"But no one can stop it, can they?" She finally reached to open the door, not waiting for him to come around.

———

Breck sighed to himself before he levered himself out of the truck, a groan coming from him. He was still very sore, after his adventures, he thought. He reached into the back for her bags, letting her take her laptop case.

"This way." Breck opened the lobby door and then watched as she stood, fascinated with the openness and the two sitting areas opposite one another.

"This is nice. Fireplaces as well. And the stained glass up there? I like that."

"Barnabas' mother had some of these ideas. We can spend time down here as friends, now that the guys are married. It helps." He pointed to the stairs. "We can walk up or we can take the elevator."

"Walk, I think. I need to do that." Neasa stopped, her eyes on him. "But are you okay to do that?"

"I'm fine, Neasa." Breck paused in front of a door, pulling out a set of keys. "This is the one for you to use. There is no charge, Neasa."

"What? That can't be right!"

"It is, Neasa. The Foundation keeps apartments here for use, such as for you. Some of the other ladies have used them as well. It's part of their mandate of encouraging others." He unlocked the door, opened it, and then waited patiently for Neasa to walk in.

Neasa entered, not quite sure what she was walking in to, a soft sound coming from her as she saw the beautiful, comforting decor and colours. "This is beautiful, Breck. So warm and welcoming." She finally made her way back to the hallway, where he still stood. "My stuff?"

Breck grinned. "Your stuff, is it? I'll drop it into the master bedroom. I think some of the ladies shopped for you, but if you need anything, let me know." He paused. "What about a vehicle?"

"Just find my motorbike." She sighed. "I need to talk to the insurance company about it, but I'm not sure how to explain it."

"I can help you with that." Breck sighed as he felt his phone vibrate. "Excuse me for a moment." He peered at the text message.

"It's Dallas. They have found your motorbike. It's okay. He says they'll take it to the police garage, go over it and then release it to you."

"Oh, thank goodness. I saved up for that. It was my first real purchase." Neasa paused, her eyes on him. "Breck? Thank you."

Breck shrugged. "It's what I do, Neasa. It's who I am. And besides, you're special." He grinned at her and then shut the door behind him, not seeing the look that softened her face.

With just a low light on, Neasa curled up on the couch, her inevitable cup of hot chocolate in her hand, and studied the living room. *This is a nice place. I can't get too comfortable, though, as I will have to leave. Eventually.* She set her cup on the end table and then laid her head on her outstretched arm, her face turning dreamy as she thought of Breck. *He is such a compassionate, caring man. I wonder that he has never married, but right now, he's the friend that I need.* Neasa reached for her phone, pulling up her text messages, finding one from Breck. She smiled as she read it, and then responded to it, telling him good night.

Breck reached for his own phone, smiling as he read Neasa's text message. *She's a sweet lady, Lord. I wonder that she's never married. I don't want to hurt her, and I am afraid that I might do just that.* He stopped as he read the one from Dallas and shook his head. *I'll call in the morning,* he thought. *Tonight, I just need to sleep.* He set his phone aside, turned out his light, and then spent the next while in prayer, Neasa one of the ones that he petitioned hardest for.

The next morning, Breck stared down at his desk, studying the paperwork that needed to be done. *Neasa, I'm sorry. I need to do this but I will catch up with you, by lunch. I promise.* He sent off a quick text to her and then immersed himself into the paperwork, looking up as his door opened.

"Brody? How are you?"

"I'm fine, but how are you?" Brody sat in one of the chairs in front of the desk.

Breck shrugged. "As okay as I can be. We were to meet the other morning."

"We were, but that's okay. I just dropped in to see how you were and ask what we can do for you."

"Right now?" Breck just grinned. "I can't think of anything but if I do, I'll certainly ask." He paused. "Neasa is in the apartment next to mine. We all felt it best that she not be at her parents' for now. Maybe some of the ladies could stop by?"

Brody grinned. "Ker is already planning that. She and Imly and Jaxcy, I think. A welcome to the building visit. Neasa won't be leaving."

"She won't?" Breck stared at his friend, his eyes narrowing at the look on Brody's face. "Not happening, Brody."

"I say otherwise. I've seen her around the church. She's your lady, Breck. She's the one that you need to complete you. But on another note, Ker has asked what the building does for holidays, if there's anything in particular that we do, decorations, etc."

"You know, we never really have, not outside our own apartments. She's wanting to decorate?"

Brody nodded. "All the ladies are. They think we need something in the lobby, just to brighten it as we come in and out. I told her that I'd ask."

Breck sat back, his eyes on his friend. "I can't see that it would hurt. Tell them to go ahead, be modest with what they do, and then bring me the bills. I'll okay with the board, but I don't see a problem, given that it is our home."

Brody stood. "That's what we thought you'd say. You're in our prayers, Breck. This time, we get to help you. Call us." He walked away, the door closing quietly behind him.

Breck rose, staring at his desk, and then cleared away paperwork before he reached for his schedule. Nothing more today, he thought. I need to find Neasa, glancing at his watch. I'm sure that she's found something to do but I need to make sure. He headed for the stairs, his steps slowing as he reached the lobby, his eyes on Neasa as she sat on one of the couches in the seating area. There were two but she had chosen the one nearest his office. He smiled, wondering if she had done that on purpose.

Sitting beside her, Breck waited. When he spoke, Neasa jumped and turned to stare at him, her face white, fear making her eyes huge.

"Breck? When did you get here?"

"Just now. You were lost in thought." He reaching for her hand, finding it cold. "You're chilled."

"No, not really. I am just trying to make sense of all this." Neasa sighed. "Can you?"

"Not at present. We don't have enough information. Has Dallas been in touch about your bike?"

"No, not yet. When I talked to him last, he said it would be a couple of days. That's what I need. To go for a really long ride. It always helps to clear my mind."

"I don't have a bike, but I have a truck. We could go for a really long drive. Grab some lunch and have a picnic." He grinned as she stared at him.

"A picnic? At this time of year? Breck!" Then she frowned. "Did you just ask me out?"

Breck thought for a moment. "Yeah, I guess I did. Would you do me the honour of going for a nice long ride and then having a picnic with me?"

Neasa tilted her head before she nodded. "Thank you, Breck. I think that is exactly what I need to do." She waited for him to stand. "Well? Didn't you say something about lunch?"

Breck laughed as he pulled her to her feet and then through the door to his truck, tucking her inside. When he had seated himself, he turned, laughter still on his face. "I did. Thank you, Neasa. You're a beautiful lady with a kind heart."

Late that afternoon, Barnabas stood and watched as Breck and Neasa walked back towards him, hand in hand before he shook his head. Brady had been right, he thought. There is interest there. Brady had been adamant that morning that Breck had found his lady. Barnabas had replied that he didn't think he had.

Breck looked up, surprise on his face for a moment. "Barnabas, you're waiting for us?"

"I am. Dallas was around. He needed to speak with both of you. He said that he'd be back early this evening." He turned to Neasa. "Neasa, my parents are around. They would like it if you would come for dinner tonight."

"They would? I really need to talk with my Dad." Neasa was hesitant.

"He's invited as is Nevin. Mom talked to your mother earlier." He grinned at Neasa groaned. "That was bad?"

"Knowing Mom? It might be. She might have let out a secret or two."

Breck grinned, mischief on his face. "You have secrets? You didn't tell me that."

She shoved at him with her shoulder, finding that she was more and more comfortable around him. "I have secrets. Barnabas, he's your old friend. Does he have any secrets that I should know about?"

Barnabas began to laugh, despite Breck's protest that he had no secrets, causing the men and ladies in the lobby to glance their way. "Oh, I think he does. One or two."

"Only one or two? That's not too many for me to discover." She tugged at her hand. "If I'm to go out for dinner, I need to go get ready. Dressy or casual?"

"Casual, Neasa. We don't dress up any more than we have to."

She stared at Barnabas. "That's not what I expected. Considering you're on the board here as is your father, I thought that you'd be in suits and ties all the time."

Breck shook his head at Barnabas. "I know from what you said that is how the boards you have dealt with him been. Not this one. We are more interested in the person than the dress. It's part of how we try to encourage others." Breck watched her face closely as she thought through his words.

Neasa finally shook her head, a grin on her face. "I'll figure it out. I always do. Breck, if you're invited for the meal, come find me." She ran quickly for the stairs and then disappeared from sight.

Breck watched her leave before he glanced around the lobby. "I see we have an audience."

Barnabas laughed, thinking that was funny. "You do, Breck. It's your turn for the spotlight. And we're all happy for you." He pointed towards the corridor to the offices. "Do you have some time?"

"I do. I should be checking on my messages." Breck was hesitant to do just that.

"Leave it for now, my friend. Let's go pray for you and your lady. I fear for you two."

Breck nodded, watching Barnabas closely. "Thanks, Barnabas. She's running from something or someone. I'm just not sure what or who."

"They all were, Breck. Every one of the ladies was. That's where our fellows stepped in."

Breck nodded, slipping down into the chair he favoured in the office. "Barnabas? There's more than what you said."

"There is, Breck. Dallas will be back out. He asked that you be available, both you and Neasa. He was almost angry if I could describe how he was."

"At us?"

"No, at whatever is going on." Barnabas leaned forward, his arms on the desk. "How can I pray for you, Breck?"

Breck shrugged. "I'm usually the one asking that, aren't I? I really don't know, to tell you the truth. I'm in uncharted waters here."

"I know that. Dad and I were talking. Neasa is going to need something to fill her time. I spoke with Dan after the board met. We're putting the work at the shelter on hold until the spring. We felt it best, given that the police may need back into the site. He said that he doesn't have anything on the books, as he put it, for now, not until spring. He's worried about her."

"I know he is. I'll see what I can find for her to do. She's a trained chef, but I got the impression that she's reluctant to take that back up."

"She is? You know, the board was looking at setting up to do meal deliveries for the seniors and shut-ins. Would she be interested in heading that up?"

Breck shrugged. "I have no idea. Let your Dad talk to her. He might get a better sense than either one of us." Breck yawned. "I'm sorry. I'm beat"

"I know. Take off, Breck. It's Friday. Come back on Monday to start over." Barnabas watched his friend walk away, a prayer in his heart for him and his lady.

—

Breck watched Neasa closely that evening, seeing how exhausted that she was. He finally reached for a small pillow, dropping it against his leg, and then leaned over to whisper to her.

"You can lay down, Neasa. They won't mind." He nodded as she looked up at him and then with a grateful sigh, did that, her head on the pillow, her legs curled up on the couch.

Elizabeth had been watching and reached for a blanket to cover her. "She's tired, Breck." Her hand rested on Breck's head.

"She is, Elizabeth. And from more than just the last few days. We have a chance to talk today, but I won't break her confidence." His arm rested around Neasa.

"Nor would we ask you to." Elizabeth exchanged a glance with Bruce. "What can we do for her?"

Dan had watched his daughter closely, seeing how she was turning to Breck, and not himself or Nevin. "Right now, Elizabeth? Just let it lie. She likes to mull things over. If she wants help, she'll ask for it."

Nevin, Barnabas, and Breck exchanged glances, knowing that Dan was reading his daughter wrong. Nevin sighed. Even he could not get Neasa to open up to him. That had never happened in the past. They were close, this brother and sister, sharing their thoughts and wishes and dreams with one another.

Dallas stood for a moment, watching the group, Bruce standing beside him.

"She's sleeping?"

"She is, Dallas. She's exhausted." Bruce watched Breck closely, thinking of him as another son. "Breck thinks that is more than just the last few days. He talked with me, told me I could tell you that."

"I'm sure that it is. She's running, Bruce."

"I know she is. I see all the signs. And she's run to Breck, not her family. I think that has surprised her father."

Dallas glanced at Dan, finding him in conversation with Barnabas. "It will be hard for him to let go, you know? I had a long talk with Will today."

"He and Dan have been friends for many years. They grew up together, just as I did with them." Bruce shook his head. "But until something happens, or she speaks freely, we can't do much."

"No, unfortunately, we can't." Dallas sighed as his phone chimed and he excused himself to answer it. When he returned, it was to simply excuse himself from the gathering. He had a crime scene to get to.

Late that evening, only Breck and Neasa were left with Barnabas, the others heading home. Barnabas handed Breck a new mug of coffee before he sat in his favourite chair, a sigh coming from him.

"You need a vacation, Barnabas." Breck watched him closely. "All this with the men have worn you out."

"It has, Breck." Barnabas sighed again, his eyes closing for a moment. "And you as well."

"Well, yeah, there's that too." Breck's hand tightened on Neasa's. Over the course of the evening, her hand had found his.

"Dan seemed surprised that Neasa wasn't turning to him or Nevin."

"We talked about that. She wants a different perspective on what she's going through. Her family is too close to her." Breck pulled his upper lip down over his teeth, a habit he had when he was uncertain about something. "I need to talk with you and the fellows, but I need to talk to Neasa first."

"About what?" Neasa sat up, sleepily pushing the hair back from her eyes. "What I'm going through? How could they help?"

"They have helped solve all the adventures, as we call them, that they each had. They all have different ideas and thoughts, work through them, and then pool them." Breck studied her, seeing the shadows in her eyes. "I won't talk to them if you say no, Neasa. I won't break your confidence."

"I know you won't." She turned to Barnabas. "How do I do it though? It's just random thoughts, ideas, impressions. Nothing really solid."

"I would say that we all meet, the ladies as well if you want. They've helped as well. We don't discount them just because they're ladies."

"That's refreshing." Neasa leaned against Breck. "I need to go home, Breck. It's late."

"I know it is. Here, up you go." Breck stood, reaching for Neasa's hand.

Neasa whispered a soft thank you to Barnabas before she walked away, tugging Breck with her. Barnabas watched as they left, a prayer for his friend and his lady rising.

The next afternoon, Neasa wandered the conference room that had been set up with computers, whiteboards, printers, faxes, and whatever supplies were needed. She was impressed, to put it mildly, and told Breck that. He had grinned at her comment before he turned to answer a question from Branigan.

Berneen, Baird's wife, approached Neasa, not sure how to do just that.

"Neasa? Have you everything that you need?"

Neasa turned. "It's Berneen, right? Thank you. I do. I understand that I have you ladies to thank for that."

Berneen shrugged. "It's what we do, Neasa. It's part of being in the Foundation family. We are encouraged to be encouragers."

"That's a mouthful." Neasa grinned. "I understand that it was named after Barnabas and also the Barnabas in the Bible. I have always loved how he was such an encourager to Paul and to the churches."

"Me, too." Berneen directed their steps to the small kitchen area. "They set this up to provide coffee, tea, water, juice. The cupboards hold snacks. We make sure the fridge has fresh fruit and veggies."

"You seem to think of everything." Neasa accepted the cup of hot chocolate handed to her by Jaxcy. "Thank you. Someone must have squealed on me."

"He did. He was adamant that we keep hot chocolate, mint flavoured preferred, here now. He's taking care of you, Neasa."

"He is." Neasa's face softened as her eyes sought out Breck. "He is. He's a good listener."

"He is. Hagen's twin sisters, Hailey and Holly, think of him as their big brother. He has helped them a lot with different things."

"He would. He's that kind of man. He also has a wonderful way of praying."

"He does, Neasa. I can't tell you how many times one of his prayers have lifted me up when I needed it." Berneen turned to face the other woman. "We'll need to tell you all our stories. I understand Breck told you that you didn't need one of our adventures."

Neasa began to laugh. "He did. I told him that I wanted one. But now that I seem to be involved in one? I think he was right. Just don't tell him that."

"Not tell who what?" Breck grinned at Neasa as he came to stand beside her.

"I'm not telling and neither are these ladies." Neasa shook her finger at him even as she grinned. "So, tell me. What have you discovered so far?"

Breck stared at her, even as the ladies began to laugh.

"She's got you there, Breck." Berneen reached to hug Neasa, surprising her. "It's not often we get one up on Breck. You just did. You're good for him."

Neasa stared at Breck for a moment before she nodded. "You know? I think you're right. Someone has to keep him in line." That brought more gales of laughter from the ladies with Breck protesting that he didn't need to be kept in line.

Barnabas turned from where he stood at the front of the room, in conversation with Buckley and Brandon, and shook his head.

"He's met his match. She'll be good for him." Buckley grinned.

"I agree." Brandon watched the couple closely, seeing how close Neasa had moved to Breck. "What's going on with her?"

"That we don't know yet. Breck just mentioned to me that she had moved back from a big city, not liking that life, but that he felt there was more to it than that. She's passed her phone over to Dallas."

"Phone? Messages?" Brandon looked at Barnabas for confirmation.

"I would say so. Neither one is saying."

"That incident at the shelter? Any word on it?" Buckley sipped at his coffee before he set the mug down on a table.

"No. Dallas didn't think there would be. He's not the one investigating it right now. Not unless his supervisor pulls him in. It will take time, he said." Barnabas was frustrated with that. "The board has decided to wait until spring to move forward with that once more." He turned as Bradon approached. "Bradon?"

"Dallas just had this dropped off for you. The officer asked that you get it right away." He handed over an envelope.

"Thanks, Bradon. Buckley, let's get our meeting started. I see all the ladies are here."

"They are. Hey, everyone, let's find our seats and spend time in prayer, just like always." Buckley watched as the men and ladies sorted themselves out into twos before he walked towards Bruce. "Bruce?"

"Sure, Buckley. Let's find our chairs. I feel that we need this prayer time today. And I have no idea why."

Neasa looked around later that afternoon, wandering the apartment that she was living in. She was tired, she thought, of having her life on hold. That was how it had felt. She missed her bike as well, normally heading out on long rides when she felt like this. Maybe a run, she thought? Dressing quickly, she headed for the stairs, finding Jaxcy heading up.

"Neasa? Just who I was looking for." Jaxcy turned to walk back down with her. "Oh! You're dressed for a run. Have you seen the gym?"

Neasa's head shot around. "There's a gym? Breck didn't tell me that."

Jaxcy grinned. "He didn't? And yes, there is. This way. Hagen has a woodworking shop attached to the back. She crafts toys and puzzles. Most of her work is sold online."

"I need to look at that. But first, the gym." Neasa stared around the gym. "This is nice. Much better than some of the gyms I've been to over the years."

"Barnabas makes sure to have all the equipment kept up to date. It's part of what he does. The Foundation looks after us."

"I can see that." Neasa moved towards a treadmill. "This is a nice one. I keep repeating that word. I need to find a new one."

Jaxcy broke out into laughter at that. "And there are trails around here that are great for walking, even taking you to the lake. But I wouldn't advise that right now." She stepped onto an adjacent treadmill and made the adjustments that she wanted.

"And why not?" Neasa was puzzled.

"Because of what you're going through. It's not likely safe. The bad guys, as Holly refers to them, have actually come right into our building."

Neasa nodded, knowing that was the case. She sighed to herself even as she began to run. *How do I do this, Lord? I feel that I*

—

am bringing a lot of danger to these ladies and the little ones. How can I solve this and then move on, without harm coming to anyone?

Jaxcy watched closely as Neasa abruptly stepped away from the machine and then left, her heart rising in prayer for her new friend.

Neasa stood outside the gym, staring around before she moved towards what she thought were gardens. Her eyes widened in surprise as she saw the fruit trees and bushes. This is so wonderful, she thought. She turned as she heard footsteps. Burnie stood there, watching, a closed look on his face before he smiled.

"Neasa? I'm Burnie. I think that we've met."

"I think so." Neasa walked towards him. "You're an author."

"I am." He turned to walk beside her as she headed for the rose garden. "This garden here? All the ladies love it. The roses bloom for months."

"They do? I would like to see it but I'll be long gone before they bloom in the spring." Neasa sank down onto a bench, her eyes on the ground. "Burnie? You had an adventure?"

"I did. It was quite the one as well. But I met my beautiful Muir and rescued her as well as her Granny."

"Granny? Oh, I know her. She makes sure that she speaks to me every time I'm at the church. She's so sweet."

"She is. She raised Muir from a baby after Muir's parents were killed in a plane crash. Long story. We'll have you over for dinner one night and tell you all about it."

"You will? I see. Making plans for me?" Mischief sparkled in her eyes as she watched him.

Burnie spluttered with his words for a moment before he too began to laugh. "Does Breck know what a treasure he has?"

"A treasure? And who has? As far as I know, we're not a couple. And not likely to be." Neasa shook her head at that.

"I think otherwise, Neasa, but it's up to Breck to tell you."

—

"Burnie, can I ask something else? I don't want to seem insensitive or impudent, but I notice that all of you have the same initials."

"We do. God laid it on Barnabas' heart that he needed to find men to bring here to work. All had to have the same initials as he does. All would be orphans. We come from every province and territory in Canada, except for Breck and Barnabas who are from this area. The Foundation pays our wages, letting our employers find others as they need to without financial hardship. We all volunteer at something as well. And our wives are pay wages from the Foundation as well. This is all part of their mandate of being encouragers."

"Wow! I didn't realize that. It's not noised around, is it?"

"No. It's not. I mean we could talk about it if we wanted to, but we don't."

"I see." Neasa grew quiet before she looked up at him once more. "Your ladies? I see that their last names are all starting with the letter "D" and that their names go in alphabetical order. But there is no one that starts with "A"."

"No, there isn't. We all think that will be Barnabas' lady. Only we have no idea who she is or where she is." Burnie stretched out his legs, his hands going into his jeans' pockets.

"You do?" Neasa nodded. "Of course, she would be. I just find it interesting how it has worked out. He looks sad sometimes when he doesn't think anyone is watching him."

"He does. It's becoming more frequent. Muir and I think that he had a lady who walked out on him. We also think that he'll take off and try and find her at some point, just to close that chapter."

"That's so sad." Neasa grew thoughtful before she was on her feet. "I need to keep moving, Burnie. I'm sorry. I'm restless."

"And you will be, until whatever it is that is weighing you down disappears. Talk to any one of us, please? Breck has always been there for us, no matter what. We want to do the same for him and for you. He's chosen you, Neasa, whether you realize it or not."

—

Breck stared at Dallas as he spoke before he reached for the picture. He stared down at it. This was taken yesterday, he thought, as he and Neasa had walked around the building.

"Where did you get this?"

"It was dropped off at the front desk. We're pulling the security feed to see if we can make out who it was. The desk officer had turned away for a moment and when she turned back, it was there."

"That's from yesterday. They're watching her closely."

"Or you." Dallas nodded as Breck's eyes shot up once more to stare at him. "You, Breck. I know that you don't have any dark secrets. At least, I think that you don't. But you're involved with Neasa. Someone is after her and they're going to go after you."

"I know, Dallas. Neasa and I have talked. She's been open with me. Unfortunately, I can't share what she has told me, without asking her for permission. We're taking all the precautions that we can, but it seems as if they're not enough."

"They're never enough." Dallas was frustrated, turning as a tap came to the door and it opened.

"Breck? I can come back." Neasa's voice was very quiet and withdrawn.

Breck was to her side, drawing her into his office before she had a chance to leave. "No, it's okay, darlin'. We need to talk with you anyway."

"About what?" Her eyes saw the photo that Breck had dropped on his desk. "That's us."

"It is. Someone has been around, taking pictures of us. We're off on that adventure that you so wanted."

"I don't want it anymore. Not at all." She thrust the envelope that she had been holding at him. "This came today. How did they know that I was here?"

"Drop it on the desk, Neasa." Dallas watched her hesitate. "On the desk, Neasa." He pulled out a pair of latex gloves. "You've read it, but I need to preserve it as much as I can."

Neasa paled as she did just what he asked. "Dallas?"

"I need to talk to you about your phone messages, but first this." Dallas carefully slid the letter from the envelope and opened it, his face growing grim as he did so. "Neasa, what did you go and get mixed up in?"

"Nothing. Absolutely nothing. I went to work, went home, went to church, when to the gym. Went shopping. I kept to myself. I really had no friends there." She paled as she saw Dallas' face before she grew angry. "I have done nothing to warrant this."

"I know, Neasa. I know. I just need to ask the questions." He read the letter before his eyes raised to Breck and then back to Neasa. "Neasa? Where did you work?"

"At some fancy-dancy restaurant in the downtown area of the town. I lived nearby. I didn't have contact with any of the customers. The wait staff was always changing over, which I found strange. I had been there for about two years when I left." She bit at her lip. "I found that strange.'"

"It is strange. Let me have the name of the restaurant and the owner's name." He wrote them down before he looked back at the letter. "This is very specific about an event. Do you remember it?"

Neasa shook her head. "Not really. I know that there were sometimes private dinners. I never saw the guests. I only cooked." She poked at the letter with a slim index finger. "What did they think that I saw?"

"That's what we have to determine." Dallas gathered the letter and envelope back up and sealed them into an evidence bag before tucking it back into a pocket. "Listen, you two. You need to take precautions. Breck, you are well aware of what needs to be done. Neasa? Do you have transportation other than your bike?"

—

Neasa shrugged. "I can get something. I need to, now that the weather's turning colder. Why?"

"Because you need to. You can't be out on your bike. It's too dangerous."

Neasa's temper flared at that. "Right now, I don't see any danger. Other than some text messages that make no sense, that letter that says I saw something that I didn't, and that picture, I see nothing to worry me." She was gone before either man could react.

Breck ran after her, finding her on her motorbike, pulling away. He stopped in frustration before he ran for his truck. Neasa, please? Let me talk with you. He followed her until she finally pulled over, just sitting waiting for him to approach her.

"Neasa?"

"Breck. Go home. I don't want you around me."

"That's not happening, Neasa. I will not walk away from you." Breck rested his hand on the handlebars of the motorbike.

"I don't want you hurt. Please? Go home?" Neasa finally looked up at him, her face haunted.

"What did you remember, Neasa?"

She shook for a moment before she nodded. "I did remember something. Take me home, Breck. I mean to Dad's. I need to leave my bike there."

Breck watched her as she pulled away before he was back into his truck and following her as closely as he could. He waited as she settled her bike into the garage and then ran for his truck, ducking inside and buckling up. Neasa prayed that her family had not seen her. She didn't know how she would explain her movements, of not coming in to see them, and just leaving with Breck.

Breck pulled into a local coffee shop, running in and out quickly with an order for them, handing Neasa her hot chocolate, setting his coffee into the cup holder. He pulled away, searching for somewhere that they could talk, finally just deciding on the parking lot at the local library. Before Neasa could speak, he simply reached for her hand and prayed for her.

Neasa blinked as he finished. She couldn't think of another friend who would do that, just sit and pray with her. She felt his hand squeeze hers and she then clung to his. She needed that contact.

"What did you remember, Neasa?" Breck finally spoke, his voice quiet.

"I'm not sure what it was. I can remember one night one of the wait staff coming back into the kitchen, her face white. She was shaking. I couldn't get her to tell me what happened. She just took off her apron, found her purse, and walked out. Someone else had to pick up for her. They never said anything. I never saw her again, but there was a report of a murder. The description seemed like her, but I never heard a name. Could that be it?"

"It could be. They may think that she said something. We'll need to let Dallas know." Breck's thumb rubbed against her hand. "What else?"

"I can remember being followed one night as I was walking from the bus. I heard the footsteps that tapped after me, stopping every time that I did. I ran the final block and locked myself into my apartment. That was about a month before I came home. I put in my notice the next day and just walked away. I didn't have much in the apartment. It never felt like home."

"You came home and then went to work on your grandfather's farm." Breck stared out through the windshield. "How did that work out?"

She shrugged. "It got me away from the city and then away from here. I needed space to think. I'm not sure how much thinking I did. I worked until I dropped every night, even though Pops tried to make me not. I was driven, I guess, Breck."

"Driven to forget?" At her nod, he sighed. "Where do we go, Neasa? How do we protect you?"

Neasa stared out the side window before she spoke, her voice sounding tiny in the truck cab.

"I don't know, Breck. How do you protect against someone that you can't see, that you don't know?"

"We have done just that, Neasa. Twelve times. Sure, they were injured, some had to be brought back to life, but God protected us in so many ways. He will protect you. All I ask?" His voice died away, not sure what to say or even how to say it.

Neasa waited before she turned to him. "What do you ask?"

"I ask, Neasa, that you let me walk beside you through this. You are a beautiful, funny, adorable lady who loves my God so much. I would like to be that man who protects you, Neasa." He didn't look at her, not wanting to see her rejection of him.

Neasa had to swallow hard. "Breck?" When he didn't look at her, she tugged at his hand, causing him to look at her. "Do you mean that?" At his nod, she closed her eyes, a tear tracking down her cheek. "Thank you. I have waited all my life for those very words." She opened her eyes to find him watching her intently. "Will you?"

"I will. I don't want to see you hurt, Neasa, but there's more there. I would like to see where we go, if we go anywhere, in our relationship. I have never ever been attracted to someone. Not until you. People think it's strange. I have talked to both my parents. Mom just hugged me and told me that if God wanted me single, then I needed to accept that and live my life for him. Dad hugged me as well, told me to wait for my Proverbs 31 lady."

"Proverbs 31 lady? I like that." Neasa stared out the side window again. "I'm just not sure that I'm a Proverbs 31 lady."

"You are to me, Neasa." Breck's voice was barely audible. "Now, what else can you tell me?"

Her head shot around as she stared at him before she began to laugh. "Only you, Breck, could tell me what you did, and then ask that?"

Breck was puzzled until he thought back over what he had said and then he too laughed.

"I'm sorry. I shouldn't have done that."

"I can see life is going to be interesting." She watched as he reached for his phone which had been vibrating for a while. "I wondered when you were going to answer that."

He shook his finger at her. "When I'm with you, you are my priority, the most important thing at the moment." He looked at his text messages. "Barnabas is looking for us. He needs to talk with us, as soon as we can make it. I don't like that. He doesn't do that unless there is an emergency."

"Anything else?" She reached into a pocket for her own phone. "Dad left a voice mail." She listened to it. "It's okay. He just wanted to make sure I was okay. He found my motorbike in the garage but not me. He'll have to get used to that."

"He will. I'll talk with him if you like. In fact, I need to, if we're to start dating."

"Start dating, is it? And talking to my Dad? That sounds serious, buster."

Barnabas watched as Breck and Neasa walked towards him across the parking lot from where Breck had parked. The men of the building had gathered in the conference room, taking the information that he and Dallas had given them and begun their search. Not that they had a lot at the present time, he thought. We need to get Neasa to talk to us, and I'm not sure that we can.

"Barnabas? You called?" Breck grinned at his friend before he sobered. "You have something to talk to us about."

"I do. Dallas was around. The crime lab had a look at the threat and the picture. They found something in the letter." Barnabas turned to walk back towards the building. "The fellows are working on what they can."

"I figured that they would be. It's different this time."

Barnabas gave a quick grin. "It is. It's you that they're investigating. Not one of them, with you leading."

Neasa paused in her walk, her eyes on the gardens. "What do they do?"

"I'm not sure if I can explain it all. Each one has their own way of searching. It always seems to work." Barnabas paused at the conference room door. "If you ask each one, Neasa, they will explain it to you."

She shrugged. "Not that it really matters. I was just curious."

"Ask them, Neasa. If you don't, I will and have them each talk to you. This is your life that we're speaking of. You need to know." Breck was firm with her, not letting her back down from her question.

"Boy, you're bossy." Neasa yanked open the door and entered, letting it close behind her.

Breck stared at it until he turned to Barnabas, to find his friend with a grin on his face. His eyes narrowed.

"You think this is funny?"

"In a way, I do, Breck. She's got your number. She's exactly what you need." Barnabas disappeared into the room, leaving Breck staring at the closed door.

Breck cautiously opened the door and peeked in, grinning to himself as he saw Neasa seated beside Baird, watching him as he worked away. He could tell that she was asking questions, just from how Baird was working.

Buckley stood beside the door, watching Breck.

"Are you coming in or not?"

"In. At least I think I am. Barnabas had information for me."

"He does. Here. This is your copy. Your lady has gotten herself involved in something pretty nasty."

"That's what Neasa and I have already decided." Breck glanced through it. "Here. This name? That's likely the wait staff that she says walked out. She thought that the lady had been killed."

"What kind of restaurant was it?" Buckley pulled out a chair and sat beside Breck.

"That I am not sure of. She says it was a high-end one, but the staff kept changing all the time. She was followed home one night and that's when she gave her notice and moved home."

"Only whoever it was followed her?"

"I would think so." Breck paused. "I wonder how she got her things here. She couldn't on her bike."

"I sent them by bus, Breck. It was the cheapest way. Not that there was much." Neasa stood beside him, her hand on his shoulder.

"Have you gone through the boxes?"

Neasa nodded. "I did. I unpacked everything and put the boxes out for recycling. There wasn't anything there that wasn't mine if that's what you are thinking."

"I am." Breck pointed to the chair beside him. "I saw you talking with Baird."

"I was. He was actually able to explain what he was doing in a way that I could understand. I don't always understand the technical terms that you use."

"No, I guess you wouldn't." Breck was distracted. "Neasa? That restaurant owner?"

"Him? What about Mr. Daniels?"

"Did you know that his father was in the mafia?"

Neasa paled. "No. I had no idea. Was he?"

"That's what Dallas is working on right now. If he is, Neasa, I don't know what we'll do."

Neasa took one look at Breck and then was on her feet, moving quickly from the room and towards the lobby. She stopped to stare out of the door before she sighed. I need to quit running, don't I, Lord? Only I don't know how to.

Guenivere stood and watched for a moment before she walked towards Neasa, the sound of her footsteps alerting Neasa to the fact that she was not alone. The two ladies stood for a moment, gazing out of the window before Neasa spoke.

"How do I do it, Guenivere? How do I do it? I think I've brought danger to Breck." Neasa's voice was barely a whisper.

"By trusting God, first of all. By trusting Breck. He's been around the block as they say. He'll do everything that he can to keep you safe. So will our guys. And Dallas and the police will as well."

"I get that, Guenivere. But how do I allow that to happen? I don't think I can." Neasa moved to sit in one of the chairs, Guenivere sitting near her.

"It's hard, Neasa. All of us have wanted to run and not put our guys in danger. Some of us married to keep each other safe. Berneen married Baird to save his life. It's who we are, Neasa. That's what we do for one another. It's part of being a family. As Breck's lady, you're part of it now."

"I know." Neasa's voice was still only a whisper. "I just don't know if I can live with myself if something happens to him."

"I don't think that matters to him, Neasa. He's indicated that he wants to be in your life, hasn't he?" At Neasa's nod, Guenivere reached for her hand, bending her head to pray for her new friend.

Breck stood and watched before he turned back towards the conference room. No, he decided, Neasa needs me. Not the guys. They can work on it well enough on their own. He walked quietly to where she sat, crouching down beside her, an arm around her. He was surprised that she hadn't jumped when he touched her.

"Thank you, Guenivere. Neasa?" Breck watched her profile.

"I'm okay, Breck. Guenivere has helped. Thank you." Neasa gave a small smile, receiving a wide warm one in return from

Guenivere. "I've never had friends such as you ladies are to one another."

"We can rectify that, Neasa. We meet on Monday morning for Bible study and prayer. We'll all off on Monday morning. Join us. We try and meet once a week with all of us. And then we pair off. I would like to pair off with you. I usually meet with Fynn. She would welcome you."

"I'll think about it. Right now, I think I need to apologize to a few fellows." Neasa turned as Breck shook his head

"Not needed, Neasa. I did for you. They understand better than you think."

"I know that, Breck." Neasa was frustrated. "What all have they discovered?"

"That Daniels was indeed a criminal and that his restaurant was a front for multiple crime deals. You were fortunate or protected, I should say, that you were only in the kitchen. That's why the staff kept changing. They would only work for a few weeks and then be made to leave in case they saw something. The waitress? Dallas has done some preliminary work on that. The feeling is that she overheard something and that they realized she had. You were the only one to speak with her that day. That's why they are after you. They think she may have said something to you."

"But she didn't. She just left. We all looked at one another after she did and went right back to what we were doing." Neasa leaned against him. "How do I get that message out?"

"I'm not sure that we can, Neasa. They are working to find enough evidence to arrest them. But for now the police there have asked Dallas to make sure that you stay safe."

"And just how do I do that?" Neasa struggled in his arms for a moment before she relaxed. "I don't want anyone hurt. Certainly not the little ones. And that's what they will do."

"We all know that, Neasa. They won't go after anyone but you, or me now that we've been seen together. They won't go after your family. It's not their code."

Neasa was not comforted, not at all, she thought. How do I do this, Lord? How do I begin to date, when I'm in such danger? How to I keep Breck safe?

Dan watched his daughter closely the next morning from where he stood just inside the church doors, Nevin walking towards her. He shook his head. Breck certainly was not who he would have chosen for her. He searched his mind for someone he could send her way and then nodded. He had the perfect candidate. He would talk with him later this afternoon. Dan felt that he had to get Neasa away from Breck, that he was bringing danger to her.

Nevin grinned at his sister as he reached to hug her, finding her moving closer to Breck when he released her.

"How are you, Neasa?"

"Just fine. You?" Her eyes narrowed as she studied her brother. "Nevin?"

"I'm fine, sis. Just fine. Breck?"

"Nevin?" Breck copied the inflection in Nevin's tone, causing the younger man to grin at him. "I see you're on your own."

"I am. Sarah couldn't make it this morning. She's not feeling great."

"Oh, no! What can I do for her?" Neasa's thoughts went to her brother's wife.

"She'll be fine, sis. Just fine. She's been fighting a migraine the last couple of days and thought it best just to stay home. Call her later. She'd like to talk with you."

"I'll do that." Neasa bit at her lip, a habit that Nevin recognized.

"Sis?"

"Nevin? Has anyone been around you, asking about me?"

Nevin shared a look with Breck, who nodded. "No, they haven't. Sarah hasn't mentioned anything either. Now, Dad?" Nevin turned towards the church. "I'm not sure if he would say."

—

"Not likely." Neasa moved forward as Breck did, heading into the church. "Where do you normally sit?"

"At the back. Is that okay?" Breck suddenly grew hesitant about his normal seat.

"No, that's where I like to sit. Nevin?"

"I'm ushering today, sis. Catch you later." Nevin's steps slowed as he walked towards his father. "Dad?"

"Nevin? How is she?"

"She's fine and she's happy, Dad. Don't do anything to spoil that for her." Nevin walked past his father, suddenly feeling that Sarah had been right. That Dan would do just that, find someone to interfere in Neasa's budding romance. His phone was out as he sent Breck a text, warning him of that.

Buckley and Locklin slid in beside them, Buckley finding it strange that he was no longer behind the pulpit of the church that he had pastored for so long. Neasa greeted them, and then shifted closer to Breck, a sudden chill running down her back and causing her to shiver. Breck frowned and looked around, not seeing anyone that he didn't recognize.

"You're okay?" He bent his head to whisper to her.

"I am, I think." She looked around. "I just feel uncomfortable, but I need to be here. Does that make sense?"

"Perfect sense, darling. Perfect sense." Breck's attention went back to the front, missing her speculative look at the term of endearment that he had called her.

Locklin leaned over. "He means that, Neasa. He doesn't give endearments to just anyone."

Neasa nodded. "I know. It's just so new. And I'm just so uncertain about things."

"We need to talk. Tomorrow, how be we do lunch? Our meeting will be over by then?"

"I would like that. Thank you."

Breck watched late that afternoon from where he stood near the Foundation building entrance, Neasa standing a few feet away

—

from him. He didn't know the younger man who had shown up, asking for Neasa.

Neasa had been hesitant to meet him, her hand reaching for Breck as she went forward. He had stopped just short of where she now stood, a whispered word in her ear.

"I'm sorry. I don't know you. You said my Dad sent you?"

"He did. He knew I was looking for a lady to date. He suggested that you would be willing to go out with me." The man, who Neasa knew from her father's work, Phil Evans, had a belligerent look on his face.

"Oh, he did, did he? Sorry. I'm not interested. I would suggest that you leave. And don't return." Neasa turned away, just as Phil reached for her arm, stopping her.

"I'm not done yet, Neasa. You will be going out with me. Starting tonight. So let's go. I have reservations at a local restaurant." He looked up as he heard a low growl and saw Breck standing in front of him. "What's your problem? She's leaving with me."

"For starters, I definitely heard her refuse and then suggest you leave." Breck's eyes saw the security guard on duty standing behind Phil. "There's a security guard there, waiting to help you leave. Besides, Neasa's my lady. We're dating."

"No way. She's mine." Phil's fist was back and driven into Breck's jaw without warning, sending Breck flying backward to lie still.

Neasa screamed and then fled to where Breck lay, on her knees, trying to raise his upper body. The guard prevented Phil from moving, handcuffs clicking around his wrist is despite his struggles and protests.

Brady was there, on his knees, his hands gentle on Breck's face. He hadn't seen what had transpired, just heard Neasa's scream as he and Fynn were heading out for a drive.

"Neasa?"

"He sucker-punched him, Brady. Oh, what did Dad do?" She looked up, anger sparking in her eyes. "Dad sent him. I refused to go with him and he took offence at that. Breck asked him to leave and that's when he punched him."

Breck's groan had her eyes on him and then her hands on his face. "Breck? Oh, are you okay? Breck?"

"Give him a chance to answer, Neasa." Amusement traced through Brady's words. "It's not broken, but it will be bruised and sore."

Breck sat up, Neasa's arms around him, and stared at Phil. The patrol officer who had responded approached him, crouching down to speak with him.

"You're okay, Breck?"

"I am. Get him out of here. I'm not sure if I'll lay charges or not."

"It's too late. He's been charged with trespassing. He was asked to leave and didn't. That can't be changed for now. Let him stew in jail for a few hours. He's known for tricks like this." He turned to Neasa. "You're okay?"

"I am. Just so angry. Go and talk to my father. He's the one who caused this. I'm not sure that I can ever face him again."

Dan's face paled as he faced Barnabas who stood on his porch. He shook his head. No, that wasn't what had happened.

"Phil showed up, Dan." Barnabas repeated himself. "He tried to forced Neasa to leave with him even after she had refused. Breck stepped in and Phil punched him, knocking him down and out. Phil has been arrested for trespass because he refused to leave. He may well be charged with assault."

"No, that's not what happened. He called me from jail, asking me to post bond for him. He said Breck attacked him."

"No, that isn't. The security guard on duty was there, making his rounds, and saw it. We also have it on our security feed, which we have turned over to the investigating officer. At the moment, Neasa is refusing to leave the building or the property, which is her right to do so. That is her home at present." Barnabas was frustrated. How had his father's friend sunk to this? "And if case you didn't know it, Breck and Neasa are dating. If you try anything like this again, I will go to the church board and we will be speaking with you. She is an adult, capable of making her own decisions."

"We'll see about that. I'll be out to speak with her." Dan moved to shut the front door, stopping as Barnabas held out a paper.

"I'm sorry, Dan, that it had to come to this. This is a restraining order that Neasa took out against you. You cannot come on to the Foundation grounds. Not at present. In fact, you cannot be in touch with her. This order is directed at you alone. Not your wife. Not your son." Barnabas turned and walked away, sadness in his heart. How did this happen, Lord? And how do we help heal this relationship? It will never be the same, that much I know.

Neasa thrust her phone at Breck, fear on her face. He took it before he looked down at it.

"Your Dad? He's that angry?"

"He is. I've never seen him like that. Barnabas said he'd talk to him, hand him the restraining order. I didn't think that I had any choice." Tears sparkled in her eyes. "Breck?"

Breck simply swept her close to his heart. "I've got you, darling. I've got you. Let your Dad cool off. Bruce and Will I know are intending to speak with him." He turned to her phone again. "It's Nevin."

"Just send him a message. Let him know I'm okay and that I had to."

"Wait. He's downstairs. Stay put, darling. I'll be right back." Breck had taken Neasa to Doc and Anna, Doc examining his jaw and then just shaking his head.

Nevin turned as he heard footsteps and then reached to shake Breck's hand.

"I'm sorry, Breck. I wondered if Dad would be up to something. He can be restrictive with Neasa. That's part of the reason that she moved away. He just doesn't understand that she's an adult and can make her own decisions."

Breck nodded. "I know. She just doesn't need this right now, not with being threatened and followed."

"I wondered. She seemed edgy this morning. She not likely will want to talk to me. Will you tell her that I love her and that I will do everything I can to make sure Dad doesn't try a stunt like this again?"

"I will. Give her a day or so and then call her. Just send her a text later telling her that. She needs your support."

"She has it. Mine and Sarah's." Nevin looked down at the bag that he was holding. "Sarah heard what happened and sent this. A care package if you like. Some of her favourite treats and her hot chocolate."

Breck took the bag, a sad smile on his face. "I'll do that. Thank your Sarah for me." He watched Nevin walk away, hearing footsteps approaching him.

"You okay, Breck?" Benen spoke from beside him, Blair on his other side.

"I am, fellows. Thanks. Where is everyone?"

"Out and about, doing fun stuff. We had just come back when we heard. Nevin okay?" Blair nodded towards the doors.

"He will be. He's hurting for his sister."

"He will. Now, we just need to solve your adventure, you two can marry, and that will be the answer." Benen grinned as he waved and walked away.

"Did he really just say that?" Breck stared after him.

"He did, Breck. We can all see your heart. You're not hiding it very well. You are in our prayers." Blair walked away as well, leaving Breck standing staring outside, a frown on his face, a thought crossing his mind that had him shaking his head.

Screaming, Neasa ran for the building, her heart racing in fear even as her feet pounded along the gravel pathway. She could hear the thudding of footsteps getting closer, and that lent wings to her feet. I can do this, she prayed. I see the end of the path. There has to be someone around. Her breath caught in her throat and her chest hurt from the exertion. Just a few more steps, but she didn't make it. Tackled and taken to the ground, Neasa struggled against the man holding her down.

"What did she say?" His guttural voice finally made it through her fear.

"I don't know. Who?" Sobs shook her body even as she continued to struggle, to no avail.

"The waitress. What did she tell you?"

"Nothing. Let me go!" Neasa screamed again, hoping and praying that someone would hear her.

The man shot a glance towards the building and with a curse, his hand was back and then thudding harshly against Neasa's temple, sending her spiraling down into darkness. She lay limp even as he shoved away from her and ran himself, heading back towards the woods and safety.

Brendon ran after him even as Branigan and Brody dropped down beside Neasa.

"Neasa?" Brody tried to rouse her. "She's out cold."

"She is. Is Doc around?"

"No, and neither is Brady. Cadee was but she was heading into town, for a class she said when I saw her earlier."

Branigan nodded, frustration at not having help for Neasa at hand. "Call it in, Brody." He ran back to the building, heading for the infirmary and unlocking it to reach for a folded metal emergency blanket. The door locked behind him, he ran again for the lobby, finding Blair and Bradon standing watching him.

"Branigan?"

"Neasa was attacked. We didn't get there in time." He continued to run, heading for Neasa, shaking out the blanket and wrapping it around her. "Has she roused?"

"No, not at all. Breck's not here?" Blair looked around.

"No, he had meetings out of town today. He thought he would be back about now."

The men stood back as the paramedics arrived and then the patrol officers.

"What happened?"

"We're not sure. We heard Neasa scream and ran this way. We found her like this. Brendon took off towards the woods." Branigan looked around. "Here he is."

Barnabas met Breck as he walked towards the building, pointing towards his truck.

"In, Breck."

"Barnabas? I just got home." Breck protested.

"I know. Neasa's been hurt, about thirty minutes ago. I need to take you to her. They're asking for you. She was awake long enough to name you as her next of kin at the hospital. Did you know that?"

Breck stared at Barnabas. "No. I mean, we talked about it, but I didn't know that she had done that." His head went back as he prayed for his lady. "How bad?"

"Branigan and Brody weren't sure. She has facial bruising, Brody said, that was starting. It looked as if she was hit with something."

Breck's head went back on the headrest as his eyes closed. "Was she outside?"

"She was. She was heading back from the gardens. Brendon took off for the woods but couldn't find anyone. He heard a car pulling away before he got there."

"They've tracked her down. How do I keep her safe? I have to travel. I have meetings."

"I know, Breck. I know. We'll work on what we can, do video conferencing if possible." Barnabas' heart hurt for his friend.

Breck's head shot up. "Her father? If someone has called him, there will be problems."

"I know. I have been praying that didn't happen, but I'm sure it has. Security said for you to head in through the ambulance bay." Barnabas paused his truck long enough for Breck to jump out before he pulled away and into a parking spot, running for the main Emergency Department doors. Blair met him, an angry look on his face.

"Blair?" Barnabas drew him aside, even as he heard the angry raised voice.

"Her father. Some nurse called him. She didn't wait to verify the next of kin. Doc has refused to let him in. Nevin is listed after Breck. She was awake again and adamant about that, as much as she can talk. Dan's not taking it well." Blair turned to watch the older man. "What is his problem, anyway?"

"That's what we need to find out. Did someone call it in?"

"Security did. Will is on his way. So is Dallas. He's worried about Breck. They received another threat today, this time from someone on the street. Breck's been targeted too." Blair blew out a breath.

"Of course he has been. Listen, Breck went in through the ambulance bay. Doc called and asked for that. We need to keep him out of sight of Dan until Dan is removed." Barnabas looked around as he felt a hand on his shoulder. "Dad?"

"Will called. First, Neasa?" Bruce was concerned about Breck's lady.

"I don't know yet, Dad. She has been awake on and off from what Blair has said. This is the problem that we need to deal with."

Bruce's hand kept his son in place. "We don't. Barnabas, this time we let the authorities deal with him. I hate to say it, but he's changed in the last year or so. He has always had a temper but has been able to keep it under control. I think that is part of why Neasa left home. Nevin has come to me and talked over the years."

"He has? And it could be."

Doc met Breck as he headed down the hall towards the desk, reaching for his arm and pulling him into an empty examination room.

"Doc? Neasa?"

"She's in imagining right now, son. She took a blow to her face. I want to ensure that she doesn't have a fracture."

Breck sank back against the wall. "Her face? It was that hard a blow?" At Doc's nod, Breck scrubbed at his face with his hands. "How long will she be?"

Doc glanced at the clock. "She should be back in a couple of minutes. But there is a situation that you need to be aware of. One of the nurses didn't listen to who Neasa said was her next of kin and called her father."

"No! And he has a restraining order against him from her. Make sure that nurse understands that."

"Oh, she has been told. She's in her supervisor's office right now. It's not the first complaint against her." Doc's hand rested on Breck's shoulder. "I was told that Dan showed up and was fighting with the security guards. They called in the police."

"And that will not go over well. Can I see her?"

"Wait here. I'll be back." Doc was back shortly. "Come with me, Breck. She's this way."

Without any hesitation, Breck walked up to the stretcher, his eyes on Neasa. He grimaced as he saw the spreading bruise that started on her temple. A hand reached for hers, finding her cold, but her fingers tightened on his. She stirred, not quite waking, before she was still again. As best he could with one hand, Breck tucked the blankets around her, before he just stood, watching his lady, wishing that it was him lying there and not her.

Barnabas paused in the doorway, an hour later, as he watched his friend. Doc had finally made Breck sit, telling him that he needed to. Breck had nodded, not taking his eyes away from Neasa as Doc explained their findings. He had sighed, asked if she was being admitted, and was adamant that he was not leaving her. Doc had nodded, said he would make that possible, and had walked away after praying for the couple.

"Breck?" Barnabas' quiet voice broke into Breck's thoughts and he looked around.

"You're here?"

"Of course, I am. We all are. No one will leave until they hear from you how Neasa is. You know our group."

Breck nodded, exhaustion seeping through him. "No fractures, thank God. Doc doesn't think a concussion but he can't rule it out. She's been up and down for the last little while."

"They're keeping her in?"

"Doc wants to, but there's a bed shortage right now. I want to take her home, Barnabas. Anna sent word for us to come to them."

"And Cadee and Brady have volunteered to help." Barnabas leaned against the end of the bed. "Has Neasa been away long enough to say what happened?"

"Just enough to give a statement. And it wasn't all that clear. She was attacked as she ran from the gardens. She didn't get a look at the man. All he asked was what the waitress had said."

"So, it is what we thought."

Breck nodded, standing to place his hand against Neasa's cheek as she moved restlessly. "It is. You're staying?"

"I will. I'll be out in the waiting room. I'll send the others home." He handed over a bag. "Cadee brought in some clothes for Neasa, that would be easy for her to put on, she said."

"Cadee is such a compassionate caring person. Thank her for me." Breck paused. "Neasa's father?"

"Unfortunately, he was arrested. He assaulted a security guard and also a police officer. I have no idea what's going on with him. Neither does Dad or Will."

"Nevin called. He said his father's temper got worse after Neasa left home. Why, he couldn't say." Breck's hand rested against the uninjured side of Neasa's face. "Take us home, Barnabas. That's where we need to be."

"I will. I'll send Doc in. He's figuring that's what you would want."

Neasa shifted restlessly, not quite asleep, not quite awake, in the early morning hours. She felt arms tighten around her and shifted again to peer through pain-filled eyes. She knew this place, she thought before she snuggled down against whoever it was that was holding her and slept, a natural sleep this time.

Breck's head rested against Neasa as he slept, holding the love of his life, he had decided, as he sat in a comfortable armchair in Doc's living room. Anna had covered the two of them and then sat in her own chair, watching. She had sent Doc off to bed, knowing that he needed the sleep, with the promise to rouse him if she needed to. She prayed for her young friends, suddenly fearful for them, and then had shaken her head. Breck had been reluctant to leave the night before and Neasa just refused to let go of him, muttering that he kept her safe and that he couldn't leave her.

Breck finally roused in the early morning hours and looked around before he yawned and rubbed at his face. His eyes went to Neasa and he smiled before he rose and headed for the bedroom Anna had prepared for her, tucking her into bed and then leaving, closing the door behind him. He left the apartment quietly, heading for his own, to shower and shave and change. The ringing of his phone distracted him as he stood for a moment in his office and he reached for it.

"Dad? You're calling? I didn't think that you would!"

"Breck, son? Are you okay? Your mother and I have had such a burden for you. I headed out last night to where I could find service. We're planning on heading home in the next week or so."

"You are? Wonderful? Me? I'm okay, I guess."

"I don't like that hesitation." Beck Curran knew his son well.

"It's like this, Dad. I came to the rescue of a beautiful lady and have found my love.'

Beck stared at his phone before he began to laugh. "You did and you have? You're off on one of those adventures like the others?"

"We are, Dad. I won't go into all the details but she is in danger. Right now, she's with Anna and Doc. She was hurt last night."

"She was? Your Mom and I will be praying. In fact, she made me promise to tell you that. She's had such a burden the last couple of weeks."

"It's been about that long. Neasa really needs our prayers. She's struggling with some other stuff as well."

"Neasa? Dan's Neasa? Oh, Breck, what have you done?" Beck hesitated before saying anything.

"Dad? I don't like the sounds of that?"

"No, I didn't think you would. Listen, I'm running low on charge. I'll talk with you when we get back. Just watch yourself around Dan. He can come across as jovial and happy but there is a dark side to him that not many see. I am afraid that you will."

"We have, Dad. We have. Give Mom my love. You're flying back when?"

"Knowing your mother, likely in the next day or so. We have accomplished what we needed to here in the village and can head home at any time. The people here are growing so fast in the Lord."

"Oh, that's great, Dad. Don't cut it short because of me."

"We're not. God has been nudging us to leave the last few days."

Breck stared at his phone before he tucked it into his pocket. His parents, Beck and Bonnie, were on their way home. He couldn't wait for Neasa to meet them. He reached for the flowers that he had had Berneen pick up for him the night before and headed back for Doc's, finding Anna waiting for him.

"Anna?" Breck looked past her.

"It's okay, Breck. She roused and couldn't find you. I managed to calm her down. Do you realize how much she needs you?"

"I do, Anna. I do. And I need her." He reached to hug Anna. "I spoke with Dad this morning."

"You did? I didn't think that they had cell service." Anna bustled around the kitchen, preparing their breakfast, her heart raised in prayer for all of the building as she did so.

"He came out to where he could get service. They'll be home in a couple of days."

"That's early." Doc stood in the doorway.

"It is, Doc. But Dad says they've accomplished what they felt they needed to and are free to come home." Breck took the mug of coffee offered to him and then leaned against the counter.

"Good. You need him here with you." Doc hesitated before he spoke. "Neasa's mother?"

"She's still away. Nevin was unclear when she would be coming home. It's almost as if he was afraid to say that she wasn't."

"I see." Doc laid a hand on Breck's shoulder for a moment. "We're praying for them all."

"Thanks, Doc." Breck's mug hit the counter as he heard a whisper of sound from the hall and headed that way, finding Neasa there, turning in a circle, her hand to her head. "Neasa?"

"Breck? You're here. I dreamt that you left me." She launched herself at his open arms, her own around his neck. "Don't leave me, Breck. Please don't leave me."

—

Three days later, Neasa wandered her apartment, restless but not sure what she should be doing. She was afraid to leave the building, and then grew angry with herself. That was not the way she wanted to live, she decided, and reached for her shoes and a jacket, heading for the stairs. A hand on her head, Neasa walked towards the doors, hesitating before she walked outside and then around the building, slower than she normally would. Paul, the security guard on duty, followed her from a distance.

Neasa paused, turning her face up to the sun, feeling the warmth from it even though the air was chilly. This is my favourite time of year, she thought, a time to head into a season of rest and recuperation. And I need that, don't I, Lord? I am afraid to love, to let go and let Breck totally into my heart. He's the one, isn't he, Lord? He's the one that You planned for me. I see that, but I am just so afraid. Teach me how to love again, Lord. Somewhere over the years, that disappeared. I say the word but I don't feel them in my heart. And that is not how it is to be.

Breck watched her for a moment before he moved towards her, his footsteps spinning her around, fear momentarily on her face. He simply stopped, arms open as she ran towards him, launching herself into them. He stood, the most precious bit of lady in his arms, he thought, feeling as she hugged him back hard. Something had changed, Breck thought. I wonder what.

"You're back, Breck. I didn't expect you until later." Neasa looked back, a happy look on her face. "I was afraid for you today."

"I know, darling. I was afraid for you. I am so glad that you ventured outside." He watched as a cloud covered her face before it cleared.

"I am taking back my life, Breck. I have been under a cloud or shadow or whatever you want to call it for years. That's why I left, I think, to try and reclaim my life, but that didn't happen."

"But it has now." Breck hugged her again, a kiss on the top of her head. "That warms my heart so much, darling. Care to share?"

—

Neasa shrugged. "God and I had a conversation a while ago. He just told me to start living and loving. So I am. I am running towards my life once more."

"Run towards me?" Breck drew in his breath. Did he really say that?

"If you want me to, I intend to." Neasa studied him, seeing the relief on his face.

"I do, Neasa, my darling. I do. I want to walk through life with you by my side." He turned her, his arm around her. "We'll talk, but first I have someone or two someones who want to meet you, very much."

"You do?" Neasa's steps slowed for a moment. "Oh! Your parents! I have met your mother. We were part of a Bible study until I left. She's so sweet."

"Mom said that she knew you, but not as my lady." Breck grinned down at her even as he felt eyes on him. He refused to look around, not wanting to give satisfaction to the watcher. But he would be out later, when it was still light, to have a look around.

Beck and Bonnie watched as the younger couple walked towards them, arms around one another.

"He's found his lady, Bonnie." Beck spoke quietly, not sure why that was.

"He has. I often wondered if she would be the one. She seemed to suit him." Bonnie reached for Neasa's hands before she simply swept her into a tight hug. "Neasa. Welcome to the family. We've been waiting for you for so long."

"You have?" Neasa stood back, her hands still in Bonnie's. "Tell me something. Is everyone in your family so open and honest, Breck?"

Breck began to grin. "You'll find Mom is. And she's right, darling. We have been waiting for a long time. All my life, in fact."

Beck began to laugh before he reached to hug Neasa as well. "That we have, Neasa. Now, let me take you all out for supper somewhere. Bonnie and I have been hungry for a good burger and fries."

"Dad has spoken, Neasa, but it's your choice." Breck and his father shared a look, Beck nodding at Breck's words.

"That it is, Neasa. We will not force you to go, but we would like it very much if you did join us."

"I'm dangerous to be around, Beck, Bonnie. Someone is after me." Neasa was suddenly afraid to do just that.

"We'll take precautions, love." Bonnie had her arm around Neasa, leading her towards the parking lot. "I could use some girl support. These two men of ours tend to ignore me."

"Not all the time, Mom." Breck laughed at his mother's comment.

"No, not all the time, but you and your father can get into discussions that I can't join in. Not that I mind." She winked at Neasa who suddenly broke out into laughter.

"Bonnie, you have no idea how much you have just helped me." Neasa quickened her pace. "Who's driving?"

Breck stared down at his desk the next day, his thoughts not really on the work piled there before he reached for a folder. His thoughts were on Neasa and his parents, and his smile grew. She had teased his father, stuck up for his mother, and just listened as they had talked about where they had been. She had asked all the right questions, he thought, not just from politeness but from genuine interest. His father had nodded at him at the end of the evening, giving his approval for Breck's choice.

His thoughts coming back to his work, Breck steadily made his way through the evaluations of the twelve men that were employed by the Foundation. It wasn't necessary, he thought, to do these, but each man had asked that it be done, just in fairness to both sides. He found no complaints from any of the men. In fact, Breck thought, the men thought that they were being given too much. He smiled at that thought. God had led Barnabas to each of the men and that showed in their character.

His phone ringing disturbed him and he absentmindedly answered it, his full attention coming to the call as he heard Dallas' voice.

"Breck? Where are you?"

"In my office. Why?"

"Because I need you to stay there. Neasa?"

"She's with Mom and Dad, I think. They were heading this way earlier today." Breck was on his feet, heading for the door as it opened and the three appeared. "Actually, they're here with me now."

"Stay in your office. Lock yourselves in. I'm on my way with patrol officers. There's been a threat made against you directly today, Breck, and it states that they will hit the building to get to you."

Breck paled even as he reached for his lady, to wrap her under an arm. "Today?"

"Today. Stay put." Dallas cut off the call, heading for the Foundation building. Will had approached him just moments before, a grim look on his face, as he handed over the paperwork Dallas had given him.

"Find Breck. Dan is out and on the hunt for Breck. He's managed to find a couple of men to go with him. They're heading for the Foundation building, fully intending on harming Breck and bringing Neasa home."

"That would be kidnapping."

Will nodded. "It would be but they're trying to play it that she is mentally unsound. I know the men. They will not stop at violence to take her."

Dallas nodded, before he ran for his car, hearing Will call that he had ordered patrol vehicles to head that way.

Breck answered the knock on his door an hour later to find both Dallas and Barnabas standing there. He stepped back to let them enter, the door closing behind them before he moved to where Neasa had seated herself.

"Dallas? Barnabas?" Breck looked between the two men.

"I'm sorry, Neasa. It was your father. He was heading this way with two men to bring you back to his home." Dallas' face was still grim.

"He was? He just doesn't let go? What will it take to make him? I tried moving away and even that didn't work out so well." Neasa blinked back tears of hurt, Breck's arm around her.

"We don't know, Neasa. This time, we have arrested your father with charges of threatening death, conspiracy, and attempted kidnapping. He'll have a high bail to make."

"He'll make it. He'll have friends who will." Neasa watched Dallas closely. "Let me guess. He's tried to declare me incompetent."

"He has, Neasa. We're working on fighting those charges."

"So, what do I do to help that? Be out and about and put everyone in danger?"

"That will help. We need you and Breck to be seen together more than you have been." Barnabas took up the conversation. He held up a hand as she protested. "I know, Neasa. It's putting both of you at risk, but we need to do something. Dallas has information that he's working on regarding the restaurant owner. In fact, he has spoken with the police in that city and the man is under arrest. He understands that you did not speak to the waitress or have any information regarding him. He has agreed to call off whoever it was that he sent after you."

"When?"

"I'm sorry." Dallas frowned. "What do you mean?"

"When did he do that?"

"A week ago?"

"Then who was it who attacked me and asked that? There has to be someone. I'm not safe, not until we find that person."

"And the fellows are working away on that. There hasn't been a lot that they have discovered yet. Brady has reached out to a friend."

"A friend? And just who would that be?"

"A lady named Emma. She finds people and information that no one else seems to be able to."

"I know an Emma who does that. She has a little boy named Isaac."

Breck's arm tightened on Neasa. "That is Emma. Once she knew it was for you, she dropped what she was working on and started on that investigation."

"She did? That sounds like her. I know her and Abe's story. It wasn't pretty." Neasa leaned suddenly against Breck. "I'm tired, Breck. Can I go home?" Her eyes closed as she slept.

Breck stared down at her before his mother spoke.

"She's been pushing too hard for too many years, son. Now that she feels safe with you, she's relaxing. And this is part of it."

Breck turned from the window that he had been staring out in Barnabas' office, waiting until his friend was finished with his telephone call. He had heard Barnabas' steps behind him.

"Barnabas?"

"Breck? Has Dallas been back in touch?"

Breck shook his head. "Not since we spoke this morning. Neasa went with my parents for the day. She's hurting, Barnabas, and I don't know how to make it better."

"Has she spoken with her mother?" Barnabas leaned against the door frame to the office hallway.

"Not that I know of. She's leery to do that, she said, just in case her mother is involved."

"Do you think she is?" Barnabas watched him closely.

Breck shrugged. "At this point in time? I have no idea. Neither does Nevin. Nevin is hurting for his sister and for himself. Sarah is trying to keep his spirits up, he said, but it's tough."

"It is. Would Neasa speak with Ker? She might be able to help, given what happened with her mother."

"I have asked Neasa, but she is not ready to do that, she said. Maybe at some point. I did, just to try and get a sense of what I can do to help Neasa."

"Good. Talk with Buckley as well, even though I know you have." Barnabas shoved away from the door frame. "Have you been to the conference room?"

"Not today. I've been swamped with paperwork and then phone calls." Breck sighed, rubbing at his temple with one finger. "I have no idea how the fellows did this."

"With a lot of prayer and support." Barnabas' hand rested on Breck's shoulder as he prayed for his friend. "Now, let's head for the

—

conference room, see what they can tell us, and then you need to head to find your lady."

The twelve men looked up as Breck entered, waving, or calling out a greeting. They had been in there since early that afternoon and were planning on breaking off soon. They watched Breck closely, seeing the strain in him that they all recognized.

Breck walked the room, studying the whiteboards, reaching for a marker to add his own comments, before he stood back, nodding. They were working well again, he thought, finding information that he had not even dreamed was out there. His head turned as Benen stopped beside him.

"Breck? How are you?"

Breck shrugged. "About how you all were at this point. I'm afraid for Neasa, but I'm not sure why or who from."

"We know that, Breck. Dallas has been around. He said you told him to talk with us, and he did. We have that information. Emma is starting to feed us information on her friend, Neasa." Benen slanted a glance at Breck.

Breck grinned. "I just found out this morning that Neasa is acquainted with a little guy who has parents named Emma and Abe. I don't know how or when they met, but Emma has been a friend to Neasa from what she said."

"I'm sure that she has been." Benen looked down at the floor, not sure how to continue. "Her father?"

"Dan? It's strange, you know, how he is reacting. Nevin has been talking with me. I can't say what all he said, but he did tell me that this goes way back to before Neasa ever left home."

"It is bizarre. To try and kidnap her? I know right well he's going to claim that she's incompetent."

"We know that. We're working on some plans. No, not marrying like some of you. Not yet." Breck thought back to his conversation with his lady. She had not wanted to make that move, not ready for it yet.

"No, she's not. Neither are you. When those of us did that, we were ready. The ladies understood why and agreed."

"That they did. Listen, I have to run. I'll be back. Make sure you fellows pack it in soon." Breck walked away, not seeing twelve pairs of eyes watching him before they exchanged glances.

"How do we do it, fellows?" Branigan spoke up. "He was there for each of us. How do we do it for him?"

"Keep plugging away at this." Bradon pointed to his computer and then the papers stacked by each man. "Find the one responsible and bring him or her to justice. And we know it could be a woman just as easily."

Baird raised his head at that. "That fellow who had the restaurant? Did we ever find anything on his wife or daughter?"

"Not yet, but we're still digging." Burnie rose and stretched. "Sorry, fellows. I need to run. Muir and Granny are expecting me for dinner and it's almost that time."

Breck paced the next morning, his phone to his ear, as he listened to the police detective from another town speak with him. He sighed to himself. This is not what he needed. One of the properties that the Foundation had been looking into buying had been damaged in a fire. He had been the name that had been given to contact.

"It's a total loss?"

"It is, Mr. Curran. I'm sorry. I know that you were in the planning stages of purchasing it."

"Any chance that it was accidental?"

"No. Our arson dog hit a number of spots where accelerants were used. It is definitely arson. We'll be working with the arson investigator on it. We'll ensure that you are kept abreast of what we find."

"Thank you." Breck tossed his phone to the desk. Now what, Lord? That was a big project that just got put on hold. He would need to bring a report to the board and right away. He dropped to his desk chair and sent off a group email, detailing what he had been told. He then sat back, a frown on his face. That property was where he had been just a few days ago. Had he been followed and someone did this as a warning to him or Neasa?

Bruce turned as Barnabas gave an exclamation, frowning.

"Son?"

"Breck just sent out a group email. The property in Purdy? It was destroyed in an arson fire."

"Arson? And Breck was just there? Any connection?" Bruce watched his son closely.

"I wonder if there is. A threat against him, perhaps? Or it could just be coincidental." Barnabas sat back in his chair. "He's hurting, Dad, and for the first time in our friendship, I don't know what to say to him or how to help him."

"Praying for him helps. Just standing beside him is what you can do. You have always done that." Bruce paused, his mind going back to the two men, watching them grow in his mind. "You two have had disagreements but nothing that ever came between you. He's moving on to a new aspect of his life, Barnabas, that he will not be sharing with you. That breaks a portion of your friendship. I mean, you two will always be friends, but it's changing and growing."

"I know, Dad. Breck and I have often spoken of what would happen if and when we ever met our ladies. He has. Neasa completes his heart, as he has often said he wanted. Just how do we keep them safe? That's a question that I don't have an answer for."

"None of us do. Tell me where your men stand right now in their investigation."

"Nowhere near finding out who it is. We've ruled out the restaurant owner. He had no idea that Neasa was the cook or that the waitress may have heard something. He's under arrest for other things. We're looking at his wife and daughter. He has no son, contrary to what Neasa was led to believe."

"Then, who was it that pretended to be the son?"

"Emma's working on that. She and Neasa are friends. I have no idea how they met but it helps. She's starting to feed us bits and pieces as she can."

"Good. She's a wonder, that lady. And has quite the story to tell, from what she has said. I've had talks with her and Abe."

"You have? I wasn't aware that you had even met her."

"I meet many people during the course of a year. Now, about Breck? Is he okay for staff in his office? I know his secretary was off for her cancer treatments."

"Becky? She has been. Breck said that she was putting in her resignation. She doesn't feel that she wants to continue to work, even though she enjoys the work. We'll be looking to replace her. He's been working without a secretary for now."

"Neasa? What is she planning? I know she's a chef but is hesitant to continue. That much she has told me, when we've talked.

And we've had many conversations, that young lady and me. Would she be willing to step in for a bit?"

Barnabas shrugged. "I can ask, but somehow I don't think so." He looked up as Amy tapped at his door.

"Sorry to interrupt, but Neasa is here. She would like to speak with both of you. She wasn't aware that Bruce was here, but her face lit up when she found out he was."

"Of course, Amy." Barnabas was on his feet, heading for the reception area, watching Neasa as she shifted from foot to foot. "Neasa? I wasn't expecting to see you today but come in. Dad and I were just talking."

"Thank you, Barnabas. I really do need to speak with the two of you." Neasa was edgy and upset, that the two men could tell.

"Neasa? What can we do for you?" Bruce shared a look with Barnabas.

"This." Neasa thrust an envelope towards him. "This came. Someone has made a complaint that I am incompetent and that I need to report for an assessment to a mental health ward."

"What!" Bruce took the letter and read it. "You do nothing without legal representation, Neasa. Let me speak with John, one of our lawyers. You stay put. Barnabas, find Breck, and get him here."

Neasa sat back, drawing in a deep breath, relieved that someone actually believed her for a change. She had never really felt that with her father. He made the decisions and demanded that she go along. He covered that with a smile when they were out and about, but she still felt under his thumb. Nevin wasn't even aware of all that she had faced. Neasa knew her mother had not yet returned and wondered at that. Was she escaping, Lord? Is that why she's not coming back? I pray for her safety. Nevin will be okay. Dad never treated him like he did me.

She felt an arm around her and leaned back against Breck, knowing he had dropped what he was doing and came to find her. Breck studied her face, seeing the fear and distress in it.

Bruce sat back down, a stern look on his face.

"John is on his way." He tapped the envelope. "He will deal with this. He did have a suggestion, Breck, and I will not push you to it."

"I know, Bruce. That we marry. I can't do that to Neasa. She needs this time."

Neasa had turned to watch Breck, seeing his concern for her in his eyes. "Breck? Is that what he will suggest?"

"He might, but then it would be used against you. They would say that you did that just to avoid the assessment." Breck shared another look with Bruce and then Barnabas. "Do we know who instigated it?"

"No. But John will look into it thoroughly. He has his secretary working on it right now. He thought something was up and had already started the process."

"It may be Dad. Is he free?"

"No, he's not. Not yet, Neasa, but his lawyer could be doing something." Bruce pulled out his phone and sent off a text.

John stood for a moment, watching Neasa before his attention turned to Breck. *Bruce is right. He is head over heels in love with his lady, and I can see that she returns that, even if she won't admit it yet.* He sighed. *This notice is not what they need.* He set his briefcase on the floor and reached to shake Breck's hand.

"This is Neasa, John, the reason that you're here." Breck introduced the two.

"Neasa? I've seen you around church. The little ones just love you. My granddaughter is always excited when you're in the children's church."

"Little Abby? Oh, she is such a sweetheart. Loves to cuddle." Her brow clouded. "But what about this?" She pointed to the envelope that Bruce had handed him.

"We'll look at it. I have confirmation that your father's lawyer is the one asking for this. Neasa, have you any idea why?"

Neasa shrugged. "Other than he can't control me any longer? I have no idea. I don't think that I have any money coming to me. At least, not that I am aware of."

"Okay. So, what we do is this. My secretary has already prepared forms for you to sign. We thought this would be coming up. I will go before the courts tomorrow. I have already scheduled it, or my secretary did. I will need you there, both you and Breck." He studied the young couple. "And don't even consider getting married today. That will go bad for you."

"We figured that out, John." Breck grinned for a moment. "We are dating but not that far. Not yet, anyway."

"Okay." John pulled out his phone and then excused himself. He was sober when he returned. "Breck, there has been a new wrinkle. His lawyer has gone to the press, stating that you are holding her here against her will, and that you are poisoning her against her father."

"What!" Breck was on his feet. "You know that's not true."

"We do. I talked to Cindy. She's the lawyer we use in cases like this, Neasa. She has already filed for an injunction against your father, his lawyer, and the press. We would like to do a video statement with you two, to put out there. But it won't go out until after tomorrow's court."

"I see." Neasa wrinkled her brow as she thought, bringing Breck's attention to it. "What if someone is forcing Dad to do this? Has that been looked into?"

Barnabas spoke from where he was standing near the window. "It has been, Neasa. Emma has found evidence of that and sent it on to Dallas. Our fellows had also had that thought and found a person of interest, shall we say, who is pushing your father. We can't say any more than that as it is an active investigation. Dallas has indicated that he plans to speak with you two in the next day or so. This may push him to do that."

Neasa sighed, relaxing back against Breck. "Why? That's all I want to know is why?"

"We don't know yet, Neasa, but we are rushing to discover that. You are still not safe, that much we know." Breck shared a look with Bruce. "I promise to do my best to protect you."

"But they have already hurt you, Breck." She rubbed at her temple, the headache starting to throb.

"You're hurting. John?"

John looked up, his attention on them again. "Neasa? Do you know anyone who would force your father to take this step?"

"No, I don't know his business acquaintances. I mean, I may have seen them but I don't know who they are. I ran the equipment for Dad, that's all. I didn't want to be involved in anything else. How does all this relate to the bones?"

"That's a good question, and I certainly will take it up with Dallas. As of now, young lady, I am your lawyer. Any questions, you send them to me. If you want me to be present when you speak with anyone, call me and I will be there." John gathered up his papers and briefcase and walked away, leaving Neasa staring after him.

"Did he just do that?"

Breck laughed, seeing the humour in it. "He did, Neasa. It's a habit he has. He states what he wants to and then leaves."

—

"Oh! I thought it was me."

"Never you, darling. Never you."

The next morning, Neasa sat near the front of the courtroom, watching John as he sat waiting for the judge to appear. Her hand was tight in Breck's and she leaned against him, seeking to find peace and comfort from that contact. Nevin sat on her other side, her hand in his, Sarah beside him. She knew that Barnabas and his parents were there as were Breck's parents. Neasa was still worried. Cindy, the lawyer, had been out the previous night and prepared their video for relief. She had smiled at Neasa and told her that the injunctions had been served.

Neasa stood when the judge entered and then re-seated herself, listening carefully to what was being said, not understanding all the legalese that was being said. She frowned as the judge nodded, made a comment, and then John approached her.

"Neasa, the judge would like to speak with you. If you are willing to do so and only if you are. He has made that abundantly clear." John shared a look with Breck, who kept his face carefully shuttered. "I think you should, but it's your choice."

"Breck?" Neasa turned to him.

"If John thinks it will help then maybe you should. But as John has stated, it is your choice. The judge will accept that."

Neasa stared at the judge, finding a kindly eye directed her way. "I guess then it's okay. Breck, pray for me."

"I am, darling. I am." He stood to let her rise and follow John to the front, moving past the tables to sit near the judge.

"Miss Deakin, thank you for your willingness to speak with me. I will allow questions from the lawyers, but if you are uncomfortable at all, turn to me. I have a few questions that I will ask as well."

Neasa nodded, her eyes on John as he rose. She answered his questions in a quiet, calm voice before her father's lawyer rose, an almost sneer on his face, disbelief, and a bullying manner in his demeanour.

"Miss Deakin, I understand that you were involved in a situation in the city. Were you not?"

"No, sir. I was not."

"Oh, but I have proof. It was regarding a murder of a waitress from the restaurant that you were employed in. You are part of the group that was involved in her murder."

"I'm sorry, sir. I am not. I didn't even know for sure that she had been murdered."

"Oh come, now. Of course, you were. You came back here to hide, didn't you?"

"No, sir, I did not." Neasa was adamant in her answers and she caught a quick look on Breck's face. Oh no, Lord, he's growing angry. Please, Lord? Calm him.

"Move on, Mr. Lawson. She has answered your question." The judge nodded at the lawyer.

"Now, Miss Deakin, regarding this claim. Your father states adamantly that you are incompetent mentally. That you are being held against your will. He wishes a mental health assessment for you. And that happens today."

Neasa's eyes narrowed and she refused to answer.

"Judge, make her answer. She has accusations against her that need to be addressed."

John was on his feet. "Your Honour, I have affidavits here that are signed by every one who resides in the Foundation building, as well as by her brother and his wife, by the minister of her church, the complete church board. She is not being held against her will. Nor is she incompetent mentally in any way. I have an affidavit from a former forensics psychologist who spoke with her at length yesterday afternoon at my request. Dr. Darcie Foster is well known for her work."

"Dr. Foster? Mr. Lawson, I am denying you this claim of incompetence and being held against her will. You will not appear before this court or any other with these claims. If you do, I will instruct the staff to contact the bar association. This is not the first time that you have tried something like this in one of our courts." He turned to Neasa. "Thank you, Miss Deakin. You are free to go. You will not face any further charges of this sort. Court dismissed." The gavel hit harder than it usually did, showing his displeasure with the lawyer.

Neasa made her way back to Breck, to be enfolded in his arms, before she turned to Nevin and Sarah.

"I'm sorry, Neasa. I didn't know that Dad was like this." Nevin was grieved for his sister.

"It's not your fault, Nevin. You didn't know. Dad wasn't always like this. That's what so strange." Neasa finally made her way out of the courthouse, settling into Breck's truck, his parents in the back seat.

"Are you okay?" Bonnie reached forward to touch her shoulder.

"I am, I think, thank you." Neasa groaned. "That sounded so positive and sure, now didn't it?"

Bonnie gave a soft laugh. "We'll take it as you meant it, Neasa. I was not surprised to have the judge ask for you to speak."

"You weren't?" Neasa twisted to watch her.

"No. He's known for that." Beck smiled at her. "He's done it before. And the lawyer that your father has? One more complaint against him and he's disbarred. He doesn't have a good reputation."

"Then why would Dad pick him?"

"I suspect that he was chosen for your father. We need to find out who is behind it all, Neasa." Breck finally pulled into his parking spot. "Mom, Dad, Anna, and Doc asked that we come to their place."

"We certainly shall. Anna called this morning, to make sure that we would." Bonnie was out of the truck, pulling Neasa with her, heading for the lobby of the building, greeting the men and women who had gathered. "Neasa is free of all that, people. The judge had her speak, told the lawyer off, and let her go."

"Wonderful." Branigan led the cheer that followed, surprising Neasa, who stared at them all before she too grinned.

"It was all your prayers that did it. Thank you." She went from one to the other, thanking them and hugging each one, touching gentle hands to the little ones held in their parents' arms. She laughed at the signs Hailey and Holly and Darbi were holding. "You three. It's a good thing that you weren't there. I couldn't have kept a straight face."

"We knew you would be okay. God told us that." Haley hugged her before running off, Holly on her heels.

Neasa stretched out on the couch in Doc's living room, her eyes drifting closed. Her head was pounding, she thought, worse than it had been. Even the prescription pain medication that Breck had handed her to take wasn't working. She slept, not hearing the movement, talk and laughter that surrounded her. She felt part of the building family, at last, she thought, just before she slept.

Breck sat where he could watch her, knowing that she had not been sleeping. She had confessed that to him just a while before that. Worry, she said, frustration and pain all contributed to that. It didn't matter how much she prayed, or wanted to move on, to find the love that she needed and craved, she still felt trapped. He prayed for his lady love, praying for her to find the peace that she needed and that she would run to him to find the love that she craved.

He frowned, suddenly on his feet, moving towards her, holding her as her body began to jerk and twitch.

"Doc? Seizure." Breck's sudden loud call broke through the conversation, stilling it abruptly.

"Anna. 9-1-1. Breck, on the floor with her." Doc helped, watching Neasa closely as the seizure stopped. "Has she had these before?"

"No, not that she's said. She did say that her headaches are worse, that even the prescription medication isn't working."

"And has she seen her family doctor?"

"No, not that I know of. She's been too scared to go anywhere the last few days." Breck moved away as the paramedics moved in, his mother's arm around him. He was following the stretcher rapidly as it moved from the apartment and then through the lobby, not seeing the building family had gathered, worry on their face.

Barnabas stepped up to Beck.

"Beck? We heard the sirens. What happened?"

"Neasa had a seizure."

"A seizure? I know she's still been having headaches. Head on in. I'll follow." Barnabas watched them almost run for their car before he turned to the group behind him.

"We need to pray, people. Neasa had a seizure."

Buckley was moving towards the door, Locklin with him. "I'm on my way. I'll update as I can."

Breck paced the waiting room, thinking of how many times that he had done just that. Only this time? It was his lady that was sick and being treated. Dear Lord, please? He could not even put into words his thoughts, but he knew that was just fine. That's when the Spirit prays, isn't it, God?

His parents watched him closely and then turned to Locklin.

"Locklin? The prayer chain is working?"

"I would think so. I called the coordinator on our way in." Locklin was distressed. "I wish sometimes that we were still the minister couple but God had other plans for us."

"He did, dear, and you are where you are needed. God knows that." Bonnie hugged the younger woman. "Now, tell me about this ministry. I haven't had a chance to talk to you or Buckley about it." Bonnie knew about it, had kept up to date on it, but was using this as a tactic to distract Locklin.

Buckley paced beside his friend, his prayers raising for the couple and the medical team.

"I didn't get a chance to talk to you earlier. Everything is okay now with the assessment?"

Breck drew a deep sigh. "It is. The judge was harsh on the lawyer, but he deserved it. Neasa was not to testify but the judge specifically asked her to. It helped that Darcie had talked to her and John had an affidavit from her."

"He did? Oh, wonderful. Darcie is such a caring person. I can't see how that police officer treated her as he did."

Breck turned suddenly as he heard his name called and almost ran towards the nurse waiting for him, leaving Buckley standing and staring after him.

"Breck? This way. Doc has asked that you come." The nurse pointed him into one of the rooms.

Breck was through the door and at Neasa's side almost before the nurse had finished her sentences. His hand reached for hers, as he studying the medical equipment surrounding her, the oxygen mask on her face, the IV line looped and taped to the back of her other hand.

"Doc?" He raised frightened eyes to Doc, finding him standing beside him.

"She's stable right now, Breck. Patrick will be in shortly to speak with you. He's run the bloodwork we needed to, the imagining studies, the tests that he needs to." Doc prayed for his young friend. "He'll have the results for you. Her medication?"

"Here." Breck pulled it from his pocket, a frown on his face. "You know, she hasn't wanted to take it. I gave her one this afternoon, just to see if it would help. I think it's the first one that she had."

"Is that right?" Doc pulled out his reading glasses and studied the medication name. "I'll be back." He was off before Breck could say anything.

Breck turned his attention to Neasa, a hand resting against her cheek. "Neasa, please? Come back to me. I can't live if you don't. I love you, darling. With all my heart." He bent to drop a kiss on her cheek, a finger flicking at the tears that she had wept. Looking around, Breck reached into his pocket, pulling out the ring that had been a grandmother's. He studied it before he reached to slip it on her finger, marking her as his, knowing that he would have to explain when she woke and awaken he was determined that she would.

Patrick watched Breck closely before he approached, a chart in his hand as well as the medication bottle. Breck turned as he sensed someone there.

"Patrick?"

"Breck? I understand that this is your lady. Let's talk." Patrick set down the chart and bottle before he reached for his stethoscope and then assessed Neasa. "She's coming back from wherever it was that the seizure sent her. It was her first?"

"As far as I know. What caused it?"

Patrick lifted up the bottle. "These. This pain medication has a side effect that can sometimes cause seizures. But we had to run all the tests that we did. We'll repeat it before we discharge her in the morning. It seems that it was a combination of the medication and the stress that she was under. Her body just reacted adversely to both."

"She'll be okay?"

"Yes. I don't expect there to be any more seizures. It sometimes happens, Breck. We can't predict who or why." Patrick stayed for a few more moments, updating Breck as much as he could. "Buckley is here?" At Breck's nod, Patrick turned for the door. "I know he's not the pastor of your church, but I'll send him in. Your pastor is here as well."

"Buckley for now, I think. I'll speak to Daniel later."

Buckley paused as he stared at Patrick. "You're sure? Daniel's the pastor, not me."

"He asked for you. As a friend, I think, Buckley. Head on back."

Neasa roused in the morning, her headache better, but still feeling off. She stared around and sighed. The hospital again, she thought. When will I stay out of one? Neasa caught movement and found Breck sleeping beside her in an uncomfortable chair, moving restlessly. Her face softened as she studied him. *I do love him, Lord, but I'm not sure I'm the right one for him.* Feeling a weight on her finger, she frowned and stared at the ruby and diamond ring. *I don't remember this. What did he do?*

Breck watched Neasa through partially-opened eyelids, seeing when she found the ring and sighed to himself. He shouldn't have done that, he supposed, surprising her like that. It was not how it was to be. He was on his feet, reaching for her finger to withdraw the ring, startling Neasa, who stared up at him, fear briefly showing on her face.

"I'm sorry, darling. I shouldn't have done that. But I was afraid that they wouldn't let me stay."

Neasa stared at him and then the finger that she had curled towards her palm. "Taking it back, are you? Didn't mean it? I won't let you have it back, Breck. Not a chance."

"Neasa?"

"I mean it, Breck. You put it there, putting your heart out there for everyone to see. I see it. I have seen your heart for days." Neasa blinked back tears as she lifted her eyes to him. "Why?"

"Why? Why the ring? Because I love you dearly and deeply. I want to walk through life with you, to have you as the helpmeet that God chose for me. Only I don't know how you feel."

"How I feel? Right now, I feel like I have drummers in my head that are finally slowing down their beat. In my heart? I find that I love this tall handsome fellow, who has tried his best to protect me from everything, who wants me to walk through life with him. How can I not?" She pulled off the oxygen mask and tossed it aside. "I don't need this. Or maybe I do. Some fellow here in the room is taking away my breath."

"Neasa, darling? You mean that?"

"What? That I don't need the oxygen? Yes, I do. I also need out of here. Where are my clothes?" She smirked at the look on his face. "Breck? Sweetheart, I do. Now, find my nurse. And my discharge papers. If I don't have them, I'm still escaping. Only, didn't we do that once before?"

Breck had begun to grin as she spoke before he laughed quietly. "We did. Only this time, we're taking my truck and not your motorcycle. Although I still want to go on a long ride with a beautiful lady."

"And we will." Neasa watched as Breck looked around and then kissed her. Her eyes closed as he did so. "Stingy. Only one?"

Breck laughed again. "I can see how henpecked I'll be." He kissed her again before he reluctantly left to find her nurse, finding instead Patrick standing in the doorway, a huge smile on his face.

"Asked and answered? Congratulations, you two. I was just on my way in to see how Neasa was. Neasa, I think we need to keep you in for at least a week. You're too sick to go home." Patrick grinned at her squeal of outrage. "Seriously, though, you can leave. I know Doc will be checking on you, to say nothing of Brady and Cadee. Now, we need to note that you can't have that medication. And you need to lessen the stress in your life." He looked up as the couple laughed. "Not happening? Do your best. Here are your papers, young lady. Now, scoot. We need the bed for someone who is really sick."

Branigan approached the whiteboards, writing down the information that he had discovered before he stepped back and then moved to the one that they had all decided would be Breck's logic problem. Burnie, the writer in the group, had set up one at one point and they had continued to use it. He added information to it, and then stood back. Something is missing, he thought. Something crucial. I'm just not sure what.

Benen stood beside him, Brennen on his other side, papers in their hands.

"What are we missing, fellows?" Branigan shot them both a look. "We are missing something."

"I know. I wish I knew what it was." Benen was frustrated. "How deep have we looked at that lawyer?"

"Not deep enough. Bradon was working on that, but he was called out on a search and rescue. He didn't know when he'd be back."

"Okay, so he's looking after that. What about the bones?" Benen was looking for anything that would move them ahead.

"Dallas is being very quiet on that. He hasn't said much." Branigan spoke up.

"No, and he can't. Not yet." Brady moved in to add to the board. "I'm looking at her father. I'm not liking what I find. He has a reputation for a temper and anger."

"We know that. What did you discover?" Brandon stood near them.

"That he has had charges laid and dropped. I have a source that has confirmed this. His wife was one of the ones who laid charges years ago, but dropped them."

"Domestic abuse?" Benen spun. "And then he tries this with Neasa? We need to talk to her mother."

"I have arranged that. Locklin and Buckley are heading that way tomorrow. She knows them and has agreed to speak with them. She sounded relieved that someone might finally believe her." Brady looked around. "I'm off. Fynn and I have a date tonight and I'm cutting it close as it is."

The remaining men watched him leave before they all looked at one another and then quietly put away their work and left, ready to pick it up on the morrow. Being married meant that they didn't spend hours and all night in the conference room. Not any more.

Neasa walked the room with Breck as he studied the walls, the marker he had handed her underlining certain names and events.

"How did they discover all this?" Her voice was barely a whisper.

"They all have sources they go to. Programs they run. They bounce ideas off of each other. Sometimes it is very quiet in here and at other times, very noisy. They joke with one another and laugh, but it is not at the person or persons. It is just a way to relieve their tension."

"I understand that, Breck. I need to be here, to talk with them." Neasa moved into his hug.

"I know. They'll be back in here as they can. I'll make sure that you're here."

"You have your own work to do, don't you? How are you managing without your secretary?"

"With great difficulty. We need to hire but at present, with what's going on with us? We have decided not to."

"Can I help in any way? I can at least answer the phone for you. And file. You do have filing that you do?"

"Darling, you are an answer to my prayer. Barnabas asked that, you know. He wanted to know if you might be interested." Breck kissed her and then led her from the room. They were meeting his parents for dinner and were running late.

"He did? I'll have to have a chat with him, I think. Putting ideas into your head. Signing me up for work without asking first." She smirked as he stared at her and then began to laugh.

"You just do that, darling. You just do that." He watched carefully as lights appeared in his rearview mirror, not sure anymore if they were friend or foe. He pulled into his parents' driveway and the car behind him flicked their emergency lights on and off. Breck breathed a sigh of relief.

Breck listened closely as Buckley updated them all on his and Locklin's talk with Neasa's mother. It was not what he had expected. Looking at the men's faces, he could tell that they felt the same, other than for Blair. Blair caught his eye and nodded. He knew, didn't he, Lord? He knew that Dan wasn't Neasa's father, that he was her step-father. But where is her father?

Buckley handed around pages of notes and documents.

"Her mother provided this for us. Her father disappeared when she was around two, Nevin one. His car was found in the lake, with evidence that led investigators to believe that he was in the car when it entered the lake. His body was never found."

Brody looked up, a look on his face that caught everyone's attention. "What if he wasn't? What if it was staged to look that way?"

"That's something that the original investigators were looking at. They didn't think that, in their conclusion. But we know that lake. Bodies can travel or be submerged and not be found."

Brody nodded. "Breck, did they ever say anything more about the bones?"

"No, they didn't." Breck stopped his pacing, his eyes on Brody. "Are you suggesting?"

"That it was her father? I am." Brody held up a paper. "This is from Emma. How she managed to get this, I don't know. It's the preliminary examination of the bones. Male. Early thirties. Caucasian. They found some bits and pieces of clothing. And a wedding band."

Breck sank into a chair, horror moving through him. "Her father?"

"They haven't concluded that yet, but I suspect that it is. Emma seemed to think so." Brody watched with compassion as

Breck scrubbed at his face. "We can't say anything, Breck. Not until it's confirmed."

Nodding, Breck reached for the papers being handed him and read through them. He sat back, a puzzled look on his face. "I don't get why there. I really don't. The shelter has been there for so many years."

"Not that long. Neasa's what? Twenty-eight? The shelter building was run-down when the Foundation took it over twenty years ago. It's possible for someone to have been buried there and not found."

Brady looked up. "We need to talk to Barnabas and Bruce. Possibly Will. They might know more."

Breck looked up. "I can remember the shelter being dedicated. Twenty-five years ago. The land around it was not disturbed. It was left as it was, other than some landscaping around the building and the fence around the three sides. The work was not done near where we are planning the playground." He rose and suddenly left the room, needing to find some open space and fresh air. Lord, how do we do this? How do we tell Neasa that the man that she thinks is her father isn't? We need Your words and guidance on this.

Neasa watched as Breck paced, a frown on her face before she moved to stand in his way. His face lit up as he saw her and he reached to kiss her, holding her tight to him in almost a desperate manner.

"Breck? Are you okay?" She tilted her head back to look up at him.

"Not really. Just heard something disturbing. Walk with me."

The couple walked in silence for numerous circuits of the building before Neasa drew him down to a bench at the front of it.

"Breck? What is it?"

"Neasa, we had some disturbing news that we have to verify."

She looked disgruntled and distracted. "You too? I finally heard from Mom. Not what I wanted to hear. She told me that Dan is not my father, just my step-father. She apologized for that. When I asked her about my own father, she grew silent and just said that he was dead, that his body had never been recovered. She was calling Nevin after she spoke with me."

"That's all she said?" Breck watched Neasa closely.

"That's all. But she left out something. Something big and crucial. I could tell by how she hesitated and by the words that she was not saying." Neasa leaned against him. "I had this horrible dream or nightmare. That it was my father that we dug up. Do you know anything about it?"

"We just heard from Emma, darling. She had some information on your father. I was trying to clear my head before I spoke with you." His arm tightened around her. "Your father's car was found in Lake Erie, with the supposition that he was in it and was washed out. His body was not recovered in the lake."

"That's possible." She thought for a moment. "But there's more, isn't there?"

"There is. Emma pulled the preliminary medical report on the bones."

"My father?" Neasa looked up, horrified for a moment, and then she nodded. "That makes sick sense, you know. Dan was all jovial about doing the work, seemed to really want to, but there was a dark side to it that I saw. I don't think he really wanted to do it. Is he responsible?"

"That we don't know, Neasa. We don't have confirmation on the body as yet. They were still processing all the evidence." Breck grew silent, content just to sit and hold Neasa, bringing what comfort he could to her.

Dallas watched Neasa closely later that afternoon before he sighed. This is the part that I hate about this work, Lord, having to notify the next of kin. Her mother wasn't surprised. Nevin was angry and I can understand that. He was lied to all his life by the person who should have been honest with him. Now I have to speak with Neasa. Breck called me, Lord, just to warn me that Neasa has guessed. Please, Lord? I need the words from You that I just can't find myself.

Neasa looked up from where she was standing in the rose garden, watching Dallas, and then walked towards him.

"Dallas? You have news?"

"I do, Neasa. Where's Breck?"

"He's on a conference call that will last the rest of the afternoon. Do you need him here?"

"I would prefer it, but let's head in. I don't like you out here right now." Dallas looked around, feeling someone watching them intently. "Someone is watching you, Neasa."

"I know they are. I have seen their shadows this afternoon, and also glimpses of them. They're bold."

Dallas stared at her before he spoke angrily. "Don't you care? Do you know what Breck would go through if something happened to you?"

Neasa stared back at him, no expression on her face. "I know exactly, Dallas. We have talked about that, many times. He knows I would deliberately put myself out there, but I can't stop life. I have to live. I have to love. Even if it only for a short time. Don't you get that?" She brushed by him, heading for the building.

Dallas' head went back as his eyes closed. Lord, how do we reach her? She's reacting differently from the other ladies. And I really don't know how to get through to her about the danger that she is in. He found Neasa seated in a chair in the lobby, her eyes watching for him.

"Neasa?"

"Dallas? I know what you're going to say. That the bones we dug up were my father." She sighed, her eyes sliding closed, a single tear appearing on her cheek. She opened her eyes, anger briefly flickering in them. "Who?"

"That we don't know. And we are trying to determine that as best we can. It's been a lot of years, Neasa."

"I get that. I lived most of my life without knowing that Dan was not my father. Did he legally adopt us?"

"He did. I am sorry, Neasa, that I had to be the one to tell you." Dallas handed over the paperwork that he held in his hand. "This is what I can give you. I spoke with your mother earlier. She has no plans to return to this town. Were you aware of that?"

Neasa shrugged. "I gathered that much. She has always hated it."

"What can we do for you, Neasa?" Dallas wasn't quite sure how to proceed. Neasa was not like the other ladies from the building. Those ladies he had sort of known how to approach. Neasa was different.

"To tell you the truth, Dallas? I'm not sure." Neasa rubbed her hands along her jeans. "I thought that when I moved home, I would be happy and content to work for Dan. This has changed all that. Finding out that he was not my father? That has changed who I feel I am and makes my life seem like a lie. I mean, he would be kind to us at times, but stern. I always felt he was sterner with me than with Nevin. Maybe that's why I rebelled. He never wanted me to have the motorbike. I just went and got it. We had a fight over that. You know, Mom just stood back and never said a word. Nevin tried to intervene but Dan bluntly told him to stay out of it."

"I can see you rebelling." Dallas gave a grin. "You still are."

"I am?" Neasa stared at him and then past him before she nodded, a slow smile growing on her face. "I guess that I am. I need to stop though."

"Why? Breck loves you just as you are. He's a bit of a rebel at times."

"I know he is. He's looking at a motorcycle. Did you know that?" Neasa bit back a smirk, seeing Breck standing behind her, reflected in the window.

"He is, is he? And how does his future bride feel about that?" Dallas had a wide smile on his face.

"I think she feels it the right thing to do." Breck simply swept Neasa into his arms and sat down where she had been seated, grinning at her mock look of outrage.

"I can see you two, heading out on the open road. Just stay safe." Dallas sobered. "I was explaining to Neasa about our findings."

"It was her father?" At Dallas' nod, Breck sighed. "Do we know how?"

"No, unfortunately, there isn't a lot of evidence for that. We're looking into his medical history as well as his associates at the time."

Breck watched his friends closely as they worked away before he looked down at the papers that he had just been shifting around. He didn't feel like working today, he thought, but I need to. These men need my attention to them, and that has been difficult. I need to get back to our weekly meetings and prayer time. He stood abruptly, a thought crossing his mind, and walked to the map that was tacked on the wall.

His finger tracing the area near the shelter, Breck paused at where the bones had been discovered and then moved his finger further away. A horrible thought came to him. What if that wasn't the only spot?

Brody had been watching him and exchanged a look with Brendon before he rose and approached him.

"Breck? You're thinking hard about something."

"I am, Brody. I had a horrible thought. That area was so abandoned and overrun with the Foundation took it over. What if Neasa's father wasn't the only one there?"

Brody nodded. "We had that same thought, Breck. I approached Dallas. They're planning on doing a search."

"They are? Good. Now, where do we stand with everything? And do you know what is strange? Neither Neasa nor I are receiving the nasty, horrible messages as she puts it. Not like you all did."

"You're not? That's weird." Bradon had approached. "I would have thought that you would be."

"No, not since that fellow was arrested in the city." Breck searched each of the men's faces, finding them all there.

"That is bizarre. No packages? No photos?"

Breck shook his head. "I mean, we can feel someone watching us. Neasa has glimpsed someone but not a good enough look to be able to describe whoever it was."

"Mind games, Breck. They're playing mind games with you. Trying to scare you without leaving any evidence. That's how they are doing it." Blair spoke from where he stood at the printer. "They'll up their game, now that it has come out about Neasa's father."

"It will." Breck leaned back against the wall, crossing his arms over his chest. "She's getting restless and is ready to revolt. I can't say as I blame her. She's never had this kind of restriction on her."

"Then, get out there. The weather is still nice enough that you could be out on her bike." Benen looked around as the door opened slowly and Neasa appeared, devastation on her face.

Breck shoved away from the wall and was to her before she could even speak, gathering her close, feeling the sobs that began to shake her body.

"Neasa? Darling? What is it?" He felt the phone that she had in her hand hitting him in the chest and reached for it, handing it to Branigan, who stared down at the photo and then at Neasa, shock and then anger on his face.

"My bike! He destroyed it! Why?" Neasa's voice was barely audible.

"What? What do you mean?" Breck looked up as her phone appeared in front of his face. He drew in a deep breath. "Your bike? Dan?"

"It has to be." She leaned back. "It is destroyed, in pieces, damaged beyond repair. Is he that angry at me?"

Breck had no words to comfort her. He could only hold her as tight as he could, his chin resting on her head, his eyes on his friends.

Anger flickered through the room before it turned to determination. The men shared a look and then dug back into their research, not willing to let Breck and his Neasa down. They all felt that there was someone behind Dan, someone driving him to do what he had. But who? Even Emma had been silent on that, and they all felt that was odd.

Breck pulled out a chair, seating Neasa, and then crouching down beside her. "You're sure it's yours?"

———

She nodded. "Look at the tank. There was an angel on it. It's there." She blinked rapidly, her tears turning to anger. "I want him, Breck. I don't want revenge. I just want to know why. What did I do to him that makes him that angry that he wants to destroy me? I don't have any riches. I have no trust funds or anything coming to me. Pops told me that." She paused, a thought crossing her mind. "What about Dad's people? Do we know anything about them?"

"We'll find out, darling. We'll find out. Right now, let's see what we can discover about Dan. Up for a challenge?" Breck grinned for a brief moment as she frowned at him and then nodded, determination on her face.

Neasa looked around later that afternoon. She was still in the conference room, deep in reading the material that each of the men had handed her. She was surprised at how much that they had discovered, each finding something different. Neasa nodded. Of course, they would. They all think differently, now don't they?

Rising, she made her way to the kitchenette and stood, watching the kettle as it boiled before she made her hot chocolate. Grasping the cup in her cold hands, she wandered the perimeter of the room, her eyes assessing each one of the men. She was beginning to know the ladies, finding each one unique but all friends. She could see how they were pairing off. Sighing, Neasa wondered who it was that she would pair off with. Her mind turned to Barnabas and she began to pray for him. Lord, I feel that he is hurting, that someone hurt him in the past. I don't know who or how or why, but You do. Is his lady the one that I will be friends with? Lord, I need someone, a female, that I can be friends with, someone to laugh with, to share life. I know I have Breck, but us women need a friend.

She turned as she felt someone near her. Berneen stood her, reaching for her cup and handing her a fresh one, setting it down on a nearby table.

"You look thoughtful, Neasa." Berneen watched her closely.

"I am. It's been a bad day, all around." Neasa rubbed at her temple. "No, I don't have much of a headache. At least, not that kind." She looked up. "Dan destroyed my motorcycle. I found out that he's my step-father. Mom isn't speaking to me. And Nevin needs to be with Sarah. Breck is on conference calls, which I understand." She gave a small smile. "How does that sound?"

"Sounds like you need some girl time." Berneen swiped her mug and then deposited the cups into the sink, running water into them. She then linked an arm with Neasa, drawing her from the room, waving at the men as they looked up. "Don't worry. If Breck is looking for you, they'll send him my way. Come on. We need to start planning."

"Planning? On what?"

Berneen just shook her head, a finger to her mouth, as she walked Neasa to her apartment and then in.

"Sit. And reach for that pad of paper and pen. I picked up that habit from Breck. He always has a pad of paper and pen handy. Barnabas said he has always done that."

"Okay. Pen. Paper. Mug of chocolate, once more. Gingerbread cookies." She looked up, suspicion on her face. "Who told you that I like these cookies?"

Berneen began to laugh. "No one. I do, so I just assume everyone does. Now, you are going to be planning a wedding, aren't you?"

Neasa stared at her before she began to laugh. "Berneen! You know, I just asked the Lord for a friend, and you appear."

"I did, didn't I? I felt Him nudging me your way." Berneen sipped at her tea. "Now, what are you thinking?"

"I have no idea, to tell you the truth. Mom is refusing to speak with me. I sent her a text to let her know and she just responded "Oh?"." That hurts, you know. But I will go on with what I want. Sarah will help but she's not well right now. So I can't be burdening her."

Berneen nodded before she bent her head and prayed for Neasa and her family. Looking up, she found Neasa staring at her in surprise. "It's what we do, Neasa. We pray for one another as we need to. That's another thing your Breck is teaching us."

"He is? Teaching us to love one another as we should? I can see that." Neasa fiddled with the pen, tapping the end on the paper. "To tell you the truth? I never ever thought that I would marry. Right now, I'm afraid to. I'm afraid that I will bring more danger to Breck."

"And you will. We all did, both the fellows and the ladies. Baird was held captive for a few days where I was. The fellows came in, got us out, and then we were taken captive the very next day. I stepped in to marry him to save his life. He was beaten very badly. Buckley was with us and forced to perform the marriage. But I will say this. No matter what we went through, we love each other more and more each day. God provided for us. He will provide for you and Breck. Now, do we plan a wedding or do we take on the fellows and try and solve this ourselves?"

"Solve it ourselves? Do you think we can?" Neasa looked up in surprise at that.

"I think we can take a stab at it. I have information that they haven't got yet. Emma, our friend, has been in touch. She sent me a whole lot of stuff. Darcie, another friend, has sent a profile of who she thinks is involved."

"Oh! Where is it?" Neasa watched as Berneen rose, heading for the office in the apartment and then sitting back down, handing over a pile of papers and keeping a stack for herself.

"Here. Read through it. I haven't yet, either. It just came, and that's when I went looking for you."

Chapter 37

Sitting back at last, Neasa looked over at Berneen, to find her watching her. Neasa grinned.

"How are we doing?" Berneen raised an eyebrow at her

"I think that we are getting somewhere. This bit about Dan? I didn't know that about him." Neasa poked at the paper she had been writing on. "He's related in some way to the man who had that restaurant. I would never have worked there, had I known that."

"That's interesting that he is. I wonder if the fellows have discovered that." Berneen sent off a text message to Baird and was surprised at his quick response. "No, they hadn't discovered that. And he wants to know how we did just that." Berneen began to laugh. "Give him ten minutes and he'll be up here."

"I say, five, and Breck will be with him."

The two ladies looked around as the door opened and both Baird and Breck appeared, as well as Dallas.

"We didn't include Dallas, did we?" Neasa grinned at Berneen.

"No, we didn't. Hmm. Should we tell them or should we wait?" Berneen looked up at Baird as he wrapped an arm around her.

"What have you ladies been up to?" Baird glanced at the clock. "It's supper time, ladies. I suggest that I fire up the grill, do some meat and veggies. We eat. We pray. And then we talk."

"Sounds like a plan." Berneen was on her feet, heading for the fridge. "I have chicken here and some burgers. I wasn't sure which we would want tonight, Baird."

Breck had been watching Neasa closely and knew that she would not make it through supper without speaking with him and Dallas. He drew her to her feet and then to the living room, beckoning Dallas to follow. He ducked his head to study her.

"Neasa?"

"Breck? Do you know what we discovered? That Dan is somehow related to the man I worked for?"

"He is?" Breck looked over at Dallas, to find him watching Neasa intently. "How did you discover that?"

"Emma sent it. We just found it out before you came in. There was a whole lot of information. And Darcie, I think it was, sent a profile. It fits Dan to some extent but not totally."

"Do you have that information that you can share, Neasa? Emma's been sending me information as well." Dallas looked down for a moment before he looked at Neasa, seeing how fragile she seemed at that moment.

"I guess." Neasa retrieved it from the kitchen. "Here. I want a copy of it."

"And you will have this one back. I just need to make some notes." Dallas scanned through it, taking photos of the pages that he needed to. "I'll investigate this, Neasa. Now, what else?"

"What else? Besides a destroyed dream?" Neasa blinked back tears. Her voice dropped to a mere whisper. "Do you know how long I had to work and save to buy my bike? And that dream is gone. Even if I were to get another one, it won't be the same."

"No, it won't, but you need to, maybe." Breck grinned as she shook her head at him.

"You're real definite there, you know?" Neasa turned back to Dallas. "What can you tell me?"

"Right now? We're working through everything that we have. I'm sorry I can't be giving out more information than that, but there is a lot of legwork and investigative work to do." Dallas grinned at her for a moment. "But right now? I think our supper is ready. Let's eat. And then we'll see where we stand."

Neasa looked disgruntled before she sighed. "I'm sorry. I know that it takes time. I just wish it was all over." She walked away from the two men, leaving Breck staring after her and Dallas watching Breck.

"Breck?"

Dallas' voice had Breck turning to him.

"Dallas? What didn't you say?"

"That you're the target now. I'm sure that Neasa has that figured out, but you both need to take extra precautions. We're still trying to determine who it is that put out the hit on you. And it is a hit, Breck. Someone wants you dead."

Breck paled before his face grew grim. "We've been through this before, Dallas. Whoever it is will not win. God's not finished with me here yet. Or at least, He hasn't said that He is."

Hitting the rough pavement with his knees and then his hands, a deep groan came from Breck as he tried to recover from the brutal blow that he had just taken. His head hung down as he struggled to regain his breath. A savage blow from the ragged 2 x 4 sent him rolling towards a broken-down building and the open door. A shove from a booted foot had him tumbling down the broken concrete stairs to lie in a crumpled heap at the bottom, not moving. The door was slammed shut by his assailant, a bent rusty piece of pipe bracing it shut.

Dan stood in the shadows watching, a vengeful sneer on his face, before he reached into his pocket and pulled out a wad of bills, peeling a couple off and handing them to the young man who flung the 2 x 4 away from him. The young man grabbed the money and ran, not looking around at all. Dan's eyes followed him before they turned to the door. He strode away, a hateful laugh echoing behind him. As far as he was concerned, Breck was dead. He could now turn his attention to Neasa. If he couldn't get to her, then he would target Nevin. One of them would pay for his being arrested and placed in jail.

The late autumn darkness closed in, bringing shadows to the dimly lit area. Breck moved, groaning as he did so. He rolled to his side, pain shooting through him. He heard the faint rustlings of the critters in the basement of the building, the sound startling him, as did the feeling of critters crawling over him. His eyes slid closed and he was once more lost to consciousness. He didn't feel the trickle of blood that soaked into his hair or the cuts and scrapes that covered his face and hands.

A whisper of sound at the door and a slight scraping sound sent the critters scattering as the door squeaked open and a shadow appeared, that descended the steps. The man stooped over Breck before he glanced around. He raised Breck to his feet, struggling with Breck's height before he draped him over a shoulder and then staggered back up the stairs. He gently laid Breck down before he again closed the door, the pipe against it as he had found it. He raised the unconscious man to his shoulders once more and made his way as quickly as he could to the only shelter that he knew was safe, a rundown building blocks from where he had found Breck.

Breck was gently dropped to the rough pallet of ragged blankets that the man called his bed before the man turned to light the small fire that he always had ready. He rubbed his hands together before he turned back to Breck, carefully assessing the younger man. He sat back, before he reached for a bottle of water in his pack, opening it. Breck's head was raised enough so that he could swallow sips before he nodded, his eyes flickering open and closed.

"What do I do with you, Breck?" The man's whisper echoed through the room. "I need to get you to help, but I can't let anyone know that you're alive. He meant for you to die down there. And you would have. The door was the only way out and there is no chance that you could have opened it." He rummaged around in the room, finding the pot and carton of broth that he had stashed there, working to heat it and then spoon it into Breck, before he ate himself.

Early morning, with the dawn just breaking, the man roused, hearing footsteps ringing on the pavement outside. He was on his feet, to the door, his demeanour changing, his clear intelligent eyes taking on a mistiness as he ducked outside, to stand with his head lowered as the patrol officer approached.

"Davy? You're up and about early. Can't sleep?" The officer handed over the takeout cup of coffee and muffin that he had brought.

"Naw. I was asleep. You woke me with your heavy feet. Can't you walk any quieter?" Davy looked around, not seeing anyone else. "I need help, Joe."

"You do?" Joe kept his voice low as well.

"I do. I heard that a hit was put on on Breck."

"That's true. What would you know about that?" Joe watched the area around them, not looking directly at Davy.

"Cause I have him with me. He's hurt, Joe, hurt bad. I can't keep him awake. But I can't take him to the hospital. They'd find him."

"That they would. Let me think about this for a moment." Joe's voice raised. "Go on back to your bed, Davy. Enjoy your muffin. I'll bring another tomorrow for you."

"I'd be thanking you, Joe." Davy disappeared through the doorway, to stand in the dimness just inside it, watching Joe walk away. A breath of relief passed through him. Joe would make sure that Breck was taken care of. That he knew. He just had to keep him hidden until then, and that meant moving around in the daylight. That's where the danger was, he thought.

Dropping to his knees beside Breck, Davy shook his shoulder. "Wake up, Breck. We need to move."

Breck roused slightly, shaking his head. "No, I need to sleep, Dad. It's not a school day."

"No, it's not." Humour lashed through Davy's voice. "But we need to move, Breck. Come on, boy. Up with you."

Breck stood on unsteady feet, an arm wrapped around himself as the pain intensified. His face was white under the scrapes, cuts, and bruises. Davy gathered his things, stuffing them into his pack, and then shoved a shoulder under Breck's arm, knowing the younger man just didn't have the ability to stand and walk, not on his own.

"We're moving, Breck. I need to keep us on the move for the day. I have help coming but I just don't know when. And I just don't know how bad you're hurt."

Davy watched Breck closely over the day, as they moved from bench to bench, ending up in another abandoned building. It was one that Davy used a lot, and he knew that Joe would find him. That's what Joe did.

Breck sank down to the cold, earthen floor, not even feeling the dampness or chill that met his body. He didn't care. All he knew was that he hurt and hurt badly all over and that this man he was with had kept him on the move all day, despite his protests that he just couldn't do it. He didn't see Davy setting up a fire or finding ragged blankets that he had stuffed into a crevice, spreading them out of the floor and then rolling Breck onto them, covering him with another one.

His head turning as he heard a noise, Davy moved towards the doorway, extinguishing his fire on the way. His hand went up to shield his eyes as a bright light flashed at him before it moved around the room. A gentle hand took him to one side and Joe's voice whispered in his ear.

"I had trouble finding you, Davy. You moved a lot today."

"I had to, Joe. I had to for Breck's sake. I saw men looking for someone."

"I know, Davy. I know. Here, let's get you out of here. Where's your stuff?"

"Here." Another man handed Davy his knapsack. "We've got him, Davy. We'll look after him. You need to come with us."

"I can't, Joe. I can't." Davy disappeared before either man could stop him, leaving them staring at one another.

"It's what he does, Ed. He helps and then disappears."

"So I am told." Ed turned to the other two men with him. "Where to, fellows?"

"I would say the building, Ed. If we can come up with some excuse to get him there." Joe looked around. "How close to the door are you parked?"

"Not close enough to. I'll move in near the back door. It's easier to get at." Ed was gone and then they heard the quiet sound of the vehicle as it stopped outside the door.

The three men in the building quickly moved Breck to the vehicle before Ed moved away as quickly as he could, the four men searching the darkness for anyone watching. Joe saw Davy briefly appear, a hand raised to acknowledge him before he once more disappeared into the darkness.

"They'll be watching the building for Neasa." Ed shot a look back at Breck, slumped in the middle of the back seat, his eyes closed.

"They will be." Joe had his phone out. "Let me call Barnabas. We can likely go into the loading dock that they have there. Barnabas? Joe Barrett. I'm good. And you? Breck? We heard that there was a hit out on him. Listen. I have a friend with me. Can we come in through the loading dock?"

Barnabas stared at the phone he had pulled from his ear before he was speaking. "Joe? The loading dock? Sure. I'll meet you there. We've upped the security around here. Branigan will meet you by the gate and lead you in."

"Sounds good. Fifteen minutes, I think, Ed says." He tucked away his phone, his own eye son Breck. "Branigan will meet us, Ed."

"Sure. I thought there would be someone there."

Branigan watched carefully as Ed drove into the loading dock before he ducked in, the overhead door closing behind him. He approached Barnabas, who stood waiting for the men to exit the vehicle, a frown on his face when they didn't, only Joe slipping quickly out and closing the door behind him.

"Joe? Why the mystery?" Barnabas stared at the officer that he knew well.

"We have Breck, Barnabas."

"Breck? You have him." Barnabas moved to go around Joe, stopping as Joe held up his hand. "What's wrong?"

"He was beaten badly, sometime yesterday, and shoved down some cement stairs. A fellow on the street found him, took care of him overnight, and then kept him on the move today. We don't want to take him into the hospital, not unless Doc or Brady says we should. Is either one around?"

"Both are." Barnabas turned as he heard Branigan running from the area. "Branigan will get them. Do we need the stretcher?"

"I would say yes, but we need to get him out of here and then have us leave. It's too obvious that we have something or someone for you, driving in as we did."

"True." Barnabas watched as Breck was carefully maneuvered from the back seat, and arms over the shoulders of two of the men, walked to the infirmary, Brady appearing as they reached the door. "Brady?"

"Got it, Barnabas. Doc's on his way, Branigan said. So is Anna. Beck and Bonnie are with Neasa."

"I know. Get him in there, and I'll head up. Joe, Ed. Thanks."

Joe and Ed simply waved, following the other two officers back to their vehicle, waiting for security to open the door and let them out. Joe stared back at the building, knowing that Breck was in good hands, but worried about Davy.

"Davy? How much trouble is he in?" Ed's voice reached through the dim lighting in the vehicle.

"A lot, I would say. But he can take care of himself, much better than anyone would think." Joe didn't let on that Davy was an undercover officer, had been for a number of years, and was due to come back into the office, taking up a position on the detective squad.

The previous afternoon, Neasa had gone looking for Breck, just needing to see him and feel his arms around her. When knocking at his door brought no answer, she headed for the main floor and his office. She knocked and then finally opened the door, finding the lights off and no Breck. She paused, a hand rubbing at her forehead, a tiny headache beginning behind her eyes. She was frustrated with those, she thought.

Heading for the conference room, she opened the door and then entered, watching as Brandon, Bradon, and Burnie were at work, looking up to greet her.

"Have you seen Breck?"

The three men looked at one another before shaking their heads.

"I think he was heading into town this morning. He said something about having to go to city hall with some paperwork." Burnie rose and approached her. "He's not back?"

"No, he's not. I can't find him." Neasa was worried and it showed.

"Neasa? What's up?" Bradon had approached as had Brandon.

"Dallas was out yesterday. He said that there's a hit, as he called it, out on Breck. Breck was trying not to let me know." Neasa wrapped her arms around herself. "And now I can't find him."

"Listen, I'll head into town." Bradon was moving towards the door. "Ennis will come with me." He didn't let on, but her words had hit home with him. Breck was the latest of them to have had a hit put out on him.

"I'll check out the gym and that area." Brandon moved away as well, leaving Burnie to reach out a hand and direct Neasa to a nearby chair.

"Neasa? Did he talk to you today at all?"

"He did. About mid-morning. Just to say he loved me and that he would be back this afternoon." Neasa rose and paced the room. "This is not the Breck I know. To say that and not do it."

"No, it's not Breck. Let me call Dallas and let him know."

Neasa shook her head. "He's in court, he said. We can't disturb him." She spun, walking along the whiteboards, studying the new information. "You fellows have been busy."

"We have been, Neasa. We were to meet with you and Breck tomorrow morning. He requested that. There is some information that we're still confirming."

"I see. What's this?" Neasa pointed to a name. "Who is this?"

"That lady? We're still confirming it, but we believe that she is your natural mother. And Nevin's." Burnie watched as she spun, shock on her face. "The woman that you knew as your mother? She is actually your step-mother. What we have determined is that your mother died from cancer about two months after Nevin was born. Your father remarried quickly, not able to make it work raising you two."

"And then he died about ten months later? Burnie? This sounds like one of your books."

Burnie grinned. "It does? That what they told me about Muir and me." He sobered. "I'm sorry, Neasa. Breck wanted to be here when you were told."

"And he's not. What else has been false about my life? My grandparents?"

"The ones that you see? They are your father's. They were adamant that they not be kept out of your life. The woman that you know as your mother is not with them. She hasn't been."

"I see. That makes sense then that I hadn't heard any other voices. I haven't had a chance to call Pops or Grams yet, with what all has been going on. And that's not me." Neasa sat, her arm leaning on the table. "I need to."

"You do, but I would wait for the moment. Right now? We need to figure out where your fellow is." He pulled out his phone. "It's Bradon. Bradon? His truck? Oh. No sign of him? Okay. Ennis

---

134

will? Sure. Call it in. I'm still in the conference room with Neasa. They are? That's good."

Burnie put away his phone, his eyes on Neasa. "Bradon found Breck's truck, but it was in the downtown area."

"Downtown? That's strange."

"It is. He sometimes heads that way when he's in town, just to check on the people there, to make sure that they don't need anything. That's what he was likely doing. Bradon will call it in."

"Oh. Okay. His parents?"

"They were on their way here. Apparently, Breck had asked them for dinner."

"He did? I didn't know that." Neasa was on her feet, heading for the lobby, not seeing Burnie reaching to stop her.

Burnie watched her move away, shaking his head. Lord, she's hurting in so many ways. Now, Breck is gone, and she has to feel like she's sinking or lost at sea or something. Help us to find him and find him quickly.

Bonnie watched as Neasa paced her apartment the next afternoon. They had stayed with her, not willing to leave her on her own. Beck had headed for Barnabas, to see what he could discover. There had been no word as yet, and both Breck's parents were worried.

"Neasa?" Bonnie watched as Neasa turned towards her. "What can I do for you?"

Neasa sighed before she sat beside the older lady on the couch. "I'm not sure. I'm just so confused right now. I don't know where to even start."

"Just start talking. We'll figure it out as we go along." Bonnie reached to wrap an arm around the younger woman, bowing her head to pray for her.

"Thank you, Bonnie." Neasa wiped at her eyes. "I had some really bad news yesterday. Breck knew and had wanted to tell me." She looked up at the ceiling, blinking as she did so, her hands twisting on her lap. "The woman I thought was our mother? Isn't. She's a step-mother. Our real mother died when Nevin was two. Then Dad was killed when about ten months later. It's just so confusing. I'm not even sure if the last name I have is the correct one."

"Let them sort it out for you, Neasa. Right now, you're needing to heal. I would like to step in as your mother, if I may. Not to replace her, but to be there for you." Bonnie watched as Neasa struggled with her emotions.

"Thank you, Bonnie. Can I call you Mom?" Neasa turned to her, hope on her face.

"You can, my dear. You can. Call Beck Dad, if you want. You'll be our daughter. I always wanted one, but God didn't send us one."

Finally stretching out and sleeping, Neasa didn't hear Beck return or Bonnie moving around her apartment. She didn't rouse as

---

the older couple ate their meal, leaving hers in the fridge for when she awoke.

Barnabas tapped at the door late that evening, finding Beck opening it.

"Barnabas? I didn't expect to see you tonight." Beck studied the younger man. "Have you word?"

"Where's Neasa? Is she still up?"

Beck pointed to the living room. "She's asleep in there. Go on in, son." Bonnie stood with her hand on Beck's back, watching as Barnabas crouched down beside the couch.

A hand on Neasa's arm, Barnabas spoke quietly.

"Neasa, can you wake up for me?" He grinned as she frowned at him before she pushed her hair away from her face.

"Barnabas? I was sleeping. This had better be good."

"Oh, I know that you'll sink so. Breck is here." He waited, opening his mouth to speak again as Neasa sat up abruptly.

"Breck? Where?"

"The infirmary." Barnabas moved quickly out of the way as Neasa shot to her feet, running for the door without a thought for her shoes. The door almost slammed behind her, she had opened it with that great of force.

"Breck?" Bonnie moved forward.

"He's in the infirmary, Beck, Bonnie. He has been hurt." Barnabas stared at the door. "I'm glad that I wasn't standing in her way."

Beck began to laugh. "I think she would have just run you down. Where are her shoes, love?"

"Right here?" Bonnie held up the shoes that she had retrieved. "And I have her keys. Let's go find our son."

Neasa didn't see the men waiting in the hallway, their ladies with them, or even see Hailey and Holly as they huddled together near the door. All eyes were on her as she ran past them, heading for the infirmary, through the door, and beside Breck before anyone could even reach out a hand to stop her.

Doc looked up and nodded towards her, Cadee turning and approaching her.

"Neasa? We need you to step back for a moment." Cadee's arm around her drew her away, even as Neasa struggled to get back. Barnabas was there as well, his arm around her, Cadee nodding at him before she returned to help Doc. Brady watched from the other side of the stretcher.

Barnabas turned her towards the door, not letting her return to Breck, even as she continued to try that.

"We'll wait right outside here, Neasa. They won't be long, they said."

Neasa stared at the closing door. "I need to be with him, Barnabas."

"And you will. Right now, Doc needs this time. He's been beaten, Neasa."

"Beaten? Is that why?" Neasa stared wildly around before she ran, not hearing the cries for her to stop and to wait. She hit the door in the lobby, running through it to the outside, the darkness covering her path. Where could she go, she wondered? Where? It's my fault that he's hurt. She continued to run, finally stopping in the rose garden, dropping to her knees beside a bench, heart-rending sobs rising from her.

Blair stood and watched, before he moved forward, reaching to gather her up, surprised that she didn't fight him. He looked around, sensing someone there.

"Who's there?"

"Just me. Davy. I just wanted to know how Breck it."

"Davy? You found him? Come. Come with me."

Davy hesitated and then moved forward, following Blair, keeping in the shadows as much as he could. He stopped as he stooped in the lobby before he moved towards the infirmary. Then he turned and left. He couldn't and shouldn't be here, he thought.

An hour later, Neasa stood with Breck's hand tight in hers, her other hand on his face. The stubble on his cheek was rough under it, but she didn't care. He was here, even though he had not awakened as yet. Doc wasn't overly concerned, he told her. If Breck didn't awaken soon, then they would need to transport him to the hospital. At the moment, none of them wanted that.

Neasa prayed hard, prayed for her fellow to awaken, for the ones responsible to be caught and brought to justice. She really had no idea how to pray. She turned her head as she heard soft footsteps.

"Hailey. Holly. Should you be here?"

The twins nodded.

"We need to be with you, Neasa. He's like our big brother." Holly whispered even as she leant against Neasa. "Is he okay?"

"Doc said he was beaten. We were told that he was likely shoved down some steps. What else happened, we're not sure." Neasa looked at Hailey. "Hailey?"

"It's okay, Neasa. We can go now. We just needed to make sure."

Neasa reached to hug the two girls. "Come back in the morning. He may be awake then." She watched them walk away before she reached to wrap a blanket around herself and then picked up the mug of hot chocolate Benen had brought her, waving away her thanks.

Barnabas raised his head after Buckley had finished his prayer. The men had all gathered in the conference room, grim looks on their faces, before they bowed for prayer. It was time, he knew, that they pulled back from their work, as they had so many times already, and worked towards finding the ones responsible for Breck's beating, to solve the mastering surrounding Neasa. And it was becoming more and more of a mystery. Just who she was? That was what was puzzling all of them.

"Barnabas?" Brennen looked around at his friends. "Do we know what happened?"

"Joe brought him out." The men recognized the name of an officer that they knew from church. "He was beaten sometime yesterday. Dumped down some stairs. A homeless man found him and took care of him. Joe said he moved Breck all over the downtown today, trying to protect him."

Benen spoke up. "An undercover officer, I have no doubt."

Brody stared at him. "I never thought of that. But likely. But where do we go from here?"

"I talked to Neasa. She's aware of what we found. Now, how far along on that are we?"

"Not where we need to be. I'm finding out all sorts of stuff about the step-mother. She had reported Dan for abuse but always backed away from it when questioned. That was in the early years. She has finally talked to me." Branigan looked up. "I pulled the legal stuff with her. Told her I was a paralegal and if she wanted help, I would see that she could get it. She's refused, for now, just glad she said that Neasa and Nevin were away from Dan."

"Only they're not. Barnabas, where is Nevin and his Sarah right now?" Brendon looked up from his notes.

"They're with friends. Not our friends, but their friends. And away from here."

"That's good. He'll go after Nevin if he can't get to Neasa. I hope he doesn't know who the friends are."

"Nevin said that he won't." Barnabas looked up as the door opened and Dallas appeared.

"Dallas? I thought you had to be ready for court in the morning."

"I was but the case was postponed. Will told me to get myself out here and stay until we solved this. He put in a leave of absence for me, letting me do that, but keeping access to all my sites and programs." Dallas sat slowly, a thank you to Brandon for the mug of coffee set in front of him. "What's going on? Will just told me to talk to you."

Barnabas nodded. He had called his father and Bruce had contacted Will.

"We have Breck."

Dallas choked on his coffee. "I'm sorry. I thought that you said you have Breck."

"We do. Someone took care of him and then some of your officers brought him out here tonight. So far, Doc thinks that between himself, Brady and Cadee, they can manage to treat him."

"How bad?" Dallas' face grew stern.

"Bad enough that he hasn't roused yet. He was beaten, Doc thinks with a 2 x 4. We think he was shoved down some stairs and then locked into a building. Whoever it was that found him took him from there and then moved him around all day. It didn't help him any physically, but it likely saved his life."

"I see." Dallas reached for a pen and paper. "If he was locked into a building, that had to be in the downtown area. And some of those buildings? You put a board or something against a door and that would block the only way out. There are no windows in some of them."

"That's our guess." Baird spoke up. "I would like to thank whoever it was."

"We all do." Dallas rose and walked towards the whiteboards, silent as he studied them. "You fellows have found a lot of information. I haven't had the time to devote to it as I should. Being one short on the detective team means a lot of overtime."

"We get that, Dallas. Emma's been sending us information. She sent Neasa a profile, she said."

"That she did. I have it. I'll gladly share if Neasa says I can. I can't put a name to the person described but he or she sounds so familiar."

"He or she?" Bradon spoke up. "You're thinking female?"

"We always do, Bradon. Now, how late do we work? And Barnabas, I'm told there is an apartment here that I am to use for the next few days."

Rousing early in the morning, Breck stared around the room, recognizing it as the infirmary at home. He sighed. Someone had brought him home, but who? He turned his head, feeling a hand touching his face, and frowned.

"Do I know you?" He stared at the young woman standing beside his bed, the paleness of her face and the dark shadows under her eyes showing her fatigue.

"Do you know me?" Neasa stared at him before she repeated herself. "Do you know me?" Her hand went up. "This is your ring on my finger, buster. We're engaged. How dare you ask me if you know me!" She swatted his arm, not seeing the wince that he gave.

"We are? I'm sorry. Everything is foggy right now."

"Foggy? Is that your excuse? Breck! How dare you forget me!" The tears that she could not contain sparkled on her cheeks as she backed away. Standing with her back to the door, Neasa faced him down.

"I'm sorry. We're engaged?" Breck lowered the bed rail and swung his feet off the bed, sitting for a moment to let his head clear. He stared down at his clothes, wondering how they got so dirty, and why he was so sore. He slid off the bed, wincing once more as the slight jar that went through his body started the pain before he moved towards Neasa. He stood, a hand flat against the door on either side of her head, and studied her.

"We are. You told me that you loved me. How could you forget? I don't need someone to forget." Neasa swiped at the tears, jumping as Breck's hand cupped her cheek.

"I'm sorry. My mind is foggy. No one should forget as beautiful a lady as you are." He stared down at her and without even thinking bent to kiss her.

Neasa shoved at him, sending him toppling backward to the floor. Horrified, she stood, hands over her mouth before she was on her knees, helping him to sit up.

"I'm sorry. I shouldn't have done that."

"It's okay. I shouldn't have kissed you."

Neasa smacked his arm once more. "Of course you should. We are engaged. And I am not letting you go. So take that, buster." She looked around as the door opened, and Doc peeked in cautiously, having heard her raised voice.

"Breck? You're up, I think. Neasa? Any reason you two are sitting on the floor?"

"Don't ask, Doc. Talk some sense into this man. He's forgotten that we're engaged. He doesn't remember me, he tells me, and then he has the nerve to kiss me." Neasa was on her feet, running from the room, not hearing Guenivere as she called for her.

"Breck? Did you really do that?" Doc helped Breck to his feet and back to the bed.

Breck stared at the door, waiting for Neasa to return. "I did, Doc. I guess that I shouldn't have."

Doc shrugged. "You two are engaged, but I don't think it was a good idea. Your kissing her, that is."

Breck suddenly grinned. "She's a firebrand, isn't she?"

Doc began to laugh. "That she is, son. That she is. She's just what you need. She doesn't back down from you, not like the other ladies do when you go all stern and dark."

"No? That's unusual." Breck sat, bemused. "I'm really engaged?"

"You are, Breck. She's going through some pretty bad stuff right now, which is why you were beaten up and dumped. Someone found you and then Joe and some fellow officers brought you home."

"I don't remember much after going to city hall." Breck slid from the bed, standing for a moment to catch his balance. "I need to go change and then find my lady. What's her name?"

Doc stared at him and then began to laugh heartily. "Don't tell her that you can't remember her name. She'll hit you again. It's Neasa."

"Neasa? A beautiful name for a beautiful lady." Breck walked slowly away, leaving Doc shaking his head after him.

Showered, shaved and in clean clothes, Breck practically inhaled the coffee that he had made before he turned to the door, opening it and then closing it behind him. He stopped. He needed to find Neasa, only where would she be? He stared at the doors on his floor before he shook his head. Right now, he had no idea which apartment she would be in if she was even in one of them. He turned as he heard Devaney's voice behind him.

"She's in the apartment next to you, Breck. You have that lost look on your face." She grinned at him.

"I do, don't I? I'm in the dog house and not sure how to get out of it."

"Grovelling is good. Lots of grovelling. Flowers are also right up there." She continued to grin. "Only I don't think you're in any shape to go out and buy her flowers."

"No, I'm not. That will have to wait. Thanks, Devaney." He turned to the apartment door, tapping at it, hearing Neasa's voice telling whoever it was to go away.

"Neasa? Please? Open the door."

Neasa flung the door open, standing with her hands on her hips, staring at him in disbelief.

"How dare you come around me? You don't remember me. Go away!"

Breck simply shook his head. "Please, Neasa? Can we at least talk?"

Neasa stared at him, before she shoved by him, slamming the door behind her, and then heading for the lobby. He reached to stop her, finding her stiffen at his touch. Lord, how do I do this? I've hurt her, without meaning to. Please, Lord? What do I do?"

Neasa stood, her back straight as she faced away from him. "Breck? What is it exactly that you want to say?"

"That I'm sorry. I know that's my ring on your finger. I recognize it. I just don't remember all that well. My mind's confused."

She snorted. "Your mind's confused? That's a mouthful, Breck." She turned, eyeing him. "And what else?"

"I'm grovelling here, Neasa. I was told to grovel to get out of the dog house. Oh, yes. And flowers. Only I was told I wasn't in any shape to go and buy you any."

Neasa looked past him, seeing Devaney standing there, a grin on her face. "Oh, I see. Grovelling, are we? How much grovelling are you prepared to do?"

Breck stared at her before his eyes narrowed, catching the smirk that she was trying to hide.

"I don't know about that now. Grovelling seems kind of low." He simply swept her into a hug, finding her struggling at first before she hugged him back. "Work with me, please, Neasa? I want to remember. I truly do."

Opening the door to the conference room, Breck waited while Neasa entered before he followed her and stood beside her, his narrowed eyes taking in the activity. Everyone is here, aren't they, Lord? That means we must be making progress. Only I have no idea and I need to know. Heal me, please, dear Lord. And protect the lady that they say is mine.

Dallas stood from where he had been sitting, approaching them, seeing not a couple but two people. He frowned as he felt the tension between them before Neasa moved away, to stand staring at the whiteboards before she turned to speak with Bradon.

"Breck?" Dallas was hesitant to even question him.

"Dallas? You're here."

"I am. Will sent me to work on this with you all. How are you?"

"Not great. I hurt all over. I don't remember what happened." Breck paused, sadness on his face. "And I don't really remember Neasa."

"You don't remember her? You're engaged. How could you not?" Dallas simply shook his head, a hand on Breck's arm steering him to a chair.

"I don't know. She didn't take it well."

"And do you blame her? Do you remember anything of what's going on with her?"

Breck shook his head. "It's like I have a huge gap there, that I can't remember things. I see flashes and bits and pieces."

"Okay." Dallas looked around, beckoning to Buckley. "First, let Buckley pray for you, and then we'll work with you to get you to where you need to be. Neasa has been in and out for the last few days, helping in any way that she can. Just thought that you should know that."

"Thanks, Dallas. I do." Breck watched as Neasa moved from work station to work station, speaking with each of the men. He frowned. "Buckley? What's she up to?"

"Neasa? You don't know? She'll come in and speak with each one of us. Not about what's going on with her. Just to see how we are, what she can pray for, how the ladies are, how the littles ones that are here are. She has a gift, Breck, that I don't see very often. A gift to reach down and find out what she wants to know about a person so that she can better understand them and then pray for them. She's like you in that."

"Yeah, about that." Breck sighed, his eyes on his friend. "I can't really remember her. She didn't take it well."

"Do you blame her? Let me pray for you, Breck. You're like Neasa. You just give and give, without asking for anything in return. It's our time to return that to you."

Breck finally looked once more, to find Neasa had seated herself beside him, her hand on his. He shared a look with Buckley before he turned to her.

"Neasa?"

"Breck? Where do we go? Sorry, Buckley. I shouldn't have asked in front of you."

"It's okay, Neasa. I can play the pastor role again if you like." He simply grinned at her. "Or I can get up and walk away."

"Stay, I think, Buckley. We may need a referee." She smirked as Buckley began to laugh, Breck staring at her in disbelief. "Yes, a referee. Breck, you tell me that you don't remember me or what we've been going through. You are about to get a crash course in it. The men all tell me that you have worked tirelessly to solve the adventures that they went through. Now, it's their turn to give back. They have amassed an amazing amount of information. Dallas was sent out here by Will to aid in the investigation and do what he does best. Make it legal." She pointed to the papers in front of her. "This is a summation that Burnie has prepared. It's good. He's treated it like a plotline for one of his mystery stories."

"He does that. It's the author in him, how he thinks." Breck reached for the papers. "May I?"

"You may. Before we start, Buckley, please pray. I sense that we are coming into a very dangerous part of our lives. Almost losing Breck to that building? I can't handle it if that really happens. He is my lifeline to reality right now, even though he says he doesn't remember me."

Breck read through the sheaf of papers, stopping as he had barely started to reach for a pen and the pad of paper Buckley had set down. He finally sat back, staring across the room, before he turned to Neasa, finding her asleep, her head down on her folded arms. Someone had found a blanket and tucked it around her. He laid his hand gently on her hair, fingering a strand, before he stood, heading for the coffee pot and refilling his mug, before he turned, watching the activity. About half of the men had left, having other commitments that they needed to get to. Breck turned to the whiteboards, moving past them slowly, reading each one, finally reaching for a pen and heading for a blank one, jotting down a concise summary of what he had just read.

Barnabas approached him, his head tilting to watch his friend.

"Breck?"

Breck nodded. "If you heard that I don't remember Neasa at the moment, it's true. And she has told me off about that." He sighed, his eyes rising to the ceiling. "How do I do this, Barnabas?"

"By doing what you are doing. Helping to solve this. Praying. Just being with her. Doc would tell you that you did this to protect someone, possibly yourself. I would say that you did this to protect Neasa, or else the person involved in one that you didn't expect and that shock has done this to you."

"That may be." Breck turned to watch Neasa sleeping. "She's wearing out, my friend. How do we solve this and soon?"

Barnabas sighed. "That we are working on. We need some more information." His voice halted as he watched Breck's face. "What did you remember?"

"Dan was there. He was off in the shadows. I saw him and slowed my steps, not wanting to approach him. That's when someone hit me." Breck looked at Barnabas. "I have no idea who that was, but Dan was there. He watched without stepping in to stop it."

"Then, he's likely the one who arranged it." Dallas had approached the two men. "Let me call that in, Breck. I know we need to get your statement and I'll have someone come out. Don't say anything more."

Neasa awoke, stretching as she did, her eyes on Breck as he stood talking with Barnabas and Dallas. Will he remember me, Lord? Or I am to walk away from the one I love so much? I can't do this, Lord, and I don't understand why You are asking me to. I know You are in control. Guide our steps. Put a watch on our mouths. She reached into a pocket for her phone, searching the messages. She breathed a sigh of relief. None from an unknown number. She smiled at Nevin's message. Neasa missed her brother but understood why they had to stay apart. She was just too dangerous for him and Sarah to be around.

Rising and heading to make herself a hot chocolate, Neasa hesitated, a thought crossing her mind. She turned instead and headed for the board holding the logic problem, her finger tracing some names before she crossed out one and added another, changing the perspective of the mystery. Why that name? Neasa had no idea why.

Brandon had been watching Neasa and rose to move to stand beside her, reading what she had done.

"Her? Why?"

Neasa shrugged. "I have no idea. I can remember her being around Dan's shop and them being in deep discussion, changing the subject if Nevin or I approached. She wasn't a landscaper. Far from it. She refused to get her hands dirty. With dirt, that is. I often wondered if she was involved in a crime."

Benen stood beside them, staring at the board and then down at the paper he held.

"How'd you do that?" He was stunned.

"Do what?" Brandon peered around Neasa at him.

"Find her. I just did."

Neasa shook her head. "I don't know. I just remembered her. Why?"

"Because she was just arrested for something else. Dallas is looking for you. He was out in the lobby." Benen turned as the door opened and Dallas entered, searching for Neasa.

Dallas paused beside Breck, studying the other man closely. He could see the pain that Breck was still in and the fatigue that was weighing him down.

"Breck, go home. Go to bed for a while. You're out on your feet."

Breck nodded, scrubbing his hands down his face. "I know, Dallas, but I don't want to leave Neasa."

"She'll be here when you come back. Go on. I'll tell her." He watched at Breck reluctantly nodded and then moved away.

Neasa turned as she heard Dallas' voice behind her.

"Dallas?"

"Neasa. I sent Breck off to get some sleep. He wasn't ready to leave you. He needs this rest, Neasa."

"I know that he does. But I don't know where I stand with him. Not anymore." Neasa moved quickly away from the three men, heading out of the door, to stand in the lobby before she ran for her own apartment, locking the door behind her. She threw herself onto her bed as deep sobs shook her body. The sobs weren't just because of Breck. Neasa had reached her breaking point. She wept for the father and mother that she could not remember. For Nevin. For Sarah. For the lostness that she now found herself in. She finally swept, sobs still shaking her body. They would be healing but she still faced danger.

Three hours later, Bonnie stared at her son before she looked at Beck, who also stood staring at Breck.

"What do you mean, son? You don't remember Neasa?" Bonnie finally asked the question.

"That. I remember the ring, but not on her finger." Breck sighed, running his hand through his rumpled hair. "I made the mistake of asking if I knew her."

Bonnie began to laugh, picturing that very event. "Went well, did it? How much did she tell you off?"

"Mom!" Breck finally nodded. "She did just that, Mom. And then shoved me away from her."

"Can't say as I blame her, son." Beck moved past Breck towards the kitchen. "It must have been a shock for her. She hadn't slept much when you were away."

"She hadn't? I didn't know that." Breck took the mug of coffee offered to him.

"No, you wouldn't. She's hurting, Breck, from what she has found out about her past. To be going through this and then have you disappear? It shook her world in a way that I can't even begin to understand." Beck slid back a chair and sat, his mug hitting the table as he watched his son.

Bonnie moved away, heading for the apartment next door, and the young lady that she had taken to her heart. Not getting an answer, she sighed and reluctantly reached for the key that Neasa had given her. She entered the apartment, searching for Neasa, standing beside her bed, seeing the traces of the tears that had been shed. Bonnie reached for a blanket, covering Neasa, and then headed for the bathroom, returning with a warm damp cloth that she used to wash away the tear tracks.

Bonnie settled into the living room, not willing to let Neasa stay on her own. Her head bowed as she prayed for her daughter, as she had begun to think of Neasa. No in-law about it, she had decided.

Neasa roused in the late afternoon, finding the bedside lamp on, and not remembering turning it on. She felt the blanket covering her and frowned before she rose, showered, and changed to fresh clothing. Heading for the kitchen, she paused as she saw lights on and grew fearful, tiptoeing forward until she spied Bonnie in the kitchen.

"Bonnie?"

Bonnie spun before she moved to wrap Neasa in a hug. "Neasa? You've slept. You needed that, child. Now, I have some soup ready for you. I hope that was okay."

Neasa shrugged. "I don't have much of an appetite."

"I didn't think that you would. Too much going on. Here. Sit. We'll eat, pray, and then decide what to do with that thick-headed young man next door."

Neasa stared at her. "Bonnie?"

"He told us, Neasa, that he couldn't remember you and that you told him off." Bonnie began to laugh, bringing a smile to Neasa's face. "I would have loved to see that. Not many people get a chance to do that."

"Devaney told him that he needed to grovel and grovel a lot. And that he needed to bring me flowers."

"So that's why." Bonnie nodded. "He called Beck, asked him to stop at the florist and find the best and biggest bouquet of yellow roses that he could find."

Blair was on a hunt, the paper held in a shaking hand. He had just discovered something about Dan that he needed to talk with Neasa and Breck about and he could find neither one of them. It was the next day, and he was suddenly afraid.

Running for the outdoors, Blair searched the grounds, finding the couple in the gym, appearing to be at a stand-off over a treadmill. He paused, shaking his head before he hid his grin. Breck, Neasa is just what you need. She doesn't back down from you. It's not that you like your own way. It's just that you have a plan in mind when you approach people, sometimes not listening to us. Not that your plans are wrong. In fact, they usually work out for the best.

"Breck. Neasa. I need to speak with you two."

"Go away, Blair. We're in the middle of a huge fight." Neasa didn't look at him.

Breck stared at her. "You don't tell friends to leave. And we are not fighting. We are having a discussion."

"A fight. One that you seem determined to win. To have your own way. That's not how couples do it, Breck. We discuss, come to a compromise. What is so difficult about that? Have you never compromised in your life?"

"He has, Neasa. Let's set that aside. Neasa, I have new information about your parents."

"Which ones? The real ones? The step ones?" Neasa still did not look around.

"Your real ones. Neasa! Please!" Blair's tone of voice got through to her at last and she turned.

"What do you have?"

"This." He handed her the paper. "This is what I've found. Your parents weren't from here. Did you know that?"

"I knew Dan and his wife weren't. That he moved here to start his business. Pops mentioned that once and then shut right up. I think that they were scared of Dan."

"Scared that if they said anything, he would refuse to let you see them?" Breck reached for the paper, glancing over it. "They were from the other side of the province? Strange that they ended up here."

"She had connections. Neasa doesn't like to say her name, I can see that."

"No, I don't. As far as I'm concerned, she doesn't exist." Neasa stared at the two men. "What does that mean?" She stabbed a finger at the paper.

"It means that she is involved in something as well. Dan wasn't involved on his own. Dallas is working on this as well." Blair stabbed a finger at the door. "He was looking for you two a while ago."

Neasa walked away quickly, needing to get away from Breck. He's trying, Lord, isn't he? But trying too hard. I don't know which is worse. His not remembering or his trying to remember and driving me to distraction? Her steps slowed as she became lost in thought, jumping as she heard voices near her.

"Neasa?" Hagen stood near her, Guenivere and Jaxcy with her.

"Sorry. I was lost in thought, trying to sort out something. What can I do for you ladies?"

Jaxcy grinned. "We've all been there. Still are at times with our guys. We usually prepare meals when they're working like they are. Come. Join us. I talked to Bonnie earlier. She and Beck are heading home. They have to travel tomorrow."

"Oh, I missed her. I'm sorry." Neasa looked sad for a moment. "He's so lucky. To have a mother like Bonnie."

"We know, Neasa. We know." Jaxcy reached to hug her. "I thought mine were killed when I was seventeen. Only they were taken overseas and kept there. Friends found them and brought them back. We're still working through issues from that, but I am just so glad to have them back in my life. I'll share with you."

———

"She shares her parents with us, just like Cadee does. And have you seen Fynn's building of creepy-crawlies yet?" Guenivere linked her arm with Neasa. "If not, we are definitely planning a field trip."

"No, I haven't. I haven't been away from this building other than to church for days. I have no transportation." Neasa looked upset. "And I need to replace my bike,"

"You haven't?" Jaxcy shook her head. "That has to change. Let's get the fellows their meal and then we're going on a road trip with as many of the ladies as I can track down. The twins, too. And knowing Berneen's brother, Darbi? He'll want to come. He insists that we need a guy with us, as he puts it. I think he likes to shop, just doesn't want to admit to it."

Standing outside late that afternoon, Breck rubbed at his head. He had a headache, he decided, and that he definitely didn't like. He also couldn't find Neasa. He had tapped at her door, without any response. In fact, he decided, he hadn't seen or heard from any of the ladies that afternoon.

Barnabas watched his friend, praying for him, asking for healing and a remembrance of his love for Neasa. For love her, he knew Breck did. He walked towards him.

"Breck? You've been standing here for ages."

"I know, Barnabas. I can't find Neasa. Dallas had word that Dan is actively searching for her."

"The ladies all headed into town, Darbi and the twins with them. Jaxcy told me that Neasa needed it. She has not been away from here except for church."

Breck groaned, his eyes closing. "No, she has not. And we need to look for transportation for her." He looked around as he heard the sound of a motorcycle. "She didn't, did she?"

"I would say that she did. She needed to, Breck. She needs to reclaim her life and this is part of it. You didn't seem willing to help her, in her eyes. The ladies were." Barnabas' hand rested on his friend's shoulder for a moment. "She's fragile right now, Breck."

"I know. I just don't know what to say to her. It seems everything I say? We end up having words."

"Remember this. Tell her that you still want to go on a long ride with a beautiful lady. You told her that the morning you two left the hospital, way back at the beginning."

"I did?" Breck shook his head. "That's not me."

"Sorry, my friend. Where Neasa is concerned, it is. You are flirting with her more and more. Trust me on this. We all saw it and welcomed it for you. She's good for you." Barnabas waved as he walked away, surrounded suddenly by ladies.

Breck walked slowly towards where Neasa had parked her motorbike, not seen the interest that she had attracted. Brendon, Brennen, and Brody watched from near the gym. He studied her as she slipped from the bike, reaching to rub the handlebar, and then stand back staring at it.

"You found a nice one, darlin'." Breck spoke from where he had stopped beside her.

"I did. It's a new year model but I got a really good deal on it. I know the owner. We went to school together. I don't think he made anything on it." She sniffed. "It's nice but it's not the same. I needed transportation, Breck."

"I know, darling. I know. I should have taken you, but I guess fear won."

"How can you say that? You don't remember me."

"I'm starting to, I think. Bits and pieces are starting to come through the thick head that Mom always says I have." Breck walked around the bike. "Does your friend have a matching one?"

"A matching one?" Neasa stared at him. "You want one?"

"I do. That way, we can go on rides together." Breck stood in front of her, his hands resting on her shoulders. "But in the meantime, you need transportation for winter."

"I do, but it doesn't matter." Neasa watched him. "We need to talk, Breck. I saw Dan in town. He and his wife. They're back together. I wonder if she even left town. He was watching the ladies. They tried to cover for me but some of them are so short. Darbi wouldn't leave my side. I can't have him hurt."

"That's Darbi. He's very protective of all the ladies here. Goes back to what happened with Berneen." Breck helped her to cover the motorcycle and then reached for her helmet and then her hand.

"Breck? What are you saying with this?" Neasa raised their joined hands.

"That I want to go on with what we had planned for our lives. I will remember, Neasa. That much I know. Right now, though? We need to keep you safe and solve whatever it is that Dan and his wife are involved with." He paused. "Do you think that she's the one behind it all?"

"Could be. Did you know that she has a sister?"

"She does? Is that the name they came up with?"

"I think it is. I never saw her that I remember. But I did see her name one day. I just need to remember it." Neasa frowned. "I don't know that I have ever said her name. It's Jessie."

"Jessie? I see. I think the fellows discovered that. They were being sensitive, not asking you." Breck held the door open. "And I have flowers for you. I didn't get a chance to give them to you."

Neasa grinned. "The best and biggest bouquet of yellow roses? Your mother squealed on you."

"She did, did she? She thinks of you as a daughter, Neasa, one that she could never have. She'll spoil you."

"Jessie's sister is Jane Light." Neasa's voice grew sad. "What did they take from us, Breck? And why?"

Neasa stood by the restaurant door, watching as Breck ran back towards her, the cool rain pelting at his hooded jacket. He grinned at her as he shook his head.

"It's wet."

"Rain usually is." She walked into the restaurant entry, looking around. "I don't know that I have ever eaten in here. We never went out for meals."

"You didn't? That's strange." Breck lifted a hand to the waitress and pointed to a table near the back of the room.

Neasa shrugged. "It's who we were as a family. We hardly had any takeout either. They just never did that." She slipped from her coat, hanging it over the back of her chair, seating herself so that Breck could move her chair forward before he sat across from her.

"Don't worry about the cost, darling. Tonight, this is for you. As a thank you for being who you are."

She stared at Breck, not quite sure of what he was saying. "Breck?"

"I remember, darling. I remember."

"Oh, praise the Lord. I thought that I was going to have to hit you over the head or something."

Breck laughed at her even as he pointed to her menu. "And you would do just that, I know."

Later, walking back towards his truck, her hand in his, Neasa kept as close to Breck as she could.

"Breck, I'm scared." Neasa looked around the dimly lit parking lot.

"I know, darling. So am I." Breck tucked her into his truck and then ran for his side, climbing in and starting the vehicle. "We need to talk, Neasa. Not just about what we want, but what we have found. Dallas has been hard at work for the last couple of days. He needs to solve this, arrest who he has to, and then move back to town."

"I know." Neasa's voice was barely a whisper. "I hate that he is giving up his life for us."

"He's okay with that. He has tracked down Jessie's sister. She was horrified to hear what Jessie had done. She lost track of her after your own father died and she moved away."

"What else? I hear the "but" in that sentence."

"There is. Dallas wasn't comfortable with some of what she said. He's speaking with someone on that city's police force." Breck drove away, watching carefully, not seeing the vehicle following him.

"What can we do for him, Breck? I don't know him that well, but he seems at odds with himself."

"That's a good way to put it. He is at odds with himself." Breck turned onto the road leading to the Foundation lands. "Some of us think that he'll resign shortly from the force and move on to something else."

Neasa nodded, her eyes on the road ahead of her. "Breck? What's on the road?"

Breck slowed and then stopped, reaching to ensure that the doors were locked. "I don't know, darling. But we're not getting out to find out. Call it in, will you?"

Neasa reached for her phone, a scream rising from her as she saw the man appear at her window. "Breck!"

Breck sat, his hands tense on the wheel, his mind racing as to how to get them out of there. He watched as the man hammered at Neasa's window, Neasa shrinking back from it.

"Neasa? Your seatbelt it tight?"

"It is. You're planning something."

"I am. I think that's just a wooden barricade. I'm going to try and ram it, to see if I can get through it. Someone has moved in behind us."

"Great. We go out for dinner and then get into danger. What next?" Neasa's fingers whitened as she tightened her hold on her seatbelt. "I would say, go for it, but it's your truck, Breck."

"Which can be replaced. You can't." Breck sent up a quick prayer and then gunned the motor, not seeing anyone in front of him. Wood flew from where he rammed the barricade, the truck sliding on the wet road before he straightened it and sped down the road, barely slowing to turn into the Foundation gate. He parked quickly, reached to lift Neasa over the console and out of his side of the truck, and then ran for the back entrance, which was the nearest. He keyed in the combination and pulled the door open, shoving her through.

Neasa stared at him in shock and disbelief.

"Did we really just do that?"

"We did. Hurry. Up to your apartment. I need you safe." Breck pulled her with him towards the stairs, hesitating for a moment. "No, I think my office." He headed that way, the door unlocked, and then shoved shut and locked behind them. He walked carefully through the office before he reached to turn on a light at the reception desk.

"Breck?" Neasa stood in front of him, arms crossed. "Why not my apartment?"

He shrugged. "Something told me not to. I have learned to listen to God when He tells me things like that."

Breck paced his office, watching Neasa closely as she sat at the reception desk, her hands busy with the mail that sat there. He had protested but she had ignored him, continuing on with what she was doing, rising at one point to head for his office, laying down a number of letters that he needed to look at. He finally shook his head and continued to pace.

Hearing a tap at the door, he raised his hand to Neasa, who nodded, moving on silent feet to stand with his ear to it. The tap came again, this time with a voice calling his name. He reached to unlock the door and Dallas and Barnabas slipped in.

"What did you go and do, Breck?" Dallas looked angry.

"Just ran a barricade. What was that all about?"

Dallas turned as Neasa approached, to be swept close to Breck. "They were waiting for you, Breck. Officers were following you and before they could get to the situation, you had moved through it. They were to take you captive and take you away."

"We gathered that. Who?" Breck's arm tightened around Neasa."

"Her step-father, Dan. The men here heard something around your apartment. They were waiting up there for you as well. We have those ones in custody."

"How did they get in?" Breck was puzzled. "Our security is good."

"They slipped in by the looks of it on the video feed when Jack was out on his rounds. They are keeping that close an eye on here." Barnabas was both angry and frustrated.

"That close?" Neasa's hand grasped for Breck. "Breck wouldn't let us go upstairs. Why not wait down here?"

"Because they are not likely sure which is his office. They have figured out the apartments here and I would like to know how."

Dallas paced. "Did you see anything off when you were out tonight?"

Breck shook his head. "Not a thing. And I was watching. Even in the restaurant. I took our favourite table, at the back, near the kitchen."

"And the staff knows us well enough to say something, if they saw anything." Barnabas paced. "The fellows are pulling an all-nighter, Breck. They are close to finding all the information. Emma has been silent, which isn't like her."

"No, it isn't. I had an email from her this morning. Abe and his team were called away suddenly on an assignment. She was called away with them."

"That explains it." Barnabas turned suddenly to Neasa. "Neasa? What can we do for you?"

"I have no idea, Barnabas. I never thought of that." She paused. "My Pops and Grams? How safe are they?"

Barnabas grinned. "We thought of that, Neasa. Andy, Brennen, and Jaxcy flew up there tonight. They're going to try and persuade them to move this way, or at least come for a visit."

"They are? Oh, that would be wonderful. I have been so scared for them."

"And you never said a word." Breck hugged her. "You need to talk to us, darling, but I know it's difficult, given what you've not said about your life."

Neasa smacked him before she moved away, fatigue suddenly weighing at her.

"How long?"

Dallas stared at her, a puzzled look on his face. "How long?"

"Right. How long before I can go home? Not that I object to your company, but sometimes a gal just needs to be by herself."

Dallas laughed, knowing exactly what she was doing. "Soon. The team is going through the hallway and the stairs, and then you'll be able to go home. I'm sorry, Neasa. Sorry that you had to face this after your date with Breck."

Neasa shrugged. "It's what I've come to expect. He seems to like danger."

"Me? Like danger? I thought you were the one who liked danger." Breck protested, knowing that was what she expected.

Barnabas stared at the three in the room with him before he too laughed. "Neasa, you are exactly what we need in this building. The other ladies have brought laughter and fun, but you add just that certain touch, like the right spice or seasoning, to our family. Have you two set a date yet?"

"A date? I thought that was what we just had." She smirked at Barnabas as he stared at her before she winked.

"No, we have not set a date, but I think we will. Let's get her grandparents here." Breck had a thought. "Her mother's family?"

"We've looked, Neasa. Brody has made this his mission. He is on the track of a cousin, he said, but he can't find any living relations. He says it looks as if your mother was an orphan when she married your father, with a brother who had married and moved out west."

"A cousin? Oh, that would be wonderful. Nevin and I were always envious of those who had cousins."

The next morning, Breck stood in the conference room, watching as the fellows dished up plates of food and then gathered around tables set apart from their work stations, their ladies with them. Neasa stood beside him, her hand tight in his. She was envious, for a moment, of the fact that the couples were married and didn't have to stay apart. She had wanted to be with Breck last night, just to be held in his arms and prayed for.

Breck's hand tightened on hers before he spoke.

"Neasa, we need to eat, but first, I need to ask you a question."

"The answer is yes. A week from Saturday works."

He stared at her. "Neasa? You didn't even know what I was going to ask."

"I did, Breck, because you want the same thing. You don't want an apartment wall between us, not when you're that concerned and frightened for me." She looked up at him, her love for him on her face. "Why should we wait? Nevin has said for us to go ahead, as much as he would want to be here."

"He did?"

"He did. I spent an hour on the phone with him last night, going over everything, just touching base. He would be saddened not to be here, but he wants us to go ahead."

"If we could get them back to the building, they could be here."

"True, but I won't put them at risk." She looked up at him again. "Ask your question."

"Neasa, will you marry me a week from Saturday?"

"I will."

Breck bent to kiss her and then looked over at the men. "I wonder if Buckley is free then. Did I ever tell you that he offered dates to two of the couples, not thinking that they would take him up on them?"

"I hope that they did. It would serve him right. He's serious and all but does like to tease and torment, as Grams would say."

"He does." Breck held their plates as she dished them up before she reached for their drinks and then headed to the tables, sitting in the spots saved for them.

Buckley watched them for a while before he spoke up.

"Listen, you two. I have a week from Saturday open, in case you want to set a date. Unless you want Daniel to do the honours."

Breck shared a look with Neasa before he too spoke.

"Quite the coincidence. We were planning on that date."

The men and ladies broke out into laughter and then talk even as Buckley shook his head.

"Got me again, didn't you?"

"We did." Breck smirked before he sobered. "We would like to try and bring Nevin and Sarah back if we can arrange that."

"We should be able to. Barnabas?" Brady looked towards him.

"I think it's time they came home anyway. Dallas is needing to spend more time speaking with him and is finding it difficult over the phone." Barnabas excused himself as he pulled out his phone. "Sorry, people. I need to take this."

"One thing that I don't understand." Benen spoke up. "You two aren't getting the text messages, the letters, the photos, the packages, the threats that we all did."

"No, we aren't." Breck shared a look with Neasa. "And that has puzzled us as well. It's as if they aren't really trying anymore. Does that mean whoever it is has moved on?"

"Or are they planning one last grand stand?" Bradon looked down at Ennis. "We've talked about that. I think they are going to make one last play and that will be the most dangerous one. Even that bit on the road? It was poorly set up. With two guys? Who does that?"

"Dan does." Neasa finally spoke. "It's the way he would work. I have watched his work over the years. He just finds the minimum that he needs. Even with the work on the playground? Nevin and I should not have been the ones. He had others that were more experienced. He used the excuse that we needed the experience, that we liked to play in the dirt." She shuddered for a moment. "I mean, I liked working the equipment, Nevin liked setting it all up, but it's not what we were used to. Nevin was the one who found the work for us, did the contracts, all the contacts. I was the one who sourced material and greenery and plants. Why put us out there like that on that particular day?"

Burnie pointed at her. "That what we want to know. He had to have known that we would find bones when we started that dig. So why you two?"

"I think it was a psychological way of keeping control of the two." Fynn spoke up. "I have seen it before. If he had used the other men, it would not have affected them the same way. Digging up their father? How has that affected Neasa and Nevin? He knew it would. He thought that he could keep control of them by using that. Instead, Breck stepped in with Neasa. Nevin walked away with Sarah. That left him without anyone. He's angry and will come after you again, Breck and Neasa. And there is someone behind him. We all know that. Who owned the property before the Foundation?"

Barnabas had stood, listening to Fynn speak, before he left the room, heading for his office. His father would know who that was.

"Dad?" Barnabas spoke to his father even as he searched his filing cabinet. "The shelter? Do you remember who owned that property?"

"I do. John and I were going over that the night before last. Your mother and I are heading your way, this time for good, son."

"You are? Oh, that's wonderful, Dad. I will be glad to have you back in town. What brought that on?"

"Your mother wants to. We've sold our property here just yesterday. It's time, son. We're not getting any younger. She doesn't want to travel as much as we have been for the Foundation. I agree. It's time to let someone else take over that."

"I don't want it, Dad. I like what I do."

"We know you do. We have someone in mind, the board and I. We're in talks with this young man. But you called. What was that about the shelter?"

"Fynn asked who owned it before we acquired it."

"That would have been Larry Light. Why?"

"Because Neasa said that she and Nevin should not have been the ones working that day. That Dan had others who were more experienced. Fynn made the observation that it would have been to keep control of the siblings."

"And from what I understand and can remember of Dan, that would have been it. I mean, we're friends, but there has always been something hidden, we felt, that he didn't want anyone to know about. This is likely it."

"It is. I'm glad you're heading here. When do you leave?"

"The movers come in on Monday. Your mother is leaving everything to them, other than our personal things. We'll head out Tuesday morning and be there that night."

"Good. Breck and Neasa have set a date for a week from Saturday. Breck would want you there. His parents are here, so that solves that."

"Her brother?"

"We'll bring them back next week. Andy is heading up to bring her grandparents here."

"They have a farm?"

"They do. Neasa mentioned that it was almost too much for him over the past summer."

"Okay. I'll speak to him. The board is looking for something like that, to set up for men or couples who want to work outdoors and want to do that. This may be the opportunity we need."

Barnabas headed back for the conference room, satisfied with his conversation. He paused just inside the doorway, watching as Neasa stood in front of Baird, tension radiating from her, Breck's arms around her.

"Baird?"

"Barnabas? Neasa remembered something, and she's not sharing. We think that she should."

"Neasa?" Barnabas' quiet voice turned her head towards him, and he drew in a deep breath at the devastation that showed.

"I remembered, Barnabas. Oh, how I wish I hadn't!"

"What did you remember, darling?" Breck's voice whispered in her ear.

"The land for the shelter? I can remember years ago, Dan and Jessie talking about it. Her brother-in-law owned it. Was he a part of this?"

"That's what we think, Neasa. I just spoke with Dad. He named a Larry Light." Barnabas shared a look with Breck. "He was killed in a suspected drunk driving accident years ago, but there was always a question about that. He didn't drink, but his blood-alcohol level was over the limit."

Dallas spoke from where he sat. "I'm looking into that, Breck. We don't have a lot of information, but we're going back through what we have. His name has come up a lot in these investigations. Will cleared it for me to talk to you about."

Neasa nodded. "What or who has Dan not touched and contaminated?"

Chapter 52

Breck and Neasa headed out the next morning, intent on living their lives. Neasa wanted to look at cars, and Breck had insisted that he take her. He had laughed when she had grumbled at him, saying he just wanted to find a matching bike to hers. He had kissed her and then led her from the building.

Their walk towards his truck stopped quickly as they saw the men waiting for them. Breck took a step backward, stopping as he felt something poke him in the back. He felt Neasa move closer to him and his hand tightened on hers.

"Just what we need, Breck. Dan and his henchman." Neasa's sarcasm came through as she spoke, her eyes on her step-father as he walked to stand directly in front of her.

Breck shot a look around, wondering that no one was outside. That was unusual for a Saturday morning. He was glad the ladies weren't, but where was security?

"You're coming with me, Neasa. This man isn't."

"No, I don't think so, Dan. You can't tell me what to do, not anymore. You haven't had that right in years, I might say, all my life. Did you kill Dad?"

"I'm your father." His hand was up, striking her across the face, a cut appearing on her lip.

Breck growled in rage and tried to reach for him, finding his arms tight to his body from the binding that had appeared from the men behind him. He struggled, finding Neasa torn from him. He lurched to the side, taking the man holding him off balance, and he freed his arms, charging towards Dan. A savage blow from the side stopped him in his tracks and then dropped him to the cold pavement, his vision darkening and then fading.

Neasa screamed, trying her best to wrench herself from Dan's grip, not able to as he pulled her towards a vehicle.

"I'm not going with you!" Her voice was loud in the sudden silence. She thought that she saw movement off to one side, but didn't dare look. "You've hurt someone I love for the last time." Her hand was up, her nails clawing at his face, her fingers poking at his eyes.

A cry of hurt and then rage came from him as he dropped her arm to cover his face. She was on her hands and knees and then her feet, scrambling away from the men, heading towards cover, she prayed. A hand over her mouth stifled her scream and then she heard Brendon's voice in her ear.

"We've got you, Neasa. We have help on the way, but they won't make it in time. Here, in you go to the building. Head for the conference room and lock the door. The ladies are waiting for you." Brendon shoved at her as she hesitated. "Go. We'll get Breck and bring him to you."

Neasa ran down the hallway, her breath catching in her throat, fear lending speed to her feet. She flew through the doorway, slamming it behind her and locking it, standing staring at the ladies, a hand on her throat, her breath coming in gasps.

"How did you know?"

"Security saw them moving in. He couldn't get to you two, so he came here." Fynn was angry. "Our guys are out there, and we're stuck in here."

"We are but what can we do?" Hagen looked around, her eyes on her sisters who held her son and daughter. "I, for one, am tired of them bringing the fight to our home. What can we do, ladies? I'm not standing back. Not anymore. Breck has helped too many of us."

"He has." Berneen moved towards the door. "You know, there are fire hoses outside the building. We could always turn them on."

"Don't we need a key to do that?"

Berneen shook her head. "No. That is one thing that is not locked down. Who's with me? Other than the ones who are pregnant? You stay put."

"That makes most of us. Let's go, ladies." Cadee turned to Berneen. "You shouldn't be going."

"It was my idea. Of course, I'm going." She was out of the door, walking as quickly and as quietly as she could for the outside. The other ladies followed, leaving the two girls to lock themselves in.

Half of the ladies went to one side of the building, the other seven to the other side, Neasa in front, reaching for the hose and unrolling it as she crept towards the front, to stand peeking around the corner at the standoff in the parking lot. Berneen peeked around as well.

"A stand-off. And Breck is still down and out. Or is he?"

"No, he's awake. Just playing possum as they say." Neasa watched Breck intently. "He's hurting."

"He is." Berneen moved backward, whispering quietly to the other ladies, who nodded. Hands on the hose, they were ready, one standing back by the valve, ready to turn the water on.

Chapter 53

Barnabas stood where Dan could see him, the other men standing in a loose circle around the intruders. He didn't dare make more of a move, not with one of the intruders holding a revolver pointing directly at Breck's head. Any move might just cause that to go off. He frowned for a moment as he saw Breck's eyes open and a slight nod from him. Okay, Barnabas thought, he's ready to move when we do. Lord, this is where it gets hard. Any false move might just get my friend killed. Give us the strength and wisdom that we need.

Dallas watched from where he had taken a position behind Dan, his revolver out and down at his side. He was ready, but he didn't want to use it, just in case one of the Foundation men were hurt. Lord, he prayed as well, guide our words and our actions.

Baird was standing where he could see the end of the building and frowned. Berneen? Neasa? I thought you were told to stay locked away. What are you planning? He frowned deeper and then a smile flickered across his face as he saw Cadee and Ennis peeking around the other corner. He caught a glimpse of the fire hoses in the ladies' hand. Lord, protect these ladies. They're trying to help. Don't let any one of them be hurt.

Dan began to pace. This was not going as he had planned. Neasa and Breck were to have cooperated with him and gone into the vehicle. That they wouldn't have never crossed his mind. Neasa had always done what he had demanded. She had changed, and that man had done it. It didn't occur to him that Neasa had come to understand just who he himself was and his character and had decided that she had had enough.

His men shifted on their feet, not liking that they were out in the open and surrounded as they were. They had the weapons, those men didn't, they all thought, but without Dan's direction, they couldn't use them. He had made that abundantly clear. If one did, they would all pay the price. And they all knew the price that he would demand.

Baird's eyes flickered to the ladies once more and then his ear caught the sound of vehicles slowing and stopping on the road. Help or not, he wondered. He glanced around, seeing the other men had also heard them. He watched Dallas for a moment as he felt for his phone on the holster attached to his belt and then nodded. Good, Friends. Now to stall this until they walked up and surrounded the men.

Dan's attention went to the road and he began to yell, his words unintelligible. He stalked towards Breck, his arms waving before a boot was out and he kicked Breck, sending him rolling away from him and more towards the building. The man who had been covering him stood where he was, not moving, his eyes on Dan.

The building men looked up as they heard female shouts and then dropped to the ground as the force of the water from the fire hoses hit Dan and his men. The ladies struggled to control the hoses, their feet digging into the ground, even as some of the men were on their feet, heading to help them. Dan and his men floundered on the ground as the force of the water kept them down and out of the way. The officers who had responded moved in, once the water was turned off, handcuffing the men, reading them their rights, and then hustling the soaking wet men away, smiles and nods directed to the ladies.

Dallas stood in awe as he watched the women run for their men, to be swept into hard hugs. Neasa was on her knees, her arms around Breck as he sat up with Brady's help, almost knocking him back down from how hard she hit him as her arms surrounding him.

"Breck? You're hurt. Did he hurt you?" Neasa's words tumbled over one another, not letting Breck say anything. Baird was on his feet, heading for where Berneen stood.

"You ladies did good, my love. But weren't you supposed to stay in the conference room?" Baird hugged her hard before he kissed her.

"We were, but we couldn't. We had to help. Breck was there for all of us." Berneen was close to tears.

"I know, my love. I know. He'll tell you off, you know."

Berneen peeked around Baird and grinned. "Somehow, I don't think he will."

Breck finally just swept Neasa close and kissed her thoroughly. It was the only way that he could stop her words.

"You're not here, darling?" He searched her face.

"No, he just made me angry. The hoses worked well, I think."

Breck began to laugh. "They worked extremely well. I'm proud of you and all the ladies. You stepped in with a solution that the men didn't think of."

"Of course, we did. Our brains work differently than men's do." Neasa smirked at him. "Now, it is over? Can we start living once more?"

Dallas crouched down beside them. "You're okay, Breck? You took a good hit."

"I'm okay. I saw it coming and rolled before he really touched me. The other blow? Nothing more than I've had playing football and been tackled." Breck took Dallas' outstretched hand to help him stand, Neasa back in his arms as he did so.

"I think that it's over, Neasa. We have everyone. I had just received word that Larry Light, his wife, and your step-mother were all arrested this morning. They were looking for Dan when he showed up here. Give us a few days, and then we'll meet to discuss what we can." He waved as he headed for his car, intent on questioning the men and women involved in all this.

Barnabas walked towards Breck, his eyes assessing his friend.

"Okay, friend?"

"I am, Barnabas. Thanks to the ladies, and to you fellows as well, I can say that. Dallas let us know that they have made the arrests that they needed to."

"Good. Now, let's get you both inside. Breck, you need some dry clothes. I don't think that you expected to take a shower out here. Give us a couple of hours and we'll meet in the chapel this afternoon."

Chapter 54

Four days later, Dallas appeared in the conference room, finding all the men and ladies waiting for him. He stood for a moment, eyeing them all, before he found Breck and Neasa, sitting off in a corner, arms around one another, heads together as they prayed. He hesitated to walk towards them but did as their heads raised. Breck was on his feet, a hand out to shake Dallas'.

"Dallas. Thank you for what you have done. I know that you've been struggling lately."

"I have been, Breck. Not related to what you have gone through. Neasa? You're okay?"

Neasa was on her feet, hugging Dallas, able only to whisper a thank you in his ear.

"You have news, Dallas?" Breck had caught the movement of the others as they found seats and were watching them.

"I do. I think it's going to be easier for you to accept, Neasa, than I expected it to be. Your brother and wife are here?"

"They are, as are our grandparents. The fellows tracked down a cousin, but he wasn't really interested in hearing from us."

"I'm sorry. That happens, but it doesn't make it any easier. Shall we?"

Breck nodded, his eyes searching for Buckley, who nodded and stood, his prayer echoing through the room.

"Thank you, Buckley. Dallas, the floor is yours." Breck moved Neasa to sit at one of the tables, reaching for the pen and paper as he always did. It was a force of habit that he just could not give up.

"Thanks, Breck. And thank you, Buckley, for your prayers. And each one of you fellows and your ladies? Once more, you have found the information far more quickly than we could. Emma hasn't been able to help this time, she said, not like she wanted to. Circumstances altered that for her. She sends her thanks as well." He paused, his eyes find the grandparents, then Nevin and Sarah, and finally Breck and his lady, Neasa. Lord, she is well. They both survived. They are in love and heading for a wedding this Saturday. Thank you, Lord, for protecting this friend of ours, who is so needed in this family. His quiet words and prayers and care and concern keep us all in touch with You and learning more and more how to love You more and each other better.

"Neasa, Nevin? I have spoken intensely with Dan. He finally admitted that it was his fault that your father was killed. He had approached him about coming into partnership with your father in his landscaping business. Your father had refused. Dan grew angry and shoved him, causing him to fall. Your grandparents did let us know that your father had a heart condition. What the medical examiner thinks happened is that with the fall, your father had a heart attack and didn't survive. Dan has admitted that your father seemed to be in distress but that he had walked away to cool off. When he returned, he panicked as your father had died. He buried him on the land that Larry Light knew, using that as leverage against Light. Light has been involved in shady deals, as they are sometimes called, substandard work and blackmail. Dan knew this and used it against him as well.

"Light has admitted to all of this and much more. His wife was pushing him to leave the area and he sold out to the Foundation, not telling them of the body buried there. They moved away. He returned voluntarily to face the charges against him.

"Your step-mother? She is something else. She knew what had happened to your father, married Dan, and then threatened to turn him in. He was abusive to her all their marriage. She did put in complaints and then withdrew them. She has admitted to another detective that she married your father in haste and regretted it. She didn't want to raise someone else's kids, as she put it. She has stated that she was heading for a divorce when he died. She didn't feel that she could place you children into care and refused to let your grandparents have you."

Neasa nodded. "Somehow, that's what I thought you would say. It's all over?"

"It is, Neasa. A bad choice that led to death and then cover up. You, Nevin, and your grandparents paid the price for years because of that. Now, you can heal. God will lead you in that." Dallas closed his portfolio and simply walked away. He was tired, Lord, he thought. Tired and burnt out. I need a change. Maybe that job offer that came out of nowhere? That might just be where You want me.

That next Saturday, Barnabas stood and watched the building family as they mingled and laughed and teased one another. It has grown, Lord, from just Doc and Anna and myself as each one of the men appeared and joined it. Then, the ladies joined, some with siblings, and some with parents, and one with a Granny, and now Neasa with her Pops and Grams. We are blessed with each one. He sought out his parents, who stood talking with Neasa's grandparents and Breck's parents.

He then sought out Breck and Neasa, who stood, arms around one another, clearly in love, as they took the good-natured teasing that he had come to expect from the men and the ladies as well. Neasa was fitting in, he thought. She is exactly who Breck has needed. He likes to tease but has a heart of gold. She has a dry sense of humour that completes his. She is already taking care of the ladies, without realizing that she is.

Breck finally made his way to where Barnabas stood, handing him a mug of coffee and then just standing by his friend. They had been friends since toddlers, he thought, having their disagreements but standing shoulder to shoulder with one another when needed.

"Barnabas? What can I say? We've been friends for so many years, but that's changing now."

"It is, my friend, but it is right and proper. We'll remain friends, but that lady there? She becomes your best friend and confidant. I understand. God brought a very special lady into your life."

Breck grinned. "He did. I pray that you find your lady, Barnabas. We all do."

Barnabas shrugged. "I'm sure that if she's out there, He will lead me to her. You're away for what, two weeks?"

"We are. And you head out that day. You need the break, Barnabas. What's happened with all the men has weighed you down."

"It has, but God has provided for us all." He grinned as he watched the ladies hovering over the little ones. "With the little ones coming now, we need to do some planning for safe spots for them."

"And we will. Nevin has taken over the company that Dan had and his first work will be the shelter and then he's moving in here, he tells me, to do a playground and fenced area for the little ones."

"He is?" Barnabas wasn't surprised. "That he will. He's part of our family." He grew quiet, sipping at his coffee, even as he watched the men and ladies. "How's Neasa after all this?"

"Hurting, as you can imagine. Questioning. Searching for answers. Have her grandparents here will help. And with Nevin and Sarah back, she has someone who lived it with her that she can talk to."

"That she does. She has a huge heart, under all her fun and teasing. And she wants to share it with the ones in the building. She told me that she didn't realize that marrying me meant that she would take on such a role."

"She will, but it is not asked of her."

"She knows that but wants to. She's also volunteering at the shelter to teach simple cooking classes when we can get that going." Breck reached out an arm to wrap around Neasa as she approached.

"Thank you, Barnabas, for this. I didn't expect it."

Barnabas just grinned and shrugged. "The board wanted to do it for you both. You're an important part of our family. Dad says that he wants to talk with you more about your work, but there is no pressure on that. He wants your input on what you see here."

"And I will gladly give it." She tilted her head to look at him. "You're hurting, Barnabas. I hear you're on vacation when we come back. Find your lady, bring her home with you."

Barnabas stared at her for a moment before he hugged her and walked away, his mug placed carefully on the table before he left the room.

Neasa watched him walk away before she looked up at Breck. "Breck?"

"You didn't say anything wrong, Neasa. He's been hurting for a while. We've all seen it. None of us have figured it out. The ladies have suggested that he's hurting for someone who walked away from him. Honestly? I don't remember him showing interest in anyone since we were in college. There was a lady then, but I don't seem to remember it being serious."

"It could have been serious, but they kept it on the light side for some reason." Neasa turned in his arms. "We are blessed with many friends, sweetheart."

"We are, my darling. That we are. Have I told you today that I love you?"

Neasa nodded, a smile on her lips as she did so. "You have, but not enough." Her head turned up for his kiss. "Hmm. I think I like this. You're a keeper."

Breck broke out into laughter, bringing eyes to them, before he spoke.

"Neasa, you do my heart good. You tell me that I have taught you to love. You have done the same for me. You have taught me to love God more and more each day. You have taught me to love you and that too grows more and more every minute I'm around you and when I'm not. Your reaction to the ones who wronged you has shown me that we can love them too, even when they plot evil for us. Thank you, my love."

"And you have taught me as well." She reached to kiss him. "Thank you for being the man of God that you are. Grams and Pops have both told me that you are what they prayed for, just for me. Sarah is Nevin's heart."

"That they are." Breck reached for her hand. "We need to mingle, my love, and I understand that there is a cake to cut." He twirled her around, studying the simple white, lace-covered dress that she had chosen, and the yellow roses that he had given her in her hair. "You are just so beautiful today."

Thank you for picking up the story of Breck and his love, Neasa. This was quite the story, not like the others but similar in ways. She was not what I expected for him, not at all. She kept rebelling about her name, finally letting me settle on Neasa. To have her riding a motorcycle? Nope, not planned at all, but it fit her personality.

As always, the characters have driven the story. I might want it to go one way but the unruly characters take over and don't share the road map or the GPS coordinators. It is always interesting and a challenge to follow where they lead.

How do we love? How do we teach someone to love? It's hard, particularly in these days when anger and hate seem to prevalent. I look to Christ. How did He teach this? First, by example. Second, by His words. We can follow no one better than our Lord in teaching or learning love.

The folks from His Guardians only came in by name this time. They didn't walk in and out of this story. Emma and Abe are in this series. Darcie's story is The Heart of a Lion.

God bless each one of you as you walk with Him. Even in the times that we are living, with the restrictions of the COVID-19 virus that is prevalent world wife, He is there with each of us, in every way.

Ronna

Barnabas: Encouraged to Live

The Barnabas Chronicles
Book 14

By

Ronna M. Bacon

Proverbs 3:5,6

Trust in the Lord with all your heart and lean not unto your own understanding.

In all your ways, acknowledge Him and He will direct your paths.

NKJV

Table of Contents

His hand wrapped around his mug of coffee, Barnabas Carey padded through his apartment in the Barnabas Foundation building, his bare feet smacking almost silently on the dark hardwood floor. He sighed, his free hand scrubbing at his face. He felt every bit of his age of early thirties that night, the last four days wearing him out beyond what he had ever experienced. He stood for a moment in his home office, staring at the pile of files and personal mail his secretary, Amy, had stacked neatly there. Tomorrow, he thought, I'll look at them. Tonight, I just can't do it. He wandered over to the window, parting the drapes to stare out into the twilight, looking up at the darkening of the sky, watching the twinkling of the stars appear and the full moon shedding its light over the property. He could see the parking lot from where he stood, and counting cars, felt comfortable that all the men who lived there and were employed by the Foundation were at home with their ladies.

He turned, heading back for the kitchen, to refresh his mug of coffee before he stood, hand on the counter, his head turning towards the hallway. Fresh mug of coffee in hand, he headed for the living room, pausing a moment to scan it out of habit. It looked the same, he thought, just as it did a month ago when I left on the long-overdue vacation. His eyes dropped to the couch and his face softened before he moved forward, mug landing on the table beside it before he sat, his eyes on the lady who slept, curled up, her head on her arm along the back of the couch. He gathered her close to him and heard her gentle sigh as she settled down in his arms.

Barnabas studied the dark red of the curly long hair, his hand brushing down it, knowing that the deep brown eyes would be covered, eyes he felt he could drown in. He sighed himself, his head of heavy black curls cropped short dropping back on the couch, as his thoughts wandered. His dark blue eyes closed for the moment. He had no idea how to approach what he had to do. He had briefly spoken with his father when he had arrived home but didn't let him in on the secret he had brought with him.

He dozed off, his head rising as he heard a tap at the door, and then shoes being nudged off and set neatly by the door.

"Barnabas?"

"Yeah, Breck?" He heard his lifelong friend and second in command head for the kitchen.

"When did you get in?"

"About four or five, somewhere in there."

"I didn't see you come in, but I saw your truck as Neasa and I were heading out for dinner." Breck lifted the coffee pot and stared at it before he dumped it out and made fresh. "How old is this coffee anyway?"

"I think I made it when I got in. I've been drinking it. But I could use a fresh mug."

"You sound exhausted. Didn't you relax at all? That was the whole point of you going away by yourself."

Barnabas shook his head, even though Breck could not see him. "I did for a bit. The last couple of weeks were rough."

Breck could hear something in Barnabas' voice, not too sure on what. He doctored their coffee the way they both liked it, and picked the mugs up, intent on heading for the living room, when he paused, a sudden deep urge to pray for his friend. Somehow, he knew that when he entered the living room, things would change for them. Lord, I have no idea what I'll find going on with my friend, but You do. You have gone before us in this. I pray for him. He's worn out, has been for a while. He's been there for each one of us, all thirteen of us, as we went through what we did. Now, we need to be there for him, without knowing why. Lord, bless my friend. Protect him. Heal him.

Breck padded to the door, intent on not spilling the coffee from the mugs he had filled almost too full. He set the one down on the table by Barnabas' elbow, a quiet thank you from his friend before he stood, freezing as he did so, seeing the lady wrapped in his friend's arms, her hand clutching at the dark blue T-shirt he had changed into after his shower and shave.

He backed away, finding the chair he preferred, his mug setting down a little harder on the table beside it than he had thought. He stared at his friend, waiting for him to speak.

Barnabas' head had gone back on the couch, his eyes sliding closed, so he missed Breck's initial reaction. But he heard the silence from his friend. The silence that asked questions that Breck would not or could not ask aloud.

"Breck?" Barnabas looked over at his friend without raising his head.

"Barnabas? What's going on? You didn't have a lady in your life when you left. At least I don't think you did."

"I didn't. Not really. I left to find her, to see if she was all right. She wasn't and I had to step in. I had no choice. God would not let me walk away without trying to help her."

"Does she have a name?" Breck's head tilted as he stared at her. "She looks familiar. Do I know her?"

Barnabas raised his head to stare down at his lady before he nodded. "You do. It's Aubrey."

"Aubrey Dorsett? That Aubrey? I thought you had forgotten her."

Barnabas shook his head. "No, I never did. I couldn't. She was the only one for me. We kept in touch for a few years, and then about two years ago, I stopped hearing from her. Letters were returned unopened. Emails bounced back. Phone calls went to a disconnected number."

"She didn't want to stay in touch."

Barnabas shook his head again. "No, that's wasn't it." He looked down as Aubrey stirred, her hand reaching up to rub at her nose before she laid it back on his chest. The soft lighting glinted off the rings on her hand.

"Wait. Barnabas, she's wearing a wedding band and engagement ring. What is going on?" Breck's voice died away as Barnabas lifted his hand, showing his own wedding band. "You didn't, did you?"

Aubrey roused even more, her head raising as she squinted, hearing another voice.

"You awake, sweetheart?"

"Not really. I thought we were here alone. Who do I hear?"

"Breck."

"Breck? I don't know a Breck, I don't think."

Barnabas shook his head at Breck. "You do. We were all friends at university. Don't you remember?"

She thought and then nodded. "Breck. I do. Why is he here?"

"He lives in the building, sweetheart. He dropped by just to make sure we're okay."

"Oh. Okay. Wake me in the morning, please." She dropped back to sleep, her head tucked up under Barnabas' chin.

Breck had listened in wonder as they had talked before he looked at Barnabas, seeing not just the fatigue but the stress, strain, and worry that had overcome him.

"Barnabas, I know you have a story to tell. Tonight is not the night. We'll meet in the morning." Breck stood, hesitating for a moment.

"Thanks, my friend. It is a story to tell and it's not over. We're on the run. I haven't slept in four days, just trying to get back here without being followed."

"Barnabas? Four days? Where did you come back from?"

"Northern Ontario. It's not that long a trip unless you're being tailed by someone who really wants to stop you and will stop at nothing to do that, including murder."

Rousing the next morning, Barnabas stared around the living room, surprised to find himself still there. He squinted at the clock on the mantle and sighed. His parents would be there shortly and he wasn't ready to face them. Not quite yet. The lights were still on, he saw, and he shifted Aubrey enough so that he could rise and shut them off, returning to stare down at her before he simply gathered her close and walked to the bedroom. She roused as he did so, a hand rubbing at her eyes.

"Barnabas?"

"It's okay, sweetheart. Just moving you to the bed."

"No, it's okay. It's morning and I need to be up." Her head went back down on his shoulder as she yawned. "What is on for today?"

"I'm not sure. Mom and Dad will be here shortly."

"They will? I have wanted to meet them for so long. I think I met them briefly."

"You did, our first year at school. Things have changed over the years." Barnabas set her on her feet. "Go on and shower, have a bath, whatever it is that you want." He frowned. "But I don't have stuff for the bath for you."

"It's okay. I'll manage." She was reaching for the clean clothes that they had purchased, turning to find him handing her a pair of scissors to cut off the price tags.

Barnabas hesitated, seeing the sadness that she was trying hard to cover up, as well as the fear. He wrapped her in his arms, a kiss delivered before he prayed for her.

Aubrey looked up at him, a smile hovering on her face. "Thank you, my love. I think I felt your prayers over the years, particularly when things were the roughest. They kept me going."

"You have never been far from my heart or my prayers, sweetheart." He watched her closely.

———

"Breck was really here last night?"

"He was. He's married now, a lady named Neasa. She's what he needs in his life." Barnabas grinned. "She rides a motorcycle."

"She does? And he loves his motorcycles. A perfect match." Aubrey turned away. "We need to talk some more, my love, but for now, I need to get ready to meet your parents."

Barnabas wandered back to the living room, opening drapes as he did so, to tidy up the couch area and then carry his used mug back to the kitchen. He set fresh coffee and put the kettle on for tea for his mother, a smile crossing his face at the anticipation of how she would react to his bride. Lord? Aubrey needs a mother. Please let Mom be that to her.

He searched the fridge, finding fresh vegetables and juice and eggs. An omelet, he decided, reaching for the frying pan that he preferred for that. Turning as he heard the door open, he knew his father had appeared. His parents had an apartment on the upper floor of the building and had just recently moved back to the area to live permanently.

"Son?" Bruce Carey's voice carried through the apartment.

"Kitchen, Dad. Coffee's ready." Barnabas wiped his hands on a towel and turned to find his father standing beside him, reaching to hug his son, holding on just a bit longer than he normally did.

"Good to have you home. You didn't call much." Bruce's keen dark blue eyes studied his son, seeing the changes the last four weeks had wrought in him.

"No, I didn't. I was on the move a lot, Dad." Barnabas pulled his upper lip over his teeth, a move that Bruce recognized as uncertainty on his son's part.

"Barnabas? Do we need to talk?"

The younger man nodded. "We do, Dad. We do. But it involves someone else, not just me." His head turned as he heard soft footsteps approaching the doorway.

Bruce turned to face the door, stopping in stunned silence at the beautiful woman who appeared and stopped, uncertainty on her face as well. Barnabas sighed and moved to draw her into the room, an arm wrapped tight around her, just as he heard his mother enter.

Elizabeth Carey moved to the kitchen, not seeing her son for a moment, setting down the baskets of muffins and biscuits that she had brought. Finally turning, she looked first as her son and then at the lady in his arms.

"Barnabas? What's going on? You didn't have a lady in your life when you left." Her brow wrinkled. "At least, I didn't think that you did."

"Mom. Dad. This is Aubrey Marie Dorsett Carey. She is my bride and the love of my life." Barnabas was not watching his parents, his eyes on Aubrey as he introduced her, finding her watching him. He reached to kiss her before he looked over at his parents.

Elizabeth stood, her hands over her mouth, surprise on her face for a moment. Bruce had hidden his surprise but interest stood on his face.

"Your bride? Your Aubrey? The lady that you used to talk about and then stopped?" Elizabeth moved around the table, coming to stand with her hands on Aubrey's arms as Barnabas tightened his around his bride. "Oh! You are so welcome to the family. We have waited for all Barnabas' life for you." She simply swept Aubrey into a tight hug.

Aubrey, surprised at first, reached to hug Elizabeth in turn, finding the mother welcoming her to the family in such a way that she knew she was loved and wanted already. Barnabas stepped back, his father at his side, an arm around his son's shoulders.

"Pulled a fast one on us, son? You had your reasons, that much I know."

"I did, Dad. I had to." Barnabas sounded like a little boy for a moment, trying to explain to his father what he had just done. "She was in danger, Dad. I had to rescue her."

"And brought her to us. We'll help you, son." Bruce slanted a glance at his son, a smile hovering on his lips. "Off on your own adventure?"

———

Barnabas groaned and then nodded. "I am, Dad. I have been for the last four weeks. The past five days or so have been brutal. We'll talk."

"We eat. We pray. And then we talk. Is this why Breck has called a full building meeting for this afternoon in the chapel?"

Barnabas' head shot around as he stared at his father and then nodded. "He dropped in last night. We didn't get much time to talk. I figured that he'd do that."

Elizabeth had turned, her arm around Aubrey, listening before Bruce moved to stand before Aubrey, his eyes kindly and welcoming before he too hugged her.

"Mother, it seems as if you now have the daughter you always wanted. Love her lots."

"Oh, I already do. I don't know what happened, son, but your bride is a welcome part of our family." Elizabeth moved past her son, a hug given to him before she began their breakfast preparations.

Barnabas moved back to wrap Aubrey in his arms, finding her shaking.

"All right, sweetheart?"

"I think so. I didn't expect this."

"You are now a loved and special part of our family. And there are thirteen men and ladies who have been waiting to meet you for years."

Her head shot around as she stared at him. "That many?"

"That many. The building family. And then there's Doc and Anna as well as Amy, my secretary, and her husband. You have been prayed for."

Chapter 3

Her hand tight in Barnabas', Aubrey stood in the hallway outside the chapel in the Foundation building. She had had no idea that the building was that big or that so many people called it home. He had tried to explain it to her, finally just telling her that he was giving her a tour of it. She was suddenly afraid for him and for the ones in the building.

Bruce and Elizabeth had found their seats inside, listening to the talk and laughter of the men and ladies they considered family. The men, other than Breck were all orphans, brought to the Foundation by Barnabas from all provinces and territories. Most of the ladies were as well, but the ones who weren't gladly shared their parents and siblings with the others. Elizabeth watched as the little ones that were starting to grace the building chattered away or sat staring at the chapel, given their ages.

Bruce leaned over. "They have no idea, do they?"

"Not at all. I know that they have prayed for a help-meet for him. I fear for him, Bruce, and for his Aubrey."

"I know. He didn't say much but I can feel the concern and fear that is driving him to do what he has done.""

Barnabas studied Aubrey, finding her discomfort coming through. She has no idea, Lord, what I am about to walk her into, and I did try, I know I did, to prepare her. She just wasn't ready for this. Forgive me, Lord, if I rushed ahead of Your plans, but You seemed to be leading in it all.

Aubrey's hand brushed down the soft yellow tunic that she wore over a brand-new pair of brown corduroy slacks. She had fled her home with very little in the clothing line and Barnabas had taken her shopping, insisting that she buy what she wanted as well as what she needed. She could never remember doing that, she thought. Her eyes found his, trust in him in hers, before he bent to kiss her and then pray for her.

"Are you ready, sweetheart?"

———

"I guess. I'm not good at this. I haven't been around people since we graduated. He made sure of that." She grew angry at how her life had been impacted by her guardian.

"I know, sweetheart. I know. We're working on that for you. These fellows in there?" Barnabas nodded at the door. "They will work their wonders again, and we'll bring him to justice. They have done it for all of them."

"All of them?" Aubrey's eyes grew huge. "All of them? Even Breck?"

"All of them. Even Breck. Some were so close to death, it was touch and go. Burnie's wife actually did die and had to be brought back. Bradon was drowned and revived. God is with each one of them, sweetheart. They will welcome you."

"If you say so." Her hand tightened in sudden fear. "I hear babies."

"You do. God is blessing our building family with little ones. We will do everything we can to protect each and every one sitting in that room." He paused, praying for them both before he reached for the door and opened it quietly enough that no one heard. He led her into the chapel, standing at the back, finding Breck watching for him. Breck nodded and rose, standing at the lectern, finding all eyes on him as the room quieted.

"Buckley, before we start, we need you to pray, and in particular for Barnabas."

Buckley rose from where he sat beside his wife, Locklin, and did that. He had been their church minister until the Barnabas Foundation board had asked him to take on a new ministry. He sat when he finished, his eyes on Breck, sensing the concern that Breck was trying hard to hide.

Breck searched each face, finding interest and concern on them, his eyes stopping on each couple, before he looked at Doc and Anna, and then Bruce and Elizabeth. He drew a breath of relief. They've met her, he thought. They've met her and welcomed her to the family. They have the daughter that they wanted so badly, but God had other plans. His eyes raised to Barnabas, finding his friend watching him steadily before they moved to Aubrey, finding her watching Barnabas, confidence in her groom and her love for him on her face.

"Fellows. Ladies. We have been through a lot in the last few years. I don't need to remind you of that. You lived it. God brought us through and has strengthened us in Him. We are now able to reach out to others under the mandate of the Foundation and be the encouragers that were envisioned when it was set up.

"About four weeks ago, we sent Barnabas off on a long-awaited and much-needed vacation. You have all asked over those weeks if I had heard from him. He was not in contact a lot, but that was okay with us all. We understand that as our leader, he needed the time away.

"Barnabas returned late yesterday afternoon. I dropped in on him last night. A situation has occurred with him, that led to our meeting today. He didn't call the meeting. I did, out of concern for him, and so that we could all be on the same page in praying for him." Breck stopped, biting at his lip, unsure of how to proceed.

"Before any of you look around, Barnabas is standing at the back of the room. He is off on an adventure, my friends, just like we all did. When he was away, he found the lady, the love of his life, that he lost touch with. I know the lady and I can safely say that they are two parts of a whole. They complete each other." He paused once more. "Barnabas, please? Bring your lady love forward and introduce us to her. And then, you need to share what adventure that you are off on and what we can all do to help."

As Breck sat beside Neasa, Barnabas strode forward, confidence in his very step, Aubrey keeping pace with him, her eyes on the front, her hand tight in his. He stopped and turned to face the building family, searching each face, his eyes lingering on his parents, before he looked down at Aubrey, finding her face tilted up to him, uncertainty in her eyes, even as her face remained calm. He simply bent and kissed her, sealing his love for her in the presence of their friends.

His eyes raising to search his friends, Barnabas drew a deep breath of relief. He found no censure on their faces, only interest and concern. He sought his father, finding Bruce watching him intently, and then nodding. Bruce knew, without being told, that Barnabas had been in difficulty the last few weeks, and that on his own, other than for their God. He wished that it had been different, but he trusted his son.

Aubrey's hand tightened on his for a moment before Barnabas began to speak.

"I need to apologize for not keeping in better touch with you all. I just felt it best not to. Not that it seems to have mattered. The one responsible for separating Aubrey and me all those years ago has been tracking us.

"First, let me introduce you to Aubrey Dorsett Carey. Breck, Aubrey, and I were friends in university. Breck, I'm sorry. You never knew how much Aubrey and I meant to each other. We didn't realize it ourselves until the last few weeks of university. Through circumstances out of our control, we were separated. We managed to keep in touch until about two years ago. At that point, my letters, emails and phone calls went unanswered or were returned or bounced back on the server. I didn't feel that I could walk away from any of you, not while you were going through what you were. When Breck married, I knew the time had come to go find out if the lady I loved had moved on or was still waiting for me." He paused his eyes on Burnie, who was frowning. "Burnie, it's going to be like one of those mystery stories that you write, and the adventures that you all underwent which you tell us are more bizarre than one of them."

Barnabas turned to Aubrey, seating her beside his mother, who simply wrapped an arm around her new daughter. His father's hand rested on his shoulder for a moment before he returned to the front, to lean one elbow on the lectern.

"This may take a while, but I'll give the shortened version. Fellows, I need you to work with me. I have been in touch with

Dallas and he'll be out tomorrow as he's away today." Barnabas swallowed hard.

"Four weeks ago, I hit the road and travelled up north, many hours and many miles up north, to a small town where I knew Aubrey had had her home. I didn't know if she was still there or not. I rented a small cabin in a neighbouring village, not wanting it to seem obvious that I was a stranger there. I went back every day, searching for her. I finally ran into someone who has been concerned about her. That person showed me where Aubrey was living. This was five days after I arrived there.

"I searched for the house, finding a huge, opulent place, that I knew was not what the Aubrey I knew would have wanted. I walked the perimeter, watching for her, and not seeing her. I had no reason to doubt that she wasn't there. There was security all around, which seemed odd at the time.

"Finally, on the sixth day, I was able to approach the house, finding no guards around. I knocked and then tried the door, finding it opening. I shouldn't have entered, but something drove me forward. I searched, finding a room on the main floor that was locked."

Barnabas had turned the key, opening the door slowly, not sure what or who he would find inside. He stepped through the doorway, searching, hearing a soft cry and then a body hitting him, arms wrapping around his neck. He felt the tears that soaked into his shirt.

"Aubrey? Is that you?" He couldn't get her to raise her head to look at him.

"Do you know how long I have waited for you? I thought that you had forgotten me." She sniffed as she tried to control her sobs.

"Never, sweetheart. Never. I thought that you didn't want anything to do with me."

Aubrey shoved away from him, anger sparking in her eyes. "What did he do? Can I leave with you?"

"That's why I am here. What do you need to pack?"

Aubrey ran for the closet, pulling out a backpack, and blindly stuffing it with the bare minimum of what she wanted. She had had months and years to plan this and knew exactly what to take.

Barnabas frowned as she pulled out the drawer on the bedside table and reached to the back of the table to pull on a packet.

"My identification." Her simple statement said a lot. "He tried to take it from me, but I hid it." She ran back towards him, a hand reaching for his, watching as he closed and locked the door. "He's away for a few days. When he's away, no one is here, only long enough to bring me cold food and water."

"You've been a prisoner?" Barnabas ran with her towards the trees, his eyes watching for someone coming to stop them.

"I have been. Since I graduated. The last two years have been the worse." She ducked down into the back of his truck, letting him pull a blanket over her.

"Stay down, Aubrey. I'm heading for the cabin I rented as if I'm heading back there for the night, but I have everything with me. I'll drop off the keys inside. That was the arrangement. Then, we'll find somewhere that we can talk."

Chapter 5

Aubrey finally sat in the front seat, brushing back her hair, turning to look behind them. Barnabas had sped away from the cabin that he had rented, even though it was still early morning, heading for a nearby city. He knew that they couldn't travel as they were. A plan had come to him, only he wasn't sure that Aubrey would be agreeable. They didn't know one another anymore.

"Barnabas? Now what?" Aubrey turned to him.

"I'm heading for the town nearby. We need to talk, Aubrey."

"I know. I need help to bring him to justice. Only I don't know how to do that."

"I can help. I have many friends and lawyers who will help." Barnabas pulled into a fast-food drive-in. "Let me grab us some food and something to drink, and we'll talk."

Their meal finished, Barnabas gathered the garbage and headed for a waste container, standing and staring at it before he angrily shoved the debris into it. *Lord, I am so angry and heartbroken for her. How do I keep her safe? I see only one way, and I'm not even sure that is what You want for my life.* He sighed, turning back to the truck, sliding inside.

Aubrey watched him closely, before he reached for her hand, his head bowing as he prayed for them and for her. *He knows, doesn't he, Lord? Without me saying anything, he knows.*

Barnabas' thumb rubbed at her hand, and he spoke without looking at her.

"Aubrey? I have a plan, a plan that would bring you away from here, but it would also put you into more danger.'

"A plan?" Aubrey's hand tightened on his. "Does it involve more than you just riding in on your white charger and taking me away from there?"

"It does." He finally looked up at her, his heart in his eyes. "I have loved you for so long. Even when I thought you wanted

204

nothing to do with me, I loved you. Will you marry me, Aubrey? Today?"

She stared at him before she had to blink away the tears. Her voice was barely audible as she spoke.

"Do you know how many nights that I have dreamed of that? That you came and saved me, swept me away to your town, married me, and brought him to justice?" She swiped at the tears on her face, taking the handkerchief that he handed her. "Yes, Barnabas. Yes. We were at that point when we graduated, I think. Only he stepped in and took over."

"He did. And we will talk about that. Now, let's see where the city hall is."

Two hours later, Barnabas tucked Aubrey back into his truck, sorrow at the fact that she had a rushed wedding weighing him down. He stood for a moment, watching her through the window before he moved to slide behind the wheel.

"Where to, Aubrey? Where can we go that he can't find you?"

"Go north a ways. There's a small town that he avoids. He was forced to leave it about five years ago." She watched as Barnabas parked at a small bed and breakfast.

"We can stay here likely for a day or so if they have rooms. Let me find out."

He was back shortly, driving around to the back of the building. "We have three days here. Then we move on. I don't have to be back at work for about three weeks."

"You don't?" Aubrey was surprised.

"No. I took a four-week vacation, intent on finding you." He grinned at her. "And I did."

"And you did." Aubrey stood in the room that they had been assigned. "This is nice. I love the white and green."

"You always liked your green." Barnabas swept her into his arms. "Still do?"

"I do. He decorated in browns and grays and blacks. I had no choice in what he did." She leaned back. "Barnabas, I have few clothes. I didn't bring what he made me buy or bought for me."

"I know, sweetheart. I know. Let's spend some time in prayer. We need it. And then we'll go find you some clothes. And a nice restaurant."

A week later, Barnabas shuddered suddenly as he shut the back door on the cab of his truck. We've been found, he thought, even moving from town to town as we did. He helped Aubrey in and then ran for his side, sliding inside.

"Barnabas?" Aubrey shot him a look and then her eyes moved to the outside. "He's found us?"

"Someone has. We need to move. I'm heading for the eastern side of the province. From there, we'll work our way back towards Lake Erie and home." He grinned at her. "Have I told you today that I love you?"

"You have. I will never tire of that. I love you, too." Aubrey watched the traffic behind him. "The white truck. That's his son's. How did they find us?"

"I should have taken off for the south. They figured that we'd stay up this way. It was a chance that we took." Barnabas abruptly turned into a parking lot, the horns of the vehicles behind him sounding, and then drove through it to emerge and head the way that they had just come. "I hope that I can shake him long enough to get away. He has no control or authority over you?"

"He hasn't since I was like eighteen. He just refused to relinquish it. I was able to send documents to another lawyer in your town, hoping that word would get to you."

"And because of lawyer/client confidentiality, they couldn't."

"His name is John. I remembered you talking about him."

"John? One of our Foundation lawyers. Wonderful. We'll go see him once we're home."

Five days before he had to head home, Barnabas stood on a street corner in a large town, Aubrey's hand tight in his. He felt it tighten and looked down, seeing fear on her face.

"Sweetheart?"

"His son. He just drove past us. He saw me, Barnabas."

He simply ran her across the road, dodging traffic and shoved her into the truck. He was behind the wheel and driving off, his eyes watchful. They had made a habit of not staying more than one night in a motel or bed-and-breakfast.

"We'll stay just outside of town tonight. It's getting late to be moving too far." Barnabas finally pulled into an out-of-the-way motel.

The next morning, they were up and gone earlier. Barnabas drove back and forth between cities, towns, and villages for the next four days, his eyes watchful, not able to sleep. His eyes were heavy but he refused to give in. Aubrey worried, but kept watch with him, sleeping in fits and starts, on the lookout for her guardian or his son.

Driving towards home, Barnabas drew a breath of relief. Here, he thought, Aubrey will be as safe as we can make her. I'll take her in to see John, to find out what our options are. He sighed. He had to introduce her to his parents and then the building family. He would not find censure from any of them, that much he knew. There might be questions but they would only be to ensure that the couple was safe. Then, the fellows would start their investigation, that much he knew.

Barnabas parked in his designated spot and sat for a moment, before he reached for Aubrey's hand, his head bowing as he prayed for them, as a couple, and for her, that they could quickly resolve what was going on and find out the reasons why. He walked her towards the patio of his first-floor apartment, her eyes taking in the three-story building. Unlocking the door, he swept her up and carried her inside, claiming a kiss as he set her down in his home office.

"Let me grab our bags and I'll be right back. Go on. Take a look around your home." He was out to the truck, and back in, depositing the bags into the bedroom, before he turned to find her still standing in the office, her eyes on him.

"You haven't moved." He walked to stand in front of her, reaching for her hands.

"No, I didn't. You need to do this, Barnabas. You need to show me your home, and then we'll make it ours."

He nodded. "Of course. Here, let's start in my office." He led her from room to room, listening to her comments, smiling as she took delight in the rooms.

They prepared a quick meal before she headed to shower and change, finding her way back to the living room. Barnabas stood watching her before he handed her the cup of apple spice tea that she seemed to have developed a liking for.

"Will it do?"

She set her cup down and spun in a circle. "It will more than do. You saw the house that he had. It wasn't mine. I had that small room for the last two years. Even before that, I only had access to two rooms beside mine. The kitchen and the laundry room. I wasn't allowed in any other rooms." She flopped down on the couch, her hands rubbing at her eyes. "I'm exhausted, Barnabas."

"Curl up there and sleep, sweetheart. I'll be back in about ten minutes or so." He watched as she curled up on the couch, an arm along the back as she studied the room. "And we will make changes here, sweetheart, to make this your place as well."

Aubrey nodded, her face thoughtful. "We will, my love, but I need to live here first to get a sense of what we want. And it will be our decision, not mine."

Barnabas came back to the present, his eyes finding Aubrey as she sat, his father's arm around her, her hand in his mother's. Thank you, Mom and Dad. You have taken her to your hearts. She needs this. He looked down, not wanting to look at his friends. He jumped slightly as he felt an arm on his shoulders and Breck began to pray for him and his Aubrey.

"Fellows, we have a mission now." Breck looked around the room, finding the silence greeting his words comforting. They had all been through too much to be surprised at what Barnabas had said. "First, we greet our newest family member. Then, we make plans."

Buckley was on his feet, heading for Barnabas.

"First, we pray for Barnabas and his Aubrey. Then we make plans. Locklin has already whispered to me that we need a pot-luck tonight, to welcome Barnabas back and to welcome his bride." He prayed for his friends before he hugged him and then stepped back, watching the couples move forward. Aubrey had simply risen as he had begun to pray, to come and stand beside Barnabas.

Aubrey stood that evening, watching as the ladies scurried around, setting out the meal before she walked forward, her contribution in her hands.

Berneen turned as she approached, reaching to take the hot pan of scalloped potatoes from her, setting it down before she reached to hug her.

"You are so welcome to our family, Aubrey." Berneen watched her. "We have prayed for you, without knowing you."

"You have?" Aubrey nodded as she thought through the words. "Barnabas said that you had been. We still need those. To find my guardian and his son? That's what we need to do. But why do I keep calling him my guardian?"

Cadee moved in, hugging her as well before she linked an arm with her. "He's not, is it? How many years?"

"I would have been eighteen or so. I was that before I graduated from university. He tried to play it that he was my guardian longer. I found the paperwork one day and took it."

"You did?" Devaney hugged her as well. "And where is it?"

"Barnabas' lawyer, John, has it. I haven't heard from him, but nothing got through. That's why Barnabas came looking for me." She looked up as the ladies grouped themselves around her. "You need to introduce me to you all, with your fellow's name. And the little ones."

Hagen nodded as she stood beside her, her son in her arms. "And we will. Right now, we eat and enjoy our fellowship. We try and do this once a month, just for fun." Her son had been watching Aubrey and suddenly launched himself at her, his arms tight around her neck before he leaned back and then moved in to give a sloppy kiss.

"I'm so sorry, Aubrey. He never does that to people that he doesn't know."

Aubrey was laughing, hugging the little fellow, who refused to look at his mother as she reached for him. "It's okay. I'll keep him for now, if you like. It's been a long time since I've been around little ones. I used to help in the nursery at church."

Barnabas reached for the little fellow as well, the little boy never refusing to come to him. He watched in amazement as the little one buried his face against Aubrey and just refused to look at anyone else. Brandon stood there as well, his daughter in his arms, who as soon as she saw her brother, launched herself from her father towards her brother.

Aubrey's face lit up with laughter as she held the two little ones, her face covered in sloppy kisses.

"I never expected this kind of welcome." She looked up at Barnabas. "You didn't warn me, my love."

"No, I didn't. They've never done that before."

Hagen and Brandon finally removed their twins, much to the dismay and protest of the little ones. Barnabas stood with an arm around Aubrey.

"I think they're in love, sweetheart."

"Maybe. They are so sweet." She looked around. "Okay, so what happens now?"

"Buckley prays. We dish up, find seats, eat and have fun." He looked around. "I have wanted my bride with me here at these dinners for so long. I'm glad you are finally a part of it."

"I am. And tomorrow, we meet with John?"

"We do. I sent him a message that we were home and that you were with me. He's been trying for years to reach you, he said."

Aubrey wandered the apartment late that night, restless, unable to settle down in one room. Her hands reached to touch the ornaments that Barnabas had sitting around. She knew that he was on a call, that he had been reluctant to take, but felt that he had to. She ended up in his office, his hand reaching for her as he paced.

"Dallas will be out tomorrow afternoon." He tucked his phone into a pocket.

———

"Who's Dallas again?"

"A detective with the force here, and a good friend. He's worked with all the men and ladies." Barnabas began to laugh. "I didn't expect the twins to do that."

Aubrey's face lit up. "I don't think their parents did either. It's not the first time I have had twins fighting over me. I have missed the little ones."

Chapter 8

His keen eyes on the couple across from him, John Tyson assessed them. They're in love, I can see that, Lord. Now, how do we keep them safe? I know of this man who claims to be her guardian. He will stop at nothing to regain control of her, even declaring her incompetent and having mental health issues.

"John? You have read through what Aubrey sent you?"

"I have, Barnabas. He is not your guardian, Aubrey. In fact, he was never your guardian. He had no control over what you did. Your mother was your guardian. I understand that she died just as you turned eighteen?"

"She did. He stepped in during my grief for her and just took over. I didn't fight him. I was too heartbroken. When I did question him, he waved off my objections and concerns."

"I see. He has drawn up papers, with your grandmother's purported signature, stating that he was to be your guardian until you turned thirty. That was two years ago?"

"It was." Aubrey stared at him before the anger grew in her. "That's why."

"Why what?" John had a good idea but he needed her to say it.

"That's why he imprisoned me. It was the day before my birthday. He just shoved me into that room, despite my protests, and locked the door. It was a lock that could only be opened from the outside." Aubrey's face dropped into her hands. "I didn't have my phone with me. He had taken it. That's when he cancelled the email, cancelled my phone, returned any letters that came to me. I had very few of those anyway."

Barnabas' arm was around her. "What now, John? You know my guys are working on this."

"That I know. Breck has already been in touch, not to ask any questions specific to you, Aubrey, but in general." He looked down at his notes. "I'll have these transcribed, Aubrey, have you sign the

———

213

statement that you have given me, register it at the court. We will need to have someone assess you, just in case he plays that card.”

“Oh, he will. He’s already told me that.” Aubrey looked frustrated. “But who?”

“We know a lady, who is a respected forensics psychologist, even though she’s retired. She’d be around your age. Darcie’s not from the area, so that will help.”

“Anything. As soon as possible. He’s not going to wait.” Aubrey sat back, a puzzled look on her face before she turned to Barnabas. “I don’t know why he’s done this. He would try and get me to meet with different people, said he was trying to help me get established as a singer. I had no interest in that. You know that.”

“I do. You have a beautiful voice, but that’s not where you want to serve. John? What next?”

“I’ll contact Darcie and see what she can arrange in the next day or so. She has always been willing to work with the Foundation. She and Doug are supporters. That may put a wrinkle into it, but I don’t think it will.” John stood, his hand out to shake Barnabas’ before he hugged Aubrey. “I have no doubt that he will try his best to trap you somehow, and take control of you. But legally? He has no standing at all. This paperwork shows that. When we go to court, and that we will need to do, he will be sent away. It’s not legal. Do you have anything of your Grandmother’s showing her signature?”

Aubrey nodded. “I do. I kept things hidden from him, receipts, bills, letters, addresses. I’ll make sure that you get them.”

“Good girl. You’ve a head on your shoulders, despite what you went through.” John watched them walk away before he reached for his phone, asking to speak with the Chief of Police, Will Peters.

“Will? Got a moment?”

“I do. Just a moment, John, while I close my door.” Will sat back into his chair after closing his door. “You’ve called. You have a concern.”

“I do. It’s young Barnabas.”

“Barnabas? I thought that he was away on holidays.”

"He was. He's been back three days. The thing is, Will, is that he married while he was away. His bride is one that Jeremy Forester has tried to force into the music scene. He gave her paperwork that said he was her guardian until she turned thirty."

"Still trying his old tricks? We've been trying to catch him for years, just never had the proof."

"We have it now. Young Aubrey was smart enough to remember my name from her talks with Barnabas and sent everything that she could find. I am sure that she paid for that. He locked her up two years ago and cut off all communication with her."

"He did? Now, we can get him. You're worried."

"I am. He has already threatened to have her declared mentally incompetent. We went through that with Neasa. I prayed that we didn't have to again."

"Me too. Darcie's onboard?"

"She's my next call. I can't see her refusing. Barnabas mentioned that he had called Dallas yesterday and that they were to meet today."

"Good. I'll find him and speak to him. Anything else?"

"Not offhand. I'll make sure your people get copies of what she has sent. He's a mean, vindictive man. I fear for young Barnabas."

"There's that. I'll have a talk with him. Married, is he? Good. What's she like?"

"A very beautiful redhead, who is clearly in love with her fellow. They're parts of a whole, Will."

"Is that so?"

Chapter 9

Dallas stared at Barnabas that afternoon when he had tracked him down to his home office, not quite sure that he had heard him correctly.

"I'm sorry. I thought that you said you were married. You weren't dating anyone."

"I am, Dallas. Aubrey is the one I found in university and then we were separated, through no fault of ours. We had kept in touch for a number of years until all contact was cut off about two years ago."

"She did that? Then why marry her?" Dallas was puzzled.

"She didn't. A lawyer claiming to be her guardian did that. I've talked to John, and I can almost guarantee you that he talked to Will."

"He might have. Will was looking for me earlier, but I was out of the office. That could be what he wanted." Dallas ran his hand through his hair. "So, what do we do, Barnabas?"

"First, you meet my lady." Barnabas had his hand out to draw Aubrey to him. She had appeared in the doorway of the office and hesitated about entering. "Dallas, this is Aubrey, my bride and the love of my life."

Dallas turned to study her, finding her brown eyes watching him carefully, a calm expression on her face.

"Aubrey? I am glad to meet you, even under these circumstances. Barnabas, it was to stop with Breck, didn't we tell you that?"

Barnabas began to laugh and had to control it before he could turn to Aubrey, her puzzled eyes shifting between the two men. "We have told each fellow that it ends with the one before him. It never worked." He grinned at Dallas. "You're next, aren't you?"

Dallas looked horrified for a moment before he grinned. "Don't think so. I'm not part of the Foundation building family." He turned to Aubrey, sobering as he did so. "We need to get as much information from you as we can. Barnabas, here or in your office downstairs?"

"Here. And John has all the information that Aubrey could give him. He said he'd send it to you, but I would ask legally for it. It's another lawyer that we're dealing with."

"It is, is it? Makes no difference." Dallas pulled out his pad and pen. "Okay, let's get started. The sooner we solve it, the better it will be."

Two hours later, Barnabas closed the apartment door after Dallas. Leaning back on it, his head dropped forward and his eyes closed. *Lord, this time, it's different. It's my lady, my sweetheart, who is in danger. And we don't know why or who all is after her. It can't just be that lawyer. Dear Lord, protect her. Help me to be the one who can do that, with Your strength. Please, Dear Lord?*

Aubrey watched him before she just moved into his space and into his arms, her head resting against his chest. *Lord, protect this man who loves me. I know that man will go after him. I couldn't handle it if he is hurt because of me.* She leaned back as she felt Barnabas move.

"You're back to work when?"

"Tomorrow's Sunday, so it will be Monday. Are you ready for church tomorrow?" He assessed her, a frown on his face.

"As ready as I ever will be. I haven't been to a church service or heard a sermon in years. He wouldn't let me. I think he was afraid that someone would help me. He couldn't take a chance on that."

"No, he couldn't." Barnabas turned her and headed for the living room, sitting in his favourite chair and drawing her down on to his knee, cuddling her close. "We're not fancy dressers if that's a concern."

She shrugged. "I wondered. I was just going to go by what you were wearing." She bit at her lip. "I need to get some more things, Barnabas. I only have the basics."

He nodded. "As my wife, you will receive a wage from the Foundation. All the wives do. But that doesn't matter. The ladies will want to take you into town, introduce you around and find some outfits for you." He began to grin. "Hailey and Hollie, Hagen's twin sisters, have likely already talked Breck into taking them to town to do that. They have done it with all the ladies after Hagen and Brandon married. He's like a big brother to them. They have him twisted around their fingers."

"They will? How sweet? And I saw a younger man there, with Berneen, I think it was."

"That's her brother, Darbie. He likely went along with the twins. He says he hates shopping but he's always up for a trip."

"He is? You have such wonderful people here. I like how you found all orphans for the men. And to share your initials? That had to be God."

"It was. I would be given a list, pray over and then find the one God directed me to. They are all different, have different occupations, and all volunteer. The ladies either work, volunteer, or are in school. Some are staying home now that they have a family."

"That's good. I remember you saying that the Barnabas Foundation was set up to be encouragers. I can see that. But where do I fit in?"

"Right now? They'll go easy on you, seeing as you're the new one here. It's up to you what you do. I would like it if you kept track of the ladies. Neasa is doing that, but you can as well."

"I don't want to step in and take over. That's not me. How be I focus on the little ones?"

Barnabas tilted his head to study her. "I don't know that we ever really discussed that, as a Foundation board. There will be a play area and a playground going in. There is also an empty room on the main floor with outdoor access. Let me talk to the board. I am sure that we could turn it into a daycare centre of some kind. I remember that you studied that as well as your business degree."

"I did. And I think that's what Jeremy was afraid of. That I would move on and away and he would lose a source of income that he was trying to establish."

$$Chapter\ 10$$

A week later, Baird stood and watched Aubrey as she wandered the gardens, a frown on his face. He realized that every time he saw her, she was on her own. That's not right. I know the ladies are great friends, but they have never shunned or ignored one of them. He turned, heading for the building, finding Berneen in the lobby.

"Berneen? Have any of you ladies talked with Aubrey? Every time I see her? She's on her own."

Berneen flushed. "I have been, Baird, but she's so quiet that it's hard to get a feel of what she wants."

"And the others?"

She shrugged. "I have no idea. They're not saying."

"This is not right, Berneen. She's part of our family, as Barnabas' wife. She was isolated for years, locked up for two. It has to be difficult for her to make the move that would make friends."

"You're right." She moved into his hug. "I'm sorry. I know better."

"You do. You know what it's like to be locked up." He reached for her hand. "Do you have some time right now?"

"I do. Where is she?"

"In the gardens. Come on. Let's go find her. I'll stay for a while and then I have to run. Invite them for supper if you want."

Berneen hesitated for a moment before she approached Aubrey.

"Aubrey?" She waited until the other lady turned. "I need to apologize. I was not the friend that you needed. Baird tracked me down. I'm sorry."

"For what? I could have made the motion to get to know you all. But you seem to be such good friends, I didn't want to intrude."

"Oh, Aubrey? Is that what you think? It would be no intrusion. We just open up our group and take in the next lady. Listen, we're meeting in about half an hour for Bible study. Did anyone ask you?" Berneen bit her lip as Aubrey shook her head. "I am so sorry. I know better. I should have asked you. Forgive me?"

"What's to forgive? I could have approached you. I just don't know how to anymore. Jeremy kept me confined for so many years. The last two I had no contact with anyone but him, or one of his security men if he was away."

Berneen reached to hug her. "That's so sad. I was kept prisoner for a few months until Baird appeared there as a prisoner. He made sure that I came with him when five of the men swooped in and rescued him. Listen. Let's head to Cadee's where the study is. And I know Hagen's sisters have things for you. They finally talked Breck into taking some time yesterday to go shopping for you. He's been running around like crazy the last week or so. And I think Darbie said he found something for you. Let's stop by Hagen's first and then head out." Berneen linked an arm with her. "From now on, if you don't speak up, I'll be your mouthpiece. I do that very well."

"You do? I never would have guessed." Aubrey bit back a grin as Berneen stared at her. "And I do want to hear about all of your adventures. Barnabas has told me bits and pieces. And he says that you ladies go into competition with the fellows to solve the mysteries."

"We do." Berneen tapped at Hagen's door. "But we all feel as if there has been something left hanging and unresolved."

"That could be, Berneen." Hagen stood in her open doorway. "Are you two coming in or are you going to continue your conversation in the hallway?"

"Coming in. Aubrey was wandering around by herself. Baird found her and then found me. We need to do better, Hagen."

"Yes, we do. I was heading your way later, Aubrey, with what the twins and Darbie found. Now that you're here, let me find the stuff, as Hollie so elegantly calls in."

Late that afternoon, Aubrey stared down at the bed, her hand covering her mouth, as she counted the outfits, sweaters, bath stuff, as Hollie called it before she reached for an eagle statue that Darbie had insisted she needed. She blinked back tears. Lord, it had to be You, to direct him to something that means so much to me. Eagles always were my favourite. Teach me to live again, dear Lord, and teach me how to fly above the storms.

Barnabas' arms came around her at that point and she leaned back against him.

"Lots of loot, as Darbie says." He grinned at her.

"The twins. Apparently, Breck had to free up some time yesterday." She held up the eagle. "Darbie found this."

"Your bird. You always wanted to try and find them, didn't you?"

"I did. Berneen and Baird asked if we would come for dinner. I didn't know what to say."

"We can go, or we can stay at home. It's okay. They understand." Barnabas was distracted for a moment.

"Barnabas?"

"Hmm? Sorry. There was a letter that came today in the mail. I need to go over it with you, but I think, if you're willing, we head for Baird's. We don't need to stay too late."

Late that evening, Barnabas stood in front of Aubrey, an envelope held out for her to take. She stared at it and then up at him, shaking her head.

"I won't, Barnabas. I don't want to read what he has to say."

"You need to, sweetheart. We both need to know what he's up to. He's very specific. He knows that we are married. How I would like to know."

"Someone from that town, likely." She finally reached to take the envelope as if it were poisoned. "Do I really need to?"

Barnabas swept her into his arms and then to a sitting position on the couch in the office.

"You do. If you want, I'll read it for you."

"No, it's okay." Aubrey shook her head, extricating the letter and unfolding it. Her face hardened and paled as she read. "Is he for real? He never said anything like that before. He was always very careful about how he worded anything."

"He's seeking revenge. They don't care how they talk." Barnabas tapped the letter. "This here? It's a direct threat to our lives. I'll give a copy to John and the original to Dallas."

"How do we stop him? I can almost guarantee you that he will have gone into hiding."

"Likely. We'll be careful, as we always are. Dallas will likely want to speak with you again, to see what new information you can give him."

"He picked my brain clean the other day. I don't know of anything more that I can tell him." She leaned against him. "Is this what the others went through?"

"Much worse for some."

Aubrey sat in silence, staring down at the letter. "How do we protect one another?"

"That we will work on. I know the fellows have started their investigations. Don't ask me how they find their stuff. They do. They all search differently from each other." Barnabas began to pray, his voice echoing through the room.

Aubrey finally rose and began to pace, her arms wrapped around herself. Barnabas watched her before he reached for his phone, which had been vibrating. He stared at the number before he just let it go to voicemail.

"Barnabas?" Aubrey sat beside him, leaning over to look at the number. "Jeremy? He has your number?"

"He does. It's on the website, so he could find it." Barnabas set his phone to one side. "I'm not listening to the voice mail. I'll do that when I see Dallas. I am sure it's not going to be nice."

"How do we do this, Barnabas? I feel like a broken record." Aubrey sighed. "I don't want to bring any harm to the ones here or to the little ones."

"I know, sweetheart. I know. For now, we continue as we are. We have to live our lives. We can't hide in fear."

"I know that. He wants us to. That's what that letter is all about. He tried so hard with me to make me fear him. I never did. I was disgusted by him, angry. I couldn't understand at first why Mom would have done this. Then, I realized that it wasn't Mom. It was him. And I don't know why."

"You don't? No trust funds? No land coming to you? No property?"

"Nothing. I had scholarships and grants to go to school. I worked during the summers to help pay my way. And I worked part-time when at school." Aubrey sighed. "I just don't know why."

"We'll figure it out." Barnabas wrapped an arm around her, praying for her as he pulled her close to him. "Now, then. What have you decided about the apartment?"

"The apartment? Where did that come from?"

Barnabas shrugged. "I guess that I just want you to feel at home here. Make it yours."

———

"I am at home, Barnabas. I would be at home wherever you are. I am not sure what you would like to change. The furniture? It's great. The floors? I love the hardwood. The walls? They are the colours that we talked about, all those years ago."

"I know. I think I decorated it for you. But there has to be something you would like to add."

"Right at the moment? I can't think of a thing." Aubrey snuggled down beside him. "There are holidays coming up. What does the building do for Christmas?"

"In years past, we would have a dinner on Christmas, but that has been changing. Some are at relatives, those who have them. The others? It's hard to say what this year will be like."

"Do you decorate the lobby?"

"You know, we never really have. How be you work on that? The ladies will likely help." Barnabas paused, not quite sure how to phrase his next question.

"Berneen made sure that I was part of the Bible study. I need that. They are all wonderful ladies, a little unsure of my role here, though. I think that is why they are hesitant to approach me. After all, I am married to the boss, as they say.'

"True, but not true. I oversee them, through Breck. I work for the Foundation more than I do oversee them."

"I know. It's just complicated. That's all."

The next morning, Aubrey stared at the security guard as he tried to hand her a package. She shook her head, pointing back to his desk. She had been studying the lobby when he had approached her.

"I didn't order anything. And I have no one that would be sending me anything." She paled. "Please. Put it down." She peered at the writing as he did so. "It's what I thought. I need to contact that Dallas. Do you know how to?"

"I do. Barnabas warned us to expect things like this, but I don't think we expected anything so soon." He turned away to call and then turned back to her. "Barnabas isn't in this morning, is he?"

"No, he had a meeting in town, he said, that would likely take him until noon." Aubrey backed away from the desk. "I don't want to even know what's in it." She almost ran from him, stopping in the centre of the lobby, arms wrapped around herself as she stared at the door. I could make a getaway, couldn't I, Lord? I could run, change my name, my appearance, but he would still find me. That much I know. She jumped as she felt a hand touch her arm.

Brandon stood there, a frown on his face. "Aubrey?"

"Brandon? He's found me, do you know that? He sent that package over there." Her finger stabbed towards the security desk.

"He has? He did? We need to call Barnabas and Dallas." He reached for his phone.

"Barnabas is not to be interrupted. I won't allow it. He's in meetings all morning."

"He would set them aside for you. You do know that?"

Aubrey nodded. "I know. Right at the moment, I am not in danger. It's a threat, just like the letter last night. And that Dallas has already been called."

"He has?" Brandon looked around. "Then, you're running away. It won't work. Barnabas would just come after you. It would put you both at risk." He pointed towards a hallway. "Come with me. I'm heading to the conference room that we use. We've been wanting to speak with you about this man."

"Don't get me started. I know too much and I don't know why." Aubrey frowned as she entered the room. She paused, studying the work stations, the kitchenette, the whiteboards on the walls. "You have it set up nicely. Does it work?"

Brandon grinned at her. "It does. We've found more information than what we really knew we could. We also have a friend who researches stuff, as Benen calls it, and finds information that no one else seems able to."

Aubrey wandered the room, her eyes taking in what had already been added to the whiteboards. She stopped in front of one and then smiled. A logic problem, she thought. How interesting!

"That's Burnie's idea." Benen spoke from behind her. "He set it up for Buckley, I think it was, and we used something similar for him, Breck, and now Barnabas."

"I find it interesting. What does Burnie do?"

"He's a mystery writer."

Aubrey spun, her eyes huge. "A mystery writer? Oh, I have always wanted to meet one."

Benen grinned. "And now you have. Aubrey, Barnabas has given us what he can. But we always like to speak with the ladies. Sometimes, they can add to what we know. They also have a different perspective than us fellows."

"Our brains work differently, is that what you're saying?" Aubrey sighed. "I can give you what I know. Right now, I am waiting on that Dallas to come out. There was a package delivered to me this morning. And Barnabas had a letter yesterday."

"We have that letter. Not a very nice fellow, is he?"

"No. And I can't figure out why. Barnabas asked last night about any inheritances. I have none. Mom scraped together what she could after Dad was killed in a motor vehicle accident when I was twelve. We never had a lot. Dad's insurance had to pay for our upkeep. I have no idea how Jeremy got involved, but he suddenly just appeared in the days after Dad's death. He wouldn't leave. Mom asked him to many times. When he was around, she made sure that I wasn't."

"Your mother knew something? And she left no papers or diary?"

Aubrey shook her head. "No. I cleared out her desk and paperwork when she died. There was nothing other than receipted bills. I used her insurance to help fund my schooling." Aubrey grew pensive. "I just don't understand."

Benen drew a chair out and made her sit, moving away for a moment and then returning with a cup of tea for her.

"Here. Cadee told me that you like this tea. Drink it." He drew out a chair beside her, his mug of coffee landing on the table before he reached for a pad of paper and pen. He grinned. "Breck has us doing this, reaching for pen and paper."

"He does? Is that what he always does?" Aubrey leaned her chin on her upraised hand, elbow on the table. "Talk to me, Benen. Tell me about you fellows. I know that you are all orphans, from every province and territory except this one."

Benen did just that, his pen moving across the paper as he made notes for her. When he finished, he tore the papers from the pad and handed them to her.

"Some homework for you." He grinned again. "I hear the ladies and you were together yesterday."

"We were, Benen. And it's hard for me. I have been so many years with just my own company."

"We know that, Aubrey, and we are praying for you and for Barnabas. You're the person who completes him. Even going through what you are, I am glad you are here." He raised his eyes as the door opened. "And there's that Dallas, likely looking for you."

Filling a mug with coffee, Dallas drew a deep breath. He had to talk with Aubrey but Barnabas wasn't there. He wasn't sure how to approach her, given what she had been through. And now this, he thought. A box with dead roses and a sympathy card for Barnabas.

"Dallas?" Aubrey stood in front of him, worry on her face.

"Aubrey? Can we sit?"

She shrugged, heading back to where she had been seated and taking her seat again.

"What did you find?"

"Dead roses. A sympathy card for Barnabas." Dallas watched her closely, seeing her pale.

"A sympathy card. Was it signed?"

"No, just had his name on the envelope." Dallas pulled out his phone, bring up a picture with the envelope and then handed his phone to her.

"That's his writing." Aubrey shook for a moment before she thrust the phone back at him. "What's his game?"

"Your life." Dallas watched closely as Aubrey paled even more. "You escaped him. He wants you dead. And why? That's what we need to discover. And if he can't get to you first, he will go after Barnabas."

"I know. I know that. I shouldn't have left with Barnabas." Her voice was barely a whisper.

"He wouldn't have left you there, Aubrey. Not a chance on that." Dallas looked up as the door opened and nodded. He had reached out to Barnabas, who had responded with shock and then fear.

Aubrey jumped as she felt arms come around her and her head turned. "Barnabas? You were in meetings. They weren't supposed to call you."

"And do you think that I would sit in a meeting, knowing that you were being terrorized? As soon as the board found out, they sent me to you." Barnabas looked over at Dallas. "Anything else?"

"Just what I told you and the picture that I sent. He's upping his game, Barnabas. He's going to get more and more vicious as time goes by."

"I know that he will." Barnabas pulled out a chair and sat, Aubrey's hand tight in his. "What do we do?"

"For now? Take extra precautions. We can't find him or I would bring him in to question him." Dallas was frustrated. "If you see him at all, Aubrey, don't approach him. Call us."

Aubrey watched as Dallas rose and walked away, leaving her with Barnabas' arm around her.

"Sweetheart? Did you open the box?"

"No. I refused to take it from the security guard. He called Dallas." She turned to watch him. "I'm scared, Barnabas. I am so scared that he will try and hurt the people here. Maybe I should just leave."

"And I would leave with you. That would mean that we would be on our own. Here, we have our friends to help look out for us. I know. I know what you are saying. I feel the same. So did every one of the fellows and the ladies as well."

"They did? Then, how do we do this? How do we stay safe and keep them safe?"

Blair hesitated as he approached, not wanting to interrupt. Aubrey looked at him with a frown before she turned to Barnabas.

"Blair?" Barnabas peered over Aubrey's head at him.

"Barnabas. Aubrey. We found some information on your father, Aubrey, that we would like to speak with you about." Blair was still hesitant even as he spoke, bringing a frown to Barnabas' face.

Aubrey spun to stare at him. "You do? What is it? I have trouble remembering my Dad, it's been so long." Her face grew sad.

"We found this. Is this your father?" Blair handed over a photo.

Aubrey took it, staring down at it before her finger moved to touch it. She blinked back tears.

"Oh, Dad! I miss you." She blinked back tears even as Barnabas' arms held her. "Blair? Where did you find this?"

"In a newspaper archive. It seems that your father was well respected in his occupation as a contractor."

"He was. He never let any of the trades do shoddy work. If he felt it was, he made them redo it. He never wanted to be associated with any building that would be condemned or collapse. He had seen that happen." She looked up. "But I don't understand. Why this?"

"It's what we do, Aubrey. We look into everyone in your family, tracing what we can. We research everything we come across, no matter how minute. We confer with one another, bounce ideas back and forth. We will keep you updated. We will keep coming back and asking the same questions, different questions, whatever it is we need to do."

"They all look at it differently, I think I told you, sweetheart. It's how they work."

Aubrey was on her feet, moving towards the door, the picture of her father still clutched in her hands. She swiped at the tears on her face before she almost ran for the lobby, stopping to stare around. She walked quickly towards one of the two seating areas, drawing a chair up near the gas fireplace. Dad? Why? God, please? I need answers. I need to feel Your presence and right now, I don't.

Neasa watched from where she had just walked in before she moved towards Aubrey, sitting in a chair near her, just waiting. She finally handed Neasa a handkerchief.

"Aubrey?"

"I'm okay. Blair found a picture of my Dad. I miss him so much." She held out the picture.

"This is your father? He looks like a kind and compassionate man."

"He was. He was." Neasa didn't realize that she had repeated herself. "To lose him like we did broke Mom. She was never the same. I still think that she died from a broken heart."

"That may well be. Aubrey? What can I do for you?" Neasa watched her, kindness on her face.

"To tell you the truth? I really don't know. I have been so isolated for so long, my social skills are rusty, if not non-existent. Jeremy saw to that." Aubrey studied Neasa. "How do I do it, Neasa? How do I get back to some semblance of who I was?"

"You'll never be her again, Neasa, unfortunately. That was taken from you. But you can become your own person once more. We are praying for you. We have been hesitant to approach you, not sure of just how to, knowing what you have been through."

Aubrey nodded, her eyes on Barnabas as he stood near the stairs, his eyes on her. She knew that he was praying for her. She could feel the prayers. "I guess that I would just come up and talk to me. If I'm quiet, it's not that I'm upset or don't want to be friends. It's just that I don't know how to converse with anyone anymore. I had two years of strict isolation. Before that, eight years or so of semi-isolation. I never saw anyone but Jeremy, his son, and his security guards." Her voice died away. "I wonder how much the fellows have looked into the son."

"I'm sure that they are." Neasa looked up as Jaxcy and Imly approached. "Jaxcy. Imly. You two look like you're on a mission."

"We are. Cadee has an idea of what we can do for the shelter inhabitants for the holidays. It means shopping, though."

"It does? Aubrey, you up to doing some shopping?" Neasa looked over at her.

Aubrey shrugged. "Sure. Why not? When?"

"Tomorrow. We're all available and so are the twins. Darbie is insisting that he needs to go with us. That we need a man with us." Jaxcy laughed. "He thinks that we can't defend ourselves."

"Even with the fire hose trick we used on Dan and his henchman?" Neasa laughed, picturing the scene. "Aubrey, you should have seen it. My step-father had appeared, had taken Breck down, the men and Dallas surrounding them. They didn't dare move in as one of Dan's men had a gun held on Breck. We separated into two teams, used the fire hoses on them, and knocked them down. It was a sight."

"It was, and it was good for you, Neasa. You know that as well as the rest of us." Imly reached to hug Aubrey. "I'm glad you're here, Aubrey. Barnabas needs you. We have all felt that he needed that special lady, and we just didn't know who."

"You did? He didn't tell me that." Aubrey seemed surprised. "Even though I have brought danger with me?"

"Aubrey, we have all done that. Some of us more than others." Imly simply shook her head. "We have learned to enjoy life, no matter how hard. The love of our men keeps us going. They try to protect us. Sometimes too much."

"Ain't' that the truth." Jaxcy grinned. "So, all day tomorrow? Or is that too long?"

"Let's start with the morning and see how it goes?" Aubrey suddenly yawned. "I'm sorry. All of a sudden I am exhausted."

"As you should be. We'll meet in the morning. Wear comfortable shoes." Neasa reached to hug Aubrey. "Have a good night, Aubrey."

The three ladies walked away, stopping to speak with Barnabas, leaving him laughing at something they said. He approached Aubrey, crouching down beside her.

"Okay, sweetheart?"

"I am. I'm sorry that I ran. I just couldn't stay."

"We know that. Your emotions will be all over the place. We understand. Ours have been too. Just don't run from me. That's all I ask."

Aubrey's hand rested against his cheek. "I won't. I can't, not even if I tried."

Chapter 15

Late the next afternoon, Aubrey shut the apartment door behind her and then leaned back against it for a moment. She stared down at the bags in her hand. She hadn't planned on buying anything, but the thirteen ladies, the twins, and even Darbie had insisted on finding things for her. Finally putting a stop to it, she had laughed and then shaken her head, telling them that she would never wear all the clothes that they seemed to think she needed. She grew sad as she thought of how she had only had one pair of jeans, a couple of sweaters and some summer shirts for the last few years.

Toeing off her shoes and then setting them tidily into the clothes cupboard near the front door, Aubrey headed for the bedroom, dropping her packages, pulling off her jacket and then heading for the kitchen. She needed a cup of tea. Squinting at the clock, she sighed. Barnabas would be home soon, she thought, and she had nothing yet ready for supper. Some wife she was, she thought.

Hearing the entry door open and close and then his footsteps, Aubrey sighed again and closed her eyes. She just couldn't do it, she thought. She was not a cook. That much, she knew. Neasa had figured that out early that day and had promised to come to help her. Neasa had been a trained chef before she married Breck. She had refused to return to that line of work, telling Aubrey that she just could not do that but she was ready and willing to help a friend in need. Was Aubrey a friend in need, she had questioned, a huge smile on her face as she did so.

Barnabas watched from the doorway for a moment before he moved towards Aubrey, his arms coming out to draw her back against him. They stood like that for a moment, his head resting against her. Aubrey felt her tension relaxing and leaving as it always did when she was near her love.

"Have a good day, sweetheart? I checked here at noon and didn't find you."

"I did. The ladies are a great group. The twins and Darbie are a riot, you know."

Barnabas gave a soft laugh. "That they are, considering that they went through a lot with their sisters." He didn't speak for a moment. "Anything happen?"

"No." She thought a moment and then shook her head. "No, not that I can put a finger on. I know I was being watched, just couldn't see anyone."

"That's what he is doing. Watching. Hoping to spook you. Trying to rattle you." Barnabas kissed her cheek. "It's Friday, sweetheart. How be I take you out for dinner tonight?"

"Really? Like we used to do?" She twisted in his arms, her own going around him. "I dreamt of those days so much that I began to look at them as just that, dreams."

"You did? I missed them. Casual or dress?" He let her make that decision.

"You don't care?" She searched his face. "No, you don't. How about casual tonight? I don't have the energy to dress up."

"Then, let me change from my dress clothes and I will be right back." He leaned down to kiss her, not letting her go until she shoved at him, a smile on her face.

Barnabas reached for Aubrey's hand as they walked across the parking lot to a local family diner. It was a favourite of his. He had been at school with the daughter who now ran it for her parents and knew that they would enjoy whatever meal that they decided to get.

Eva looked through the door and then held it for Barnabas, reaching to hug him before she studied Aubrey.

"Barnabas? Who is this lovely lady that you are holding so tight to?" She grinned at Aubrey.

"This is my bride, Aubrey. This is Eva. Her parents had this restaurant when we were growing up. We used to congregate here after school and on weekends. They never chased us away, always interested in each one of us."

"Hi." Aubrey smiled shyly at Eva. "It's good to meet you. Barnabas used to talk about this diner. He always was going to bring me here."

"Then, I am glad he finally has. Your booth is waiting for you, Barnabas. I'll be back with your coffee and menus. Aubrey, what would you like for a beverage?"

"You don't happen to have an apple spice tea, do you?"

"We do. I'll bring that to you." Eva watched as Aubrey slid onto to bench seat, Barnabas sitting beside her.

Her mother stood watching. "Who's that with Barnabas?"

"His wife, Mom. He's married. Her name is Aubrey. Didn't he and Breck used to talk about a friend named Aubrey?"

"They did. Wonderful. He always had a certain tone in his voice when he talked about her. She's the reason that he's never looked at another lady."

"That would be it, Mom. Like all the building guys. They're one-lady fellows, and each has found their lady."

"Just as you found your fellow, Eva. God leads us to that one."

Barnabas shifted uncomfortably towards the end of the meal, his eyes searching the patrons in the diner. He frowned as he studied the younger man sitting near the front, in such a way as he could watch their booth.

"Aubrey? Jeremy's son? How old is he?"

"About our age. Why?"

"There's a man around our age watching us. I wonder if it's him."

Aubrey leaned against Barnabas just enough that she could see. "It's him. That's Jason. We can't even have a meal."

"We can and we will. We will continue to live our lives, sweetheart." Barnabas sent up a prayer for protection. "You're finished?"

"I am. How do we escape? Through the kitchen?" She smirked at his look.

"Good idea. I would like to introduce you to Eva's parents. I know that they're usually here on a Friday night." He stood, reaching for her had as she did and then leading her towards the kitchen. He could feel the eyes on his back.

Eva's husband, Jim, a patrol officer, took one look at Barnabas' face and reached for his keys.

"Stay put. I'll bring your truck around front. And who is it that you're concerned about?"

Aubrey shifted on the truck seat, looking through the back window before she faced front again. She was on edge, knowing that Jason had been in the diner. She was suddenly afraid for Barnabas but didn't know how to tell him that.

"It's okay, sweetheart. I'm scared too." Barnabas reached for her hand. "Jim will have a talk with him, find out why he's here."

"He will?" Aubrey turned to study Barnabas, as much as she could see him in the dim lighting.

"He's a patrol officer. We were in school together as well. He was a close friend. We're not as close as we had been. Time and circumstances and just life have changed that."

"That's sad, you know? I lost touch with all my school friends. Jeremy saw to that. I miss them." She wiped at a tear, angry with herself for that tear.

"Go ahead. Cry, sweetheart. Get mad. Yell at me. I'll find some rocks for you to kick." Barnabas gave a sad smile. "I can't imagine how your life was."

"I know. But God allowed it, didn't He? And I must accept that and then move on. I just don't want you hurt or any of the others hurt."

"It's a risk we take every day, sweetheart. We could get hurt in so many ways." He pulled into his parking spot at the building and shut off the truck before he turned to her, reaching for her hands. "Let's pray, sweetheart. I feel the urge to bathe us in God's protection for the next few days."

"This is real, isn't it?" Aubrey bit at her lip. "I'm scared, love. I am so scared."

"And I am too. But we know that God will protect us. He will allow things to happen. That's part of life. We're not wrapped in cotton wool and put on a shelf. He expects us to continue going about our daily walk, trusting in Him."

"I know that, love. I know that in my heart. It's my head that I'm having trouble convincing of that." She blinked, a thought coming to her. "I don't get why Jason would be here, though. It should have been Jeremy."

"Jim said he saw an older man hanging around a vehicle near ours. He disappeared before Jim could approach him."

"That was likely Jeremy then. They're in town. Now what?"

"Now what? We continue. Buckley has asked if he and Locklin could have us for dinner tomorrow night. That came up late this afternoon. It's up to you."

"We need to, love. We can't continue to hide. Not at all." Aubrey drew a deep breath. "I'm going to be bold and you know that is not me. We need to go out and about. Go on the offensive, isn't that what they say?"

"It is. I'm just not sure if this is the right time."

"Barnabas!" Aubrey's voice held a note of shock. "I have lost ten years or so to him. I can't do this anymore."

"I know, sweetheart. How I know that! We need to make some plans. Dallas said he'd be around tomorrow, just as a friend, not an officer. Why don't we talk to him?"

"We can. Do you know anyone in security that you can talk with?"

"I do. A good friend. In fact, why don't I put Dallas off until Sunday? We can take off early in the morning and go see my friend. It's not that long a drive."

"We could do that?" Aubrey was still amazed at the freedom to live that she had once more.

"We can. If we leave early enough, we can stop at the Irish bakeshop for breakfast."

"Oh! I like that." She was out of the truck and running for the building before Barnabas could respond.

"Hey! Wait!" He ran after her, the locks on the truck clicking closed behind him.

She spun and then ran back towards him, feeling his arms hugging her tight. "I love you, Barnabas. Thank you." She reached up for his kiss.

Her hand tight in Barnabas, Aubrey looked around the town of Riverville the next morning, surprise and then joy on her face. *This is what I needed, Lord. To get away and do something for fun. Thank you.*

Barnabas held the door to a bake shop open for her and they entered, Aubrey's eyes closing as she drew in a deep breath. The aroma of fresh baking and spices filled her senses. Her eyes popped open as she heard someone stop in front of them.

Dave Allison stood there, a grin on his face, even as he reached to shake Barnabas' hand.

"Barnabas! It's been a while. Good to see you! And who is this?" Dave's attention transferred to Aubrey.

"My bride, Dave. This is Aubrey. Aubrey, this is Dave, a friend. His wife runs this cafe with her grandmother and Dave's sister. Is Rylee around?"

"No, she's not in right yet. But what can I get you?"

"Whatever you want. I promised Aubrey breakfast here." Barnabas sat Aubrey at one of the tables and then approached the counter. "Dave? Is Abe around today?"

"He should be." Dave peered at the door. "In fact, there is Abe and Murphy."

Barnabas turned, then moved towards the two men who had just entered.

"Abe! Just the man I was looking for."

Abe Finlay looked around in surprise. "Barnabas Carey! You're in my town. That's a switch."

Murphy O'Brien reached to shake the other man's hand, a frown on his face. "You're looking ragged somewhat, Barnabas. Don't tell. You're in the middle of an adventure." He grinned.

Barnabas nodded even as he smiled. "I am. I ran away today with my bride, Aubrey. We're needing to pick your brains. I was hoping and praying that you'd be around."

Abe looked around, finding Aubrey watching them intently. "This is your bride?"

Barnabas reached out a hand to draw Aubrey to him. "This is Aubrey. It's a long story, but if you have time today, we'll run it by you and then see what suggestions that you can offer us."

"Aubrey, welcome to our town. It's good to finally meet the lady of this man's heart. Listen, how be we get what we came for? You bring your breakfast and then we'll head for Emma's business. She'll be anxious to meet you. She's been putting in some extra hours, not willingly, I might add, but necessary."

Aubrey stared around the reception area of the business Abe led them into, hearing his voice speaking with a lady in the back. She stopped in front of an enlarged picture of an eagle couple, drawing in her breath. Murphy had been watching her and approached.

"Emma took that picture. She had been watching these eagles for years. She and Abe had been separated and kept apart for years. She told Jace, who works for her, that if she ever got that photo, then she knew what was unresolved in her life would be resolved. That was finding Abe once more."

"It's sad that they were kept apart. It's like Barnabas and me. I was kept imprisoned by someone who said that he was my guardian. Two years ago, he locked me into one room, cutting off all contact with Barnabas and everyone else. He's tracked me down to town. His son was in the diner we had dinner in last night. I need to know how to stay safe while trapping him. Is that too much to ask?"

"Not at all. Abe and I have a security team. His father started it. Abe took it over and then asked me to come into partnership with him. We have six other men on the team. Each of us has our specialties. We can meet and then come up with some ideas for you two. And if I know Emma, she'll want in on the search."

"She will? I'm sorry. I'm not sure that I understand." She looked past Murphy as Abe and a beautiful russet-haired lady approached.

"Aubrey, this is my wife, Emma. She's the one who has been helping out on the adventures your fellows have been on. At least some of them."

Emma simply hugged Aubrey and then drew her back to her office, seating her and then perching on the edge of the desk.

"Talk to me, Aubrey. I understand from Abe that you were imprisoned for a number of years. And that the man's son was watching you last night."

"I was. And Jason was." Aubrey explained it all to Emma, ending with a sigh. "What do I do, Emma? How do I stay safe, keep Barnabas safe, and not harm anyone else in the building?"

"That's a tough one. Abe will work with his team, come up with a plan, and then we'll come to see you. He'll need a day or so. Do you work?"

"No. I don't. I wish I could but it's not possible right now." Aubrey sighed, her eyes closing for a moment. "I had such dreams when I was at school. I took business courses, took courses in early childhood education. I wasn't sure quite what I had planned, but I wanted to work with children. Now, I'm not sure. Not seeing anyone for ten years other than just a few? That changes your perspective. A whole lot. I had time to read, what little he allowed me. I hid my Bible. He wanted it. Said it was full of lies and that I wasn't to read it. I memorized a lot too, just in case. I wasn't allowed a computer. A television. I had a phone but only limited access to it. There was an email that I refused to let him access."

"And you didn't ask for help?" Emma moved to sit beside her, hugging her.

Aubrey stared through blurred vision at the tears slashing off her hands. "I couldn't." Her voice was barely audible. "I couldn't. He had threatened to kill anyone who came to help me. I didn't want to be responsible for that."

"And that is part of how he kept control of you." Emma looked up as Barnabas appeared, on his knees beside Aubrey, wrapping her in his arms, and listened as he prayed for her.

"Barnabas? Do you have to head back today?" Abe spoke from the doorway.

"We do. Dallas is heading out late this afternoon to meet with us." Barnabas looked around.

"Then, we'll get what information that we can from you two. Murphy? Ready, I see." Abe grinned as a pen and pad of paper was shoved at him.

"Let's move to the reception area." Murphy stepped back that way. "I have beverages out here. Aubrey? Emma has some of that apple spice tea that I am told you like."

Stretching out on the couch once they were home, Aubrey tucked one hand under the pillow her head was on, the other under her cheek. She smiled as she thought back over the day. Barnabas was still the fun man that she remembered, liking to tease and torment as her mother would have said, but with a steadiness and seriousness to him that she appreciated. It had always been there but was more enhanced now, she thought, reflective of what he did for a living and also what he had been through with his friends. A smile was still on her face as she drifted off to sleep, to sleep without dreams for once.

Barnabas pocketed his phone and turned from where he had stood, looking out the French doors in his home office. He sighed. He hadn't wanted to take that call but had no choice. John, one of the Foundation lawyers, had needed to speak with him. He had listened as well as Barnabas had brought him up to date on what they knew. John's wisdom of the years came through in the words and advice and the prayer that he offered.

Walking back through the apartment, he found it quiet, but not the silence that he had grown accustomed to over the years. He heard the soft instrumental music that Aubrey had turned on and smiled. He usually liked no music but knew that she needed this. He would not say no to her, not on something this minor, he thought. Barnabas stood for a moment, his eyes on his bride, before he moved forward on silent socked feet, to reach for the green, yellow and cream plaid velour blanket that she had found and bought for the living room. He covered her gently before dropping a kiss on her cheek, bringing a soft smile to her face.

Hearing a tap at the door, he headed that way, standing back as both Dallas and Breck entered. He frowned. It was only to be Dallas.

"Breck? You're here? Where's Neasa?"

"On her way. She knew that you two had been away today. She had been looking for Aubrey. She decided to make your supper, hoping that you hadn't eaten."

"We haven't. We've only been home for about thirty minutes or so. Coffee's on. I'll go wake Aubrey."

Dallas shook his head. "No, let her sleep. I can only imagine what poor sleep she has had over the years."

"That she has had. She's starting to talk more about what it was like. Middle of the night in the darkness talks. He was brutal with his words, Dallas. I don't know how she managed."

"God." Breck looked around before he set the mugs of coffee that he had filled on the table and pulled out a chair to sit. "Neasa hasn't said much but she did say that Aubrey told her that she spent a lot of time in prayer and memorization, just in case she lost her Bible."

"And he would have done that, wouldn't he?" Barnabas sent up a prayer for his bride, asking for healing and restoration for her. He looked at Dallas. "Dallas?"

"Barnabas?" Dallas grinned as he mimicked Barnabas. "I am here today as a friend. Nothing more. I have left the work and the case at the office, as they say. You need friends to come around you."

"I know I do, but I have one question. Jason?"

"Jason. Now that's an interesting man. He was arrested early today. Break and enter into the shelter. Cadee's father found him in the office and held onto him until the patrol officer arrived. He's not saying anything, but he had drugs, stolen jewelry, break and enter tools on his person. He's not able to make bail. No one is responding to his phone call."

"That is interesting." Barnabas looked around as he heard a tap on the door and then Neasa appeared, a basket in her hand. He rose and took it from her. "Supper, Neasa?"

"It is. If we put the oven on low, it will stay hot. I also have fixings for a tossed salad. Aubrey has expressed her desire to eat more of those."

"She has. Thank you." He hugged her before setting the casserole in the oven. "Tell me, Neasa. Has Aubrey said much?" He held up a hand. "I don't want you to break confidence with her. I just want to know that she is talking with someone, getting a female point of view."

"She is starting to, Barnabas. I have suggested that we contact Darcie and see what Darcie can offer."

"That's a good idea." Barnabas looked towards the doorway and then walked that way, finding Aubrey standing in the hallway, a confused look on her face. "Sweetheart?"

"Barnabas? Where is he? He's here, isn't he?" Aubrey spun in a circle before Barnabas swept her into his arms.

"No, he's not. Just Breck, Neasa, and Dallas. All here as friends." He frowned. "Did you hear him?"

"I thought I did. How would that be possible? I could hear him as plain as if he was standing right here."

Dallas had approached, a grim look on his face. "Let me search your apartment, Barnabas. Breck? Can we move the ladies and our meal to your place?"

"Absolutely." He was on his feet, helping Neasa gather the meal back up, turning off the oven, reaching for Aubrey's hand. "Here, Aubrey. Come with us." He nodded at Dallas as he swept the ladies out of the room.

Dallas grew even grimmer as he searched, finally turning to Barnabas.

"I need you out of here, friend. I have to bring in a team."

"He's been in here?"

"Someone has. Aubrey wasn't hearing things. If it had been different, then that would have been used against her. Knowing you and being here when she said it? That helps. I could search right away, without someone coming back in to remove what they had placed. I also asked for a locksmith to come out. Your locks are changed today."

Barnabas paled. "Okay. Whatever needs to be done. How do I tell her?"

———

"I'll be up as soon as the team gets here. I'll talk to you there. For now, you're just another one in danger, Barnabas. This time? You need to step back and let the rest of us work."

"I know. It's hard to do that."

"It is. Go on. Find Aubrey. I am praying for you both."

Staring at Barnabas in horror, Aubrey felt his hands tighten on her shoulders. She knew Neasa and Breck were behind her, watching them closely. Her eyes closed as tears started, trickling down her face as she was unable to stop them. Barnabas gave an inaudible sound and simply swept her into his arms, holding her as tight as he could, his face pressed to her hair.

"He was in our apartment?" Her voice was low.

"He was, sweetheart. Or someone else was, setting up what Dallas found." He prayed for them, feeling her relax against him as he did so. Lord, I could use some help. We need to live our lives, but he keeps interfering in them. How do we do this, Lord? How do I keep the love of my life safe?

"What do we do, love?" Aubrey leaned back to look up at him. "What do we do? Do we stay there or move?"

"We can do that, even on a temporary basis. The apartment right next door is available. It might be best. That way, we're not on the main floor. Until this is solved." Barnabas looked up at a sound from Breck. "Breck?"

"You took the words out of my mouth, Barnabas. I was going to suggest that very thing. Dallas has the team in, you said?"

"He does. He didn't say how long they would be." Barnabas turned Aubrey around. "Aubrey, this has to be our decision, not mine. Not Dallas'. Not Breck's. It involves both of us."

Aubrey nodded, a sober look on her face. "I get that, Barnabas. Can we eat and then have a time of prayer? We need that, I think. Neasa has gone to all that work of preparing a meal." She moved away from him, towards the kitchen, Neasa following after stopping to hug Barnabas.

Breck motioned Barnabas back to his home office.

"What aren't you saying?"

Barnabas shrugged. "I really don't know. It's so puzzling. Dallas was heading to talk with the security team here." He blew out a breath, scrubbing at his face. "I wish I could just take her away until it was all over."

"And you can't. You mentioned that you had seen Abe?"

"I did. He had some ideas that I need to discuss with you and the other fellows. Can we set up a time on Monday, if we can do that? We need to keep Sunday as normal as possible, for all of us."

"It's already done. Buckley asked that we meet. Said he felt so burdened for you two, a that he wants to pull everyone in and work on this." Breck paused, his eyes studying his lifelong friend. "Barnabas? You have been there for each one of us. We have been friends pretty much all of our lives. We have had differences, but I don't remember us never being able to work through them or pray through them. This time? You're the one in need, the one who needs to be protected. Let us help you."

"It's humbling to have to say yes, but it is what it is, isn't it?" Barnabas sank down onto the couch, his head in his hands for a moment. "What can I say but thank you?"

"Nothing. It's what friends do. Let me pray with you right now." Breck prayed for Barnabas and Aubrey, Barnabas finding comfort in his prayer.

Mom is right. He has a powerful way of praying, of bringing a person right before God. We need to learn that. Not many of us do.

Neasa hesitated a moment, waiting until the men had lifted their heads before calling them to come and eat. Barnabas moved ahead of her to find Aubrey, while Neasa walked into Breck's hug, stifling a sob as she did so.

"Darling? What happened?"

Neasa shrugged. "It's so sad, Breck, what she was put through. How she had to live. She has a good attitude but I wonder what she was like before this."

"She was a lot of fun. A spitfire, Barnabas used to say. I see pieces of that, but this has changed her. It had to have. We'll pray for her, darling, and him. Let's eat. I know that we need to do that, even though not one of us feels much like it."

———

The meal was quiet, no one feeling much like talking. Barnabas looked around, sighed, and then began to speak, to talk about what Abe had told him.

Breck nodded. "He has more, doesn't he?"

Barnabas nodded. "He does. This is just what he and Murphy came up with. He'll speak to the others, talk to Doug and Caleb, he said. He threatened to send Eddy and Ben or even Frankie our way."

"Any one of those would be a help. The last three? They were or still are officers."

"That they are. I wouldn't mind talking to Eddie or Ben. Abe said to call them if I felt that I needed to."

"Probably a good idea." Breck rose as he heard a tap at the door and then stood back to let Dallas in. "Dallas? Sit. Have your dinner. Then we talk."

Dallas nodded, accepting with thanks the plate Neasa handed him. "I need this. It's been a long week. Neasa, your casseroles are always so delicious." He looked over at Barnabas and then Aubrey. "Let me eat. Then, we talk. And talk we will."

Dallas finally shoved his plate away, a word of thanks as Breck rose to remove it, then sat back down. He eyed the other four at the table, his gaze stopping on Aubrey. *She's calm, Lord, and I don't know how she can be. Not after what she heard. And we heard what she heard. He's a brute, Lord, and we need to stop him before he hurts either one of these two. And, dear Lord, I don't know that we can. He's so elusive.*

"Dallas? What did you find?" Barnabas had an arm around Aubrey, feeling her leaning against him.

"Not what we wanted to. That's for certain. But what we expected." He looked at Aubrey. "I apologize. I should have swept the apartment but didn't think that there was a need, given the upped security. We are still determining how whoever it was got in. We have a suspicion on how. What did we find? Microphones. Some listening devices. A recorded message that was triggered at certain times of the day or night. How long have you felt that you were hearing something?"

"Just today. I haven't heard anything before tonight." She looked up at Barnabas. "I would have told you if I had."

"I know, sweetheart. Does that mean that they were in there today? They knew that we were away."

"I suspect that they had someone following you and when they found out that you would be away for a while, moved in and set up their devices. We are confident that we have found all of them." Dallas stared down at the papers in front of him. "Barnabas. Aubrey. I can't begin to tell you how dangerous this has just gotten for both of you. They will be watching for each of you, either alone or together. Aubrey, I know that you like to walk around the gardens, and then around the building. All I can ask is that you have one of the security guards with you if Barnabas isn't. They're trained for this."

Aubrey shrugged. "I guess. It's not like when I was imprisoned, is it? At least, I have a choice as to what I do or don't do."

"That you do. Barnabas, now you. You move around a lot some days. Other days you are here. How much can you do with a conference or video calls?"

"Probably most of it. There are times when I do need to meet, to sign documents, etc. The board would come here. They have already said that. John said that he and the other lawyers would do the same. For now, some of what I do I can shift to Breck. He's offered to take up that."

"Good. Now, what did Abe have to say?"

"About what you said. He's meeting with his team and will send further advice. Emma has taken up the hunt, and I am sure that she'll soon be sending information and documents to you."

Dallas grinned. "She already is. Interesting fellow, this Jeremy. Aubrey, when I can sort through what she has sent, I want to meet with you and Barnabas. And I spoke with John earlier about what he has. He is sure that Jeremy will try to have you committed under a mental health assessment. John's already working on that. Darcie Foster will be in touch with you either tomorrow or Monday. Talk with her. She's a resource that is used, not as much as we would like to, but she is very picky about how much she does that now. And it is usually just for friends or their family."

"She does?" Aubrey was hesitant to agree. "But why would she want to speak with me? Who is she?"

"She has an arts and crafts store and sells it online as well. She is well respected among artisans in her area. But she was a forensics psychologist who was treated poorly by the law officer she was employed by and withdrew from the force. She has kept up her credentials, which is good. We have used her with a couple of the ladies here. Neasa was one."

Aubrey's attention turned to Neasa, to find her nodding.

"She did. She provided expert witness documentation as well as a profile on who was after me. She nailed him. Darcie will work with you, Aubrey. She will not come across in a threatening manner. I found her very calming, in fact."

Breck nodded. "She is that and more, Aubrey. She and her husband, Doug, had a horrible experience with someone on the force targeting different towns and emergency personnel. He almost killed her."

Aubrey's eyes had been steady on Breck. "So, she knows what it is like? Then, I do want to speak to her. Her experience is of course different from mine, but I feel that I need to talk with someone, someone with training, and someone who can understand."

"We'll make sure that happens, sweetheart." Barnabas tightened his arm on her. "For now, let's set all this aside. We need to spend hours in prayer. We don't have that tonight, but we can spend time with our friends, finding the peace and wisdom that we need to go forward."

Late that night, Aubrey stood in Barnabas' office, looking around, feeling very uncomfortable. He watched her before he approached her.

"You okay?"

"No. No, I'm not. I hate that someone was in here." She looked up at him as she stood in the circle of his arms. "I can't sleep, Barnabas. I can't even think about living here right now. But that's not fair to you."

"No, it's not fair to you. This is your home, one that someone has walked into. Let me pack up some stuff for us. We can move up to the one beside Breck. It's all ready for that."

"Do you think we should?"

"I do." He hugged her tight. "If that brings peace to you, then we do. We take what we need for tonight and tomorrow morning. Then, we come back down, take up what we need for the week and go from there."

"Okay. I'm sorry."

"There's nothing that you need to apologize for. You didn't invite them in, now did you? They made the decision to invade our home. We will step back from it, assess how we feel after a few days. If it means that we move to another one, then we do. We do what is best for you and what is best for us as a couple."

Aubrey stood on her tiptoes, reaching to kiss him. "Thank you, Barnabas. You are not downplaying my concerns or belittling me. I can't tell you how many times Jeremy did that."

"No, I won't. I may have to act suddenly if you are in danger, but if I can discuss it with you, then I will. Come on, sweetheart. Let's grab some of our things and head on upstairs."

Aubrey settled down to sleep, not knowing that Barnabas had settled down in the living room, his Bible open on his knee, but his heart raised in prayer. This was the dangerous time, he thought, with their enemy hitting in spurts. They never knew when he would. It would be wearing on them as individuals but also as a couple. Lord, we need to be connected and together. We are just young in our marriage and already facing what many couples never do. My friends here know what it is like to some extent. But, Lord, we need to rely on You. Teach us how to do that. Please, dear Lord, protect my Aubrey? Keep her from harm. And keep me from harm, dear Lord, so that I can protect her.

Aubrey rose in the night, looking for Barnabas, pausing in the living room doorway, a smile on her face. Barnabas had fallen asleep on the couch, his head resting on the back of it. She simply moved to snuggle up against him, setting his Bible to a table and spreading the blanket that she had wrapped herself in over them. She slept as well, not realizing the danger that would start hitting at them that week, harder and harder, and putting both their lives in danger.

Barnabas rose the next morning, stretching, a frown on his face before he shook his head. Fell asleep on the couch and Aubrey came to find him. He smiled as he watched her sleep before he headed for a shower and shave and then to the kitchen to make his coffee.

Another Sunday, Lord. Another week. And this week? I am not eager to start it at all. I fear for what is coming. I have this sense of doom and gloom, as Mom would say, hanging over us. Please, Lord? Go before us. Protect us. If we are hurt, heal us. That's all that I can ask, isn't it? Except to say thank you. Dear Lord, You are right here and I need to remember that.

A few hours later, Barnabas stood at the back of the church, watching Aubrey as she was surrounded by the ladies of the building, Hagen's young son in her arms. He had taken one look at her and launched himself into her arms, hugging her tightly and then covering her face with sloppy kisses. He refused to return to his mother, his head tucked under Aubrey's chin, thumb in his mouth as he grinned at his mother. Aubrey just stood and rocked slightly, a hand rubbing at his back.

Breck stood beside him, eyes watchful, knowing that the other men in the building were doing the same, on the lookout for someone out of character.

"Did you decide what you are doing?"

"About the apartment? For now, we'll move out for a week. Aubrey's not happy with that. She hates being chased from her home."

"And I can understand that. After not having a home for all those years? Being caged like she was? I can almost guarantee you that she'll change her mind and refuse to leave the apartment. I spoke with security this morning. They're working on upping what they need to on your apartment. They have asked that you not use the French doors in the living room or the office for now."

Barnabas nodded, having already reached that conclusion. He had been watching Aubrey closely that morning.

"I agree. I suspect that we won't be moving. We can agree to not use the doors. That's not an issue. How strong a lock are they putting on them?"

"Not so much a lock as stronger sensors. That way, if you or she needs to escape through either one, you can." Breck reached for Neasa's hand. "Call me, Barnabas. We need to talk about relieving some of your duties. You're stretching yourself thin and have been for a while. Your Dad knows that. I would not be surprised to hear that he is talking with the other board members."

"He is. He already spoke to me. He wants to shift some things to you, more of the acquisitions line. That's what you already do. And some of the investigations into new missionaries." Barnabas paused. "He did say that they were setting up a new position and had already spoken with someone. Dallas would be good to come on board, but I am not sure that he's ready to leave this force."

"He's ready." Neasa spoke up. "He's more than ready, Barnabas. He did say that he was looking into something, but hasn't said much more."

"He did? Now we know how to pray for him better." Barnabas tucked Aubrey under his arm as she approached him. "Where's Heath?"

She laughed. "His father finally claimed him. Hannah wasn't happy that she couldn't come to me. I need to go visit them tomorrow." Her face was aglow from the love the little ones had shown her.

"Sounds like a plan. Come one, sweetheart. Mom and Dad would like us to come for dinner if you want."

"I want. Your mother is such a special lady. She did well raising her son."

"She did, did she?" Barnabas shot a look around before he kissed her. "Then, let's go find them. And we do need to discuss where we're living. I don't think you want to move."

"No. I don't." Aubrey shook her head. "He would win again if we leave. Breck said that we can't use the French doors, at security request. I can live with that. Can you?"

"I can. I talked to him too. Let's go, sweetheart." He tucked her into his truck and stood, looking around. Someone is out there, aren't they, Lord? Protect my lady, that's all I ask.

The next day, Aubrey packed up what they had taken to the other apartment, ready to move back downstairs. She wandered the apartment, tidying it, cleaning as needed even though she had been told the cleaners would be through to do that. She was making work, she knew, feeling impending doom handing over her like a storm-darkened rain cloud.

Sighing, Aubrey picked up the bag that she had set by the front door and moved out of it, locking it behind her. She walked down the flight of stairs, heading for the second flight before her footsteps slowed. Fear coursed through her.

"Jason? How did you get in here? This is a private building."

Jason sneered at her. "That's what you think. There are ways to get in." He walked towards her even as she backed away from him. "You're coming with me. You don't have a choice."

"I don't think so." Aubrey felt for the stair railing, hoping that she could make it down the stairs and to the security guard before Jason could reach her. "This is my home."

Jason sneered as he laughed, a cruel, menacing laugh. "Nope. You're coming with me. We're leaving this town. Dad promised that you would be mine."

"He did?" Aubrey's brow grew dark. "Sorry. Not happening." She threw the bag that she was carrying towards him and turn, almost falling, as she took the steps at a run, her breath catching in a sob.

Jason dodged the bag and sprang after her, catching an arm and pulling her with him as he tried to descend the steps. Aubrey's hand clung to the railing even as she struggled to free her other one, the one that he was twisted viciously in his determination to move her down the stairs and away from help.

Her hand slipped from the railing and Aubrey flew forward, her body slamming into Jason as he pulled her towards them. This sent the pair off balance and they tumbled down the stairs, Aubrey's scream ringing through the lobby. They lay in a crumpled heap until Jason staggered to his feet, disoriented. He looked around and then grabbed Aubrey's wrist, dragging her unconscious body across the dark hardwood floor of the lobby, muttering to himself that she was his and no one else.

Branigan and Bradon had heard Aubrey's scream, took a look at one another and then were flying from the conference room, Bradon's dog, Kade, forging ahead. He shot a look back at his master who ordered him to take down the man. A threatening growl erupted from Kade's throat and his toes dug into the floor as he surged ahead, his jaws clamping down firmly on Jason's arm. The force of the dog's body hitting him took Jason to the floor, even as Bradon ordered Kade to release and stand guard. Kade stood back, a growl coming from him even as Jason tried to crawl away, Kade circling around him to keep him from doing just that.

Branigan and Bradon were on their knees beside Aubrey, feeling for a pulse, their faces holding shock before they darkened with anger. Bradon's phone was out as he called for help.

"Where's Paul? I thought that he was on duty." Branigan looked around before he was on his feet, heading for the security desk. "He's here. He's out cold." Branigan stood back up, before he walked towards Jason, his booted feet preventing the man from crawling forward. "What did you do to them?"

"She's mine. I'm taking her with me." Jason lay still, even as the sirens sounded and red and blue emergency lights flashed in the parking lot.

Branigan didn't move, even when the patrol officers poured into the lobby. He heard a sound and turned.

"Brady? Good. I was praying it would be you."

"What happened, Branigan?"

"We don't know. We found them like this. He was dragging Aubrey towards the door. She has not moved."

"Okay. Patrick?" Brady turned to his partner who was already on his knees beside Aubrey.

"Backboard, I think, Brady. And collar. I wonder if she fell down the stairs." Patrick shot a look towards them.

"That's possible. Barnabas mentioned this morning when I saw him that they were coming back down to the first floor."

Bradon stood near them, his hand on Kade's head. "More than likely, Brady. There's a bag of Barnabas' on the floor at the foot there."

The two paramedics worked quickly, assessing Aubrey before shifting her to the backboard, neck collar in place. They moved through the lobby, heading for the paramedic rig, whoever lived in the building and were there, standing watching, horror, concern, and then anger showing on their faces. Buckley and Locklin headed for their vehicle, intent on being there for Barnabas. Locklin's phone was out before she paused.

"Where is Barnabas today?"

"Andy flew him up north for some meetings. He said he'd be back late this afternoon." Buckley sighed. "Call Bruce. See if he and Elizabeth can come. I didn't see them there."

"No, they weren't. I hate this, Buckley. I just pray that she's not hurt too badly."

"As am I." Buckley parked at the hospital and then was out of the truck, reaching for Locklin's hand as they ran for the Emergency Department.

Doc looked around as he heard Brady's voice before he moved towards him, a frown on his face.

"Brady?"

"It's Aubrey, Doc. We think that she took a tumble down the stairs at the building, but we're not sure. She hasn't been awake since we got there."

Doc shot him a look before pointing to an empty room. "For once, I have a room that I can put her in. They've been hard to come by today." His stethoscope was in his hands as he listened to Brady's report. "Okay. Barnabas?"

"Not there. I'm not sure where he is today." Brady had helped to shift Aubrey to the stretcher in the examining room. "I'm off, Doc. I'll be back." He took a look at Aubrey before he shook his head, finding Patrick waiting outside for him.

"Brady? What happened?"

"I have no idea. Branigan said that Barnabas had told him that they were moving back down to his own apartment after it was searched. This is frustrating, Patrick. We don't know who or why."

"And I'll talk to our supervisor. You'll be pulled back in to help." Patrick slammed the back door of the rig before he stood, his fingers rubbing together. "Barnabas?"

"Not sure. Buckley was following us, so he'll track him down. I imagine that he'll have already called Bruce and Elizabeth."

"I'm sure. Let's hit the road, pal. It's going to be a long day."

Andy, the Foundation pilot, watched as Barnabas ran towards him, his briefcase swinging beside him. He followed Barnabas up the stairs to the plane, pulling them in and locking it.

"All set?"

"I am, Andy. It's been a long day. Thanks for sticking around."

Andy grinned. "It's not like I was going anywhere. But you are welcome. Buckle up and we'll be home in an hour or two."

His briefcase tucked away, Barnabas sat back into his seat, his head on the headrest, his eyes closing as fatigue weighed them down. He was tired, he thought, but today had been necessary. He would be back in time to meet with the men, finding out what all they had discovered, and he was sure that they had discovered facts and people. Aubrey needed to be there, he thought. He slept, weary from the last six weeks or so.

Andy landed the plane, did his post-flight check, and then stood, watching as Breck walked towards him, Neasa standing by Breck's truck.

"Breck? You're here?"

"I am. Barnabas?"

"He was still asleep. I was heading up to wake him. Something's wrong?"

"There is. Barnabas, you're on your feet." Breck looked towards his friend as he descended the stairs.

"I am. But you're here." Barnabas frowned.

"I am. I need you to come with me. We'll get your truck later." Breck's hand on his arm stopped Barnabas in his tracks.

Barnabas stared at his friend. "Aubrey? Is she okay?"

"No, she's not." Breck's hand tightened on the arm. "She was hurt this morning, Barnabas. She's in hospital. Your parents are with her."

"How?" When Breck didn't respond, Barnabas spoke again. "How? Tell me, Breck, how was she hurt."

"Jason made his way into the building. He took down Paul. And then searched for Aubrey. We think that he found her and that she was trying to escape him. We found one of your duffle bags on the main floor. What we think happened is that she fell down the stairs to the lobby." Breck paused, unable to continue for a moment. "Bradon and Branigan heard her scream and ran for there. They found Jason dragging her body across the floor, intent on taking her with him. Kade took him down."

"How bad?"

"I don't know. Doc was on duty. Brady and Patrick were the paramedics who responded. Come on, my friend. Into my truck. We'll get you to your lady."

Barnabas paced the Emergency Department waiting room, a short time later, dodging the people moving around, the little children who were tired and cranky and just wanted to go home, the security guards who walked among them. He knew his friends were there. He had greeted each one of the men, being told that the ladies had gathered in the chapel. Bruce had stood waiting for him, just enveloping his son into his arms, feeling the shudders of fear running through his son's body.

"Dad?"

"No word, yet, son. We've been back. Apparently, we're listed after you are." He turned his son to the door, an arm across his shoulders. "In we go. Mom is here. She refused to go with the ladies, said that she had to be here for you."

Elizabeth held her son, feeling the sobs that he refused to release shaking him. She prayed for her son, a man grown and married, but still needing his mother at a time like this. She finally drew him to a chair.

"Mom?"

"I was back just now, son. She's still unconscious. Doc said that they were waiting on some imaging results before he would know more. Breck called us as the plane landed and we got word to Doc."

Doc looked around from where he sat at a computer, his reading glasses on his nose, as a nurse approached.

"Barnabas is here."

"He is? Thanks, Stacy. Now, the results are back?"

"We have everything, Doc. The imaging, blood work, anything that you asked for." Stacy paused. "Do you want me to find him?"

Doc stood, a sigh coming from him. It had been a hectic, overly busy day. Having Aubrey arrive as she did had not eased a burden from him.

"No. I'll go find him. Thanks. There's a room available on the medical floor?"

"There is. A private room came up. We'll move her upstairs now if you want."

"Please. I'll find him and bring him upstairs." Doc stopped in his tracks, a prayer raising for both Barnabas and Aubrey. She's a fortunate lady, isn't she, Lord? It could have been so much worse, but she's not out of the woods, not by a long shot. Heal her, please, dear Lord?

Doc paused once more outside the doors to the Emergency Department rooms, his eyes on Barnabas as he paced, Breck at his side. Those two young men? They have been friends for so long. Together in trouble, what little they got into, together in fun, standing shoulder to shoulder with one another. Barnabas was there for Breck with Neasa and now Breck was there for Barnabas. Their friendship is changing and evolving, like it will as they live life, Doc thought.

Barnabas turned towards Doc and then moved to him, his parents at his side, Breck stepping back and reaching for Neasa's hand as he watched. Breck prayed for his friend, not sure how to pray.

"Doc? Aubrey?" Barnabas had trouble even speaking, his fear that great.

"We're moving her upstairs right now to a bed on the medical floor. Come on. I just finished my shift and am heading that way, to sign her off to the physician there. Bruce, Elizabeth?"

"We're coming, whether you allow it or not, Doc." Elizabeth's arm was around her son. "We're not deserting these two."

"Didn't think you would." Doc remained quiet until he stood outside the room where Aubrey lay. "Let me talk with her new physician and then I'll be right back."

Doc was as good as his word, back in no time to beckon the three to the waiting room, finding it empty.

"Sit. Barnabas? I'll let you go in but first, we need to talk."

Barnabas sat as requested, his parents on either side of him, Bruce's arm around his shoulders, his mother's hands on his.

"Doc? What aren't you saying?"

Doc nodded. Right to the point, as always.

"I can't tell you what happened. That's not my place. Besides, I don't have that information. The patrol officer who came in with her was heading out to speak with Dallas. Dallas has been by and will be by later, he said." Doc hesitated for a moment, bringing fear to Barnabas' face. "As to her injuries? She has a concussion. Multiple bruising and bumps. It is the spine that we have been concerned about."

"Her spine? Please, Lord, not that!" Barnabas buried his face into his hands.

"Right now, son, there is some swelling around the lower spine. There doesn't appear to be any injury, but she has limited response and movement in her lower extremities. We need to keep her here and still until the swelling can go down. How long that will take, I don't know."

"Will she walk?" Barnabas searched his friend's face.

"I don't see why not, but she will need to take care. No stairs at all. If she has to be in a wheelchair for the first while, that is what will be recommended."

"We're on the first floor, so that works. And we have the elevator." Barnabas' mind had started to race. "Special bed or anything like that?"

"Not yet. We'll see how she does. I expect her to be here for at least a week. Dallas has said that he is arranged for security to take over here from his officer and they will be here all day and all night as long as she is here."

"Did he say who? Do I know them?"

Doc grinned before he sobered. "Oh, I think you do. It's Abe and his men. And he has indicated that if he needs to, he has friends who will gladly step in and take over."

"Oh, that's good. Dad, apartments?"

"Done already, son. Dallas approached me not long before you came in." Bruce's arm tightened around his son's shoulders. "Let us pray with you, son, and then Doc will take you to your lady."

Barnabas finally stood in the doorway to the room where his bride lay, sorrow in his heart that she had been hurt and that he had not been there to protect her. He walked forward on quiet feet, a prayer rising, before he stood, his eyes on the medical equipment surrounding her. He studied that and then dropped his vision to Aubrey.

"Oh, Aubrey! Sweetheart! I'm so sorry. So, so sorry. I didn't want you hurt and he came after you when I wasn't there to protect you. Please? Forgive me." He laid a gentle hand against her face, finding her skin cold and damp, before he reached for a hand, holding it, finding her fingers limp against it. Lord, please? Please heal my lady? I don't know that I can go on without her.

Sobs rose once more within him. This time, he didn't try to control them. Tears flowed down his face, dropping to the pillow as he laid his head beside her, a kiss on her cheek. Lord? Why? I don't understand it. Why Jason? Where was Jeremy?

Two days had gone by since the accident. Aubrey was still sedated, letting her body heal, the physicians watching the swelling around her spine. Barnabas had refused to leave her, telling Breck to search for what needed to be done in the office and take care of it, if he would. Bruce had disappeared with Breck to do just that, the two men working to clear off as much as they could. The board had moved in as well, doing what they could to help, knowing that Barnabas would not leave his bride. And it was as it should be, they decided among themselves. It was nearing the holidays, anyway, Bruce had stated. They would soon be taking the time to spend with their families and what could be put off to the new year, would be.

Aubrey's eyes flickered late that afternoon, as she roused slightly. Barnabas was on his feet, his hand resting against her face, the other hand holding hers tightly, feeling her fingers tighten on his.

"Sweetheart? Can you hear me? Come on, sweetheart. Open your beautiful eyes." Barnabas knew that he was pleading but that was all he could do. He could not take her place, as much as he wanted to.

"Barnabas? Where am I?" Aubrey spoke without opening her eyes, her tongue licking at her dry lips.

"You had an accident, sweetheart. You're in the hospital."

"Take me home, please? I can't do this." Aubrey slept without knowing that tears of pain were trickling down her face, breaking Barnabas' heart.

"I will, sweetheart, just as soon as I can." He reached out to wipe away the tears, knowing that God was healing her, but just how much before she went home, no one knew.

Bruce stood for a moment watching his son, praying for the younger couple, before he walked forward. His arm around his son, he prayed for them before he directed Barnabas from the room, nodding at Murphy who stood at the door. He knew others of Abe's men were around.

"Sit, son." He handed him the takeout cup of coffee that he had left in the care of Imly, who had approached him earlier that day worried about Barnabas.

"Dad? I thought you had a meeting today."

"I did. Breck is sitting in for me. It's the last one before the holidays."

"It is? I thought we had a number scheduled for next week."

"The board has met. We have put off anything that we can until the new year. It is only right. They want your mother and me to spend the time with you and Aubrey." He nodded towards the room. "How is she?"

"She roused enough to recognize me. She wants me to take her home. And I can't do that."

"No, not yet. What have the physicians said?"

"The swelling is down a bit but not where it can be for her to leave. It wasn't supposed to be like this, Dad."

"I know, son. I know that." Bruce sighed, sitting back and sipping at his coffee. "We never told you that your mother had an accident before you were born. She had some spinal damage, not a lot, but enough that some of the nerves to her right leg were damaged."

"She did? Is that why she limps sometimes?"

"It is. Arthritis has also set into that hip."

"I wish I had known, Dad. She did things for me when I was young that she shouldn't have."

"Your mother has never asked or wanted to be pampered. If she did things for you, it was because she wanted to. She didn't want her injury to play a part in your life." Bruce sipped at his coffee again. "What has Dallas said?"

"I haven't talked to him since the day it happened. He hasn't been around." Barnabas pulled out his phone. "Oh, a text message. He's heading this way. Wants to know that I have security tight to me."

"And you do. Murphy is on the door. That Luke and Joseph are around here, somewhere. They are working in shifts, Abe rotating around as he needs to. He also has other friends moving in to help."

"He does? Who?"

"Men by the name of Eddie, Ben, Frankie, Doug, Dave, Gideon." Bruce shook his head. "All of the younger men have been involved in adventures as he terms it. Eddie is his uncle. Ben a good friend who is a retired officer."

"I will owe so much when this is over."

"Not at all." Abe sat down beside Barnabas. "You have provided so much over the years, Barnabas. I don't think you understand how you have been a source of encouragement to others. You live your name, every day." Abe nodded towards Bruce. "How's Aubrey?"

"She was awake, sort of. Asked me to take her home." Barnabas grew tense for a moment. "I don't know how to do this. I really don't."

"One day at a time, Barnabas. One day at a time. That's how Emma and I did it when we were separated by her aunt's third husband. She thought I was dead. I thought she didn't want anything to do with me. We reunited and are stronger as a couple." Abe looked pensive. "If you ask any of my men, my friends, they will tell you the same. That what they went through brought that to them. God protected all of them, even when they were at the point of death. The same as your friends. My sister, Rebecca? Her first husband was killed when they had been married for three months. Gideon was from our town, had left and then returned. He was able to step in and protect her."

"I see that you have interesting friends as well." Bruce watched his son closely. "Now, Abe? You said you had your security expert going over our building."

"I have. He is impressed with whoever it is that did your security system. He has talked to the head of security there, made a few minor suggestions regarding access and in particular, Barnabas' suite."

"Thanks, Abe." Barnabas was on his feet, moving towards Aubrey, his steps slow as fatigue hit him. Murphy watched him, a hand out to help him as he paused at the door before he nodded and entered the room, the door swishing closed behind him.

Chapter 26

Four days later, Aubrey frowned past the physiotherapist who stood at the side of the bed, frustrated that Aubrey refused to look at her.

"Aubrey, we need to do this. You have to be able to walk to leave."

"Says who? That's not what I was told. Please? Leave?" Aubrey watched her walk away before her head went back on the pillow. Forgive me, Lord? I am just so tired, hurting, and uncertain of anything any more.

Cadee and Jaxcy watched for a moment before they approached her. The ladies of the building, including Anna, had been coming in twos to visit her, spacing them out so they didn't tire her out.

"Aubrey? Rebelling?" Jaxcy grinned at her as Aubrey raised her head. "Not wanting to do the exercises?"

"No. I know why they want that, but I just can't. Not here. I need to go. I feel like I am still Jeremy's prisoner." Aubrey studied the two women, seeing them nod.

"That's what we thought. Here. Let us help you up. Cadee has some clothes for you. Barnabas is speaking with the physician. He's taking you home today, he says."

"He is? He didn't tell me." Aubrey accepted Cadee's help to dress.

"He was watching when the physiotherapist walked in. He knows how you feel without you saying anything. Here. We have a wheelchair for you. What do you want to take with you?"

"Just the flowers, I guess. There are so many."

"Then, pick what you want and we'll take off the cards and let the nurses distribute them."

"No, that's not right."

273

"It is. There are some here who have no one who visits them, receive no flowers. These will be a source of encouragement and pleasure to them." Jaxcy was working away as she spoke, pulling off the cards and tucking them into a pocket.

"Wow! You know, I never thought of it that way." Aubrey looked up. "Does the Foundation have a ministry that does that? Provides flowers and what not to those in the hospital or retirement homes?"

"Not that I am aware of. There you go. That can be your ministry." Cadee grinned at her, looking around as Barnabas appeared. "Barnabas, Aubrey just came up with her own ministry."

"She did?" He crouched down beside the wheelchair. "Ready to leave?"

"I am. The ministry? Jaxcy and Cadee suggested that I leave the flowers here and let the nurses distribute them. Does the Foundation do that for the ones who don't have anyone?"

Barnabas shook his head. "No, they don't. I'm not sure if we have discussed it. But we will. You're volunteering?"

"I am, I guess. I know what it's like to be alone. To not live life as it is meant to be." Aubrey watched him, seeing how he was processing her words. "Not right now, of course. And not without approval."

"We'll look into that in the new year. Right now, you need to be home." He stood, his hands on the handles of the wheelchair before he prayed for her, for himself, and for his friends.

Nathaniel watched as they walked towards him, a grin on his face.

"Blowing the joint, Aubrey?"

She laughed. Each of Abe's men had walked in and introduced themselves, endearing themselves to her. "I am. Thankfully. That means you get to go home."

"Oh, we will. Once we're satisfied that you're okay and settled, we'll hit the road. Ben and Marg and Eddie and his Peggy are staying put for now. They like the building and the area."

"They are?" Barnabas was surprised. "That's good, I guess."

"It is. They are a wealth of information, Barnabas. Talk to them."

"We will." He gently scooped Aubrey up and set her on the seat, reaching to pull her seatbelt over her to snap it shut. He studied her and then reached to kiss her, her hand resting on his shoulder. "I love you, sweetheart."

"I love you. But can we leave? I feel someone watching us."

"And there is. Jason isn't out. He hasn't been able to make his bail. Jeremy has been seen around."

"Will he haunt me forever? How do we catch him?"

Late that night Barnabas walked the apartment, his mind working overtime as he thought about what had happened. He sighed. He was no further ahead, he decided, then he had been, other than more worried about his bride. He turned and walked towards the bedroom, a frown on his face as he didn't find her. Hearing muttering, he headed for the kitchen, pausing in the doorway, a smile crossing his face.

Aubrey had decided that she was hungry and needed her apple spice tea. Only she couldn't find it.

"Lose something?"

"I did. My tea. It's not where I left it."

Barnabas froze. "It's not? I didn't move it." He gently moved her back from the cupboard and to a chair at the table. "Let me have a look." He searched, finding it in the wrong cupboard. "This is not right." He spun, heading for the lobby, finding Murphy and Ian there. "Fellows? Can you come to our apartment? We just found Aubrey's tea out of place. I don't know that the cupboards were searched, but if they were, the team would not have moved anything from cupboard to cupboard."

The two men were on their feet, heading after Barnabas, frowns on their faces. This is what they had expected, Ian thought. It wasn't just that things were placed, but that things were moved.

"Okay. Where should it be?" Murphy nodded as Aubrey pointed to the cupboard over the coffeemaker.

"I always keep it there. The kettle is underneath. I don't get why it would be in another cupboard."

"Because someone has moved it and moved it for a reason. Did either one of you touch it?" Ian looked at them as they looked at one another and then shook their heads. "Can you call that friend of yours? I need to know if they searched the cupboards and moved anything. And he needs to get out here. This is something that we have seen before."

Barnabas nodded, making the call to Dallas. "He was on his way out, he said. Now what?"

"Now what is that you and Aubrey move from this room and into another room. Or even another apartment."

"Not again!" Aubrey's voice was almost a sob. "I thought it was safe."

"And it should be. We just need to go through everything again, just to see if anything has been tampered with."

Aubrey paled. "Tampered with? As in poison?"

Murphy nodded as he crouched down beside her, an arm resting on the table. "Or an explosive or something corrosive. One of our ladies couldn't get her phone to shut off. It triggered an explosion. So, you see, we need to ensure that nothing like that is here."

Barnabas drew her up and away, exchanging a look with Murphy as he stood. "Our fellows will be working on this full time now. If you need to speak with any of them, the conference room is where you'll find them."

"Abe said he would tomorrow. I need to let him know about this." Murphy's phone was out.

Breck paused in the hallway, having come to see what he could do for the couple.

"Barnabas?"

Barnabas sighed, his arm around Aubrey. "Her tea was moved from cupboard to cupboard. Dallas is on his way out. Can we come to visit you and Neasa? I want Aubrey somewhere she can rest."

"Sure. Neasa was concerned enough that she sent me down." Breck watched as Barnabas scooped Aubrey into his arms. "What can I bring for you?"

"Her pain medications. The anti-inflammatories. They're on the counter in the bathroom. I just put them there." Barnabas sighed once more. "I'll head for the elevator."

Murphy watched them walk away before he turned to Breck. "Her medications? They're safe?"

"They should be. I had them filled at our regular pharmacy." He paled. "You don't think?"

"I do."

"Then, let me talk to Doc. He might have something here that we can use." Breck was away, hating to disturb Doc, but knowing the man well enough that he would be willing to do what he needed to.

Neasa turned from the spare bedroom where she had turned down the blankets for Aubrey, praying for her friend. She doesn't need this, Lord, not when she's hurting so badly. She walked out of the room, into Breck's arms.

"Breck?"

"I gave Barnabas the medications from Doc. He's talking with Dallas right now. What can we do for her?"

"Right now? She's not even sure herself what she wants or needs, other than her husband. I promised her a cup of tea."

"Okay. Let's do that. Some toast or crackers?"

Neasa nodded, reaching for a tray. "I think so. She's nauseous, she said. Crackers will work." She paused, her eyes on the ceiling as she tried to control her own tears. Breck just wrapped her into his arms.

"We'll help all we can. She's independent, not wanting to be a burden. She also doesn't want to be locked away somewhere, and that's a possibility."

"I know." Neasa whispered her response. "I hate this for her. She's had one-third of her life taken away from or almost that. How close are you to finding him?"

"Not close enough. We need to talk to her again, to pick her brain to find out what else that she can tell us."

"Let me or one of the ladies do that. She might open up more to one of us."

Barnabas wandered the conference room the next morning, a mug of coffee in his hand that he sipped from once in a while. He was on his own, it was that early. The fact of the matter was he had not slept. He had held Aubrey all night as she slept, her body twitching and twisting, the pain medications not working. To say that he was worried was an understatement. All he could do was pray for his bride.

Reading the whiteboards as he stopped at each one, Barnabas nodded. They are finding more and more information, aren't they, Lord? I see Emma's hand in some of it. Thank you for such a friend as she is. He turned as he heard the door open and close and footsteps approaching him.

Burnie stood watching his friend. How do we do this, Lord? How do we encourage him? And Aubrey? She has to be hurting, and he's hurting because she is.

"Burnie?"

"Barnabas? I see you're here bright and early. I thought that I would be the first one."

"Not today." Barnabas rubbed at his burning eyes, lack of sleep exacerbating that. "You fellows have been busy."

"We have. Breck pulled us all back from work. He talked to each one of our employers, you know."

"I suspected that he would. He's done it in the past."

"But not for you. They're concerned, my friend. Your encouragement over the years, not just in finding us to work for them, but in other ways? They want to repay it, but they're not sure how. The word on the street is that they are looking for Jeremy and whoever it is that he has employed. The Foundation has done too much down there for the people not to help."

"I'm sure that they're looking. He's likely coming back and forth, not wanting to stay around. Not just yet."

Blair spoke from his other side, coming in and just standing beside him. "Paul said that they've found signs of someone watching the building. Not enough that they can get a sense other than it's a female."

"Female? That's different. It's usually the men who are watching us."

"Jeremy's a different foe than we have faced. We still don't have a sense of why."

"Why? Aubrey?" Barnabas turned as he heard other footsteps and found all the men there. "That's what's puzzling us. She can't give a reason, other than he wanted her to take up a musical career. Jason told her that she had been promised to him. She doesn't understand that, either. Jeremy was careful, she said, to limit her exposure to him."

"That is weird." Benen pulled out the chair he usually sat in. "What would cause him to say that?"

"Revenge, maybe." Baird sat as well, booting up his computer. "I've come across some news articles about him. He's tried that before with other ladies. They've had to take out restraining orders against him."

"He has?" This from Brennen. "Has he been able to make bail?"

"No. Not that I know of." Barnabas turned back to a whiteboard. "Logic problem again? How is that working?"

"Not so well this time. We only have Jeremy and Jason. That's not enough." Buckley stood beside him this time. "How be we break off and pray and then get to work?"

Barnabas nodded, his eyes on his friends before he approached Brady. "Brady? Pray with me today?"

"I was going to ask you the same thing."

Barnabas finally sat back, watching and listening as the men bounced ideas from one to the other. They work well as a team, the adventures they all underwent concreting that, he thought. He sighed to himself. Lord, how do we do this? How do we find Jeremy? And now this woman? Who is she? Why watch us? He sat upright before he rose and headed for the whiteboard, Brandon following him.

"You had a thought."

"I did. This female who has been watching us. Whose side is she on?"

Brandon stared at him. "Whose side? Jeremy's?"

"But what if there is someone else? Someone behind Jeremy?" Barnabas staggered for a moment, Brandon's hand going out to steady him. "I just had a horrible thought. What if it hasn't been Aubrey? That she was hidden away, to get to me, and through me to the Foundation?"

The men's heads all raised abruptly from their work, their eyes on Barnabas before they looked at one another. The silence in the room was deafening, so deep that if the proverbial pin had dropped, it would have sounded like a cannon shot.

"Are you saying that you think someone else is involved?" Branigan rose to walk towards Barnabas.

"I am It makes sick sense, you know?" Barnabas dropped into a nearby chair, unsure if he was even on the right track. "I mean, I share the name with the Foundation. Dad did name it in part after me and in part after the Barnabas in the Bible."

Breck nodded. "We've thought that over the months when we have all been through this stuff. We never did find out who it was for some of what we went through." He began to pace. "We never did figure out who was driving that ATV that ran Neasa and me down."

"No, we didn't." Barnabas rose, heading for a clear whiteboard. "Okay, let's think about this. What would be a motive?"

"Money. Bribe you to pay out money to stop it." Benen spoke first.

"Revenge?" This from Brendon.

"I agree. Who wanted something from the Foundation and never got it?" Baird spoke up.

"Or wanted on the board and was turned down?" Branigan was thinking aloud.

"Or wanted to go out on a mission through the Foundation and was turned down?" Burnie spoke as he rose, heading for Barnabas.

"Someone who felt that they should run one of the charities we deal with?" Bradon looked up from where he was writing on a pad. "If we make a list of the charities and go from there?"

"Talk to Darcie. See if she can profile something for us." Buckley rubbed at his head. "I can do that if you like."

"If you would." Barnabas began to pace before he left the room, heading to find his father. Bruce was in the lobby, speaking with Abe.

"Barnabas?" Abe looked at him before he exchanged a look with Murphy.

"Dad? I had a thought and the fellows are working on it. What if it wasn't Aubrey?" Barnabas drew a deep breath, a bleak look around his eyes. "What if she was taken, to get to me, to get to the Foundation through me? Someone who knows me well enough to know that she was a good friend in college?"

Bruce studied his son. "I had that thought, son. I was just asking Abe about that. Emma will start working on that premise, he tells me. And that Darcie is sending over a profile. She had the same thought."

"Buckley was approaching her about that." Barnabas rubbed at his face. "Maybe I should step back from the Foundation, step back from what I do."

Abe shook his head. "That is likely what they want. If you do that, they win, whoever they are. Let us work through this first. Is Aubrey up to talking to us?"

Barnabas shrugged. "I can see. She was still sleeping when I left this morning." He turned, not even thinking to excuse himself, heading for his apartment.

Hagen looked around as he entered, pointing to the living room, a grin on her face.

"In there. She's been pretty good all morning. The alternating ice packs and heat have been helping. Although right now, she's held captive."

"Captive?" Barnabas grinned as he peeked into the living room.

Aubrey was seated on the couch, her feet and legs up on an ottoman, a blanket covering them. Heath and Hannah stood one on either side of her, competing for her attention. Barnabas grinned as Heath covered Aubrey's face with kisses and then Hannah had to copy her brother. Aubrey's face was alight with laughter before she asked the little ones if she could read.

Heath plopped down beside her, pointing to the book, Hannah standing with an arm around her neck, leaning against her.

"Aube. Read,"

"I will, but you need to listen. Okay?" Aubrey looked up, a huge smile on her face as Barnabas leaned over them to kiss her, one hand on the back of the couch to balance himself.

He began to laugh as Heath pushed at him. "Mine. Aube mine."

"No, she's mine, but I'll share." Barnabas simply picked up the little fellow and sat tight to Aubrey, settling Heath on his knee. "Here. Aubrey will read to us for a bit. Then I think your Mommy is looking for you for your lunch."

"No lunch. Aube read." Heath's bottom lip came out in mutiny.

Aubrey touched it gently. "No lip, Heath, or I don't read. We talked about that."

Hagen finally rescued Aubrey from her twins, laughing at the protest they put up before she headed home. Aubrey's head went down against Barnabas as his arm swept around her.

"Tired?" He watched her face closely.

"I am, but a good tired. Those twins are just so special."

"They are." Barnabas began to laugh. "Heath has certainly claimed you."

"He has. Hagen had a horrible time getting him away from me." She laughed as she remembered the struggles that morning before she sobered. "I just don't want them hurt."

"We'll take care, sweetheart." Barnabas just sat, content for the moment, before he spoke. "We had a thought this morning, sweetheart, that I need to speak with you about. Abe would like to as well,"

Aubrey twisted her head to look at him. "About who is it? I've been thinking about that. There's a list there on the end table of Jeremy and Jason's known contacts. The names of his security guards. It's been so strange what has happened. I can't see that

Jeremy profited any by holding me prisoner. And I know that Jason was never around that much. I think that I said Jeremy made sure of that."

"That's what we're thinking. We are now wondering if someone knew how much you meant to me back then, had Jeremy hold you captive, to come after me and through me, the Foundation." He watched her face as she thought through what he had said.

"I have often wondered that very thing, love. I had so much time to think. Is that what you think?"

"It seems to be the consensus. I would hate that this happened to you because of me."

"God knows, love. He knows."

That evening, Barnabas turned from his home office, a deep sigh drawn from him. They were no further ahead, he decided, and he did not like that one little bit. Lord? This is so hard. Now I understand what the others went through. It doesn't make it any easier. He stood for a moment, deep in thought and prayer before he looked up as Aubrey reached to hug him.

"Love?" She tilted her head to look up at him, deep shadows under her eyes and pain in them.

"You need to be sitting down, sweetheart. You're in pain." He turned her towards the bedroom, intent on tucking her in, but she resisted.

"No, I don't want that. We need to talk, Barnabas. But more than that, we need to pray. I fear for you."

"I know, sweetheart." He tucked her up on the couch. "I'll be right back." He was as good as his word, returning with her tea and his coffee and then sitting beside her, snuggling her tight.

"Have you talked with the fellows?"

"Not since late this afternoon. I don't want to hover over them. They understand, but they don't need that." He sighed again. "I just wish this was over, but it's not. Not by a long shot."

"Me too. Was that list any help?"

"Brendon took it and then copied it for everyone. They will all take a look at it, do what they do best in their research, and then compile a report. They all have different ways of looking at things."

"I know. I gave a copy to Muir when she stopped by this afternoon. She said the ladies were in competition with the men and they had a secret weapon."

Barnabas grinned. "They are and they do? Did she say who?"

"No, she didn't." Aubrey's voice softened as she thought about their conversation before her mind turned to the twins. "Those twins are special, aren't they?"

"They are. Hagen didn't want twins, she said, not sure that she would be able to manage. She has done well. Her sisters help a lot. Brandon is so proud of them. He can't wait to get home at night now, just to be with his family."

"And there are other little ones. I need to get to know them, but I am so hesitant to be around them."

"They understand. The ladies will not deny you an opportunity to see them or the little ones. I know that for a fact. We just need to be careful, that's all."

"Do you think there is someone behind Jeremy? I could never understand why. He never really gave an answer whenever I spoke with him."

"I am sure we are. Who it is? That's what we're working on." Barnabas grew quiet, content he thought for the first time in years.

"Your Mom and Dad were around earlier this afternoon. Your Mom is spoiling me."

"She will. They always wanted a daughter but couldn't have any more children. Mom is so happy right now. She will spoil you, I know. You deserve to be."

"No. No, I don't. But I understand why she wants to." Aubrey shifted how she was sitting, to ease the pain in her back. "Where do we go from here, love? How do we find this person or persons?"

"We keep digging. Dallas is digging as well. The new detective, Davy, has been assigned to help him." Barnabas frowned. "He looks familiar."

"Didn't someone say a homeless man named Davy helped Breck? Could it have been him?"

"It may well have been." Barnabas yawned, his fatigue catching up with him. "How be we spend some time in prayer and reading our favourite verses? We haven't been able to for a few days."

Baird was on a hunt two days later. He had come across some information that he needed to talk to Barnabas about and just could not find him. He paused, a hand rubbing at his neck before he headed for the parking lot and then nodded. Barnabas isn't in the building.

Turning back, Baird headed for Barnabas' apartment, hoping to find Aubrey. He watched as the door opened carefully and Aubrey peeked around it.

"Baird? You're here?"

"I am. I was trying to find Barnabas."

"He's in town. He said it would this evening when he got home. Can I help?"

Baird stared at her. "You know, you might be able to. Are you feeling up to coming to the conference room for a bit?"

"I can. Just let me grab my keys." Aubrey was back in short order, pulling on a cardigan. She stared down at her feet. "I can't change my slippers, though."

"That doesn't matter." Baird held out an arm for Aubrey to take, to give her balance if she needed it.

Aubrey stared around the room, amazed at how much activity was going on. "Those boards. They have a lot more information than when I last saw them."

"There is." Bradon had approached. "How are you today, Aubrey?"

She shrugged her attention not on him but on the boards. She moved that way, not seeing the looks the men exchanged. Bradon followed her, watching her closely.

Aubrey stopped, her finger on a name. "Who is this?"

"That is Jeremy's ex-wife. Jason's mother. Did you ever meet her?"

"No, but I have heard that name. I just can't remember where." Aubrey was frustrated at that.

"It will come to you." Bradon studied her face. "You've thought of something."

"I have. I just don't know how to express it." Aubrey found a chair to sit in, her back starting to ache. "How do I do that?"

"Just start talking. I can take notes or we can record your thoughts." Bradon reached for the laptop near her, bringing up a word processing program and pointing to the little microphone icon. "We can use this or you can use your phone."

"This works." Aubrey bit at her lip, not sure how to proceed. "Okay. So, I just start talking?"

Bradon grinned at her. "You do. Would you like me to find Heath and Hannah and you can pretend to be reading them a story?"

Aubrey stared at him before her eyes narrowed. "Funny man, aren't you? Hagen must have talked."

"Actually it was your husband who did. He was laughing as he told us about the other day."

"Those twins are quite the pair. Brandon and Hagen will have their hands full in the future." Aubrey smirked at Brandon as he grinned at her.

"That we will, Aubrey. But Heath is insistent that he needs his Aube and so does Hannah."

"I love those two little ones. Now, to go back to what I was thinking. I guess I have to go back to when Mom was still alive."

"Go back to where you need to." Burnie had moved closer, a pen and paper ready to take notes. "I'll listen and jot down what I think is important or what we would need to question further."

Aubrey finally nodded, her mind slipping back in time, back to when she was about sixteen. She knew Jeremy had been around, trying to get her mother to sign paperwork. Her mother had told him to leave and not return, that she would not sign any paperwork he presented. Aubrey had asked her mother about him and had been told to avoid him.

Her mind drifted forward, to when she was eighteen and her mother slipped away from her overnight. Aubrey had been in shock, not realizing that Jeremy had stepped in, taking over. She had turned to her friends and her own lawyer, leaning on them.

Aubrey came back to the present, her eyes on the men gathered around. "He was never my guardian. I was eighteen when Mom died. I had my own lawyer and he would have told me. He didn't."

"Let me know your lawyer's name and I'll contact him." Branigan reached for the paper she had written on. "I'll do that later. For now, continue, Aubrey."

Aubrey began to speak, her voice low at times, as her mind traced back to her university days. Breck nodded at some of her comments, a frown in place at other times.

Knowing that her mother would have wanted her to complete her education, Aubrey had struggled with finances, working hard and long over the summers, finding grants when she could, not wanting to go into debt if she could avoid that. She had known that Jeremy had been hovering around at the edge of her life and she learned quickly how to watch for him and to not let him near her if she could at all help it.

She had treasured her growing friendship with Barnabas, falling fast and deeply in love with him, not expecting that he would ever return her love. When, during their last few months of school, he had approached her, asking if she would consider moving to his town, that he wanted to explore their friendship and see if she felt the same as he did, she had agreed. What she hadn't known was that Jason had been nearby and had gone to his father.

Jeremy had begun to plan at that point, to plan how to trap her. She hadn't suspected anything when she had been asked if she wanted to work with some young children at a home. Seeing as it was her line of work, she had agreed, planning on only staying for the requested two months and then moving to Barnabas' town.

Once there, she had been imprisoned by Jeremy. No amount of pleading or escaping had worked. If she got out, he found her and dragged her back. Doors were locked from the outside. Windows were sealed shut. She was allowed her phone and internet access but under direct threat to those that she would communicate with. Her calls and emails from Barnabas had been the highlight of her weeks until Jeremy had decided that he would end those. She had been asleep the night the lock was installed on her bedroom door.

Aubrey had pleaded and sobbed with him to let her out, but he didn't respond. Two years had gone by, two years of despair alternating with hope. She had tried to think of everyone who might be involved, writing them down. She had researched the Foundation in the past, remembering the name of a lawyer involved who Barnabas had mentioned on occasion. That information she had mailed to him, somehow getting it out. She still wasn't sure how that had happened. The envelope had been on her dresser one day and then gone the next.

Having kept a copy secreted, Aubrey had frequently pulled it out and added to it as she could. She came back to the present, finding the men watching her closely.

"That list, Aubrey. Do you still have it?"

"I do. But I don't need a written list." She began to name names, listing what she knew about them.

Breck frowned at a couple of the names. "Does Dallas have these?"

Aubrey shrugged. "John has most of them. I don't know if he handed them over. I didn't ask him that."

"I know about four of them. They are from here. Now, that makes sense. If someone is trying to get to the Foundation, they would need someone from this area, now wouldn't they?"

"Tell us which ones, Breck, and we'll concentrate on those. Male or female?" Bradon looked up from his notes.

"Both." Breck named them, seeing the men exchange glances. "We all know them, I think. Barnabas has had a run-in with the men over the years regarding the Foundation." He paused, lost in thought for a moment. "I think that he was right. That Jeremy was working for someone to get to Aubrey and through Aubrey to Barnabas and then the Foundation."

"It makes sick sense." Baird looked around at the other men. "I have had my own difficulties with one of the men. About a couple of years after I moved here. He wanted me to provide documents for him, documents that I had no access to. I told him no, walked away, and never thought much about it. I did talk to Bruce at the time."

"That's strange. I think he has approached all of us, am I correct?" Buckley looked around, seeing the nods. "The last time was what, about two years ago?"

"That would be it." Brady looked up as Aubrey gave a sound. "About the time that you were locked up tight?"

"About that. Oh, no! He was using me." There was devastation on Aubrey's face. "I didn't know."

"No, you wouldn't." Buckley sat beside her. "Aubrey, what else can you tell us?"

She shrugged. "Not much more." She frowned. "I don't know how Jeremy made it as a lawyer. I don't remember that he had an office. He was around the house a lot the first few years, barely on the phone with clients. He has a loud voice and I could hear him clearly."

"Okay. We can look into that. I can talk with John if I have your permission." Breck studied her. "In fact, I think it's a good idea if we did that."

"Sure. Whatever it takes." Aubrey rose, excusing herself, her back beginning to be painful.

Brady followed her as she walked back to the apartment, keeping an eye on her gait. Please heal her, Lord. And help us to bring whoever it is to justice.

Aubrey had wandered the apartment that evening, worried that Barnabas had not returned. She squinted at the clock on the mantle. It was after seven and no word from him. She reached for her phone, scrolling through her messages. Not a one from him since mid-afternoon.

She sighed, stretching out on the couch, a hot water bottle against her back, a cold pack on the coffee table. She eyes the glass of ginger ale that she had sat there and shaken her head. No, she didn't want it. Aubrey had found some crackers early, hoping they would suffice until Barnabas was home. Elizabeth had been around earlier, her concern for Aubrey having been uppermost in her mind.

Awakening, Aubrey sat up abruptly, not sure what had roused her. She was on her feet, heading for the door, hearing the knocking that seemed to be getting louder and louder. She peeked through the peephole and then unlocked the door, swinging it open for Breck and Neasa to enter.

"Breck? Neasa?" She stared between the two, seeing the grim look on Breck's face and the compassion on Neasa's. Fear drove a sharp pain into her heart. "No, he's not. Please, God. No! Not that!"

Breck's hand came out to steady her. "He's in the hospital, Aubrey. I don't have a lot of details, other than we need to bring you in. Dress warmly. It's starting to sleet and the wind is cold."

Aubrey stared at him before Neasa touched her arm.

"Aubrey? Where are your boots? Your coat?"

Aubrey turned, moving as quickly as she was able to, heading for the bedroom, struggling into her coat and picking up the backpack she preferred to a purse. She stared down at her feet, reaching to pull off the pair of Barnabas' heavy wool socks that she had put on earlier, heading back for the closet in the hall, to pull on her boots.

Breck's hand was under her arm, Neasa's arm linked with her as they walked as rapidly as they could for Breck's truck.

Aubrey stared out of the side window as she listened to Breck and Neasa's conversation about the roads. Breck was glad that he had an all-wheel-drive on his truck, but the slick roads still meant he needed to be cautious.

Neasa turned to watch Aubrey, concern on her face.

"Aubrey?"

Aubrey turned her gaze to Neasa. "Neasa, what do you know?"

"Not a lot, Aubrey. I was called by a patrol officer. They couldn't raise you on your phone. I was just told that he was found in a parking lot and had been hurt. That they needed you to come as quickly as you could." Breck's eyes watched her for a moment in the rearview mirror.

"He was outside? In this?" Aubrey was horrified. "Who? How?"

"That we don't know, Aubrey. They didn't say much." Breck pulled to a stop near the entrance to the Emergency Department. "Stay put, Aubrey. Let me come around and help you. You won't do Barnabas any good if you fall in your rush to get to him." Breck was as good as his word, around the truck, helping Neasa out and then Aubrey and then walking them to the door, watching carefully as they entered before he moved quickly to park his truck.

Hearing his name called, Breck paused, his shoulder hunching up towards his face as he turned. Bruce and Elizabeth were coming towards him.

"Breck? I just got the call. We were in town at a dinner. How is he?" Bruce reached for Breck's arm. "Aubrey?"

"I just got her in. Neasa's with her. I haven't been told much, other than he was found outside in a parking lot and unresponsive."

"No!" Elizabeth's hands covered her mouth. "No, please, Lord!"

The three found Neasa and Aubrey seated in the waiting room. Aubrey was on the edge of her seat, her knee bouncing with her frustration and anxiety. Elizabeth dropped to the seat beside her, an arm around her.

"Aubrey? Any word?"

Aubrey shook her head, a hand wiping at the tears on her face. "Not yet. They said that they'd come to get me. He is still being assessed." Her tortured eyes raised to Bruce who had crouched down in front of her. "Why?"

"I understand they are working on that, Aubrey. They will want to speak with Barnabas when he awakens. Can I get you anything?"

"No, thank you. Just find who it is." She looked up at Breck. "Breck?"

"We're working on those names, Aubrey. I spoke with both John and Dallas. John said that you wanted to sign something that day he spoke with you that would let him speak with us."

"I did. Barnabas and I had talked about it." She was on her feet, moving towards the physician as he beckoned for her to follow him, her limp pronounced.

Aubrey moved with the physician towards the room where they had placed Barnabas, stopping at his hand on her arm.

"Aubrey? May I call you that?" At her nod, he continued. "Now, I am not sure what all you have been told. Barnabas was found outside, just as the rain was turning to sleet. He's suffering from hypothermia, among other things."

"What else, doctor?" Aubrey's eyes did not move from the closed door.

"He was beaten, by the looks of it. He has numerous nicks and cuts on his face and hand, from the window that was broken."

"Broken window?" Aubrey's eyes shot to him. "What are you talking about?"

"The patrol officer who came in with him said that the driver's window was shattered. We don't know why or by whom." He paused, drawing in a deep breath. "At the moment, we are working to warm Barnabas back up. I won't go into all the details, not until later. As a start, he has been to imaging. He has deep bruising along the left side of his body. No rib fracture that we can see. But he is in critical condition, Aubrey."

Aubrey paled even more. "Critical? Oh, no!" She looked up at the physician, devastation on her face. "Can I please go to him?"

"You can but before you do I need to let you know what you will find. He is on oxygen, warmed to help heat his interior core. Heated intravenous. He is wrapped in warming blankets. Barnabas has not awakened as yet nor responded to us." The physician watched with compassion as Aubrey wiped at her face. "You can stay for a while, Aubrey, but we will need you to leave from time to time. Have you family here?"

"Just his parents. I'm an orphan. And good friends. Breck brought me in."

"Breck and Neasa? Good. Anything else that I can get you right now?"

"Just whoever it was that did this." Aubrey walked away from towards the stretcher that held Barnabas, a hand covering her mouth as she stared down at him. Please, Lord? Heal him. I just don't understand why.

She laid her hand against his cheek, feeling the chill on it. Bending, Aubrey kissed him, her tears splashing against his face. She stood even as the nurses and therapists worked around her, trying to warm Barnabas. It was a slow process, they told her. As soon as he was stable enough, they would move him to a floor.

"ICU?" Aubrey's voice was barely a whisper.

"It might be. We'll see how he comes around." The charge nurse smiled at Aubrey, her eyes compassionate. "Right now, though, we need you to step back into the waiting room. We'll come to get you in a bit."

Aubrey bent to kiss Barnabas on the cheek once more, her hand lingering on his jaw, before she turned, walking away, her steps slow and halting as she made her way back to the waiting room. She knew that she would need to give an answer to the unspoken questions but she hesitated just outside the doors, her eyes on the floor. Tears trickled down her face.

Bruce was waiting for her and simply reached to hug her, holding her as she wept before he turned her back to where Elizabeth sat. He simply shook his head at his wife as Aubrey sat beside her.

"Aubrey?" Elizabeth shared a look with Neasa and Breck when the younger woman didn't answer. "Did you see Barnabas?"

Aubrey nodded. "I did. He's not waking up." She swiped at her face, mad at herself that she was weeping but unable to stop herself. "They're trying to warm him up from inside the doctor said." She looked around at them. "Why? Why Barnabas? Who hates him that much?"

Bruce wrapped her in his arms as he would have his own daughter and became to pray for her. When he was done, he watched her face before he rose and motioned to Breck.

"Bruce?" Breck was curious as to what Bruce was thinking.

"Have we considered that? What Aubrey said?"

"That someone hates Barnabas that much? The fellows and I have discussed that. Buckley and Branigan have made it their concentrated duty to look into that." Breck hesitated, not sure how to continue. "He would send us out, teams of six, when he needed to, to bring people or information back that was needed. He hasn't done that since the fellows went in and brought Baird and Berneen out."

"I wonder if it's something to do with that. Do you know the circumstances on those?"

Breck shook his head. "He would tell us what we needed to know. He often never said who had requested that."

"No, he wouldn't. He would keep it quiet so as not to break a confidence." Bruce paced as Breck divided his attention between Bruce and the three ladies. "I'll have to see what I can find out. He keeps things confidential and I will not break that trust."

Breck watched as Aubrey as she spoke with a nurse before she turned, distress in her demeanour.

"Bruce. I think something has happened." Breck nodded towards Aubrey. "Aubrey was just speaking with a nurse."

"She was?" Bruce had spun and was across the room, his arm around his daughter-in-law. "Aubrey?"

"They're transferring him to the ICU, they said. He still hasn't awakened. She said it was not unusual, but I hate this. I really do." Aubrey leaned against Bruce as she wept, afraid that Barnabas would never wake up and would indeed slip away from her forever.

Waking up during the night, Bruce looked around at the ICU waiting room. Elizabeth sat beside him, her head on his shoulder, her hand in his. Breck was slumped on a couch, his arm around Neasa as she curled up beside him, a sheet that he had found wrapped around her. Both were sound asleep. Bruce's eyes turned to Aubrey and he gave a sad smile. Aubrey was curled up on another couch, her backpack as a pillow. Elizabeth had found a blanket to cover her with before she had stood, hand on Aubrey's head, and prayed for the younger woman. Bruce sighed, his heart raising in petition to their God, asking that Barnabas would awaken and if he didn't that they would have peace. He knew the dangers of hypothermia even at this stage.

Aubrey roused, sitting up and pushing her hair away from her face before she was on her feet heading towards the doors to the unit. She had sought and been granted permission to enter when she could. The nurses had looked at her and then one another. They only knew too well the dangers that faced the young couple.

Standing beside Barnabas, Aubrey stared at the equipment surrounding him, frowning. She wasn't quite sure but she felt that he had improved. Her eyes dropped to his beloved face before she stooped to kiss him.

"Please, Lord? I need my best friend, my husband, my soul mate. Please, Lord? Don't let him die." She stood with a hand on his cheek, before she began to speak again. "Barnabas, I love you so much, more and more each moment. We tell each other that in words and actions. I can't handle it if you do leave me. Please, love? Wake up for me?"

She finally turned away, not seeing the flickering of Barnabas' eyelids as he tried to rouse before he slipped back into the darkness. Bruce was standing waiting for her, an arm out to hug her as he turned her back to the waiting room.

"Aubrey?" His voice was low as he spoke.

"About the same, Bruce." She drew a deep shaking breath. "I'm so afraid."

"I know, Aubrey. I know. We are too. But he is still here. God had not chosen to take him home yet."

"No, but He could at any time." Aubrey dropped back to the couch before looking up at the older man. "How do we do this? Have we heard anything?"

"Not yet. Will Peters was around earlier. He's the police chief whom I am not sure that you have met yet."

"No, I don't think I have. I have heard the fellows talk about him. Did he know anything?"

"He didn't say much other than they had the truck towed to their garage and the techs and mechanic would be going over it in the morning." Bruce sat beside her, a hand reaching for hers as he began to pray for her.

Breck had roused as they spoke before he shook his head. Lord, he thought, this is getting old. We need our friend. Please, Lord? He has taught us so much on how to live for You and for each other. Please, dear Lord? Barnabas and I have been friends for so long there would be a gap in my life if he wasn't in it. I mean, our friendship has changed with us each married but we still need one another. He's my brother that I never had.

Will Peters stood for a moment, eying the five in the waiting room before he approached Aubrey. Bruce had looked up at the footsteps and was on his feet, his face turning grim.

"Will, you're here?"

"I am, Bruce. As a friend, not in my normal capacity. This is Aubrey?" He sat beside her, a hand out to shake hers. He introduced himself and then watched her, seeing the fragility that she was trying hard to hide. It's not just this, is it, Lord? It's more and more what's going on. And that we still have not figured out totally.

"Hi." Aubrey eyes him carefully. "You shouldn't be here."

"But I should. Bruce and I have been friends for years. I watched Barnabas grow up. He's an important part of my life. I can't be anywhere else. But what can we do for you, Aubrey?"

She shrugged, turning her eyes to the hands that she had clasped together in her lap, her diamond engagement ring catching her attention. "Find who did this. Find who it is that is behind it all. I think." Her voice died away. "I think that whoever it is has been using me. They knew that we were important to one another. Likely because he was the only one I was getting mail or phone calls from. Jeremy was likely monitoring that without me being aware of it. They are after him. Why?"

"That's what we are all working on, Aubrey. I think Dallas will likely be around tomorrow or later today to talk with you. He said he had something that he needed to verify. And no, I don't know what it is. I keep hands off from their work unless I need to step in. He has the new detective, Davy, working with him."

"I see." Aubrey grew quiet before her eyes closed and she slept. Will stood, shifting her so that she once more laid on the couch and reached to cover her.

"Will? What didn't you say?" Bruce knew his friend well.

"Nothing that is definite, Bruce. Just a question that I had." Will sat down in a chair near where Elizabeth was still sleeping, watching as Bruce sat beside his wife. "I think Aubrey hit the nail on the head with her comment."

"Someone using her to get to Barnabas?"

"That. It has never made sense that she was kept captive unless she was a pawn in a huge horrible game of chess that just doesn't end. There has been no checkmate yet."

"No, there has not been and that is worrisome. Elizabeth is not sleeping at night like she needs to."

"None of us are. I talked with Barnabas a few days ago. He is worried about Aubrey, and I think that concern is legitimate. How we go forward with this has many avenues. Dallas and Davy are working on some. Davy has a lot of resources that he can turn to."

"Davy? As in the Davy that found Breck?" Bruce nodded when Will didn't comment, just watched him. "I see. Then we need to pray, my friend. My son is in critical condition because someone chose to attack him and leave him to die. I want that person. I want to stand in front of whoever it is and ask why, what did he ever do to them?"

Standing beside Barnabas' bed two nights later, Aubrey watched him closely. They had been able to move him to a regular room, he had improved enough that they had been able to do that. He still had not roused and that scared Aubrey. She looked around, then lowered the bedrail and crawled up beside him, an arm under his shoulders as much as she could, her other hand on his cheek even as she kissed him, feeling the growth of beard under her lips, and then laid her head on his shoulders. She slept, not seeing the woman who stopped in the doorway or the look of rage on her face. Their enemy had tracked them down.

The night nurse paused for a moment before she shook her head. I would likely do the same thing, she thought, and turned and headed to find a heated sheet that she tucked tight around Aubrey. She continued with her duties and then left, stopping to frown at the woman standing down the hall. It was after visiting hours, she thought, and walked towards her. The woman shot an angry look at her and then almost ran for the stairs, heading out and away from the hospital, pausing beside a younger man who was waiting near the entrance to the parking lot. He nodded as she spoke to him before he headed for the hospital, his employee card swiped in the lock, allowing him entrance.

His eyelids flickering, Barnabas gradually returned to his senses. His eyes cracked open as he peeked around. A hospital room? What did I go and do, he wondered? What happened to me? I hurt all over and it is difficult to breathe. He shifted his position, a weight on his shoulder holding him still for a moment. He frowned before his face softened and the hand with the IV in it lifted to brush the deep red curls from Aubrey's face. His hand then rested on her arm as his face turned towards her as much as it could and he slept, this time a natural sleep.

The young man stood in the doorway, looking towards the nurses' station before he entered, anger on his face. He stood over Barnabas and then turned and walked away, knowing that he could do nothing at that point. The woman would have to wait, that's what he decided.

Aubrey roused as the nurses began their morning rounds, rubbing at her nose before she raised her head, finding herself facing Barnabas. She frowned for a moment before her face lit up. His eyes were open and he was smiling at her, as much as she could see through the oxygen mask covering his lower face.

"Love, you're awake! Oh, praise God1"

Barnabas' hand traced her cheek before he reached to pull down the mask, kissing her.

"Barnabas, put that back on." Aubrey's face was rosy even as she reached to replace the mask.

"Are you okay?" His hand reached to pull the mask back down.

"I am. You're not. Now, behave." She looked up as she heard steps and found the physician standing there. "Dr. White? He's awake!"

"So I see. How be you pop down off the bed and head out to the waiting room? Just long enough for us to check him over. You can come back, I promise." He watched with compassion the struggle that Aubrey went through before she nodded, reached to kiss Barnabas, and then was off the bed, heading for the waiting room.

Bruce looked up as she almost danced towards him and was on his feet, hope on his face.

"Aubrey?"

"He's awake, Bruce. He's awake. Oh, Dad! God is good. Barnabas is awake!" She threw herself into his arms, feeling his tight hug and then hearing his prayer of thankfulness.

Bruce blinked back tears of happiness before he thought through what Aubrey had said. He paused and then smiled. She had called him "Dad". They had asked her to do that and she had refused until now.

"What does the doctor say?"

"He kicked me out so that he could examine him." Aubrey spun, whirling around the room in her happiness. "I can go back in when he's done. You're coming with me." She paused in front of him. "Mom. You need to call Mom and let her know. Please?"

Bruce simply hugged her again and reached for his phone, to do just that, handing her his phone.

When Elizabeth answered, all she heard was silence for a moment and her heart fell until she heard the happy voice wafting across the airwaves.

"Mom? He's awake. Barnabas is awake and talking. God heard!" Aubrey's voice could hardly contain all the happiness she felt.

"He is? Oh, praise the Lord. Aubrey. Is Bruce with you?"

"Dad is. Thank you, Mom. Can you come?"

"I can and will. Let me talk to Bruce for a moment?"

Bruce took his phone back and moved away, turning to watch Aubrey as she stood, arms wrapped around herself and praying, he knew.

"Bruce?"

"Yes, Elizabeth. He is awake and talking she says."

"Oh, thank God. But she called me "Mom"?" Elizabeth's voice had uncertainty and yet joy.

"She did. I'm Dad to her now. She didn't realize that what was she had called us, I don't think."

"It doesn't matter. It shows that she is healing and beginning to live again. I'm on my way."

"Wait, hon. Breck sent a text that he was heading in about this time. He offered to stop by and bring you in."

"He did? Oh, okay." Elizabeth peeked through the window of the door. "He's here now. See you in a bit." Elizabeth just opened the door and hugged Breck.

Breck stood for a moment before he hugged her back, not sure what was happening.

“Elizabeth?”

Elizabeth stood back, wiping at her eyes, causing Breck’s heart to fall.

“Aubrey called us Mom and Dad.” She laughed, a happy laugh filled with tears. “She also told me that Barnabas is awake and has spoken.”

“Oh, praise the Lord! Well? What are we waiting for?” He grinned at her, a grin he used to give when he was a teen and wanting her to go with him somewhere. “Are you up for a fast trip through town?”

“I am and this time, I won’t complain if you speed. Neasa is with you?”

“She is.” Breck helped Elizabeth down the sidewalk to the truck and then into the back of the cab. “Neasa, Barnabas has woken up.”

Four days later, Barnabas sank into his chair in his home office, staring at the pile of folders and mail awaiting him. He sighed. He didn't feel up to it but knew he needed to make a start. Aubrey watched him before she set his mug of coffee beside him, standing with an arm around his shoulders.

"You need help with this. What can I do?"

Barnabas looked up, a grateful look on his face. "Dad and Amy have done what they could with Breck's help. But these?" He lifted a corner of the pile of file folders and then let it drop. "These are what I need to go through."

"And you don't feel like it. Let me help. Where do we start?"

Two hours later, Barnabas sat back, exhausted but content. With Aubrey's help, he had sorted through what he needed to accomplish, done just that, and then had sat and watched as she sat, her hair disheveled from running her hands through it as she answered the last of the letters for him.

"Thanks, sweetheart. I didn't think that we would get through all this."

Aubrey looked up, a smile on her face. "We did. I just need you to sign these and I can take them out for mailing."

He watched as she walked away before he pulled up his email, his face paling as he read the email that he had received. This is vicious, he thought. Whoever it is doesn't threaten Aubrey. They threaten me, and then her if she gets in the way. I don't get why. He sighed to himself as he forwarded the email on to Dallas.

Dallas had been around two days before, his eyes watchful as he studied the waiting room, taking in the visitors sitting there, in particular, one couple who seemed out of place and uncomfortable. He had taken a photo of them and sent it on to Davy, asking that he try and confirm identities. He was surprised at how quickly Davy had responded, giving their names and then asking why? When informed, Davy had simply stated that he was on his way, if that was okay with his boss. Dallas had grinned. Even though Davy was slightly older than himself, they were comfortable working as a team.

Barnabas had looked up as Dallas had entered his room, a nod greeting him before his eyes dropped to Aubrey, who was curled up against him once more, sound asleep. He had smiled, a somewhat sad smile as he watched her.

"Dallas? How many times have you been around?"

"Enough that the nurses just look past me. How are you?" Dallas pulled up a chair near the table, his laptop coming out as did his portable printer.

"Getting there. Not something that I would recommend for anyone, that's for sure." Barnabas' head went back. He still hurt all over, partly from the beating that he had undergone. "Where do I start, Dallas?"

"From early that day, I would think." Dallas watched him closely. "Your heart is hurting, my friend."

"It is. I know that Aubrey is being threatened. I want whoever it is to answer for that. Only I don't see that will happen."

"We're doing our best. Your Dad picked up your truck. Will authorized it. He's taken it in to have the window replaced." Dallas paused as Barnabas' head shot up and he stared at him.

"The window?"

"It was shattered. Don't you remember? Your face, at least the left side, took a beating from the shattered glass.

Barnabas' eyes closed. "I do remember that now that you have mentioned it." He looked down for a moment, his hand rubbing at his chest. "I need to give you my statement and I'm not sure I should with Aubrey here."

"She's asleep?"

"She is and she will need to find out what happened. I'm just not sure if I'm ready to tell her. Not like this."

"She's a lot stronger than any of us give her credit for. You know that, Barnabas. She told me yesterday that she was mad at God for letting this happen. That she needed you to continue to teach her how to live."

"She said that? I can't have her mad at God. Not at all. And I guess if hearing what happens fixes that, I have to let her hear."

Barnabas thought back to that morning. He had taken reluctant leave from Aubrey, seeing the lost look in her eyes that she quickly shuttered. Knowing that he would be away all day, he had hugged and kissed her, promising to text or call as he could. Barnabas had walked away, heading first to do some shopping, his list of Christmas presents for Aubrey quickly finished. He had stared at the florist and decided to stop in on his way home, hoping that it would still be open.

His meetings finished, he had headed for the florist shop, finding it still open and quickly purchasing the daisies and carnations that he knew she liked from their university days. He had headed home, stopping at an out-of-the-way store to make an impulse purchase. The box tucked into a pocket, he had headed for his truck, his coat collar turned up against the cold rain that lashed at him.

Barnabas had pulled out of his parking spot, the last to leave, he thought, delayed by a phone call. Even the store that he had just exited was dark, everyone heading home. He had slammed on his brakes as someone appeared in front of him and then he took a look in the rearview mirror. He sighed. Someone just had to appear there, now didn't they?

He had flinched as a hand banged at his window before an iron bar kept hitting at it, finally shattering it. His arm had gone up in reflex, to protect him as much as he could from the pieces of glass. A hand had reached in, unlocking his door. A voice had ordered him to put the truck in park. When he refused, the man reached angrily across him to do just that.

Pulled roughly from the vehicle, he had stood watching the men, trying his best to get as much of a description of them as he could, to no avail. Woollen hats pulled down as much as possible and scarves wrapped around the lower faces prevented that, that and the stinging rain that lashed at him. He had sensed movement to his left side and tried to move away, the iron bar meeting his ribs and driving him to his knees where a second blow to the same area dropped him to the ground. He lay, an arm wrapped around himself, drawing in ragged breathes, unable to understand the words driven at him. He had felt the kicks driven into his legs before he was on his own, his vision fading as he passed out.

Not knowing if he was still alone or not, Barnabas had roused, pain lashing through him still. He had pushed himself up with one arm, bracing himself to stay sitting up. His other arm was wrapped around his chest to try and ease the pain. He had drawn up his legs, his feet slipping on the wet pavement as he tried to rise, unable to get traction to do so. Barnabas had raised his head, his eyes closing against the cold rain that was changing over to stinging sleet. Unable to stay upright, his arm had begun shaking until it could no longer support him. He slipped back to the pavement, his head hitting hard before blackness overwhelmed him and he slipped away into that dark well of forgetfulness. He didn't feel the cold driving his body to shiver and then past that as hypothermia set in.

How long he lay there, they were never quite sure. A patrol officer had pulled in, seeing the truck. Running the plates, he was out of it as he was advised that it belonged to Barnabas. A flashlight held high, he had walked around it, stopping as he stared at the open driver's door and the shattered window. He turned, the large light slashed through the darkness, moving across Barnabas' still form and then quickly moving back. The officer was on his radio, calling for help before he was on his knees, hands reaching to assess Barnabas. A quick return to his car had him retrieving the emergency blanket, spreading it over Barnabas to help keep him warm. Keeping him dry was not an option.

His supervisor stood beside him, having heard the call and the name.

"What do you know?"

The officer shook his head. "Not a lot. I saw the truck, came in to check it out, found out how it belonged to, and then found him." He watched closely as the paramedics worked on Barnabas and then moved to help them lift the stretcher into the back of the rig, seeing the grim looks on their faces.

"Do we have any idea how long?" The senior paramedic questioned him even as he reached for the heart monitor.

"No, I don't. Sorry. I found him about ten minutes ago. He's been there for a while I would say."

Rolling the stretcher quickly into the Emergency Department, the paramedics were ready with their report, helping to shift Barnabas to a stretcher in the department before they left. It was a busy night and there were just too many calls, they thought.

Medical staff worked quickly to stabilize Barnabas, the imaging and testing done that was requested, and then the work began to gradually warm him up. They exchanged glances, all of them unsure that he would even make it.

Barnabas finally looked up, shaking his head at Dallas' words as he informed Barnabas of what had transpired. He looked down at Aubrey as she slept. He frowned and then smiled. Faking it, sweetheart. Just so you don't get asked to leave me.

"Do you know who?" Barnabas hoped that the men responsible had been arrested and the burden having over him had been removed.

"No. No, we don't. We have taken the security feed from the stores but it's not much help. The cameras were iced up."

"So, we are no further ahead." Barnabas shook his head. "I want this over, Dallas, and now."

"I know you do, my friend. I wish the same. We're working on some leads, but they are few and far between. Even our contacts on the streets have no idea who or why." Dallas sorted out his papers, had Barnabas sign his statement, and then packed everything away. He hesitated for a moment and then shook his head, moving quickly to the door and then out of the hospital. He stood, his face raised to the sky, questioning why it was not evident who it was.

Aubrey sat up, her eyes on Barnabas as he stared across the room before she just reached to hug him.

"You heard?" Barnabas's voice was low.

"I did. Who is it?"

"That's what I can't figure out. Whoever it is has a vicious streak. They had to know that my life was in danger by leaving me there." He looked up, devastation on his face. "I can't think of anyone, sweetheart."

"When you get home, we'll start listing everyone who has reacted negatively to you. I think Breck and Bradon were working on that."

"I'm sure they are. Do you know when I can leave?"

"In a day or so. They just want to ensure you're healthy enough to."

Coming back to the present, Barnabas reached for a pad of paper and a pen and began listing names and what he could remember about each one. He vaguely heard Aubrey speaking with someone and looked up before he shrugged and looked back down at his list. He sat back at long last, lifting his eyes to find Branigan and Baird watching him.

"How long have you been here?" Barnabas shook his head. He needed to do better. He could lose himself in his work. That didn't help when someone was after him.

"About fifteen minutes." The two men exchanged glances even as Branigan spoke. "Aubrey said you were involved in something, just what she wasn't sure, and that we could come and just sit and wait for you."

"She said that?" Barnabas shook his head. "I'm sorry. I was listing names and what I could remember. I hadn't done that yet." He handed over his list. "Take a copy of that for everyone."

Branigan reached for it and then headed for the printer to copy enough for all. He was concerned, he had to admit, that Barnabas had ignored them. He would need to speak with Breck, he decided.

Baird took his copy of the list and glanced through it, nodding as he did so. It had to be God, he decided. They were finding all the same names. That didn't happen by chance.

Barnabas watched them and then looked towards the doorway as Aubrey appeared, a tray in her hands. Branigan reached for it, a quiet comment to her before she nodded and looked towards Barnabas.

"Sweetheart?" Barnabas was on his feet, walking towards her even as she backed away. "What is it?"

"I just wanted you to know that I left some sandwiches in the fridge if you fellows get hungry. I'm off to bed."

She walked into his hug, his kiss on her lips before she stepped back, her eyes on him before she turned and walked away. Fear was in her heart. Fear for him. She knew it was only going to get worse and that scared her. She knew what Jeremy was capable of, she had lived that for so many years. But the ones behind him? They were vicious and had little regard for anyone's life. They had proven that with what they had just done.

Barnabas watched her walk away before he turned, hesitating for a moment. He headed for the kitchen, finding the tray of food that she had left, a smile crossing his face for a moment. Baird stood watching him before he reached for the tray.

"Aubrey takes care of you, Barnabas."

"She is learning how to live again, Baird. So much was taken from her that she will never get back. And I am at a loss as to how to help her do just that." Sadness crossed Barnabas' face as he spoke.

"We know, my friend. We know that. But we see the change in her over the last few days. She has become very protective of you."

"She has?" Barnabas shook his head. "I don't see that."

"That's because you weren't awake." Baird grinned even as he headed back for the office, Branigan clearing a spot on the coffee table for the tray. "We lived it with her when you were unconscious. She was aggressive in ways that we didn't expect. Questioning. Having us research. The ladies spent a lot of time with her, as much as she would allow. Breck talked with your Dad. She tried to look after him and your Mom as well."

"She had that nurturing spirit in school. We all saw that. Jeremy drove it deep inside her. I'm glad it's coming out." Barnabas bit into his sandwich, chewed, swallowed, and then looked at his friends. "Where do we stand on the investigation? I know that you have all pulled back from your work. You don't have to say a word."

"We have." Branigan wiped his mouth on a paper napkin before he continued. "We have eliminated Jeremy has to be responsible for the attack on you. We've talked to people who knew him. Andy flew Brandon and Blair up there. They came back with more information regarding him. That included names from here."

"Names that you aren't willing to share or can share?" Barnabas looked between the two.

"We can. There are four names, two male, two female, that Breck zeroed in on. He says that you have had problems with them. I had issues with one of the men at one point." Baird hesitated.

"The one who wanted the papers from you?" At Baird's nod, Barnabas sat back, his sandwich forgotten in his hand. "I can't see what he wanted those for. They were just researching on a property that went nowhere."

Branigan looked up at that. "Property? Was the board looking at buying it?"

Barnabas shook his head. "No. It was next door to a property that they were looking at purchasing and then decided not to. There had been legal issues of improper lot lines and they didn't feel that they wanted to subject the Foundation to lawsuits over it."

"Okay. So, he wanted it to sue?"

"That's a possibility, I guess. There would not have been anything in it for him. He was the aggressor in it, building over the line and then claiming it as his property. I heard that whoever bought it sued him and he had a huge expense to undo what he had built." Barnabas rubbed at his face. "I don't get why he would be after me, though. I wasn't involved in that. I didn't even have that paperwork."

"We know. Your Dad clarified that. He had been the one involved, he said." Baird paused. "Unless they thought that going after you would get to your father?"

Barnabas paled. "Now that makes sense, doesn't it? Dad's the one who set up the Foundation. He had all this money that he didn't know what to do with and wanted to do something for God. If they could sully his name, it would go against the Foundation, now wouldn't it?"

"It would. Baird, I think that you just found the missing link that we were looking for." Branigan rose, heading for the desk to retrieve a pad of paper and pen before he sat back down. "That list you just gave us? How many of those would have something against your father?"

———

"The list? Everyone single one. I wasn't thinking that way but it's true." Barnabas bowed his head, his heart praying for his father, knowing that he would need to talk with him and not quite sure how to proceed.

"Let's pray for you and Bruce, Barnabas." Blair didn't wait for a response, simply began to pray.

Bruce studied his son the next morning as he paced his father's office. His arms on his desk, he rolled a pen under the fingers of one hand, not sure what Barnabas was bothered by.

"Son?"

"Dad? I need to talk to you and I'm not even how to begin." Barnabas dropped into a chair in front of the desk.

"We pray first, son. Then we talk." Bruce was as good as his word, looking up at last at Barnabas. "Now, you have concerns. You have never not been able to talk with me."

"I know, Dad. This time is difficult." Barnabas pulled his upper lip down over his teeth for a moment. "What I'm going through? What Aubrey went through? I think it was to get at you."

"At me?" Bruce frowned. "Explain, son. I'm not quite following you."

Barnabas handed over the paper that he had been rolling in his hands. "This. I came up with this list last night. Baird and Branigan stopped in. They have a lot of the same names. We were talking about it and all came to the conclusion that someone was after you and through you, possibly the Foundation."

"I see." Bruce reached for the paper, not taking his eyes from his son. "And you think that I wouldn't listen to you?"

"No, not that, Dad. I'm just not sure that we're on the right track. That's all."

"I have had the same thoughts. John and I have been going back over everyone that we have had dealings with that were hostile or wanted something from the Foundation that we were not willing to give." Bruce studied the list. "I see you have a good memory. Some of these are recent but I can see two that go back to when you were a baby and I had just set up the Foundation. They didn't think my money should be used for charity. They wanted it for their own use. One of them? He actually sued to stop us."

"He did? Who?"

"Sam Pine. That's someone who has always hovered around the edge of our Foundation. We suspect that he has tried things over the years." Bruce sat back, thinking when a grim look came over his face. "He's from up north, son. Not too far from where you found Aubrey."

"Then he would know Jeremy. Aubrey said Jeremy is notorious in that area. In fact, he has been banned from one town. We stayed there when I first rescued her, assuming that we would be safe for at least a day or so."

"You were likely correct to do so. Now, we need to find out who all he is related to. I am sure, knowing his character, that he will not bring in outsiders to do his dirty work."

"Emma or Kataleen, I would think." Barnabas pulled out his phone, irritated at the incessant vibrating. "It's Kataleen. She has sent an email to both of us, she says. We need to look at it."

Bruce was already pulling up his email program and as he read the email, his face grew grimmer.

"We're on the right track, son. Now, let's get together with the fellows and see what we can do to solve this. Your first Christmas with Aubrey is in a few weeks. I don't want this overshadowing it."

Barnabas rose and followed his father to the conference room, pacing along the edge of the room, reading the whiteboards and realizing just how far the fellows had come. He stopped at the logic problem and gave a grim smile. They had nailed the person, he thought. Now to speak with Dallas. He turned his head as he heard footsteps.

"Dallas? You're here?"

"I am. Will has sent me, once more, to work from here. Davy will be in and out, he says. He's working on other cases. Given what happened to you, Will wants this solved. And no, we're not favouring you because of the Foundation. The public relations officer is putting out a statement later today."

"They are? I'm surprised. I'm not that important."

"But you see, Barnabas, you are. You have not heard the praise and conversations that we have had since it broke in the news about you. You don't realize the impact that you and the Foundation have in our community and from here to other areas. Someone is trying desperately to bring you and the Foundation down. That includes destroying your father."

"I know. I was about to call you. Here." Barnabas handed over the papers he had been holding. "This is what we have come up with. This particular man? He's been after Dad since I was small."

"That's a long time."

"It is. He has had years to plot and plan and refine his revenge."

Looking around at the ladies who had gathered in her apartment, Aubrey shook inside. She wasn't used to this, she thought. At one time, it would not have mattered. She would have welcomed them. But now? Going through what she was? She felt that she was putting everyone in danger and that she hated.

Neasa had been watching her closely. "Aubrey, do you mind if we pray first? It's how we usually start. We share if we have specific concerns or know of specific concerns. Today? That would be you, Barnabas, and his parents."

"It would be." Aubrey looked down, not wanting to see pity on the face, missing the looks of caring and compassion. The ladies knew what she was going through. They had all been there.

Ker spoke. "Aubrey, you have heard our stories. We know, to a certain extent, what you are facing right now and will likely face. We want to bathe you in prayer, for wisdom, for peace, for understanding, and for courage."

Aubrey nodded, biting at her lip as she tried to control her tears. "You have no idea what this means. I was so isolated for so long. I shut down, just because that was how I could keep sane. He took that from me. I want him to answer for that. And I have no idea how many others he did this to."

"And he will. The fellows are working on it. We want to as well. We can bring a different perspective to it. We've done it in the past." Guenivere looked around.

"That's okay. We can, but I think this time it needs to be a joint effort." Cadee spoke from where she had stood for a moment before she sat back down. A puzzled frown was on her face. "I don't get why."

"It's about the Foundation." Devaney spoke up, Berneen nodding her agreement. "We have always felt that something was left unresolved in whatever we went through. Neasa, they never did find out who ran you two down. Breck is next to Barnabas here. If he had been removed, who would have taken over that position?"

Neasa stared at her. "They would have had to hire, and whoever it was could have brought in someone no one would have suspected." Her phone was out as she sent off a text message to Breck. "He'll bring it up with the fellows."

Aubrey finally sat back, refreshed from the fellowship of prayer with the ladies and looked at them all. They are all so different, aren't they, Lord? Yet they fit together so well. I can see Your hand in all that.

"Fynn? You were working on ideas for the lobby for Christmas?" Imly looked at her.

"I was. I have some thoughts but it's not my building. It's ours. The fellows will not likely care what we do but we need to keep it simple and tasteful. It's an office building as well as a residence."

"And that we can do." Jaxcy reached for the plans. "Oh, I like these. You're an artist, did you know that? Hagen. Here. Take a look." She handed over the papers.

"Fynn? These are wonderful. I know the fellows will help with setting up the trees. Artificial or natural?"

"I would say artificial. That way it's easier to maintain them." Fynn looked around, happiness on her face. "You know, this is the first Christmas that we are all married. It's special. We all have plans I am sure, but we need to plan an afternoon or evening when we get together, just to do that without any thought of what we've faced or are facing."

"Oh, I like that idea." Muir raised a hand. "I volunteer to organize it if no one else wants to. Once we decorate, we can plan. Buffet? Finger foods? Fruits and veggies?"

"Yes!" Ennis turned to Aubrey who was sitting beside her and hugged her. "I am so glad you are here. You are the one who we were missing. Now, let's set aside those plans and work on solving this."

Aubrey blushed and then shrugged. "Except we have no idea who." She was on her feet, heading for the door. "Let's find the fellows and see what we can do to help."

———

The men looked around as the ladies entered, even as Barnabas was on his feet heading for Aubrey. He swept her into his arms, holding her tight as she shuddered.

"Sweetheart?"

"Barnabas, love. We've come to help. We want this over because we have plans for a building party for Christmas. And this cannot interfere with it. How do we make that happen?"

The men exchanged glances even as their wives drew up chairs beside them. They watched the ladies, seeing the determination on their faces. Dallas stood back, his eyes on his friends. He was glad that they had found their special helpmeets but he was just a bit envious. Aubrey watched him, catching the wistful look on his face, and began to pray for him, asking that God bring him that special lady.

The man stood watching the ladies the next day as they shopped, Aubrey kept carefully in the centre of the group. He was frustrated. He needed to grab her to get to Barnabas, but that wasn't happening. His boss was unhappy. That person wanted whoever it was that had beaten Barnabas and left him to die.

Aubrey looked around, feeling the eyes of her. Ker was watching her and spoke quietly.

"Being watched?" At Aubrey's nod, Ker looked around, her gaze finding the man. "Listen. Stand with your back towards that way. I see him. I want to take your picture but I'm really taking him. Then I can send it on to to the fellows." She was as good as her word, the other ladies nodding their agreement.

Aubrey was frustrated. "I can't even shop without being followed. I'm still a prisoner, only I don't know who my captor is."

"No, you don't." Locklin spoke from beside her. "We all had that. So we know somewhat of what you are saying. It was different for each one of us, though. Now, how be we find somewhere for lunch? I for one am starved."

"The diner. They have a room we can use." Muir had her phone out, putting in a request. She looked pleased as she pocketed her phone. "It's free and we are welcome to use it. That's what is so nice about this town. They care about people."

Hagen stared at her. "Muir, what did you say?"

"What? That we had the room?"

"No." Hagen shook her head. "About this town. That they cared about people. That's what we've been missing. The Foundation has driven that for so many years. I know we've talked about someone wanting to take down the Foundation. My question is why? Who have they stopped?"

Ennis nodded. "That. That's so true. Ask anyone and they'll have been helped by the Foundation or know someone who has been. Cadee? Any word from your parents?"

"No. Running the shelter they should have heard something and haven't. Dad thinks whoever it is has brought in someone from out of town. There are strangers around here all the time, just given the location of our town near the canals and the lake."

"Too true. Let's sort ourselves out and head out for the diner." Berneen linked her arm with Aubrey. "Aubrey, you stay in the middle of us. That way, he, whoever he is, has to get through all of us. And we are a formidable group when we're together and angry." Her comment was met with howls of glee and agreement.

Seated in the restaurant, Aubrey shrugged out of her jacket and looked around. This is what I need, Lord, these friends. They are helping me to live once more. I was so afraid and uncertain when I arrived. Barnabas, bless his heart, has tried, hasn't he, dear Lord? But sometimes it takes a feminine perspective to help balance everything again."

Barnabas sat back in his desk chair. He had just finished a very disturbing call with someone that he didn't know. How that woman had known to reach out to him, he wasn't sure. He looked down at his notes and then rose, looking for Dallas.

Dallas looked up as Barnabas dropped down beside him, his notes hitting the table. He tilted his head to watch his friend.

"Barnabas?"

"I just got off the phone with a Lucy Logan. She contacted me out of the blue. I have no idea who she is or if she is even legitimate. She had quite the story to tell. Here. These are my notes. Read through them."

Dallas took them, scanned them, and then read through them. "She has a lot of information, doesn't she?"

"She does and I would like to know how." Barnabas blew out a breath. "She is adamant that someone is trying to nab Aubrey again, with the goal of getting to me. They get to me, then they get to Dad and through Dad, you know where."

———

"We know. I spoke with Abe this morning, just to get his perspective. He is concerned but given that we have no real information as to why or who, he is suggesting that you be very cautious where you go, be cognizant of those around you and your surroundings. The same goes for Aubrey. As much as you two want to be out and about on your own, and I totally get that, he has suggested that someone be with you. Some of the fellows here. Myself. The security people."

"That really throws a damper in spontaneous romantic dates." Barnabas sounded glum. "I know why and I can understand that. I just don't have to like it."

Dallas began to laugh. "The fellows would tell you the same thing. Let me see what I can find on this woman." He looked up as Bruce sat beside him. "Here, Bruce. Do you know this woman?"

"Who? Her? Sure. She applied to work here when we first opened up, but something was off about her. Her words didn't match her lifestyle. Is she the one?" Bruce looked over at his son.

"She called today, Dad, out of the blue. Read my notes, if Dallas will share. Tell us what you know about her."

Bruce thought back over the years to Lucy Logan. He frowned as he remembered how desperate she had seemed to land the position. He had not had a good feeling about her, something was off, and he had gone to the board, knowing that they would either confirm or recommend what they needed to.

The board had gone over all the applicants and Lucy's had been questioned. One of the older men on the board, long since gone to heaven, had shaken his head. Not her, had been his comment. She says the right words but her lifestyle belies them. She was into the shady side of life as he had called it. They had prayed over the applications and made their choice. As he recalled, she had not taken it well, swearing revenge on him. He and the board had discussed her reaction, documented it, prayed about it, and moved on.

Bruce looked at the two younger men and sighed. What the board had thought was in the past was coming back. How did they now deal with it?

Lucy Logan stared at the Barnabas Foundation website, anger growing inside her. They had destroyed her life by not hiring her all those years ago. That's what she had been told. She didn't doubt now that the person telling her this was correct. At the time, she had shrugged and decided whatever. She had moved on until about four years ago when she was approached and offered a large sum of money to bring down the Foundation in any way that she could. She had stared at the money, shaken her head, and walked away. The man kept coming back, the money offered increasing to the point that she had reached out a hand, taken it, and then walked away, to plan just how she could do that.

Lucy had looked at all the men employed by the Foundation and decided to work through them all. What she had not counted on was that someone else was after the men as well. That had frustrated her. By the time that she arrived at Breck's turn, she was angry. She had waited for Barnabas, knowing he was the one that she needed to go after. By that point, it really didn't matter if he died or not. She had not planned on him leaving town and then coming back with a wife. How dare he! She had put her life on hold, she thought, and never married. How dare he go on with his life! After what his father and the Foundation did to her. Alcohol and drugs fuelled her anger. She didn't understand that she was being used and likely would not even care if she did.

Rising, she headed for her vehicle, trying to come up with a plan, any plan, that would bring Barnabas to her. She decided that somehow she would find Aubrey and use her to get to Barnabas and then use Barnabas to get to Bruce. She drove around the Foundation property for two or three days at different times of the day, finally picking a spot to stop. Lucy pocketed her keys and walked towards the gardens, sneaking in without as much fanfare as she could.

She watched the ladies and men and the small children as they roamed the gardens, her eyes on Aubrey as she moved around with the ladies. This frustrated Lucy that she was never out there on her own. How could she get to her?

Then, one late afternoon, Lucy found her moment. Aubrey had stopped in the gardens, her hands touching the lamps that would soon be lit before she turned. She was restless, Aubrey thought, expecting something bad to happen. It just hadn't yet.

Hearing a footstep, Aubrey spun and began to back up from the woman in front of her. She studied her, seeing the ravages of the rough life Lucy had lived, of the alcohol and drugs that had ruined her beauty, the rage that kept building in her.

"I'm sorry. I don't think that you belong here. You need to leave." Aubrey continued to back away, hoping to make it to the path where she could run for the building.

Lucy simply shook her head, a gun appearing in her hand.

"Stop moving. You're not getting away from me."

"I'm sorry. I don't know who you are, but you don't belong here." Aubrey still moved backwards as she could, judging the steps that she could take with the way the gun was wavering.

Lucy strode towards her, the gun now pointing at Aubrey's head. Aubrey froze, seeing the instability in Lucy.

"No, you're coming with me." Lucy grasped her arm and pulled her roughly with her, her eyes searching for anyone who was coming to help. "I said, you're coming with me." Her gun jammed into Aubrey's side, stopping the younger woman's struggles to release her. Lucy stopped by her car. "In. I said, get in." She shoved Aubrey in, the gun pocketed and a syringe instead in her hands.

Aubrey began to please, begging that she be let go. That she didn't know who Lucy was or what she wanted. Lucy gave a cackle of glee, knowing that she had Aubrey where she wanted her.

"I want you. I want Barnabas. And then I want Bruce. He has to pay."

"Pay? For what?" Aubrey tried to find a way to escape but Lucy blocked her line of flight and Aubrey knew that she would never make it across the console and out the driver's door before she would be shot.

"I'll tell you that when I'm ready." Lucy studied her impassionately and then studied the syringe. A swift movement on her part and the syringe needle plunged into Aubrey's arm.

Aubrey struggled to get away, her vision darkening as the drug took effect. She slumped down, her head sagging forward, even as Lucy slammed the door and then walked to her own door, opening it to slide in. She drove away rapidly and aimlessly, her eyes on the road ahead of her, not worrying about being seen. In her mind, she had done nothing wrong.

She pulled into a garage in a remote location, turning off the vehicle and then moving to unlock and open the door to the house. Lucy returned to pull open the passenger's door, staring down at Aubrey. She tugged her from the car and then dragged her across the garage floor, up the stairs and to a room on the first floor. Aubrey was shoved into an antique wooden armchair.

Reaching for the rope that she had left handy, Lucy tied Aubrey securely to the chair before she turned away and headed for the kitchen. She reached a shaky hand for the bottle that was on the first shelf of the cupboard. She needed that drink and a large one at that.

Turning from his desk, Barnabas pulled out his phone about the time that Lucy had appeared. He sent a quick text off to Aubrey, just to tell her that he loved her before he headed down the hall. Shoving open the door to the conference room, he paused, his eyes on the fellows. Most of them were there, he could see. Brady was absent, off on duty. Burnie had to be out of town that day to meet with his publisher. The rest were there. He could tell that they had been busy.

He walked about the whiteboards, reading what had been discovered. Barnabas paused as he came to the name of Lucy Logan and frowned. She really is involved in a lot of things, crime and whatnot, isn't she? He hazarded a guess that Dallas knew a lot more than he could tell, and that was okay with him. It was how it was to be.

Bradon approached him, his head tilting to watch him.

"Barnabas?"

"Bradon?" Barnabas turned to him. "You fellows have been busy. I see that you have found a lot of information."

"We have. And still are. Kataleen and Emma are sending on what they can and copying it to Dallas." Bradon turned to watch Dallas. "He's not saying much."

"No, he can't." Barnabas turned to watch him. "He's burning out, Bradon, not just from us."

"He is. I asked him how long he planned to stay a detective. He just looked at me, a bleak look on his face, and shrugged. He's hurting about something and he doesn't feel comfortable enough to share."

"No. All we can do is pray for him." Barnabas excused himself, moving away to stop and speak with each of the fellows, ending up at Breck's side.

"Breck? They're quitting in good time?"

"They are. We're making sure of that. This cannot affect their brides, even though the ladies are willing to let them." Breck handed Barnabas a mug of coffee. "How are you doing, my friend?"

Barnabas shrugged. "I'm not quite sure, to tell you the truth. I worry so much about Aubrey and she is doing the same about me. It's making it tough. And now this with Dad? That has added an extra layer to our stress. God is there, but sometimes it is hard to remember that."

"It is, Barnabas. It is." Breck looked around. "We all know that, even though this is much worse for you, just because it affects the Foundation." He paused, his eyes on his own mug. "Listen. Can you and Aubrey come for dinner tonight? You need time to just relax and maybe, just maybe, take your mind off this for a while."

"I'll ask her." Barnabas sent off a quick text, staring at his phone with a frown on his face. "That's odd. She hasn't responded to my other text. And she always does right away." He spun, almost running from the room, the fellows looking up and then at Breck as he followed Barnabas at a rapid pace.

Barnabas flung open the apartment door, rapidly searching and not finding Aubrey. Where is she, he thought? He spun, running for the door and then outside, Breck at his heels. They searched the grounds, not finding her, before Barnabas slid to a stop, his hand reaching for Aubrey's phone, Breck's hand on his wrist stopping him.

"No, Barnabas. We need to call it in." Breck looked up to find Dallas watching from just behind them. "Dallas?"

Dallas nodded. "I called in it. They're on their way." His hand out, he led Barnabas back from the area. He nodded as Bradon appeared, his dog, Kade, at his side. "Go ahead, Bradon. See what you can find."

Barnabas stood near the edge of the building, his arms wrapped around his chest, eyes not moving from the officers and techs that searched the area. Bruce stood beside him, his arm around his son's shoulders. Elizabeth had been out there and he had sent her back in to wait where it was warmer. The fellows from the building had gathered around them, quiet, grim looks on their faces. Aubrey would not be the first one to disappear from the building. They had all prayed that she wouldn't. God was in control, Baird commented, even when they could not see it. They knew the ladies and Anna and Amy were gathered in the chapel, petitioning the gates of heaven.

Bradon reappeared, waiting for Dallas to approach him. He shook his head.

"There was a vehicle waiting there. Kade tracked Aubrey to there. She disappeared into it."

"Again? I'll send the techs that way." Dallas turned to watch Barnabas. "We need to get him inside. This dampness is not going to help him."

"No. I'll see what I can do."

"Bradon?" Dallas called after him, waiting until he turned back. "Say nothing. Let me do that/"

"I will. He may not ask."

"He will. Trust me. I would in his position." Dallas turned to find one of the techs and a patrol officer that he could send that way.

Barnabas looked up as Bradon approached, hope dying in his heart at the look on Bradon's face. He drew a deep, shaky breath before he spoke.

"Let's go on in, Dad, and find Mom. I need her." Barnabas staggered as he turned, his father's arm out to come around him and lead him away, away from where his beloved Aubrey had last been.

Bruce shared a look with Bradon, who simply shook his head. Bruce nodded. She's gone, and now we have to find her. Lord, why? I don't understand but I do know that you are in control.

Elizabeth sat beside Barnabas, a hand on his back as he leaned forward, his head buried in his hands, elbows on his knees. For once, like Bruce, she was unable to make it all better for him. That disturbed her. She looked up as Will appeared, shaking her head at him. Will nodded before he sat beside Barnabas.

Barnabas turned his head to watch his friend, not quite sure why Will was there and not Dallas.

"Will?"

"I'm here as a friend today, Barnabas', not as an officer. That's Dallas' job right now. His and Davy's. He said that they would be in shortly." Will prayed for his young friend. "What can you tell me?"

"Not a lot. I was working all afternoon. Aubrey had planned to do some reading she said. She can't get enough books now. I sent her a text late afternoon, just before I went to the conference room. She didn't respond and that's when Breck and I went searching." Barnabas drew in a deep breath. "Where is she, Will?"

"We'll find her, son." He watched as Barnabas shook his head and then stood, staring at the floor.

"But will she still be alive? It's to the point that I don't think that anyone cares whether she lives or dies. Not us, but whoever it is. They seem determined to bring as much hurt as they can and don't care who it destroys." He walked away, the fellows gathering around him as they stood, heads bowed to pray for their leader.

Will watched him, a frown on his face.

"He's right, Will." Bruce spoke from where he stood. "I don't think they care if someone lives or dies. And I wish I knew why."

"The Foundation. You've used your money as a trust to help. People resent that. They want the money for themselves and they really don't care how they get it. Right now? I would say that Aubrey is hidden somewhere close, where they can watch the activity here."

"Have you found Lucy Logan yet?"

"No, we haven't. Not that I am aware of. The detectives may have but we are swamped right at the moment with cases."

"I know, Will. I know that. Whatever it takes to help let the Foundation know. I don't want to be put to the forefront and ahead of anyone else if it's a matter of life and death."

Will stood, his hand on his friend's shoulder. "But it is, Bruce. It is. It is a matter of life and death for Aubrey and likely Barnabas. Not one of the officers will have it any other way but that they work on this. They are working on it in their own time. I have said not to, that they need the downtime. It doesn't matter. You and your organization have done so much for our town. This is how they pay you back."

"I didn't do it for payback. You know that."

"No, you didn't, but the town feels a debt that needs to be paid, one of so many. Even the council has approached me, asking what they can do. This will accelerate that giving. Take it as it is meant."

"I will." Bruce looked around. "I need to go and call the board."

"It's been done. I talked to John. They are heading this way, Bruce, just to be with you."

"Thank you, Will." Bruce stood for a moment, unsure of what to do, before he headed for the chapel, pushing the door open and then entering to sit at the back, not disturbing the young ladies who had gathered.

Neasa looked around and then moved to sit beside him, her arm linked with his, as she prayed for him. Bruce was loved by all in the building and it hurt them all to see the suffering that the family was undergoing.

Two days later, Barnabas looked up as he heard footsteps approaching him. He had been searching, on his own, not letting the fellows know that he was. They knew, without being told. One of them always followed him, keeping him in sight, but not close enough that it would cause him distress that they were putting themselves in danger. The man who stood in front of Barnabas was well-groomed. Barnabas frowned, not knowing who it was.

"Mr. Carey. I need you to come with me."

"I don't think so. I have no idea who you are." Barnabas stood and moved back, towards the street where he could run if he had to.

"Oh, I think you will. Check your phone." The man waited patiently as Barnabas pulled out his phone.

Drawing in a deep breath as he stared at the photo, Barnabas looked up in anger.

"Where is she? What did you do to her?"

"I did nothing to her. That's not to say something more won't happen. That's why you come with us." The man pointed towards a luxury vehicle. "In there." He reached out a hand. "Your phone."

His hand tightening on it, Barnabas almost refused before he reluctantly handed it over. He watched as the man simply tossed it into a trash container before he pointed once more to the vehicle. Given no choice, Barnabas headed that way and was soon seated. His eyes searched the area, seeing Branigan approaching the trash container. Good, he thought. He'll grab my phone. Dad has the password to get in.

"Where are we heading?" Barnabas shifted to watch the man.

"Not your concern. Not yet." He drove seemingly in random circles before he pulled to the side of the road. He handed Barnabas a bandana. "Put this on. And once it is on, you don't move it. Your wife's life depends on how well you follow instructions."

Branigan fished the phone from the garbage and then stood staring after the car, his mind memorizing the license plate number before his phone was out and he was making that call all of them had dreaded. Now not only was Aubrey missing, so was Barnabas. The next one would be Bruce. That was a given, he thought before he began to pray.

Breck approached him, a frown on his face.

"Branigan? I got your call. What happened?"

"I was staying back just like we agreed on. Barnabas was sitting there when some well-dressed man approached him. Barnabas ditched his phone, got into some high-end vehicle and they disappeared."

"Did you recognize the man or the car?"

"No. But I got a picture of it as well as a description and plate number. I have his phone."

"Okay. I think Bruce can access it." He looked around. "Are you done here?"

"I am. Can you give me a lift back to my truck? Then I'll follow you home."

Thirty minutes later, the two men stood in Bruce's office, watching as he sank back into his chair, his face white.

"Barnabas? He just went with him?"

"I'm sorry, Bruce. He did. I wonder if Aubrey was threatened or you." Branigan handed over the phone. "This is his. He threw it away. I think he saw me."

Bruce reached for the phone. "He did? Then he knows we have it." He hesitated, spending a bit of time in prayer before he unlocked the phone and then searched the text messages. "Here. Oh, no!"

Breck reached gently for the phone and turned it, a deep breath drawn as Branigan muttered under his breath. The photo showed Aubrey slumped in the chair, her arms bound to it. They could not get a sense of if she was alive but assumed that she was.

"I need to get this to the investigators, Bruce. Do I have your permission?"

Bruce nodded, unable to speak. He rose, stumbling somewhat and Breck's hand went out to steady the man he considered a second father.

"I need to find Elizabeth. She needs to hear it from me."

"I'll go with you. Branigan?" Breck looked over at him.

"I'm heading for the fellows. We're not leaving that room until we come up with some answers. The ladies have already told us that is what they expect." Branigan was away, stopping outside the conference room to pray before he entered.

A sudden hush dropped over the room and several of the men rose, their eyes on him.

"It's bad, fellows. Barnabas was just taken. I saw it and could do nothing." Branigan held up his phone. "I have photos that we can work with." He searched the room, finding Dallas heading his way. "Dallas?"

"Send it to me. I'm heading in." He was gone before anyone could respond.

Staring at her husband, Elizabeth shook her head even as the tears started and her hands covered her mouth. Bruce swept her into his arms and just stood, holding her as she sobbed. He had no answers for her. Not yet.

The ladies in the chapel with Elizabeth watched in horror before Neasa's head was down and she began to petition for the couple's safe return. The others picked it up one by one. When they finished and raised their head, the older couple was gone. Muir looked around.

"Okay, ladies. This is what we expected but prayed would not happen. We put our plan into effect. Group 1, you're on for supper and late-night snacks. Group 2, we're on in the morning. And in the meanwhile, we work our own searches and try to keep our fellows' spirits up."

Two days went by before Bruce was approached by the same man as he walked across the parking lot from John's office. He was forced by gunpoint into the same vehicle as his son had been and driven away, no one around to see anything. The man had made sure of that. He had been promised good money if that happened, and he could always use the money, he thought.

No one was aware that Bruce too had gone missing until Elizabeth looked at the clock and realized that it was mid-afternoon and Bruce had not appeared for lunch. There was no answer to her phone calls or her text messages. Frantic, she ran from their apartment, heading for Breck, meeting him coming towards her.

"It's Bruce. He's gone."

"Elizabeth? Bruce?" Breck's hands on her arms stopped her.

"I just realized that he had never come home for lunch. I can't get an answer when I call or text him."

Breck's face grew grimmer as with his hand on her arm he directed her to the conference room.

"Fellows? Bruce has disappeared. Where was he, Elizabeth?"

"He had a meeting with John early this morning. He said he'd be home by noon. I didn't realize it until just a few moments ago." She took the handkerchief that Brennen handed her, wiping at her face and then twisting it in her hands.

"Brennen? Find Dallas." Breck's voice was quiet even as Brennen had nodded and walked away rapidly, heading for the lobby so that he could call in private.

Dallas had appeared, not surprised that Bruce had disappeared. He had been the target after all, hadn't he? John was there as well, aghast that Bruce had disappeared as he left their meeting. He had been in touch with the board, who would gather at the building to make plans.

The fellows had taken a look at Elizabeth and then dove back into their research. Blair had been on the phone to Emma, begging her to help. She had simply stated that she was, that she was sending on more information and did they need Abe and her to come?

Chapter 48

A few hours after she had been abducted, Aubrey had roused and begged to use the facilities. The sedative had sent nausea roiling in her stomach. She had rinsed out her mouth after she had been sick, staring unseeingly at herself in the mirror before she was dragged back to her chair and shoved down into it. A bottle of water had appeared as well as a sandwich. Shaking her head at the food, she had simply downed some water. Her arms were once more bound to the chair. She had wept, pleading to be let go, but silence had met her demands.

This had been the routine for the next day or so, Aubrey sleeping from the sedatives that she was slipped in her water. She didn't hear the curses of the woman as she paced, hateful glares sent her way. She also didn't hear the woman on the phone, demanding that Barnabas be found and brought to her.

Barnabas was pulled from the car and then shoved forward, his shoulders moving away from the push, and through the door into the house, his blindfold still in place. He stumbled as he hit the tile floor and had to fight to keep his balance. He felt the hand on his back leading him to another room where he too was shoved into a chair and bound. The blindfold was roughly pulled from his head. He blinked and squinted as he tried to once more become accustomed to the light.

He squinted as the light became bearable and he looked around. He gave a cry and fought to free himself, spying Aubrey slumped in a chair across the room. The rough rope dug into his wrists and ankles. There was just no way that he could free himself.

"Let me go. Let me go to her!" Barnabas was pleading, he knew. The only response was a gun barrel jammed against his temple, stilling his movements.

There was the tapping of high heels and Lucy appeared, a sneer on her face. She studied the younger man before she handed over another wad of cash.

"There. Now, hide until I need you again. It will not be that long." She watched as the man carelessly stuffed the money in his pocket and left before she turned to Barnabas. "So, Carey. You are now in my control. Good. It's been a long time coming." The alcoholic haze that she was in had her convinced that she was in control and that she would win. She didn't see the determination on his face to somehow free himself, free Aubrey and leave. Only, he had no way of knowing where they were.

Two days later, Barnabas looked up as he heard footsteps. His heart sank. He recognized his father's. Dad, they got you. I was praying that they didn't.

Bruce sat where he was told to. He had not been surprised that he was not blindfolded. He had recognized the property and knew that the men of the building had been right all along. They had insisted that the Logan property was still kept up and that Lucy lived there. Boys, I apologize and I will do that in person when I come home. Only, Lord, I don't know that I will.

Lucy stared at him and began to laugh, an evil laugh that turned into a cackle and then choking. Her lifestyle was not conducive to good health. Bruce studied her, seeing the changes that life had made in her. He sighed. Even if she had been given the work, he didn't think that she would have lasted. Sin had pulled at her and pulled her hard.

Lucy paced around them, her words muttered and incoherent before she abruptly walked away. Bruce could hear the clink of a bottle and grew suddenly afraid for his son and daughter-in-law. What was she planning? Nothing for their good.

"Dad?" Barnabas kept his voice low.

"Son? You're okay?"

"I am. I mean, I haven't been treated the best." His eyes went to Aubrey. "It's Aubrey. She's been kept sedated, I think. She doesn't even know that I'm here."

"I see. You haven't been able to loosen your bonds?"

"Not really. I tried." Barnabas looked over at his father, his eyes narrowing at the satisfied look on Bruce's face. "Dad?"

Bruce shook his head. "Not now, son. Let me think about this for a moment." Bruce continued to twist at his bonds, finding them loosening. He had not been bound very well, he thought, and wondered at that. He didn't think the man really cared but Lucy would. His right hand slipped free and he quickly moved to untie his left wrist.

On his feet, his pocketknife out, he slashed at Barnabas' bonds and then at Aubrey's, gathering Aubrey into his arms before he pointed at the front door with his chin.

"Out that way. Lucy's drunk. I think I heard her hit the floor"

"I think you're right. Dad, let me have Aubrey."

"Not yet, son. Hurry. I don't know if anyone else is around."

The men headed for the nearby trees, walking as rapidly as they could, deep into the area before Bruce paused. Barnabas was beside him, his hand on Aubrey's face, and then her wrist.

"She's sedated, Dad. They kept doing that. She kept being sick and begged them not to give her any water. Lucy forced her to drink if she refused." Barnabas looked up, fear for his young wife on his face. "How do we get home, Dad? And do you know where we are?"

Bruce looked up at the deepening night. "I do, son. It's the old Logan place, not too far from home. Here, you take your wife." Barnabas reached for her and then watched as his father bent over, to pull a slim tiny phone from his shoe.

"Dad?" His questioning voice caught Bruce's attention.

"Will and I talked. We thought they would try and take me. They did. We came up with this." He held up the phone. "It's a pay-as-you-go. He found one as small as he could. Now, let's pray that I have enough signals to get help." Bruce punched in Will's number and waited.

"Bruce?" Will's voice over the phone carried to Barnabas.

"Will, they made that attempt. They had me but I managed to escape. I have both Barnabas and Aubrey. We're in Weaver's woods, near the old Logan place. What's that? The Logan place? Yes, it's the one. The boys were right when they said it would be where she was. But we had no evidence, now did we?"

"No, we didn't. Hang on for a moment." Will's voice softened as he turned to speak with someone. "Davy's on his way. Brady's with him. Doc is waiting in the infirmary for you three."

Doc stood back at last, his eyes on the young couple before he moved to the hallway, finding the whole building family waiting, children included. Heath and Hannah had been begging for their Aube, in tears because they couldn't see her. He looked around at the men, seeing the worry, concern, and determination on their faces. On the ladies' faces, he saw the same but also the peace that only God could bring.

"Doc?" Breck spoke for the group.

"Bruce is okay. Just some abrasions on his arms. Barnabas is the same. He tells me that he tried his best to escape the ropes but he just couldn't. Aubrey is sleeping. She roused for a bit and then went back to sleep. She was kept sedated, Barnabas says."

"Praise God that we have them. But do we know why?" Blair looked around.

"Not yet. Will said Dallas and his team are working on that. Something about arrest and search warrants and needing to confirm facts." Bruce stood facing them, back to the room where his son and his wife lay, his arm around his own wife. "Thank you, men, ladies. Your prayers protected us, I have no doubt. I recognized the man. He's a hired assassin, among other things. I have no idea if Lucy is the one who hired him or not." Bruce gave a weary sigh. "How be we head to the chapel? Elizabeth, I know you're staying. I'll be back." He kissed her quickly before he moved among the building family, hugs to all, and then headed for the chapel, Buckley and Locklin on either side of him.

Will stood for a moment watching before he turned to Dallas.

"Get their statements. Then, take tonight and get some rest. I think that you won't be getting a lot in the next few days."

"I will. Just a question. They were in the Logan place? Didn't we search there?"

"We did. It looked as if someone had been there and then locked it up to be away for a time. We need to speak with that patrol officer again." Will's phone was out as it vibrated and he paled. "We can't do that."

"We can't?" Dallas was confused. "I don't understand."

"They just found his body next to his patrol car. A head shot, the responding officer said."

"The assassin?"

Will gave a grim nod. "I would guess that. Don't let those three out of the building. I don't care if you have to lock them into a room and keep the key. They'll be after them." Will walked away, heading for his vehicle. This was one part of the job he hated. Having to notify next of kin of a death.

Barnabas slipped from the bed that he had been lying on and headed for Aubrey, a kiss on her cheek, and her hand in his as he bent over her, watching her beloved face. He saw the whiteness of it, the black circles under her eyes, and the hollow cheeks. He frowned. She must have been sick a lot, he decided.

Doc stood watching him before he approached, an arm around the young man who he loved like a son. His prayer whispered in the quiet of the room.

"Doc?" Barnabas looked up at him. "Is she okay?"

"I would think so. We'll let the intravenous run and then decide if we need to do another one. I suspect that we will. Brady took the blood we drew into the hospital lab for me. We'll know if there is anything off. She's in a natural sleep, son."

"I know. I just worry. She didn't eat and barely drank the water. She tried to refuse and Lucy made her drink, even as she sobbed and begged her not to." Barnabas knew that he would never forget his helplessness in being able to help her.

"It will haunt you, Barnabas. We'll pray for you about that." Doc's hand rested on his shoulder. "I'll be back. Anna was heading up to heat some soup for you two."

"Aubrey won't eat. She'll think that she's still a prisoner." Barnabas rested his hand on her hair.

"We'll see. I'm sure that you can convince her."

Doc stood with his back resting against the door before he looked up. Dallas stood in front of him.

"Doc?"

"They have survived. We'll need to find someone that they can speak with. You've gotten their statements?"

"I have. Even Aubrey's although she faded on me just as she finished and signed it." Dallas shook his head, fatigue hitting him.

Doc watched him. "Head off to bed, Dallas. You've been burning the candle at both ends. As Will said, take the time tonight to sleep."

"Thanks, Doc. I will."

Aubrey stared at Barnabas, shock on her face. She shook her head. There was no way that Bruce had been able to get free and walk out with them.

"That can't be right. You were tied up, weren't you? And I know that I was. Besides I couldn't stay awake. I don't think that I even knew you were there."

Barnabas wrapped her in a hug. "I love you so much, sweetheart. My heart broke when I couldn't get free and get you out. Dad somehow was able to loosen his bonds and walked us out."

"I don't believe you. I mean, I know it's possible, but where was that woman?"

"It happened, sweetheart. We think that she passed out and dropped to the floor in the kitchen. We heard what we thought was a body hit the floor."

"Is it over?"

Barnabas shook his head, sorrow on his face. "Not yet. They're still working on search warrants and arrest warrants, Dallas said. He's not sure how long it will take. They need to round up everyone, he says, before we're safe."

"And we're prisoners again, aren't we? Kept in our home. I need to get out, Barnabas. I can't handle being locked up, even for a day or so. I just can't." She wept against him, feeling his kisses on her hair.

"Then, we won't. We'll take all the precautions that we can, but we will not be kept in." He set her back from him, his hands on her arms, his eyes searching her face.

"So, how do we do this, then?" She watched him, not quite sure that she should have spoken.

"We go out and about. Today, we go out for lunch. It's Saturday. I was told not to work until Monday. Then, tomorrow, it's church and we will be there."

"Of course, we will. We need that." Aubrey stepped back, heading for her coat. "If we're going out for lunch, then let's go. Fast food or diner?"

"I think the nice Italian restaurant. And yes, you are dressed just right." He reached to stop her, kissing her thoroughly, a finger drawn down her flushed cheek when he finished.

Bruce watched them head for Barnabas' truck and shook his head. He figured that they would make the decision that they had and feared for them. He turned to find Elizabeth beside him.

"They have the right idea, love."

"I know. I just fear for them." He looked down at her. "I suspect that they are heading out for lunch. Care to do the same?"

"With my best beau? Any time." Elizabeth tucked her hand around Bruce's arm. "Where to?"

"I don't really care. That Italian restaurant? We haven't been there since we came home."

"No, we haven't."

Bruce paused as they entered the restaurant and began to laugh. Barnabas looked around and grinned.

"Running away, Dad?"

"Escaping, son? I didn't know that you were heading here."

"Nor me you. Shall we take separate tables or pretend that we are on a double date?" His grin widened as he looked down at Aubrey. "Care to double date with my parents?"

Aubrey studied him, studied Bruce, and then looked at Elizabeth, finding the older woman barely containing her mirth. She gave a deep pretend sigh. "If we must, we must." She reached for Elizabeth's arm. "Seeing as they are so undecided, how be we find a table?"

Bruce and Barnabas shared a look before they broke out into laughter.

"I think that we just got told, Dad." Barnabas followed the ladies, holding their chairs while they were seated and then moving them into the table before he sat himself. He looked around the restaurant, nodding at friends and acquaintances before his eyes rested on a man seated near the front of the restaurant. He excused himself as he sent off a quick text to Dallas, who he knew was looking for that very man.

They watched as an officer entered and approached the man, speaking with him and then leading him from the building. Bruce caught the look on his son's face and nodded. He reported him, didn't he, Lord? Is this why we were here today? To find him? If this is why, thank you for bringing it up.

Aubrey turned to Barnabas before a frightened look covered her face. Barnabas started to turn to see what she was looking at but a prick from a knife against the back of his neck stopped him. He saw the fear on the other patrons and prayed, harder than he had in the past.

"Look who we have?" Lucy Logan's slurred voice sounded in his ear. "Just the people I wanted to find. I don't know how you escaped, but you won't again. Never again." The knife shook against Barnabas' neck. "You will pay for not hiring me. You and that Foundation that you are so proud of."

"Lucy? You know as well as I do that you were not qualified for that position. You would never have stayed. Your lifestyle would have drawn you away."

"That's what you think. I can stop the alcohol and the drugs at any time." Her face twisted with her words and then twisted more, fear showing on it, as a hand reached for her chest and then she dropped.

Bruce was on his feet, calling for someone to help, before he knelt beside her, a hand reaching for her wrist before he bent his head, ear to her chest, and then hand to her neck. He stood, his arm reaching for his wife and drawing her away. Barnabas moved away with him, Aubrey tucked up against him

"Dad?"

"She's gone, son. God has chosen this route for her. He has spoken. We will never likely know exactly what drove her." Bruce turned as he heard the sounds of the emergency vehicles and pulled his family out of the restaurant.

350

A day later, Will and Dallas faced the building family, gathered in the conference room. They had sorted through the details, finding it not quite as it had seemed. They had worked all night, Dallas and his team and the techs sifting through evidence. There were still some details that needed to be finished but they could finally say what it had all been about.

Buckley had been watching them and then stood, calling for attention. He stated simply that they needed to spend some time in prayer. When they had finished, they looked around, their eyes on Barnabas and Aubrey as they sat, his arm around her, his parents near them. A sense of relief filtered through the room. This was it, wasn't it, they all thought? The end of it?

Dallas stood at the front of the room, his eyes on Will before he looked at Bruce and then Barnabas and Aubrey. He swallowed hard, knowing that this was the end for the investigations for these men. He had not known them well, other than for speaking at church when it had all started with Baird but as he had worked with them, he had gotten to know each one and their ladies and valued their friendship and walk with God. He had come to some decisions about his own life and this was the final investigation, he had decided. He had spoken to Will, who had questioned him, prayed with him, and then given his blessing.

"Aubrey, we'll start with you. Jeremy has confessed that he was paid to keep you captive, to interfere in your relationship with Barnabas. Someone had been watching you that closely. We'll come to who. When things started to heat up about two years ago, he was ordered to cut all contact off between you two. What was not expected was that Barnabas would go looking for you, enter the house and then disappear with you, marrying you in the meantime. He was paid well for his trouble, I must say, but he is now through as a lawyer, has been for quite some time. His son was not part of it. He decided on his own that you were his. You suspected that Jeremy tried to keep you two apart and you were correct in that.

"Barnabas? Now it's your turn. Lucy Logan was behind it, but there was someone behind her. I'll come to who it was. You were right when you suspected that two different people were involved in what went on with the fellows. And you are correct in thinking that it was escalating with each one. The ATV that ran down Breck and Neasa? It was Lucy herself on it. She apparently thought that if she took him out, you would be more vulnerable. She left a detailed diary of everything she did, and everyone she hired. We're working on sorting through that and arresting each one. You all can rest easy that we have that solved.

"As to why she was after you? Your father was correct in thinking it was because she had been turned down for work here. But someone had approached her, trying to bring down the Foundation. From her diary, we have determined that she kept refusing until the money was just too much. Alcohol and drugs had taken over her body and mind. Her thoughts were becoming more and more muddled. She would have faced multiple charges, including murder and kidnapping among others. You are not the first that she went after.

"Bruce? What can I say? I wish that we could have solved this before your son and his wife were hurt. But we couldn't. Lucy is not the one who hired the men who attacked Barnabas and left him for dead in the parking lot. I'll come to him, I promise. Lucy was after you for revenge before you shoved her aside, in her words. But she was not the only one. I am sure you will recognize the name."

"Dallas? Who is it?" Bruce exchanged a look with Elizabeth. "You speak as if I know him."

"You do, Bruce. Only too well." Dallas paused, praying as he did so. "The name? A well-known entrepreneur in the area."

"William Thomas?" Bruce's voice was quiet even as Elizabeth's hand tightened on his.

"You are correct." Dallas nodded, his eyes not leaving Bruce's face. "He was infatuated with Elizabeth and had determined that she would be his. Only she never looked at him. Never spoke with him. You and Elizabeth were friends for years, best friends through high school and university. Am I correct?" He nodded as Bruce looked at his wife. "He felt slighted and thought that she only wanted anything to do with you because of your money. It didn't matter that the money was inherited and that you invested wisely and with the Lord's leading to increase its value. When you set up the Foundation with its goal of being an encouragement and aid to others less fortunate, he again thought that this was a slur again him. His mind became warped in this thinking. All he has accomplished in his life has been in competition with you, or so he thought. He married but his wife left him in less than a year, not telling him that she was expecting. She moved from the area and he has had no contact with his son. That he blames on you as well. We have had him assessed. He will not face any charges. He has been committed under a mental health assessment. He also has cancer, which is terminal."

Bruce grew sad as he listened. "I never really knew him. We had a couple of high school classes together, but we never had anything to do with one another in them. Our interests ran differently. Would it have made any difference if I had?"

Will spoke up from where he stood behind Bruce, drawing the attention to himself.

"I spoke at length with him, Bruce. He was becoming more and more incoherent as time went on. It would not have made any difference. In fact, from what he did say and that I am not at liberty to divulge, it would have made it worse. He has admitted that he went after all the men, including your son, as a sick kind of revenge. In his mind, you ruined him. And you took the woman that he wanted."

"God protected us." Bruce hugged Elizabeth and then turned to Barnabas. "I'm sorry, son."

"For what?" Barnabas' brow wrinkled as he looked at his father

"For involving you in this. A mad man as we used to say, out for revenge."

"But you didn't know, Dad. No one did, did they, Dallas?"

Dallas shook his head. "No one. He kept it hidden. He did become prominent in the community but never in a church. He refused to step inside one, not even for a funeral. I'm sorry that we didn't catch him before he put all of you through what he did."

353

"It's not your fault, Dallas." Aubrey spoke up. "It's life. It's how God has worked. He has taught all of us something different, something that we needed to learn. For myself? He has taught me how to live. With help from my love." Aubrey turned to Barnabas. "We can become angry, bitter, or let God fill us with His peace. I had so many days, weeks, months and years to work through this. I choose to live, to let God work through me."

Buckley's voice raised in a hymn of praise, the others adding their voices before he prayed. He looked around when he finished before he just hugged Locklin. Lord, Aubrey is so wise. You have taught us so much. Thank you, Lord.

Six months later, Barnabas stood in the newly dedicated playground and family activity area that Neasa's brother, Nevin, had created for them. He was so thankful, he thought, for the friends who had become family. Friends from all over Canada. Even some of the ladies, he thought, came from outside the area. He turned as Breck stopped beside him.

"I never thought when we were teens and talked about what we wanted to do that both of us would be working here." Breck smiled.

"No, I never did. I wasn't going to come and work for the Foundation, you know." Barnabas grinned before he grew pensive.

Breck laughed. "I know. It wasn't in my plans either. God had other plans for us." He looked around at the men. "And to think that this all started with that strong impression you had about finding orphans who all shared your initials and hiring them to work for you. To send them out as ambassadors of encouragement to the community."

"And that has worked out so well. I hear nothing but praise from their employers and their volunteer coordinators. Having the ladies join us has added to that. It has made us a family."

"A family that keeps growing." Breck smiled. "I wanted you to be the first to know after my parents. Neasa and I are adding to our family." He nodded to the play area. "This is going to be used well."

Barnabas reached to hug his life-long friend, a prayer uttered for them. "That's great news, Breck. I am so happy for you." He watched as Breck moved away before he reached for Aubrey who had approached as he prayed. "Happy, sweetheart?"

"I am, love. I am. All those years that I thought I had lost? God was working in me, fitting me to become the helpmeet that you needed."

"He was. Enforced study I guess you could say." He stood, his arm around her, content as he watched, naming each couple and the little ones that had blessed the families. Muir and Burnie were almost parents, he thought, as were Brady and Fynn. He turned to Heath and Hannah, smiling as they waved at their Aube. She was still important to them, right up there with their parents.

Baird and Berneen, Benen and Cadee, Blair and Devaney, Bradon and Ennis, Brady and Fynn, Branigan and Guenivere, Brandon and Hagen, Brendon and Imly, Brennen and Jaxcy, Brody and Ker, Buckley and Locklin, Burnie and Muir, Breck and Neasa, he thought of each one as he named them. Thank you, Lord, for each and every one of them.

Bruce approached his son, dropping a kiss on Aubrey's cheek, and then laying a hand on his son's shoulder.

"Okay, son?"

"Double okay, Dad. You and Mom just got in?"

"We did. We tried to get here earlier but the traffic was backed up coming from Toronto. I wish that we had been. I have seen the playground is already in use." He grinned at his son.

"It is, Dad." Barnabas bit at his lip, an action that Bruce recognized as uncertainty on his son's part.

"Something that you need to tell me, son?" He looked over at Aubrey to see her blushing. Elizabeth stood with her arm around her daughter. He smiled as he remembered her adamant words that Aubrey was a daughter in love, not in law.

"There is, Dad. Aubrey and I are taking off for a couple of weeks, and I promise. This time we are not running for our lives or across the province to keep alive." He looked down at her, to find her eyes on him, confidence in him showing. "When we come back, I need to talk to you about something new that Aubrey would like to set up. A music program for the little ones and whoever in the community would like to take part. She feels burdened about this."

"That's a good idea, son. Aubrey, just get me your proposal and I'll put it to the board. I doubt that it will be refused." He studied the two. "But that's not all."

"No, it's not, Dad." Aubrey had taken to calling them Mom and Dad. "I don't have my parents. I wish that I did. They would make wonderful grandparents." She paused, blinking away the tears, not seeing the look of amazement and then joy the older couple exchanged. "You two will. You have shown it so many times with the little ones." She stopped, unable to continue.

"What my sweetheart is trying to say, Dad, is that the love of my life and me will be parents by Christmas. That makes you grandparents. And you can't say no."

Bruce blinked rapidly. "Not that we would." He hugged the two, watched as Elizabeth did and then hugged the three of them, a prayer raising for them.

Late that night, Barnabas found Aubrey curled up in his favourite chair. He lifted her and then sat back down, cuddling her close.

"Did you ever think we would go through all this?" She tilted her head to look at him, accepting the kiss he dropped on her mouth.

"Not at all. That day I took off? All I wanted was to know if you were okay and if you still wanted anything to do with me. I didn't dream that we would have our own adventure."

"I prayed so hard for someone to find me and rescue me. Your face was always the one that I saw. Thank you, love, for being my knight in shining armour. And for teaching me how to live again."

They grew quiet, their eyes on the flickering flames of the gas fireplace that Aubrey had lit. They were with the one that God had meant for each of them, although it had taken time for that to happen.

———

Thank you for picking up the story of Barnabas and his love, Aubrey. Who knew that Aubrey was the one that had shadowed his life throughout the books? Some of the ladies had guessed. Learning to live once more was what Aubrey faced. Barnabas was there to provide the encouragement that she needed, to help teach her to do just that.

It is the end of a series, the end of the adventures of the Barnabas Foundation family. It has been a challenge to write, but each story has had to be told, to lead to this one. Friends from previous books and series have walked in, at just the right time. I miss the guys from *His Guardians, The Heart of a Lion, A Touch of His Garment, Under His Wings,* and *The Haven of Rest.* The friends have added to the story, moving it sometimes when it was stilled.

We are all prisoners in some way to something. God can and will open the door of the prison and free us. We just need to ask. He has promised us that. We can rise up with the eagles and fly above the storms of life. It doesn't mean that Christians don't face danger, sickness, and death at the hands of others. Sin sees that we do.

We are called to be encouragers to those around us. It is difficult, especially in 2020 when we are facing the COVID-19 pandemic and life is restricted. It sometimes is just a kind word that helps.

As I end the series and look to what comes next, Dallas is quite vocal about his story. He was to be only a minor character in a book or two, just to be the investigator. His role grew until he became an important part of the story. This has happened with so many of these men and ladies. A minor character, such as Muir's Granny, or Darbie and Hailey and Hollie, and how can I forget Heath and Hannah, such sweet little ones.

Let God have all your worries and cares. He loves you so much. As I write, I am listening to Christmas carols and reminded again of His great love and His desire that we live for him.

God bless.

Ronna